STEP DOWN,
ELDER
BROTHER

By Josephina Niggli

MEXICAN VILLAGE

STEP DOWN, ELDER BROTHER

A NOVEL

STEP DOWN, ELDER BROTHER

BY JOSEPHINA NIGGLI

RINEHART AND COMPANY, INC.
NEW YORK · TORONTO

Copo de Nieve, by Salvador Díaz Mirón, and the excerpt from *La Tierra del Faisan Y del Venado* by Antonio Mediz Bolio were translated by Josephina Niggli.

Para mi comadre, Elsita Larralde

GLOSSARY

cuate, a Mexicanism meaning twin. Men use it in the special sense of meaning "best friend."

Quintana Roo, a territory of deserts and savage Indian tribes which lies between Yucatán and British Honduras.

Río Bravo, in Mexico the Rio Grande is known as the Río Bravo (the untamed river) even by the people who live along its banks.

Arabe, a term used for Syrians, who own most of the small mercantile stores.

Muy codo, patting the point of the bent elbow is a gesture used to indicate penuriousness. Any person who hates to spend money is referred to as being *Muy codo,* very elbow.

Reineros, the general term for the people of Monterrey.

aguacate, Persea gratissima, a smaller, more delicately flavored member of the avocado family.

machacado, jerked beef with scrambled eggs.

Avenida Beirut, a port in Syria. Morelos, the principal commercial street of Monterrey, carries this nickname because of the number of Syrians who own stores on it.

Juárez, Juárez liberated Mexico from the French in 1867 and gave the Republic its first constitution.

Tenorios, all legitimate theaters in Mexico present *Don Juan Tenorio* every year on the night of October 31. These presentations are known familiarly as *Tenorios.*

mariachi, a group of street musicians, usually consisting of a violin, two guitars, and sometimes a flute.

Fulano de Tal, Mengano de Tal, the Spanish equivalent for John Doe and Richard Roe.

Xtabay, pronounced ēsh-tä-bī with accent on the last syllable.

Nacimiento, the Creche. Scene representing the Nativity set up on altars at Christmas.

The Virgin of Guadalupe, the patron saint of Mexico.

cante hondo or *jondo, cante flamenco, cante andaluz,* all names for the same thing; the "deep song" of Andalucía, betraying the survival of Byzantine-Oriental influences.

Manuel Acuña, author of poem, *The Nocturne.* Born in 1849, Acuña, one of the greatest of Mexican lyricists, committed suicide at the age of 22 when a girl rejected his love.

toloache, Jimson-weed. Its dried leaves, *Datura stramonium,* when taken internally, cause insanity, and, in excessive amounts, death.

jacal, a hut, generally built from woven straw thatched with mud.

mezcal, a cheap Mexican liquor made from the fermented juice of the maguey (*agave americano*). It is highly intoxicating.

The Ten Days, February 8-18, 1913, marking the end of Madero's presidency, and Huerta's seizure of the government. Sometimes called *La Decena Trágica* (the Tragic Ten), over a thousand civilians were trapped in the two armies' crossfire.

atole, a drink made from thin gruel, flavored with either chocolate or vanilla.

Old Master this, and Early the other,
Nor dreaming the Old and the New are fellows,
The Younger succeeds to the Elder brother.

Browning: *Old Pictures in Florence*

STEP DOWN,
ELDER
BROTHER

I

Monterrey in February is not a happy place. The tourist season, which lasts from middle March until the end of January, is splashed with sunshine and the ever-changing panorama of flowers; but February is winter, and winter in Monterrey is very dull. Even the mountains reject their city, drawing a gray veil of mist between themselves and the town. The sun retires behind a curtain of heavy clouds; the begonias in the patios take this month to rest from blooming.

Since most of the wealthier families choose February to go to the ever-golden beach at Acapulco, to México City, to Cuernavaca, for one last burst of gaiety before the mourning days of Lent, their fine automobiles are frugally kept in storage, and even the traffic dims from its usual brilliance.

Of course there is no lack of cars. The traffic still snarls through the streets. There is great need for the signal light at the corner of Zaragoza and Padre Mier. But it lacks the fine elegance, the arrogance, of traffic in season.

The people on the streets do not stroll in February. They hurry, with their heads bowed. Some of the poorer classes wrap handkerchiefs across their noses to prevent the dread "catching of air." Woolen shawls lie heavy on the shoulders of old women, and old men wrap their bodies in blankets.

It is cold in February, and the brilliant sun has so thinned the blood that there is no resistance to the winds that come down from the mountains to whistle across the flat roofs. In the poverty sections of San Luisito and Guadalupe, pneumonia and influenza brush the houses, and the gates of the cemeteries on Avenida Carranza are always open to the diggers of new graves.

February is a bitter month, a month of tears and death, a month to be endured while it is present and forgotten as quickly as it has passed. And yet, to Domingo Vázquez de Anda it was, in some ways, the most satisfactory month of the whole year.

This afternoon—it was still early, not yet five-thirty—as he walked up Escobedo Street to the offices of the morning newspaper: *El Despertador del Norte* (the Awakener of the North), he moved much more slowly than was usual to his restless long stride. The wind danced around his London trousers and London overcoat, trying to pierce the wool, but without success. Domingo liked the feeling of cold on his face, and the rest of his body was warm and comfortable, his hat pulled low over his eyes, his throat protected by a blue wool scarf, and his hands, in heavy gloves, thrust deep in his pockets.

Once he paused and leaned against the wall of a shuttered house so that a shivering little boy in a ragged sweater might snap a buffing cloth across his already shining shoes. The boy chattered about the lack of tourists, and Domingo enjoyed the conversation, not so much for what the boy said as for the high sweet voice. He thought, Undernourished, and thrust the thought from him with a reminder that he must not think in terms of health any more, never any more, when he saw people. He had been reminding himself of this fact for ten years, and for ten years his subconscious evaded his vigilance and set up people in front of him, not as personalities, but as skeletons clothed in transparent flesh through which the branching arteries and veins showed clear.

When the boy finished, Domingo thrust a silver peso into his fingers, and walked on, followed by the boy's cry of "Why, you're a stranger, and I thought you were from Monterrey!"

This cry often followed Domingo, whose generous habits were much deplored by his uncle Agapito, and Domingo did not really hear it. He was concentrating on the effort of keeping his mind a blank, because he had found that to think was to remember, and remembering was too painful. Better not to think at all, but he was a thinking man, and sometimes, as now, the effort was almost too much for him.

She had come to Monterrey once, to visit, she said, the Mexico he had told her so much about, and he had walked with her up this same street, so that she might enjoy the picturesque aspect of these long rows of houses with their iron barred windows, their heavy carved doors, and now and then the brass plaques that informed the passerby that here lived a doctor or a lawyer or an

4

engineer. He remembered the brightness of her eyes, the swift tilting of her head from side to side as she exclaimed over this house being painted purple, that one yellow, another green. Nothing had ever set up the difference between them so strongly as that walk up Escobedo Street.

Even as she laughed over the narrow sidewalk, so narrow that it was difficult for two people to walk abreast, he knew that she was puzzled by his behavior, that she was waiting for him to say, "This morning I am going to take you to meet my mother." But he never said it, he never took her to the huge house with its Spanish coat-of-arms on Padre Mier, East. What was the use? She was as American as popcorn, and he, as Mexican as tequila.

In New York it had been different. In New York there had been laughter, and gay parties, and they had met and fallen in love as simply as any two people anywhere in the world. But Uncle Agapito had changed all that, and now she was North American and he was Middle American, and even the language between them was rusted with disuse. So the laughter had faded from her eyes, as it had long ago faded from his, and she had gone back to New York while he had stayed in Monterrey.

Now and then in the night he would wake up and think of her: of how the silver blond hair curled against her throat, of how the golden tipped brown lashes framed the clear blue eyes, and to get rid of her image he would do what he was doing now, furiously concentrate on real estate prices, and how much more he could get for that land on 15 de Mayo if he cut it into two lots instead of leaving it in one piece.

By this time he had reached the newspaper building. He turned into the narrow doorway marked "To offices," and climbed the stairs. From some place in the back came the rumbling of presses, and in the air was the sharp smell of printer's ink. Although it was still so early, the gray afternoon diffused little light, and the stair hall, which opened directly onto an inner patio of bare cement was dark. On the first floor he went into a desk-filled room where the overhead lights were on. The men and women at the various desks threw shadows from their own bodies across the galleys of classified ads over which they were toiling. One girl looked up at his entrance, recognized him, smiled and returned to her work. The others paid him no attention.

The sound of the presses was not so loud in here, typewriters from a back room almost drowning them out. Domingo paused in the archway and measured the breadth of the wall against the breadth of his shoulders. Tito Gómez stopped typing and swung around to watch him.

"The true soul of the real estate man," he said dryly. "Some day you are going to sell this old building, and then the slaves of the *Despertador del Norte* will have to find newer and better offices. What a sad fate."

Domingo laughed and perched one hip on Tito's desk. "You wrong me, friend. This is a good building. There are not many left in Monterrey."

"That is progress," the plump little man said seriously. "The old must go to make way for the new." As though he had not already said this to Domingo every day for years, he launched into his glowing eulogy of Monterrey's growth since 1921 when, the fighting days of the Great Revolution finished, Monterrey shook herself, exchanged her rags for a fine new dress, and strung a chain of factories about her neck. "Think of it, six hundred factories. I ask you, Domingo, has any other city in the Republic . . ."

"Guadalajara," said Domingo flatly. "It has more commerce. Its people make more money. It just doesn't boast about it as much."

"What patriotism." Tito was really shocked. No matter how many times he encountered Domingo's casual disregard of Monterrey's industrial magnificence, it always shocked him anew like an early morning plunge into icy water. "Have you no love at all for this city, friend?"

Domingo shrugged and pulled some typed sheets from his pocket. "It's my city. It is stamped in my flesh. Let the stamping be my patriotism. My father sends these ads to be printed in your magnificent newspaper. He's opening a *colonia* on the Saltillo Road."

Tito took the sheets and scanned them without curiosity before tossing them into the wire basket near his hand. "You have a name, of course, a magnificent name."

"Not too magnificent. We plan to open it in May. My sister's saint's day is in May."

"Is Brunhilda's saint's day in May?"

"Sofía. I have two sisters, Tito, as you should know, friend of my childhood. How love blinds the intellect."

6

Tito smiled ruefully. "Love from a single torch. Brunhilda seldom remembers my existence. And so you will call the *colonia* the Santa Sofía?"

Domingo slid off the desk. Someone in the front had opened a window, and a cold draft prowled through the small office. He ran his hands under the lapels of his overcoat, pulling them closer together. "In here," he murmured, "is the odor of printer's ink and burning gas. Next door is the fragrance of steaming coffee."

"You tempt me from my duties." Tito shook his head sadly, then quickly brightened. "But what is life without temptation? Also, I must buy a present for my mother." He took his coat and hat from a chair behind the desk, opened a locked door into the narrow hall, and the two went down the stairs together.

They made a sharp contrast, Domingo tall and thin, Tito small and plump. Domingo walked with well-oiled muscles, and when he had on his overcoat, as now, it was his habit to keep his hands thrust into the pockets. His family often made fun of this, telling him that he looked like a *pistolero,* with two guns always ready against his palms. Their teasing had no effect on him, and he continued to walk as he pleased, his flat crowned hat pulled low over his eyes, his coat collar turned up, his hands deep in his pockets.

But small Tito could not keep his hands long in any certain spot. He used them constantly, sketching vivid images in the air. In order to keep up with Domingo's long strides he had to take small darting steps that gave him the appearance of dancing. Sometimes, to emphasize a point, he would dip his body sideways and tilt his head to peer up into Domingo's narrow face. Brunhilda sometimes acted this out for family reunions, calling it "Domingo and his performing puppy." Domingo's lips would smile, but his eyes would stay grave, because Tito was his friend, his *cuate.*

When they reached the sidewalk, they could not decide whether they wanted coffee or something stronger and finally compromised by walking down Zaragoza Street toward Zaragoza Plaza. If their feet carried them into a saloon, then the fault would be in their feet, not in their minds.

They paused on the corner for Tito to light his inevitable cigarette, which he fitted into an amber holder. The wind whipped their coats around them and pierced the wool to touch their shoulders with icy fingers. People hurried past, heads lowered.

7

Automobile horns honked incessantly at intersections. From small restaurants floated the aroma of frying onions and garlic, and over everything was the cold grayness of the cloud-packed sky. Most of the stores had their window lights turned on, and Tito and Domingo paused here and there to look in jewelry windows at the heaped displays of religious medals, the delicate filigree of rosaries, jet and turquoise earrings, and the inevitable silver combs. Tito's mother was having a saint's day on the twenty-first, and he still had not bought her a present.

"A shawl is better," Domingo protested. "Everyone will give her medals, and as for earrings, I heard your father asking my mother the other day to choose a pair at the *Alemana*."

"My mother is an angel," said Tito indignantly. "A shawl is not good enough. Besides, she has a shawl, five or six, I think."

"A fan then. At the *Nueva China*. . . ."

"A fan? In February?" Tito pulled his coat closer about his throat and shuddered dramatically.

"It will not be February always," Domingo pointed out, "and the *Nueva China* has some elegant fans. Sofía has been referring to them in honeyed tones for weeks."

"My mother has a fan," Tito said. "This must be something special that only I can give her." His eyes ranged up and down the street with dissatisfaction, and then his attention was caught by a display farther down the block. Clutching Domingo's arm, he walked rapidly toward it. Domingo, who was never surprised at his friend's tempestuous actions, shrugged and allowed himself to be dragged along, not really caring where they went so long as they were moving with the crowd.

They had to wait for a bus to pass in order to cross the street. Someone shrilly called Domingo's name, and the bus ground to a halt in front of him, driver and passengers waiting while a young boy swung perilously from the entrance step. "Eh, brother, I have a message for you. Our mother says you are to come home for dinner tonight. Uncle Agapito is expected."

The shrill voice was drowned by violent honking from the stalled traffic. Domingo touched his ears and shook his head. Four boys on his side of the bus yelled in unison, "Your Uncle Agapito is coming to dinner."

Domingo nodded, and Tito danced and waved in thanks. The bus moved on and the traffic flowed smoothly past them. Tito,

8

seeing Domingo's frown, jerked at his friend's arm. "Light a candle to that saint when you reach the church. At the moment we have important business."

Domingo said gravely, "It would give me much joy if Uncle Agapito removed himself to Quintana Roo."

"Silence, Domingo. He is your uncle."

"Did I choose him?" The rest of his words were drowned in a new discord of honking as they weaved their way between the cars, escaping serious injury by inches. "Such exertion," Domingo grumbled, "for a small present. I know," he added hurriedly, seeing Tito's expression, "your mother is an angel. And now what miracle of gift is on this side of the street?"

Tito dramatically pointed toward a lighted display box that was stapled to the broad stone wall. In the box was one object only: a tinted photograph of a bride, the face blank as a doll's, the white satin gown draped into rigid, unnatural folds. "You see," he said dramatically, "that is something no one else can give her but myself. I know. Only this morning I was writing an advertisement for the photographer Sausedo. 'The gift that is truly personal,' I called it." He snapped his open palm to his forehead. "All morning I worked on this advertisement. I am truly stupid."

Domingo examined the photograph with distaste. He intensely disliked tinted pictures, although he had to admit that in this instance the tinting was much superior to the photography. "If this is your choice, then let us go to Sausedo. You don't want cheap work."

Tito stepped back and looked at the name plate beside the door. "Estudio Bárcenas," he read aloud. "Bárcenas. The name is new."

Domingo, who could guess what was passing through his friend's mind, said quickly, "These places have little money. They cannot afford to pay for advertising . . ."

"Listen," said Tito, "such arguments are very well for the rest of the Republic, but this is Monterrey. We are men of business, of industry. Also, I learned in the States that what you do not start, you never finish!" He opened the door and walked in, with Domingo, still protesting, at his heels.

II

Tito said over his shoulder, "Soon I will have enough funds to open my own advertising agency. It is little accounts like this one which make the money. Besides, with my genius, I can build him into as great a man as Saucedo."

"But Saucedo is a photographer." Domingo stumbled on the dark stairs and cursed under his breath. "This man's work is no good."

"Who cares? It is the fame that matters."

They emerged on a narrow gallery that hung out over a patio. There were no lights, and none of the doors were marked. It was colder here than it had been on the street, and the dust lay thick on the gallery floor. Domingo had a doctor's love for cleanliness, and this third-rate building, covered with the grime of years, revolted him.

"Let's get out of here, Tito. We'll never find it."

But his little terrier of a friend was already darting from office to office, hot on the scent of new business. He would push open a door, thrust in his head, bark, "Estudio Bárcenas?" and at the negative reply, would slam the door shut and try a new one. Finally an irritable voice suggested that he inquire at the last room on the left.

There was no lettering on the proper door, not even a small handwritten card. Tito, his Monterrey soul shocked, muttered, "Such business methods," as he turned the handle and opened the way to a small dreary room.

An electric bulb burned dimly in the ceiling. Photographs of wedding couples in gray folders stood too close together on small tables pushed against the wall. At the back was a counter showing badly framed pictures, all of them tinted and most of them brides. To the right was an arched opening through which could be seen cameras and spotlights.

Domingo was surprised at the lack of dirt. Even the woodwork had been scrubbed until the wood shone whitely through the flaking red paint. The large brass cuspidor on its rubber mat near the end of the counter glistened from polishing. Its elegance dared anyone to use it, and obviously no one had.

There was something about this office that both intrigued and repelled Domingo. It was everything that a third-rate photographer's studio should be, and yet it lacked truth. It was more like a window display which is so close to reality but is really nothing more than furniture for sale and the illusion of paint on canvas flats.

He tried to identify what it was about this silent room that repelled him, but he could not quite discover it. Perhaps it was the extreme cleanliness: there was not so much as a breath of dust on the tables. Perhaps it was the absence of the photographer himself. Perhaps it was the baize curtain that hung behind the counter, cutting him off from the room beyond. From it should come sounds of movement, of chattering voices, even a muted laugh, but there was only silence. This was a room in which once there had been life and now there was no life. Even the cemeteries on Avenida Carranza had more personality. And then he knew what it was: this room was not the studio of a photographer named Bárcenas. It was the studio of third-rate photographers from the Río Bravo to Quintana Roo. Bárcenas had followed all of the conventions in establishing it. He had merely forgotten to impress upon it his own personality.

Domingo said, "You're not going to have a picture made here, Tito, surely."

"Silence, friend." Tito went to the counter and pounded on it. "This is a challenge to me. Next year you will be saying, 'I remember he once had a small studio on Zaragoza.' Then you will add, 'Of course, all of this new elegance is the result of my friend's genius, my friend Tito Gómez.' "

Domingo picked up one of the gray folders, noticed that it had been recently dusted, and set it down again. "What elegance?"

"Why the new studio this man will have to rent on Morelos Street in order to take care of all the clients my advertising will bring him."

"Clients? For this sort of thing?" Domingo thrust a photograph of a bride and groom under Tito's nose. "Take a good look at it. Who, in his proper senses, would pay money to own such a picture?"

"Don't be stupid, friend." Tito slipped another cigarette into his amber holder and impatiently walked over to the counter as he lighted it. "When assistants with talent can be hired for twenty pesos a month? I tell you it is a challenge to me, to take *this* and build it into *that!*"

Domingo could read from Tito's expression all of the images that were passing through his mind. Instead of this cold small room there was a salon appropriately draped in gray velvet, with three large photographs carefully framed, carefully lighted, and a curved modern desk with a beautiful girl enthroned behind it to sort the vast number of requests, most humbly made, for a sitting, perhaps two months, three, even six months in advance.

"Mere advertising cannot work that great a miracle," Domingo said dryly.

"Silence!" Tito pounded on the counter with his fist. "I tell you this is a challenge to me. I like challenges."

The green curtain was suddenly pushed aside, and a little man allowed it to drape behind him. His short stature was intensified by the forward curve of his thin shoulders. White hair receded from his wrinkled forehead. Domingo, noting the shape of the high bridged nose, the slant of the cheekbone, the curve of the skull, thought automatically, A strong strain of Indian blood. Probably comes from around Mexico City—near Xochimilco. The brown skin lay in leathery folds along cheek and throat, as though fat had been removed too quickly for the skin properly to contract. A sparse gray beard and mustache intermingled along the chin and upper lip. He looked at them with blank eyes hidden behind shell-rimmed glasses. The pupils and iris were so near a shade of blackness that they were more like flakes of soot.

He made no attempt to solicit their patronage but stood there in silence, waiting for one or the other to speak.

After an uncomfortable moment, Tito murmured a few polite phrases and asked how soon he could have an appointment.

"Now, or later," the man said indifferently. His voice was a monotone, as dead as his eyes. "Will you want it tinted?"

"No, Tito," said Domingo.

Tito said, "I want your best. And the price?"

Bárcenas looked helplessly up and down the counter, then called, "Márgara! Fetch the sample book."

Now that Tito had spoken of his best, Bárcenas acquired more tolerance and suggested that the small man seat himself on the only chair. He did not notice Domingo. Since Domingo did not want a picture made, he was, said Bárcenas' attitude, of little worth.

The green curtains parted slightly, and a woman's hand tossed a large black album on the counter, then vanished into darkness again. This small action added another facet to Domingo's mental painting of Bárcenas. He's not all Indian, he thought. There's a strong streak of Spanish dating back to the Moors if the cloistered woman means anything.

To amuse himself while Tito was looking at the samples, he glanced through the photographs on display. Monterrey was his home. He had been born and reared in it, and as a real estate man he came in contact with many people. He knew that amongst such a large collection he would recognize at least one face, but these were pictures of strangers. Some of the bridal couples were photographed near tables, and this gave him the relative heights. They were, on the average, small . . . too small for the north. He said over his shoulder, "You are from the south, señor Bárcenas?"

The murmuring voice discussing the merits of tinted photography halted for a moment. The answer was cold. "Yes, señor."

"Michoacán, perhaps, Morelos, Jalisco?"

Again the slight pause. "Yucatán." And then the voice returned to its murmuring. Not Yucatán, Domingo thought, not with that bone structure, that accent.

For the first time in ten years, the first time since he had watched Doris' train pull out of the station New York bound, he felt a glimmer of interest in something beyond the mere dull routine of his life. The studio, the man, the hidden, silent woman, and now Bárcenas' lying—all fashioned a mystery at which he sniffed as a puppy sniffs a strange bone.

He realized that to Tito this was also an adventure, but in a different sense. For the advertising man this was a chance to create something out of nothing. Beyond the economic aspect he was not interested. Undoubtedly he would have scoffed at the idea of any mystery. Black was always black to Tito, and white, white, without any shadings of gray in between. This, Domingo thought, was a very convenient point of view, but at the same time slightly monotonous, even though that monotony could become charged with a certain amount of excitement, as Tito's voice was now when he

13

said, "The señor Bárcenas is going to make a very elegant portrait of me seated in a chair. Do you want to watch it?"

Domingo's shrug gave consent, and they followed the stooped man between twin arches into the photographic gallery. It had a slanted sky window that filtered gray light over the room. At one end were two painted backdrops, one representing a formal Italian garden, the other a seashore with mountains in the hazy distance. Tito finally decided on the garden, and Domingo wandered over to examine it while Bárcenas pushed lights into place and carefully centered the carved chair that was more elegant than comfortable.

Looking at the panorama, Domingo began to frown slightly. The work was too good for the subject. He glanced curiously at the photographer, who was paying him no attention, and then more carefully examined the backdrop of seascape with distant mountains. The waves had life. The pale mist that shrouded the mountains glowed in spite of cheap canvas and cheaper paint.

Bárcenas said coldly, "Forgive me, señor, but would you have the kindness to step to one side?"

Realizing that he was in the sight line of the heavy camera, Domingo strolled to the back of the room. An oil painting in a heavy gold frame hung on the wall, but one glance told him it had been done by a much inferior artist. On a small table easel, however, rested a miniature. It was a portrait of a stern, mustached face, with a black cap of hair, and it was a painting, not a tinted photograph. He started to pick it up, but a hand darted forward and snatched it away before he could touch it. "This was a mistake," said Bárcenas quickly. "It does not belong in here." In his voice were notes of repressed fury. He screamed "Márgara," before he could control himself. Almost immediately he attempted a pleasant laugh, and hurried into the other room with the miniature.

Tito, from his throne, said quietly, "He could not work for watching you, Domingo. Sit down and make yourself inconspicuous. Is it not my picture? Am I not the center of attraction?"

Domingo obediently sat on a folding chair near the archway. Bárcenas returned, wiping his palms together. He had acquired an air of business-like activity, and the task of portrait making was soon completed. "This is Tuesday," he said, counting on his fingers. "Saturday at noon you may see your proofs. That is agreeable?"

"I must have the picture on the twenty-first, two weeks from Thursday."

"But naturally, señor. On next Wednesday you shall have it. A week and a day in advance."

Domingo said abruptly, "It will be tinted, of course?"

Bárcenas' lids flicked across his blank eyes, but he said nothing.

Tito spoke with some annoyance. "I thought you did not like painted photographs."

"In this case, I think yes. The work is very good. It will be the same work as on the sample downstairs, yes?"

"But certainly, señor, the same work. It will, of course, take more days. You cannot have it until the following Monday."

"That is time enough," said Domingo. Tito started to protest, but checked himself and shrugged. Both young men murmured their goodbyes, and went to the door. Domingo turned for another look at the small photographer, and his eyes caught the movement of the green curtain. It lifted and for a moment he saw a woman outlined in the darkness. She seemed but a shadow; and her face, in its frame of dark hair, was a pale mask. Then the curtain dropped. He nodded to Bárcenas and followed Tito out of the building.

III

"You're a strange one," snapped the plump little man. "First you say one thing and then you want another." He brushed off the sleeves of his overcoat like an angry cock smoothing its ruffled feathers. "There are times, Domingo, when I do not fully understand you."

Domingo ignored this, his mind still focused on the woman in the curtained doorway. He had seen her, and yet, was she young or old? Was she ugly or beautiful? The moment of sight had been too fleeting. Only the impression of the shadowy body and masklike face remained.

Tito punched at him with his elbow. "You have a car somewhere, doubtless?"

"No, my father took it this afternoon. Our chauffeur has left us for the elegancies of my uncle Agapito's bank and five pesos more a month. My uncle Agapito preferred our chauffeur's driving to his own. My uncle Agapito is very clever at getting what he wants."

There was a slight pause. Domingo knew that his bitterness toward his uncle always made Tito uncomfortable. Tito was a great admirer of the Monterrey banker.

Ashamed of his outburst, Domingo said gently, "I am afraid we will have to walk."

Tito's usual good humor bounced into place. "You ask me to walk, I, who am your friend? I, whom you lured from my office? I, whom you persuaded to buy a cheap tinted photograph on the chance of my getting a client?"

"Am I so evil?" Domingo murmured.

"More than evil. You are brother to the seventh prince of hell. And how do you expect me to reach don Primitivo's saloon? The dirt in that building settled in my throat and demands strong beer to wash it clean."

"The *Estudio Bárcenas* was clean—clean as an operating room."

"The paint was peeling, the plaster was chipped on the walls . . . wait until he moves into his fine new studio. Ay, what a difference there will be then. Domingo! You're not listening to me."

"I'm sorry. Let us walk. . ."

"Walk!" Tito's feet stuttered in mock rage. Some of the pedestrians smiled at him in sympathy. He winked at a pretty *Arabe* girl, who winked back at him, then blushed and giggled as she hurried past. Tito sighed and tipped his hat to a saucier angle while Domingo warned him, "If we go in a taxi, you'll pay for it."

Tito sniffed and patted the point of his elbow. "You are a true son of Monterrey. A peso is closer to your heart than your arteries." He hailed a passing bus and pushed Domingo on ahead of him. "The trouble with you, Domingo, is that you have Monterrey in your blood."

The bus was crowded and they had to stand in the entrance. The man against whose back Tito's nose was pressed turned his head slightly so that he could glance over his shoulder. "Have you heard the new one, friend, about the Monterrey man whose wife would not allow him to sit down because sitting wore out his trousers?"

There was a shout of laughter from the nearer passengers which was cut off abruptly by the bus pulling to a grinding halt. The driver rose and glared at the joker. "Is it not bad enough that the rest of the Republic makes jokes about our thriftiness? Must we make them about ourselves?'

"True words!" shouted the passengers enthusiastically, some of them relaying the conversation to those out of earshot.

"Or, perhaps," added the bus driver silkily, "you are not from Monterrey?"

The big man in front of Tito squared his shoulders. "Am I not from Monterrey, and my name Elizondo? Go down to the governor's palace and see it written for yourself. The Elizondos were here before the mountains, all the world knows that."

"There are many Elizondos," snorted the driver, "all over the Republic, all over the world."

"Who speaks against the Elizondos?" yelled a voice from the back of the bus. "And I an Elizondo?"

"I speak," shouted the bus driver, and repeated it in a louder shout to top the inevitable honking that had started behind the stalled bus. "Me, I am a Martínez."

"So am I!" shrilled a lean young man, standing up on a seat. "Is there any here who says a Martínez is not as good as an Elizondo? That is the trouble with the bourgeoisie, always trampling on the heads of the workers . . ."

Several voices yelled at him to leave red syndicate speeches to the red syndicate. Domingo tapped Tito on the shoulder, and the two young men swung to the sidewalk.

"That bus will be here until midnight if they bring the communists into it," Domingo said pessimistically. "Besides, we are only two blocks from don Primitivo's. Perhaps we'll find my uncle Lucio there."

Tito nodded and sighed. "Ay, well, nothing is lost. Our fares were not collected."

He tripped along, enjoying the dusk, paying no attention to his friend's silence. They were on the street of Padre Mier, and he amused himself by gazing in the windows of stationery and book stores.

Domingo ignored Tito, his mind still tugging at the mystery

of the photographer's studio. Was there really a mystery? Here on this prosaic street, moving amongst the stream of home-bound workers, he was uncertain whether his own imagination had not taken a few facts and woven them into a romantic tapestry. The only photographers he had previously met had been men like Saucedo, true artists, their artistry flowing into their own personalities and their world.

Bárcenas was certainly not an artist. His father had doubtless pushed him into the profession without regard for talent. The result was those stiff wedding portraits, all of them of strangers. But it was a new studio. Perhaps the man had not had time to photograph any Reineros.

Monterrey was nearly fifteen hundred kilometers from Yucatán. He said he came from there. That might not be a lie. His people did not necessarily have to be Yucatecos. (That accent had never been absorbed from the ruins of Chichen-Itza.) And as for the almost antiseptic cleanliness of the studio, simply because Bárcenas was in a grimy building did not mean that he had to live in dirt.

But the woman. What of the woman? (Was she young or old?) There had been no occasion for her to come into the gallery. Her natural curiosity must have prompted her to peer through the curtains. (That pale mask of a face, as expressionless as the man's.)

Domingo drew a deep breath, pleased at the manner in which he had reasoned away a stupid romantic notion. (Ay, that pale mask. Was she beautiful? Was she ugly?)

He felt a jerk on his arm and gazed stupidly at Tito.

"Stop daydreaming," snapped the little man. "What are those fools staring at?"

Domingo blinked his eyes and returned to an awareness of his surroundings. A large group of people was pressed around the open doorway of a billiard academy. As the sidewalk was very narrow, the two men had to step into the street to circle the crowd. Far in the distance the great clock of San Fernando Cathedral tolled the hour of six. The outer darkness made the interior of the academy visible as a brilliantly lighted stage set.

Tito jumped up and down, trying to see over the massed heads. Domingo, who had the advantage of height, came to a sudden pause, then plunged forward, elbowing his way through to the entrance, Tito clinging firmly to the back of his overcoat.

There were two billiard tables, the green felt shabby with

much punishment from cues and balls, but only one was in use. A solitary man presided at it, a book propped on a holder in front of him. He had a small head perched like a ball on a long thin neck, which was attached to an angular body clad in dingy black. His old-fashioned stiff collar was too large, and his tie was twisted around to a spot almost under his right ear. His gold rimmed spectacles were perched halfway down his nose, so that he could peer over them to see the table.

From moment to moment he would consult the book, his face contracting into a frown. Seemingly unaware of his audience, he would read a paragraph, then bend from the middle to concentrate on the balls laid out in precise pattern in front of him.

When Domingo approached him, the academy's proprietor hastily stepped forward. "Forgive me, señor," he whispered loudly, "but this is a *maestro*. He is doubtless practicing for a big match. We must not disturb him."

"Do not concern yourself," Domingo whispered back. "The *maestro* is my uncle. It is time to take him home.

He dropped his hand on the smaller man's shoulder. "Eh, Uncle Lucio, the hour grows late."

Don Lucio's frown dissolved into anger, then cleared when he recognized Domingo. "Your voice is too much like Agapito's. I thought that bag of wind was interrupting me." He chalked the end of his cue with a flourish, but his eyes carefully avoided Domingo, who had picked up the book and was reading the title page, which was printed in English: *Dr. Clarkson's Easy Method for Mastering Billiards.*

Tito, peering around Domingo's shoulder, also read the title and snorted to conceal a giggle. "I thought you were studying the mandolin, don Lucio."

"Can a man not study two things at the same time?"

"Of course he can," said Domingo soothingly.

Tito grinned and blinked his eyes at the older man. "We are bound for don Primitivo's. We would enjoy your company."

"Besides," said Domingo, "it would be a kindness to the crowd. How can these good people go home and leave a *maestro* to practice in solitary grandeur? That would not be polite."

Don Lucio raised and lowered his bushy white eyebrows. "As you say, a *maestro* must always act for the good of his audience. Let us go to don Primitivo's."

After he had consigned the book to the proprietor's awed hands with instructions to guard it with his life until the next morning, the three went up the block to don Primitivo's.

This saloon had a name which was used by strangers, but to its clientele it had been for sixty years simply "don Primitivo's." There was nothing about it to attract attention. Although located directly across from that tourist's delight, the big Central Market, no tourist had ever set foot in Monterrey's oldest saloon. The men who patronized it were very careful to spread its fame abroad as little as possible. For don Primitivo's was not really a saloon. It was an institution where gourmets went to enjoy the best draft beer and the finest lunch in the northeast.

Don Primitivo himself was a tall, large boned man, whose age sat lightly upon his broad shoulders. In his youth he had been a bull fighter. To devotees of the art, he was a hallowed person, because he had once fought in the *caudrilla* of the great fighter with the mustache: Ponciano Díaz. Many an evening the toast was drunk, "Ole Ponciano!" and don Primitivo would beam and bow as though the tribute were to himself and not to his long dead *maestro*.

Unlike most Monterrey saloons, there were no victrolas, nor any radios, although once in a while street musicians were allowed to play harps, guitars, and violins. Don Primitivo did not approve of modern music. "These new composers," he would snort, "Agustín Lara, Barcelata, with their little manufactured tunes. What do they know of music that touches the heart?" His customers would sometimes argue with him, explaining that next to Irving Berlin, Agustín Lara had probably the finest gift for popular melody on the continent, but such arguments he would brush aside with a wave of his great hand, and an order to the musicians to play a ballad of the Revolution, or, usually, his favorite song, "Farewell, Mamá Carlota."

He would always tell the history of this song as his father had told it to him. "The year was 1866. There was General Riva Palacios sitting at breakfast, my father waiting on him, when the aide came in and whispered in his ear that the Empress Carlota had sailed for France to beg help from that puppy of a Louis Napoleon. Ay, what fine news that was. It told the world that Maximilian admitted our wild Mexican troops were better fighters than his pretty Frenchmen. Did my father's general say a word?

He did not. He told my father to fetch him a piece of paper, and my father, knowing no better, handed him an envelope. An old dirty envelope. Can you imagine such a thing?"

His audience invariably assured him that they could not. "And what did the General do?"

"He laughed and took it, and wrote the words:

'From the distant beach, watch with saddened eyes
All her stupid nobles, her traitors and her fools.
As the boat sails eastward, she knows her empire's finished,
Farewell, Mamá Carlota. Farewell, my tender love.'

Ay, such magnificent sarcasm. Is there any other song that says so much, so cruelly? The soldiers fitted the words to a tune, and before the month had ended every Republican was singing it. Some of the men wanted to sing it when Maximilian climbed the Hill of Bells to be executed, but it wasn't allowed. He was a poor, good man, not responsible for his shrew of a wife. What a devil of a woman that one was!"

"But beautiful," someone would invariably say, and don Primitivo would nod his head. "My father saw her once. He said she was beautiful enough to make a man forget even his horse." Then he would sigh and hum a little of the song and sigh again as everyone remembered that she had gone empty-handed from Louis Napoleon's court, not to the Mexican shore, but into insanity, to spend the rest of her life in the dark spaces of the mind. The musicians would play the song then, very softly, almost in apology to a great enemy who had tried to forge an empire and fashioned instead a ghost-haunted castle in Belgium.

Don Primitivo's two brothers also sighed a little, then one would hastily draw more beer, while the other bustled over to the long tables where the food was prepared. Their attitudes said, "Leave sentiment to our good brother. We are men of business."

The beer was always icy cold and amber as champagne, with a proud head of white foam. And the food! Beef dried carefully in caves to preserve the rich juices, then cured with chili and mixed with scrambled eggs; thin strips of veal, wrapped in tripe and popped in and out of bubbling fat; large hunks of young goat slowly cooked in a pit over charcoal; broiled chicken with a sauce of black chocolate and chili. Meat, all meat, for this was man's food, with added helpings of brown beans and mashed *aguacate* to add variety.

21

Only men whom don Primitivo liked were permitted the freedom of this paradise. The others were so grossly overcharged that they made no attempt to return a second time. Luckily, don Primitivo's judgments were passed on individuals, not families, or the Vázquez de Andas would never have been permitted to pass the swinging doors. Of all the men in Monterrey whom don Primitivo most detested, Domingo's uncle Agapito headed the list. He had once condescended to visit the saloon, but after being charged a peso for a ten cent glass of beer, he never returned.

"That man is a miser," don Primitivo would tell Domingo, folding his lips between his false teeth, shutting his eyes and solemnly nodding his head. "There is liquid silver in his veins, not blood, and in place of a heart he has a dollar sign cut from platinum."

"Diamond," Domingo would correct him. "A diamond is harder than platinum."

Then they would both drink a toast to their hatred of don Agapito.

Don Primitivo was not overly fond of Tito Gómez but tolerated him for Domingo's sake. "I can't understand," he would grumble, "why you have such a pin-head for a *cuate*."

"You call Uncle Lucio your *cuate*. Can you explain that?" Domingo would retort, and don Primitivo never had an answer. No two men could be less alike than Lucio Vázquez de Anda, the shambling, shy failure, whose only joy was his collection of correspondence courses, and forthright, brusque don Primitivo. But they had been friends for thirty years, good friends as men from two social levels often are, drawn together by their very differences.

Every evening don Lucio locked the doors of his little drugstore, and with his catalogue under his arm, would trot off to don Primitivo's saloon. Sometimes they played checkers with beer bottle tops on a piece of home-painted oilcloth, but mostly they would pore over the catalogue, weighing the merits of a course on "How to raise mushrooms" against, perhaps, "How to become a cabinet maker." Once the course was decided upon, don Lucio would send off for it, and the two men waited with much excitement for the first lesson to arrive. If it were in English don Lucio would patiently translate it, and don Primitivo would listen, his lips slightly parted, a frown between his eyes, nodding his head now and then at the wonders of such knowledge trapped between the pages of a book.

After the first two or three lessons, don Primitivo lost interest, but don Lucio would plod ahead until the course was finished. In this way he had acquired a large collection of diplomas, which assured him that he was proficient in radio mechanics, elementary electricity, bookbinding, ornamental tin work, bookkeeping, and dressmaking. The last course was an accident. He thought he was getting instructions on how to construct dressmakers' forms. The first three lessons puzzled him by the variety of samplers he had to send until Domingo clarified the mistake. With his usual stubbornness don Lucio refused to give up the course and for six months was often to be found in his sister-in-law's sewing room, fluttering back and forth between the sewing machine and the ironing board. Domingo's mother and sisters cold-heartedly refused to let him make them any dresses; but the little upstairs' maid, Serafina, was pathetically glad for any donations and would stand patiently for an hour at a time while he pinned and fitted materials around her slight body.

When don Agapito heard of this foolishness there was a family explosion, only calmed by don Rafael's suggestion that don Lucio would not send off for any more correspondence courses unless the choice was approved by either don Agapito or himself.

Don Agapito could not be bothered by such foolishness, so Domingo's father, when approached, would merely make sure that the course had to do with men's business and not women's, and don Lucio was allowed to go his way in peace.

Domingo, as he and his uncle and Tito left the Academy, decided that his father must be growing broadminded to allow poor Uncle Lucio to take two such frivolous courses as billiards and the mandolin; then remembered with a flash of pity that don Rafael had dreamed of becoming a great composer, but sold real estate instead.

They went into the saloon, and don Primitivo himself brought over the beer, two large steins in each hand. He and don Lucio embraced each other, with much patting of backs, and then they all drank a toast, "Ole Ponciano!" for no particular reason save that the night air was chill, the saloon was cozy, and the beer was very good indeed.

Don Primitivo, who always knew the latest news before anyone else, beamed at Domingo. "I hear your sister Brunhilda returns tomorrow."

Tito let out a shriek and turned reproachful eyes on his friend. "You call yourself my *cuate,* and you never told me!"

Domingo raised both hands, palms upward, then dropped them to the table. "I did not know it myself. Are you sure, don Primitivo?"

"Would he say it if he were not sure?" snapped don Lucio.

"I had the word from that fool of a chauffeur who was once yours and now belongs to your uncle Agapito, may the devil twist his tail."

"Amen!" said Domingo automatically.

"Twice amen!" muttered don Lucio.

Tito said nothing, but crossed his fingers under the table to keep himself from entering the curse. "Two years she's been away," he said blissfully, "and now she's coming home again."

"I wonder how changed she will be," Domingo said thoughtfully.

Tito bristled that anyone, even her own brother, might offer a breath of criticism against Brunhilda. "How can she be changed? When she left she was perfect. Can perfection excel itself?"

"Eh, you'll think differently when you're married," don Primitivo grinned.

"That must be the reason for Uncle Agapito's coming to dinner tonight," Domingo mused. "I knew some mischief was on foot, but I was afraid he was trying to tamper with Sofía or Cardito."

"Is that bag of wind coming to dinner? Then I'll eat here!" Don Lucio jerked at his necktie, trying to pull it back into place.

Domingo glanced at his wrist watch, frowned, rose. "I'll leave you, then. Uncle Agapito likes to eat early. It's the only North American habit he has ever admired."

"A barbarous custom," don Lucio muttered. "How any human being can sit down to dine at seven in the evening is a matter beyond my imagination. How can one feel hunger before ten?" He swayed sideways so that don Primitivo's brother could put some *machacado* in front of him and moodily began to consume it. "If the night is still young when that old fool releases you, come back here. I'll play you a piece on my mandolin."

"He is learning 'Farewell, Mamá Carlota,'" said don Primitivo with the fond tones of a proud parent.

Domingo smiled warmly at the two old men, promised to

return if it were possible, promised to telephone Tito all the news he could gather of Brunhilda's arrival, escaped to the sidewalk, signalled a passing taxi, and gave the address of his house, seven long blocks to the east on this same street of Padre Mier.

The taxi driver, who knew Domingo by sight, sniffed a little. "I can't understand, friend, why you continue to live on such an unfashionable block. Your father has all these fine houses in the *colonias*. Why don't you move into one of them?"

Domingo wondered how many times he had answered this question through the ten years since he had returned from the States. "It was my grandfather's home. We are all used to it. And it is convenient."

"But very unfashionable," said the taxi driver with a patronizing shake of his head.

As traffic on Padre Mier was routed from east to west, they had to go down Morelos Street and make a turn onto Padre Mier to reach the proper block.

By now it was six-thirty. Although most of the stores were still open, there was a festive air of "Going home" about the crowds. All of the neon signs were on, and they made a gay pattern of red and green and yellow against the night sky. The shop windows were filled with merchandise left over from Christmas, and most of them had huge signs pasted up reading, "Great sale. All prices slashed." One *Arabe* store had built a gallows on the roof, from which dangled a larger than life-sized effigy of a gypsy woman. Above her head fluttered a sign reading:

"High prices are hanged. Only low ones remain. Great sale."

The taxi driver shrugged. "The *Avenida Beirut* is very gay this evening."

"Carnival. Lent comes early this year."

The taxi slowed to a stop for a street signal. A group of young students were standing, half on the sidewalk, half on the street, near Sanborn's Restaurant. This was their general meeting place, and they could be found there every afternoon from five to seven, flirting with all the passing girls. Domingo leaned forward to see if he could find his younger brother Cardito. A boy from the medical school recognized him and came to the car.

"Cardito has a bad cold. His number for the examinations is listed for tomorrow morning. He should get enough sleep tonight."

Domingo grinned. "So soon a doctor?"

The boy laughed and shrugged. "It's not that. The Counselor Farías gives the examination, and he does not love Cardito."

The driver stretched and turned around. "The light has changed, señor. Do you want further conversation?"

Domingo shook his head. "Drive on. And thank you!" he called to the boy, who waved after him.

"That Counselor Farías," said the taxi driver. "My cousin made the mistake of hiring him for a law case one time. A street dog knows more of law than that one. It was stupid of the governor to appoint him to a professorship in the University."

But Domingo refused to be drawn. He got enough of University politics at home from his brother, who was secretary of the Students' Syndicate. At the moment he was more concerned with the thought that his sister Brunhilda was coming home after two years in New York studying piano.

She was don Rafael's ambition projected through his child. Every morning at breakfast don Rafael would say fretfully, "I wish she would write us what she is learning. All these concerts she attends are very fine, but I want to know how her technique progresses."

Doña Otilia would murmur soothing noises, and Sofía, Domingo, and Cardito would exchange winks. "Poor father," their winks said, "how much he wanted to study music, and now this stupid Brunhilda cannot comprehend he would rather have a sheet of original composition than descriptions of the finest concerts in the world."

Domingo knew that his father had made a sacrifice to send Brunhilda to New York to study. Although she lived with a cousin, which was a great aid with living expenses, the drain on the family bank account was still tremendous. He had himself sent her as much as he could from time to time; because, as Brunhilda wrote, being a woman she needed more money than a man, an argument which Domingo was never quite able to understand. He knew that of the four Vázquez de Anda children, Brunhilda was the most extravagant—and the most stupid. She was soft as a flower, her flesh plump, her eyes liquid, her brown hair fine and silky. Her femininity was greatly approved by her uncle Agapito, who called her "All woman."

At first don Agapito had grumbled about sending her off to the States to study piano. A woman, he contended, was born for marriage, and needed no excessive education; but when don Rafael, excited by her progress at the Monterrey conservatory, decided to send her to New York instead of México City, don Agapito made no objections. Indeed, to Domingo's surprise, he approved the plan, provided that she stayed with a cousin who was married to the Mexican counsel general, one señor Fernando Jaime (related, through his mother, to the great banking family, Palafox).

A letter was immediately dispatched to the señor Jaime, whom no one in the Monterrey branch of the Vázquez de Andas had ever met. Domingo disapproved of the plan, because he felt that his Uncle Agapito was using Brunhilda as an opening wedge to meet the Palafox. But he said nothing because he knew his protests would be blandly ignored. The señora Jaime had a strong feeling for family solidarity, so her reply was prompt and gracious, and Brunhilda was launched, like a ship, upon her musical career.

Later Domingo heard his uncle often refer to his niece who was staying with, "our cousin, the Jaimes, of the family Palafox."

But now don Agapito could say this no longer because Brunhilda was coming home. Tito would worship at her shrine, along with the most of Monterrey's eligible young men, and in about two months, probably in Easter week, the conservatory, proud of their ex-pupil, would present her in concert, accompanied by their orchestra. Monterrey society would attend in formal dress, and don Rafael would have to be firmly held in his seat to prevent his popping up every two minutes to exclaim, "That's my daughter!"

After that, what? She was a Vázquez de Anda. It would not be appropriate for her to appear in paid performances in México City, and she certainly was not talented enough to be invited to play at any of the great music festivals for which such conductors as Stokowski and Sir Thomas Beecham were imported.

Don Rafael would definitely never allow her to teach. The instruction of small children was a closed profession to the Vázquez de Anda pride.

Domingo shook his head sadly. He dearly loved his sister, but he was well aware of her limitations. So much money, so much time away from home, to what purpose? One concert appearance in Monterrey.

Yes, he thought, it would have been much better planning to send Sofía. With her inheritance of the family banking talent she could have returned from two years' study to prove herself a great aid to her uncle. Don Agapito, however, blocked this idea. Women, he maintained, should only be used in banks as stenographers. He sniffed at the fact that all the other Monterrey banks had recognized the feminine invasion five years ago. There were even a few women cashiers. "Never in my bank," said don Agapito. "Never in my bank so long as I live."

He's got to train someone to fill his shoes, Domingo thought. It would be amusing if he settled on our ex-chauffeur. Sofía, his own niece, not good enough for a position an ex-chauffeur could fill. His bitter little joke made Domingo laugh, and the taxi driver jerked his head around.

"So, you're awake, and here's your house. I still think you should move to one of the *colonias*."

Domingo paid him, then added a tip as he said, "Every man to his own saint, friend."

The driver rubbed the tip with his finger. "No one would know you were related to don Agapito Vázquez de Anda. Eh, have you heard the new one about the Monterrey man who came home, exhausted but happy? His wife said, 'What is wrong, my heart, that you are so hot and tired?' The man answered, 'I ran home behind a streetcar and thus saved ten cents.' And do you know what that woman said to him? She said, 'You should have run home behind a taxi and saved fifty cents. There's no pleasing the women, as I should know, and I a married man.'"

Domingo laughed at the joke which had already been told to him several times, and went into the house.

IV

He loved this house. As he had told the driver, every man to his own saint, and this house was Domingo's saint. It had been built in 1759. The date was graven in the stone beneath the family coat of arms with the motto: *Animo et fide* (By courage and faith).

It was a very big house, with iron barred windows that

28

stretched from the tiled floors to the eighteen-foot ceilings. The vestibule was wider than an average room, and doña Otilia had banked the walls with wrought-iron stands loaded with fern filled boxes. It opened on the formal patio with its mosaic paving that curved around magnolia and pecan trees and drew back from the great central fountain where the water from a stone maiden's cornucopia splashed into a basin which was really a hollow circular bench of decorative Pueblo tile.

Doña Otilia did not approve of people sitting on this bench. She believed that the water kept it damp, so she used it as a support for her flowerpots of begonias, geraniums, carnations, and dwarf roses.

Behind the fountain, broad stone stairs rose to the second floor. When Domingo was small his nurse had terrified him with the story that on moonlit nights the shadowy figure of Juárez, who had once sought refuge here in the days of the French war, could be seen climbing the stairs to his room. Domingo watched for the ghost in vain on many a moonlit night, not realizing until years later that his concentration gave his nurse opportunity to flirt with the gardener.

But this patio really belonged to visitors. The family patio, reached through a side arch, was slightly smaller than the first. Its walls were enclosed by a gallery, where the family could sit when it rained. Here were chairs and tables, and hammocks slung from trunks of giant *aguacate* and walnut trees. The servants lived in the back wall, with windows which faced their own patio in the rear. Sometimes one of the servants would play on a concertina while the others sang, and the family would sit in the moonlight enjoying the muted music. This central patio was home to Domingo, as it was to all the Vázquez de Anda children, and none of them except Brunhilda (who detested it) would ever willingly change their house for a fine modern mansion in the *colonias.*

As Domingo stepped into the vestibule, he heard his father's bellow topped by his mother's tearful soprano, both resting on the platform of Sofía's contralto.

Following the sound, Domingo jerked open the door on his left, crossed the lofty, seldom used formal parlor with its gilt Louis XVI furniture, and entered the library.

Don Rafael was pacing up and down, his tall thin body bent

forward, his hands clutched behind his back. Doña Otilia crouched in a large chair, her soft stoutness overflowing its upholstery, sobbing into her handkerchief; while Sofía hovered over her, uselessly waving a bottle of smelling salts.

At Domingo's appearance, all three of them started howling at him. His family usually addressed him in concert rather than as individuals, and he had long ago learned how to listen to three or four conversations carried on in unison. At the moment it was not at all difficult for him to interpret the news that his brother Cardito was a young fool, that he would inevitably disgrace the family, that don Agapito would be furious, that Brunhilda was coming home the next morning, and that they did not know what to do.

Having progressed this far, Domingo raised his voice to a shout so that he could himself be heard. "What has Cardito done?"

"He's drunk!" stormed don Rafael.

"Cardito drunk? Impossible. He never touches liquor."

"At this moment he is in the dining room stretched out on the floor in a drunken sleep."

"Do something, Domingo," wailed his mother.

"Get him sober for Uncle Agapito," Sofía shrieked above the uproar.

Domingo nodded and went back across the hall into the small dining room. Save for its gaily painted furniture, it was vacant. His drunken brother did not decorate the red tiled floor. Remembering with a muttered curse that the household liquor was kept in the formal dining room, he hurried through the front patio to the gloomy room, filled with hand carved furniture that had been shipped from Spain in the late eighteenth century.

Here he found Cardito sprawled in front of a large armoir, his head propped on the knees of a weeping Serafina.

Domingo buckled his hands on his hips and looked down at the boy. "Saints in Heaven, he *is* drunk! Stop crying, Serafina!"

She wiped the tears from her eyes like a child, with the back of one hand. "I can't help it, s'ñor Domingo. He looks like he's dead."

"Well, he's not. But he will be if he stays on those cold tiles much longer. I hear he has a cold."

"That's the reason for all of it—his cold!" The words came in long drawn moaning syllables.

"Tell me about it later. We've got to get him to bed."

He allowed Serafina to help after she assured him that she had learned how to care for drunks from her father who was famous for his drinking. Between them they carried the boy's limp body up the patio stairs to his room.

By the time Domingo eased Cardito onto his bed, Serafina had already hurried to the kitchen to bring black coffee, with the footnote that a shower, very cold, would be ready by the time the boy's clothes were stripped off.

During his thirty-five years, Domingo had, on more than one occasion, put drunken friends to bed, but he had never had more competent aid than now. He had always considered Serafina a nonentity incapable of performing any task save by strict command and even stricter supervision. It fleetingly occurred to him that it was strange that the upstairs maid should be in the dining room at all, but his concern for Cardito dissolved the thought almost before it was projected.

He sat on the edge of the bed and felt the boy's pulse. It was throbbing much too rapidly, and the body heat warned of fever.

As he labored over his brother a great tenderness flowed through Domingo. The boy looked so young—many years younger than his twenty years. The straight black hair grew back from a peak on the high forehead. Bushy brows shadowed the eyes, and the short lip beneath the straight nose had an indentation in it that was as deep as a woman's. In the square chin was another indentation, more cleft than dimple.

His young neck still had a prominent Adam's apple. He looked so vulnerable lying there, so helpless with the helpless vulnerability of a small child.

Looking at him now Domingo knew that in all the world he greatly loved only one person, that that was his brother Cardito. He gently pressed one slightly protuberant ear against the boy's well-shaped head. "Don't worry, Cardito," he whispered. "I hope you know how much I want to help you, but I can't. You must fight your battle with the Counselor Farías alone. Only such battles can give you strength enough to fight Uncle Agapito later."

31

Afraid that Serafina would catch him in this moment of intimate tenderness, he hurriedly finished his work. When she returned with the coffee, Cardito was already in pyjamas, the covers were snug to his chin, and the gas fire lighted to take the chill from the room.

Her eyes widened as she realized that he would not be present at dinner.

"Ay," she whispered, putting the tray on a table, "don Agapito will be very angry."

Domingo poured out a cup for himself and calmly sipped it, although his wrist watch warned him that the great man should be arriving within the next ten minutes.

"Let him be angry. The niño Cardito is sick."

She gasped and pressed her hands together against her thin chest. "Just a little sick? Please, s'ñor Domingo, just a little sick?"

"That depends upon how much whiskey he drank."

"Not whiskey, brandy. He drank a tumbler full."

Domingo almost dropped his cup in his surprise. "A tumbler full! What was he trying to do, kill himself?"

"Doña Otilia was concerned for his cold, and ordered him to drink a glass of brandy."

"Dear saints, she meant a liquer glass!"

Serafina's head dropped like a child's. "Doña Otilia said a glass, s'ñor Domingo. She did not indicate the size."

He nodded impatiently and again bent over his brother. The tempo of Cardito's breathing told him that the boy had passed out of stupor into heavy sleep. At Domingo's orders, Serafina turned off all the lights save a shaded lamp near the bed. As she gracefully moved about, he was conscious of her as a human being for the first time. She was a bit below medium height and very thin. Yet her small arms were rounded, and the hollows of the collarbones were delicately shadowed. Her face was broad at the temples, narrow at the chin. The nose was short, with an Irish tilt, and the black eyes were large beneath high arched brows. Her heavy black hair was glossy and well kept, and she wore it in a coronet of braids around her small, well-poised head. She was not beautiful, but she was very pretty, and it gave a man pleasure to look at her.

Her pink dress, which gave warmth to her toasted skin, was

32

partly covered by a pale blue apron, and she wore a darker blue wool shawl over her shoulders.

Although she had worked in the house for three years, Domingo was surprised at his own ignorance of her. Beyond the lately acquired fact that her father was a drunkard, he knew nothing at all about her. He stared at her so intently that she glanced at him several times in nervous confusion.

Aware that he was embarrassing her, he smiled and gestured for her to tiptoe after him from the room. On the gallery he told her to go back to her duties, that Cardito would sleep quietly through the night.

Disappointment washed across her face, leaving an expressionless servant's mask. She dropped a quick curtsy, and floated down the stairs, her pink skirts rippling around her ankles. Although most Monterrey servants wore short skirts, Veracruz born doña Otilia was old-fashioned, and clung to the southern tradition of servants in long dresses.

Domingo looked after Serafina for a moment, annoyed that her mask of a face should remind him of another face. (Was she young? Was she old? Was she ugly? Was she beautiful?)

This reminder irritated him, and while he was bathing and dressing, he gave himself a stern lecture on the absurdities of the romantic imagination. "Because," he told himself firmly, "she is the first woman to excite your curiosity in ten years means nothing. You will never see her again. Besides, you have lived through hell once. It would be absurd to return there because you have fancies. Now forget her and think of something else!" (Was she tall? Was she short? Was she old? Was she young?)

He rigidly set his mind to finding the best phrases for the apology he would have to make to don Agapito for Cardito's absence at dinner. While he was fixing his tie, Sofía called through the door, "Hurry, Domingo. Uncle Agapito is entering the house."

He opened the door for his sister, who stood shivering on the gallery in a long dress of purple crepe with its necklace of gold and turquoise beads embroidered at the throat. Her thick black hair was piled high on her head in an intricate arrangement of curls.

"You look very handsome, Sofía."

"Thank you, Domingo, and so do you," she said automatically, her slanted eyes anxious with her question. "What of Cardito?"

"He's sick."

"But, Domingo, Uncle Agapito . . ."

"Will for once have to accept the knowledge that human beings do get sick. Cardito has a wretched cold."

"He's drunk!"

"He's not, Sofía. He's really quite ill. And take that expression off your face. You look exactly like Uncle Agapito in his most flint-like moments."

"Well," Sofía tapped her satin shod foot on the tiles. "You'll have to tell him yourself. I won't. And do hurry!" She turned and almost ran for the stairs.

Domingo's reason urged him to haste, but his movements slowed until he felt as though he were putting on his coat in slow motion. He went to the mirror, picked up his silver-backed military brush and gave a final sweep to his hair.

He usually saw himself with blank eyes, but he stole a moment now to look in the mirror with its curved Venetian frame of tarnished gold.

Behind his right shoulder he could see the carved dark footboard of his bed, and beyond it the tall windows draped with faded yellow curtains of Spanish brocade. To the left a corner of the great clothes press was visible, and on the red tiled floor was a turquoise rug he had brought back from New York.

This was his room. It fitted him somehow, and he took the time to wonder why. Even on the sunniest days it was filled with shadows. Did he live in a shadowed world? Was that the reason? It had a somber dignity. Was he cursed with a dignified somberness? He tilted his head to one side and thoughtfully examined himself. Yes, perhaps "somber dignity" was the descriptive phrase. He knew that he rarely smiled without conscious effort. In the old New York days he had laughed quite a lot, but now there never seemed any occasion for inner laughter. But this loss of a sense of humor as he grew older was characteristic of his family. Vázquez de Anda men had looked exactly like this for generations. If Cardito and the girls married, their children would grow up in the same image. Even Uncle Lucio, with his little round ball of a head had what people called "the Vázquez de Anda expression," and now, looking at it, Domingo concluded that what the Váz-

34

quez de Anda family really needed was new blood. After all, he thought, we're related to three-quarters of Monterrey.

His watch told him that he had dallied enough. As he crossed the gallery to the stairs, a movement in the shadows attracted his attention. He saw that it was Serafina, her shawl pulled closely around her, her hands locked under her armpits for warmth, swaying slowly back and forth in a low rocking chair near Cardito's door.

His voice was sharper than he meant it to be as he said, "What are you doing here?"

"Just rocking, s'ñor Domingo." She rose and came to him. "Indeed, s'ñor Domingo, I'm not needed in the dining room. Doña Petra said to get out from under her feet. And here I'm not under her feet."

"But it's cold, Serafina."

"I don't feel the cold. My hands are warm. See?" She thrust them out and brushed them fleetingly across his fingers. "And if the niño needs anything. . . ."

She drew back from him with an odd little gesture of defense, almost as though she expected him to hit out at her.

He made no reply, but as he went down the stairs, he decided that it might be more politic if she found another job. His mother would protest at training a new servant, but Serafina was pretty and Cardito was young, and it would soon be spring.

V

Domingo cursed with irritation the next morning as he struggled into his clothes, savagely demanding of an unkind fate why trains from the States insisted on arriving at the unchristian hour of seven forty-five A. M. An incessant knocking at the door did not soothe him.

"Go away!" he shouted. "Can a man not dress in peace?"

"It is Serafina, s'ñor Domingo. Ay, the saints be merciful!"

The image of a very ill Cardito burst across his mind, and he fairly leaped to the door. "What is it? What has happened?"

Her eyes were larger than ever, and there were purple shadows along the cheekbones. "I didn't mean to go to sleep. I stayed awake all night, but at dawn my eyes must have shut . . ."

He caught her arm and shook her into silence. "Begin again, quietly."

She gulped and took a deep breath. "He's gone."

"Impossible! He's . . ."

"He's gone, s'ñor Domingo. The moment I found his bed vacant I ran to the kitchen. Doña Petra says he drank some coffee and went to his examination . . ."

Domingo gasped in relief and relaxed against the wall to fight off a surge of dizziness which he knew was caused by too much adrenalin pumping into his system.

"S'ñor Domingo! You're not sick, too?" Her voice rose to a wail.

He opened his eyes and shook his head at her.

"Don't be more of a stupid than necessary, Serafina. The sleep and the liquor probably worked a better cure than a hundred doctors. He's perfectly all right. Stop worrying, and stop worrying me."

Again that expression of disappointment washed across her face. She bobbed him a curtsy and walked slowly away, while he turned to snatch up his hat and overcoat. He reminded himself to speak to his mother about dismissing Serafina. It was a pity. She was a nice little thing, quiet and easy about the house. Good servants were a problem these days, since so many of them preferred to go to the States where they could get higher wages. But Serafina was much too interested in Cardito. The situation would inevitably take a serious turn if it were not stopped now.

Domingo's mouth twitched as he remembered his own first love affair with the pantry maid. He had been seventeen and she fifteen, and her heavy braids curled like thongs about his wrists. When they were discovered, the girl . . . what was her name? He no longer remembered. . . . At any rate, she had been promptly dismissed, while he had been cowed with dire threats of don Agapito's anger, should the affair ever come to his attention.

He tried to recall the girl's face, but it was too dim. Odd, because when he moved his fingers, he could still feel the texture of her glossy braids.

He shrugged the memory away and hurried down the patio

steps to the rear of the house where Sofía, slender in brown, with an orange and yellow scarf at her throat, was already sitting in the car waiting for him.

They drove in their usual silence to the railroad station. With few common interests, they never bothered to manufacture small talk. Once Sofía asked him if he thought don Agapito had really believed that Cardito was ill, and Domingo shrugged his shoulders for answer.

As they waited for traffic-free passage across the wide expanse of Avenida Madero, she said irritably that she would be glad when they found another chauffeur as she was sick of riding busses. "One of the companies is going on strike this week, and then it will be worse than ever."

"You should learn to drive yourself." He was aware immediately after he said it that the suggestion was unkind. They both knew that don Agapito did not approve of women driving cars.

Domingo parked in front of the long red stone pile that was the station, and they went into the chilly waiting room to be greeted with the news that the train was fifteen minutes late.

Sofía pulled her long coat with its high collar of brown fur closer about her.

"I refuse to stand here and freeze, Domingo. Can't we get some coffee?"

"The only place is the Chinese restaurant here in the station. The coffee leaves much to be desired."

"But it's hot?"

"It's hot."

She turned on her heel and walked ahead of him. Watching her slim elegance, Domingo was suddenly proud of the good taste with which she selected her clothes. Her dress allowance was considerably smaller than most of her friend's; but she had the gift of style and was generally considered the best dressed girl in Monterrey. He wished that he liked her more. He loved her very much, but he did not really like her.

She was too restrained, too remote, for his own warm nature to understand. I pity the man who marries her, he thought idly while he watched the waiter put thick cups in front of them.

At this hour in the morning the white tiled restaurant was nearly empty. Two men were sitting at the imitation mahogany counter, dipping *tortillas* in plates of steaming beans and drinking Coca-Colas. The other tables were empty. Behind the cash register a young man, chewing on a toothpick, was perched on a high stool.

The absence of other women did not disturb Sofía's poise. She stripped her gloves from her hands without haste and patted a curve of hair into position beneath her hat brim.

On impulse Domingo asked her why she wore a hat in Monterrey. "Even our mother seldom puts one on."

Sofía shrugged and sipped her coffee before answering. "You were right. It is vile, but hot. I wear a hat because it pleases me."

"Do you always do what pleases you, Sofía?"

Her eyes slid past his. There was a pause while she watched the cashier make change for one of the men at the counter. "In small things, why not?"

Domingo stared at his coffee cup. "Small things," he repeated bitterly. "Some day one of us will lose our temper and tell Uncle Agapito the truth . . ."

"No!" Her clenched fist hit the table with a small bang. "None of us must ever tell him!" Seeing his expression of surprise, she added in a lower tone, "Why should his money go to the other branch of our family? We've had to endure his beastliness for too many years."

"Blessed Saints, Sofía! Surely you're not counting on an inheritance . . ."

"And why not? He has plenty of money; he has no children. If he leaves his money to that milk-faced wife, she'll spend every cent of it within a year, and he knows it."

"After putting up with Uncle Agapito for fifteen years Tecla deserves to spend it."

"She was a fool to marry him. She knew when she did it that he would keep her on a short rein. Let her take the consequences."

He sat back and carefully lighted a cigarette. "You're almost as granite as Uncle Agapito."

"He should not have taught his lesson so well," she retorted. They could hear a train whistle far in the distance, and she gathered up her purse and gloves. "Did you invite me to this coffee, or do you expect me to pay for my own?"

He suddenly laughed. "Yes, my young miser, I did invite you. Do I not always?"

"Cardito doesn't."

His voice softened as it always did when he spoke of his brother. "But then he gets only five pesos a week for spending money."

"I get ten," she said dryly, "but I save five. That's the difference between us."

He quirked an eyebrow at her and went to pay the check. The cashier was a stocky young man with coarse black hair and a tilt to his snub nose. Although his shoulders were propped against the wall, vitality swirled in him.

He switched his toothpick from the left side of his full-lipped mouth to the right as he took the check. Suddenly his eyes widened. He flicked the toothpick to the floor and jumped to his feet. "Forgive me, s'ñor, but aren't you the young Vázquez de Anda?"

"Some people call me that."

"Of the real estate firm?"

At Domingo's nod, the man bent forward across the counter. "I've heard that you need a chauffeur. Me, I am Mateo Chapa. I would like to apply for the post."

Domingo frowned, then was amused by the impudence. "I'm not sure . . ."

"Let me make myself plain, s'ñor." He started to come out from behind the counter, but Domingo checked him.

"One moment. The train approaches. I must meet it. I'm afraid I have no time . . ."

"May I come to see you when there is time? I only heard this morning that you needed someone. I was planning to come to your office. I could do that. Indeed, s'ñor . . ."

Sofía said impatiently, "We must hurry, Domingo."

He nodded and started toward the door, saying over his shoulder, 'You might have to wait quite a while. I'm showing some lots . . ."

"I'll wait," Chapa called after him, "all day if I have to. I have much patience."

Domingo waved and hurried toward one of the long cement fingers thrust out into the railroad yards. A cold gust of wind made him plunge his hands deeper into his overcoat pockets.

Sofía pattered beside him, then came to a jerking halt. "I forgot my handkerchief. I'll be back in a moment."

Before he could offer to fetch it for her, she had turned and darted through the restaurant door. He shrugged and moved toward the Pullmans that were slowly backing into place.

Outside of a few railroad employees, the platform was deserted. Monterrey business men traveled by air, leaving the train to tourists. Brunhilda had wanted to fly south from New York, but doña Otilia, an avid reader of a weekly magazine called *Policía* (borrowed from doña Petra, the cook), was convinced that air travel was synonymous with sudden death. *Policía* showed all plane accidents, complete with mangled corpses, in photographs which so worked on doña Otilia's imagination that the thought of Brunhilda high in the air made her cry herself into a state of exhaustion. Even don Agapito was upset by her grief, and wired his niece to stay on the ground.

To the banker, however, a plane was the only sensible means of travel. He made the two hour trip back and forth to México City as though he were shuttling from his office to his home.

Leave such speed, Domingo thought, to Uncle Agapito. Brunhilda's homecoming is the important thing. A warm glow dilated his heart as he visioned the four Vázquez de Anda children together again. Tonight there would be the intimate jokes of years, and Brunhilda showing off her new musical adeptness under don Rafael's proud eyes. Uncle Lucio might even play "Farewell, Mamá Carlota" on the mandolin. Uncle Agapito's presence would not dampen the happiness too much.

Domingo remembered that there had been some talk last night of his uncle's having to attend a banker's convention in the Capital. Although he felt sorry for the bankers, he hoped that don Agapito would leave this afternoon. Then the family reunion could truly be held in peace.

Sofía came up to him and slid her arm through his in a rare gesture of affection. "I found it," she said blithely. "I'd left it on the table."

Domingo frowned. "I must be getting old, or not noticing any more. I can't remember your ever taking your handkerchief out of your purse."

Her eyes slid sideways toward him and then toward the Pullmans. "Soon you'll be as absent-minded as Uncle Lucio. Ay! The train has finally stopped."

She pulled on his arm in her excitement at the thought of Brunhilda's homecoming. He noticed that there was added color in her cheeks, and her lips were slightly parted, almost as though they were waiting to be kissed. This fancy made him smile, for Sofía, in spite of her smooth elegance, was too cold a type to attract the attention of Monterrey's eligible young men. Even the usually dense don Agapito would snortingly demand, when he was angry with her, why she had to exist at all, since she was obviously doomed to die an old maid.

Domingo felt a great admiration for her also, because he knew how much she had wanted to go to the States to study finance. She had never shown any jealousy of Brunhilda's being chosen instead, and was now as excited as her nature would permit her to be over Brunhilda's return.

He slipped his hand from his pocket and laid it over her gloved fingers. Immediately she shrank into herself and, under the pretext of waving, drew away from him. This broke the intimacy between them, and he felt alone again, and cold, and a part of the cloud veiled February day.

The porter had descended to the platform and was helping tourists to alight, warning them that the train would stop in Monterrey only twenty minutes before plunging south to México City. The men and women and a few children passed Domingo in a haze of faces. They meant nothing to him. He was intent on only one face, and it was appearing in the Pullman vestibule now.

He waved excitedly, and the next moment he and Sofía and Brunhilda put their arms around each other all at once. They laughed and kissed each other's cheeks, and patted each other's shoulders, and even cried a little, because two years is a long time, and Brunhilda was home again.

He saw that her face was as plump and soft as ever, but even prettier. He told her so, and she glowed in answer, although she was disappointed that Cardito had not come too. Giggling a little, Sofía described their younger brother's experiment in brandy drinking with flashing gestures that were underscored by Domingo.

As they passed some of the strolling tourists he overheard a little boy say, "They're speaking Spanish, Mama. I thought you just spoke that in school," and found time to grin and wink before his sisters swept him through the station to the waiting automobile.

The train agent from the Ancira Hotel bustled after them. "Eh, Domingo, there has been a call from your house. You're to go by the University and pick up Cardito."

Domingo called his thanks. As the car rolled out of the station yard, Brunhilda gave a trilling little laugh as foreign to the old Brunhilda as were the saucy green hat and the magnificent fur coat. "I'd forgotten that the people below called one by one's first name."

Sofía answered her, but Domingo mentally raised his eyebrows. He wondered if our cousin the Jaimes (related by marriage to the Palafox) had taught Brunhilda a few things not scheduled in her music course.

The three were pressed into the front seat with Brunhilda next to him, and he found difficulty in maneuvering the car because of her bulky coat, the fox skins long and silky and obviously new. He tried to calculate the price and was glad when Sofía exclaimed over it.

Brunhilda stroked its shining beauty with almost simpering pride. "I think it was so sweet of Uncle Agapito to send me the money."

The shock of her statement made Domingo jerk the wheel. The next few moments were consumed in attempts to pacify wildly shouting fellow drivers.

Once the turn toward Juárez Street on Avenida Madero was accomplished Domingo relaxed a little. "Do you actually mean that Uncle Agapito sent you some money?"

Sofía's voice held a strong note of warning. "If he ever discovers you spent it for a fur coat . . ."

"Nonsense." The trilling laugh floated again through the car. "He sent me money for the coat, my little geese. Ay, there's the old Lírico! Remember when we used to come and see the Tenorios?"

There came a flood of reminiscences excited by the buildings they passed. Domingo allowed this chatter to swirl about him while he wondered why Brunhilda had told them such an obvious lie. That Uncle Agapito would pay out good money for a fur coat was too absurd to be stated, much less believed.

Poor Brunhilda was as stupid as ever. Even her lies still held the overtones of her well-remembered, pathetic little efforts to draw attention to herself—to hold the center of the family stage as much and as long as possible. He smiled in his mind. In spite of the pseudo-sophistication, the foreign laugh, the elegant clothes, the true Brunhilda still lurked beneath the new façade, and it was wonderful to have her home again.

He settled back and allowed the life and color of the Avenida Madero to absorb him. To him it was the real heart of Monterrey, although actually its three miles of parkway formed the city's northern boundary. In the old days before the Great Revolution, when Morelos Street was called Commercial Street, it was too narrow to take care of the quickly growing business section brought into being by the railroad and the new factories, and many of the merchants had moved out here. Downtown property holders, horrified at losing so much good rent, widened the street, renamed it for the patriot Morelos, and tried to entice the merchants back with modern buildings. But their efforts came too late. Tourists spent their money on Morelos Street; Monterrey spent hers on Avenida Madero.

Here were little shops that dealt in everything from ice-cream cones to grand pianos. The "Jew of the Bazaar" lent money here to the financially embarrassed. Here were the theatres: the glamorous film palaces with tickets that sold for three pesos each, and seats that swung back and forth so that no one need trouble to rise to allow a late comer to pass down the row; the tiny hole-in-the-wall movies that had never been wired for sound, and for twenty *centavos* offered such stars as Wallace Reid and Gloria Swanson; the legitimate theatres where the Capital's best talent could sometimes be tempted to come and perform; and the burlesque shows with their flashing signs and performer photographs to entice the wandering eye.

Branching off from this street was the great Market of the North that imported southern folk art for Mexicans instead of tourists and also housed a branch of the liquor store that sold the same bottles downtown at four times the price.

Three miles of barbershops, hardware stores, leather workers, tinsmiths, fruit stalls, clothing stores, furniture stores, bookshops,

43

music stores, marked on the east by a giant smelter (on the east, said Domingo, was Industry) and on the west by the city hospital (on the west, said Domingo, was Death).

This street was Domingo's passion. Whenever he was free, morning, noon or night, he would drive down it. Only in the hour before dawn was it ever silent, and even then it had a quivering stillness, as though it were aching to burst into sound again at the slightest opportunity.

To him it symbolized Monterrey, clanging with music from a thousand radios and victrolas. It was as hard and garish as a painted woman, as full of laughter, as full of warmth. Lacking the subtlety, the charm, the sweet placidity of the south, it was frankly interested in only one thing: money.

"Loving Monterrey," his Uncle Lucio had often told him, "is like loving an evil woman. You know she is evil. She parades all her faults for you without shame. If you fail her, she will leave you without tears, but you can't resist her. You will crawl on your knees to win a smile from her, and you will endure any shame, any humiliation, if she will only love you. Monterrey is not for the poet, the artist, the dreamer. She belongs to the warrior, to the iron-fisted man. Monterrey is no city for the feeble and weak. Keep strong, Domingo. Keep strong and conquer her."

Uncle Lucio had been very full of beer the night he made that speech. Domingo had never forgotten it, because it put his own feelings into words, just as this Avenue put them into symbols.

As always, it was with a slight feeling of regret that he turned off it onto Juárez Street. Brunhilda gave little squeals of delight as she recognized familiar homes and businesses. "It's as though I've been away a million, million years," she kept repeating, "instead of just two."

She exclaimed again as he swung the car around the small Colegio Civil Plaza and stopped in front of the University. The white building with its rose granite door-case filled the entire block. Although modern, it had kept the colonial architecture of its predecessor, the old Colegio Civil.

"Why, it's been painted, Domingo. How elegant it looks. And have they moved the law school over here? I thought this was just for the Schools of Bachelors and Civil Engineering."

44

Domingo raised his brows at Sofía. "Our poor brother Cardito has encountered a few difficulties in getting out of the School of Bachelors."

Sofía sighed. "He has a professor, the Counselor Farías, who keeps on failing him. All his other courses he takes in the law school downtown, but for three years the poor boy has returned here to take and retake this one course."

Brunhilda's full red lips curled slightly. "If he studied more and played less . . ."

Domingo slid to the sidewalk. "I fear you will not recognize our solemn younger brother. There are times when he makes even me in my ancient glory feel as though I should just be entering kindergarten."

Brunhilda's new laugh followed him across the sidewalk. Then he was inside the front patio with its gallery of pink arches and cherry colored tiles. Classes were going on, and the tree shaded oblong was empty save for a boy who was pacing up and down, nervously puffing on a cigarette.

Seeing Domingo he gave a gasp of relief, tossed the cigarette into a rosebush, and hurried up to him. "You are the Vázquez de Anda?" At Domingo's nod, he clutched his arm and maneuvered him toward the auditorium doors. "We wanted to call a doctor, but you know how the Rector is—always nervous. And that fool of a Farías . . ."

Domingo, with a flare of worry, tried to make the boy stop long enough to explain what had happened, but he only shook his head and led the way into the darkened auditorium.

The change from daylight to this shadowed room blinded Domingo for a moment. All he could see were the great arched windows, with their designs in ruby, emerald, and sapphire glass of mighty male figures surging upward through intricately twisted tropical fruits and flowers.

Someone tapped his arm nervously. "Perhaps we should have called a doctor. He kept insisting he wanted you. You are his brother?"

In order to see better, Domingo tightly shut his eyes, then opened them to watch a small nervous man emerge from shadow into substance. He was nervously waving his pince-nez like a fan, and had to tilt his head back to peer nearsightedly into Domingo's face.

45

"I am the Rector—this is all most unfortunate. The Counselor Farías says it is a stupid game, but I don't think he would fall down the stairs headforemost if it were a game. I mean it isn't logical, and I am a man of logic."

Domingo wanted to scream at him for an explanation. With a great effort of will he kept his voice reduced to its usual quiet level. "If you would explain what has happened . . ."

His student guide burst into voluble speech, to be snapped off by the Rector. "If you please. I will explain it. Return to your examination."

"I haven't any. I've taken mine."

"Then go back to where you came from. Go away!"

The boy took himself off, and the Rector settled himself more comfortably on his tiny feet. "The Counselor Farías was giving an examination to your brother's section. The difficulty, of course, is that all of the questions had been given out to the students, and your brother had time to read them to see if he knew the answers."

"What has happened to my brother, señor Rector?"

"One moment. I must tell this in logical sequence or you'll never understand it—and neither will I. I was saying something. What was it?"

"The questions . . ."

"Don't interrupt, *if* you please. The Counselor Farías contends that your brother, realizing that he would again fail the examination, immediately acquired a sickness, staggered melodramatically from the room, pretended to faint on the upper gallery, and fell headforemost down the stairs, all to make a sensation and attract pity to himself."

"Blessed saints! Where is my . . ."

"If you will please not interrupt. This I cannot quite believe. He could pretend to faint just outside the door. Why risk great injury, even the possibility of breaking his neck, by tumbling down the stairs? Vázquez de Anda has always impressed me as being a most sensible young man. . . ."

Domingo took three deep breaths. "If you please, señor Rector. Where—is—my—brother!"

"He's stretched out on one of the front seats. Now you, señor, as an intelligent man, will agree with me . . ."

Domingo did not wait to hear the end of the sentence. He

46

ran down the aisle and saw, with a sharp contraction of his heart, a limp body stretched on one of the long pew-like benches. His nervous fingers felt throat and wrist, and the raging fever seemed to burn his skin. He said gruffly to the little Rector who had pattered after him, "Present my compliments to the Counselor Farías and tell him he holds the distinction of being the most stupid idiot in Monterrey. Have you sent for a doctor?"

"Naturally not. If it were only pretense, a doctor would quickly spread the rumor that a student had actually hoodwinked us . . ."

"And if he had died, the police might have put you all in jail for criminal neglect."

"Such melodrama, my good soul. He's not dead. You can actually hear him breathing."

Domingo gave a snort of disgust, took off his overcoat, and tenderly wrapped his brother in it. The rasping breathing terrified him even more than the fever. He said through his teeth, "If it would not trouble you too much, be so kind as to call an ambulance."

"But, man, surely there's no need . . ."

Domingo thrust him out of his path with such a savage push that it tumbled the little dignity against the opposite row of benches. He paid no attention to the sputters of indignation as he sprinted up the aisle to the back door and plunged into the maze of offices. One of the stenographers was using the telephone. He snatched it from her with a muttered apology, wasted precious moments arguing with central, who insisted that he look up the hospital number in the book, finally grabbed the book and almost tore out the pages in his frantic haste.

The stenographer calmly took the book away from him and gave him the emergency number. This time he was connected, and he sagged with relief when a placid voice informed him help would immediately be on the way.

The girl patted his arm. "Do not worry too much. Cardito has the body of a young horse."

He looked gratefully at her. She had the alive face of an intelligent little monkey. He said, "But he might have gotten concussion in the fall. And the fools moved him."

She lifted her shoulders in a high shrug. "As long as state politics governs the University, what would you? Now if it were autonomous we might get men here instead of the governor's poor relations."

He nodded, and they shook hands in a sudden feeling of fellowship. "We're in the auditorium. You'll bring the doctors as soon as they arrive?"

She pushed back her chair and hurried to the door. "I will wait for them on the steps. Do not worry, señor, and when Cardito is better, tell him he's a fickle fool." She winked at him and was gone.

The ambulance arrived in an amazingly short time, and Cardito was tenderly conveyed to the large Catholic hospital on the Saltillo Road.

Domingo was not sure whether he should take the girls to the hospital or home. Sofía said, "We are closer to the railroad station than any place else. Take us back there, hire that man for your chauffeur, allow yourself to be dropped off at the hospital, and he can drive us home. You know that our mother will have hysterics between the joy of seeing Brunhilda and the agony of a sick Cardito. She'll need us more than Cardito will."

"But I don't even know if the man can drive or not . . ."

"He would hardly apply for a job as chauffeur if he couldn't. And he seems quite capable. Did you watch him making change this morning? I could not have done better myself."

"Stop hesitating, Domingo," Brunhilda snapped, "and do something."

Realizing that Sofía's plan was filled with common sense, Domingo agreed to it. Nevertheless, all the way to the station a nagging little voice deep in his mind kept warning him against the young cashier.

VI

The doctors at the hospital said that Cardito had pneumonia. So far as they could tell from preliminary examinations, he had suffered no concussion from the fall. "The faint undoubtedly relaxed him enough to save him. He is not even bruised."

They put the boy on sulpha drugs and told Domingo that nothing more could be done until the fever was lowered. "Wait," said the doctors. "All anyone can do now is wait." They advised him to be thankful for the miracle of sulpha. In the old days the crisis was a matter of days; now it was a matter of hours.

He assured them that he was thankful, but as he sat down stairs on a leather sofa, his elbows on his knees, his hat twisting and turning in his hands, he felt as though he were swimming in a sea of guilt. "If only I had known enough about medicine. I would have called a doctor last night," he repeated over and over. Once more he felt fierce resentment surge against don Agapito's cool dismissal of his medical ambitions.

"An heir is needed for your father's real estate office," don Agapito had said ten years ago. "Socially your ambition to be a doctor is a very fine thing. Economically it is most unsound. Consider: six years to study, another four or five years to attract sufficient patients to make you self-supporting. And where is the money to come from during that time? Not from your father and he with four children. Certainly not from me. No, no, the real estate office is much the best."

"I could work my way through," Domingo answered. "In the States many boys . . ."

"In the States," said don Agapito, who did not approve of the States, "perhaps. But this is México and you are a Vázquez de Anda. You will go into the real estate office."

After ten years, the words should have lost their power to wound, but their knife was as sharp now as the day they were first honed. As a protecting shield, Domingo kept his personal library filled with medical books, which he read and re-read, until he felt confidence in his ability to diagnose family ailments.

"I was so sure it was only a bad cold," he told himself in partial apology, against which his inner mind argued. "He had fever. You can't play tricks with fevers. Serafina knew he was sick, but you were too wise, too sure of your medical knowledge. If he dies it will be your fault. Your fault. Your fault."

The phrase rang louder and louder in his ears. Unable to endure it, he paced up and down the floor, trying to count each green tile as he set his foot on it. But his usual refuge in mathematics was proving no refuge now. "Your fault, your fault, your fault!" The phrase chained itself to the rhythm of his movements, and he found himself continually hovering near the entrance with the dread-sprinkled hope that a nurse or doctor was coming to him with news.

He was familiar with the new treatment for pneumonia. In the old days it was whiskey every hour and a freezing room. Now the room was kept warm, and large doses of sulpha were administered to force down the raging fever. The temperature should drop within twenty-four hours, and at the end of five days the lungs should be clear, the patient safe in life again.

The battle now was between Cardito's fever and the sulpha. Domingo knew that it was much too soon to expect any change, and yet every rustle of a nurse's starched apron focussed his attention on that empty doorway.

When his mother and sisters arrived, quickly followed by his father and Uncle Lucio, he startled them out of tears by the abrupt announcement that he was leaving the hospital. It was their custom, when any of the family fell sick, for all relatives and friends to cluster around the sickbed. Domingo had often protested this attitude, pointing out how bad it was for the patient.

"Everyone does it," they answered. "Shall we appear heartless to the world?"

He felt now that if he heard one more sob from his mother, one more breast beating phrase from his father, one more lamentation from his Uncle and sisters, he would lose his mind. He loved them, but there were occasions when his only relief was to escape from them completely.

Also, he dared not remain until don Agapito arrived. His uncle had ruthlessly destroyed his life's ambition to be a doctor and in destroying it might have been responsible for killing Cardito. Don Agapito was the last man Domingo wanted to see at this moment.

He fled down the front steps and paused beside the automobile where the new chauffeur waited, a toothpick drooping between his lips.

"If the family inquires for me, tell them I'm using the bus."

"I could drive you to town and return, s'ñor Domingo . . ."

"No. I want to walk. What did you say your name was?"

"Mateo Chapa."

"It's a good name." He started away from the car but impulsively turned back. "Tell me, is it your life's ambition to be a chauffeur?"

"Ay, no, s'ñor—señor Domingo. I want to sell real estate, and yours is the best office in the city."

"You really want to sell real estate?"

Chapa slid out from under the wheel and stretched his stocky body to its full height. "From the time I was a little boy. Not small lots for homes, you understand, but big sites for factories. I will be a man of money when I die." There was a look of exaltation on his face, and strength flowed through him as water flows through rich farm earth.

In Domingo's eyes Chapa ceased to be a single man and became all Monterrey's young men who, like don Agapito, saw life in terms of economics instead of human values. All his curiosity about Chapa was abated in a wave of revulsion. He turned without comment and went off down the Saltillo Road.

A bus was waiting, but he passed it, preferring to walk. He barely noticed when the Road changed into Hidalgo Street. In order to keep from thinking about his brother and his intensifying hatred for his uncle, he tried to compute real estate divisions, but this involved the thought of money which returned the circle to don Agapito.

As he passed the Quinta Calderón, he started to turn into the large gardens for a glass of beer, decided it was too early, and strolled on. He wondered how many other men had gone along this street with hatred seething in them and anxiety for someone they loved. There must have been thousands of them in the three hundred years since Monterrey first came into existence.

Hidalgo Street was the old Camino Real. Along it rode messengers from the Viceroy with orders for His Christian Majesty's most loyal Governor of the Province of Nuevo León. Some of those messengers must have hated the Viceroy or the Governor; some of them must have left behind them weeping wives, sick children. In those days it took six months to travel from the Capital to Monterrey—six months of not knowing if your family would be alive to greet you when you returned. No, not six months, a year—more than a year.

And what of the French soldiers who had marched down this street to capture the city for Maximilian? True, men from the Foreign Legion were used to serving on foreign soil. But there were other soldiers, little Frenchmen, torn out of the only world they knew, to be plunged into a strange war in what, to them, must have been a barbaric country, to keep an emperor's crown on the head of a man who was not even French, but Austrian.

They were surely bewildered, Domingo decided, but resentment must have invaded their bewilderment, and a dull, gnawing hatred for Louis Napoleon. The Mexican fiasco had helped to lose him his crown, had made the Spanish Eugenie forever unpopular in France. And the story of that fiasco had been written home in nostalgic letters by men in Veracruz, Guadalajara, Tampico, Monterrey.

Hatred could lose two emperors their crowns. Hatred could kill and maim and destroy. What, then, of Uncle Agapito? Did he sleep well at night, knowing that his pillow was poisoned with hatred? But was he really aware that he was hated? He was so satisfied with his life, so certain of his own power that he probably never took into account the feelings of those who surrounded him. Domingo remembered an old proverb: "The satisfied cat forgets the rat." Uncle Agapito gobbled down the cheese of his own desires and never bothered about the hungry mice who tumbled out of his way.

Domingo curled his fingers inside his palms and thrust them deeper into the pockets of his overcoat. It was not right that one man's ambitions should so dominate the lives of others. His father, his uncle Lucio, himself, and Sofía had all been flattened under the great iron hand. The only ones to escape thus far were Brunhilda and Cardito. Brunhilda, of course, could never be flattened, any more than could a piece of sponge rubber. But Cardito?

If he tries to dominate Cardito, I believe I could kill him, Domingo thought savagely. He ruined my life but he shan't touch Cardito. The boy shall have his chance if he lives. If he lives, dear God. Let him live, dear sweet God.

He found himself near the new church which had been built in place of the beautiful old Purisima. To his mother's horror he called it the stone quonset hut because its ovaloid shape had an extraordinary resemblance to the war-born buildings. Of rough gray granite, it had a bell tower at one end, built in what an architect friend of Domingo's called the "stove-pipe design."

It was, in Domingo's eyes, a monstrosity. He would have thought it ugly even if he had not known that don Agapito con-

52

sidered it a gem of modern architecture, had actually contributed money toward its construction. Don Agapito was a firm believer in all things modern—except women—and he saw no reason why churches should continually follow the plateresque of Mexico's golden age of cathedrals. Domingo agreed with this reasoning, but he did not agree with the idea that everything modern was good simply because it was modern. He privately believed that the architect had visioned this church in a nightmare; but nevertheless it was a church and at the moment he felt great need for communion with God.

Like many Mexican young men, Domingo's religion was painted on his soul with tinsel colors. He loved its pageantry, its peace, the fragrance of its incense, but its duties fell lightly upon him. He went to mass when he pleased, usually just at Christmas and Easter. Since Father Andrea died he seldom went to confession, although his mother was always introducing him to priests with the hope that he would find a confessor whom he liked and respected. But when his spirit was troubled beyond endurance, he would go into a church and pray for a little while to St. Anthony, the Monk, on whose day, January 17, he had been born.

He felt a great kinship to St. Anthony, whom the devil had lashed with whips and tempted with fair women. Somehow St. Anthony was always able to calm him and bring him peace.

Now, seeing the church, he went into its cool interior and knelt at the lofty altar. He prayed for a long time for Cardito's life. When he went out onto the street again, he telephoned the hospital from a sidewalk fruit stand.

There was still no news, so he continued down Hidalgo toward the center of town. He was completely unaware of other pedestrians. Afterwards he knew that he must have passed many people, for the streets of Monterrey, especially in the commercial sections, were always busy, but he walked through a mist that was even grayer than the cold light of the February afternoon.

Still intent on his prayers to St. Anthony, his feet carried him along of their own volition, with no guidance from his conscious mind.

It gave him a start of surprise, therefore, when he found himself on a vaguely familiar balcony. At first he felt dazed, as though wakening from a dream, and then he recognized the grimy walls and doors, the dreary patio a floor below him to the right.

His feet had brought him here. His hand opened the studio door. The little anteroom was empty.

Even as he rapped on the counter, he wondered what he would ask the photographer when Bárcenas appeared. He wondered if his tongue would ask for the woman, and again the memory of that pale mask suspended in darkness flowed through his mind. Why had she haunted him, this woman? He knew her name, Márgara, and that was all. Was she ugly? Was she beautiful?

The green curtains drew slowly aside, and the woman came through.

Staring at her, he felt as though all of his senses were surrounding her, probing her, seeking to discover what she was really like. The carnation fragrance of her body, too faint for any other man to notice, was strong in his nostrils. His tongue tasted her sweet flesh, and his hands felt her velvet softness. His ears could hear the pulsing of her blood. As he looked at her, the room faded, while her head enlarged to fill his mental screen.

She was tall for a Mexican woman, nearly five feet, five inches. Her black hair was parted in the middle and fastened in a heavy knot at the nape of the long neck. Her forehead was broad, her eyes long under the arched brows, while the high cheekbones seemed to cut through the flesh. The chin was rounded, and the mouth wide but delicately cut.

Sensing her so completely, he knew that he had been right: it was a mask of a face, revealing nothing of the woman trapped inside the skull.

As though aware of his intensity, her lids drooped until the thick lashes lay like a fringe on the honey colored skin. Realizing that he had embarrassed her, he flushed and nervously shifted his weight while he searched his mind for some explanation as to his being here at all. It would have been very simple to have tossed off any excuse to Bárcenas, but he could not lie to this waiting face. He breathed deeply to quiet his jumping nerves and stumblingly asked for the photographer.

Her lids raised again. For answer she turned her head and glanced down the counter. He looked in the same direction and saw a clock. The hands, pointing to one, mutely explained that the man was out to lunch. As she looked back at Domingo, he mut-

54

tered the first words that popped into his head, "But the door was open."

Her lips parted and he was aware that at last she was going to speak. She was so completely a definite Indian type that he knew before the notes sounded that they would flow in the sweet singsong of the flower venders of Xochimilco.

She spoke. The shock of hearing destroyed the meaning of the words. There was no accent at all. Her voice was as unidentifiable as a piece of blank paper. He had been so certain of what he thought he was going to hear, that what he really heard startled him as no phrase could have done. There was no singsong. There was not even a section accent so that it could be identified with the tumbling words of Veracruz, the slow pace of Michoacán, the flat tones of Jalisco, the clipped syllables of the frontier. Her voice was as great a mask as her face, disclosing nothing beyond the shape of the words.

She did not seem at all surprised when he asked her to repeat what she had said. There was no impatience in her, and yet she was not stolid. She was as tranquil as a quiet evening, as the hour before dawn in the mountains.

"I was just going to close the door, señor. We open again at three o'clock. If you wish to return then. . . ." She did not shrug as a northern woman would have done. She simply allowed the words to trail into silence.

"You have a telephone? I wonder if I might. . . ."

Again her head turned toward the counter. He saw the telephone with the book laid neatly beside it. The cover was very new, as though no one had ever used it. He found his number and gave it to central but quickly turned as she moved toward the green curtains.

"Please don't go." He meant to be casual, but his voice in his own ears held an almost pleading note. She heard it also, because, for the first time, her black eyes reflected an expression. Then the surprise was gone and the eyes were blank again.

The placid hospital tones sounded in his ear. There was no further news of Cardito. He slumped a little as he dropped the instrument back into its cradle.

The soft contralto rippled around him and warmed him. "Someone you know is ill, señor?"

"My brother. He has pneumonia."

55

"You do not stay in the hospital with your brother?" She asked the personal question quite simply, as if she had said, "This is an interesting phenomenon which needs further investigation," and in the same spirit he answered her with his belief that the very sick needed doctors, not weeping relatives.

Slowly her head nodded. She evidently found this an intelligent reason, because her hand gestured toward a chair, and without waiting to see if he obeyed, she slipped between the curtains.

He bit his lip in perplexity, not only at her but at himself. What was he doing here? True, this studio had captured his interest yesterday evening—was it only yesterday evening? Now it seemed a hundred years ago. The brief glimpse he had had of her in the shadows had intrigued him more than any woman had done for years; but none of these reasons was sufficient to explain his actions now.

She came back through the curtains carrying a tray on which were coffee and a plate of sweetbread. He took the tray from her, and she moved some photographs off a table so that he would have a place to put it.

Neither spoke as she poured coffee and steaming milk into the cups. As she gestured toward the sweetbread, he murmured, "You are very kind."

She shook her head, and the small gold earrings vibrated against her throat. "There is no kindness when one is in trouble. Only necessity, and perhaps a little comfort."

The words surprised him. The women of his world would never have been capable of such phrases, but then they would not have offered coffee to a man whose name they did not even know.

To correct this omission he said, "My name is Vázquez de Anda."

Again she surprised him. He felt as though she were continually giving him a series of small electric shocks. She said, "I know. You are Domingo Vázquez de Anda. Someone told me your name on the Plaza one Sunday evening."

"My name? But why? I am a person of no importance."

She bent forward and poured more coffee into his cup. The honey colored mask was as impenetrable as ever. "I asked who you were. You sold the building next door to us three months

56

ago. I was worried for fear you might sell this one. It is very difficult to rent space for a photographer's studio."

"You mean you've known me for three months, and I never knew you existed until yesterday?" The question was wrenched out of him before he had time to weigh its implications. •

"Why should you know me? You are the Vázquez de Anda, and I. . . ." Her head titled to one side, and the full red lips smiled slightly. "I am a person of no consequence."

"You say my name as though it were a title. It means nothing . . ."

"In Monterrey it means everything. Your uncle Agapito is a king . . ."

"A pirate king."

"Does it matter? He has power."

Again there was silence while Domingo turned her words over in his mind. He asked slowly, "Why do you say 'power'? Anyone else would have said 'money.' "

"To me it is the power that is important, not the money. Of what good is money, of what good is anything without power?"

He bent his head and crumpled a flake of sugar paste between his fingers. "I wish you hadn't said that. I wish you hadn't."

For the first time the mask broke as a dusky flush rose to her cheeks. The red glowed beneath the honey skin, and then receded as quickly as it had risen. "You have so much security, señor. How can you judge what you do not know?"

He peered through the cracks of the mask and what he saw frightened him a little. Here were long years of poverty, of trailing, perhaps, from one city to another, seeking the security of daily bread and daily shelter. The coffee and sweetbread in front of him took on a new aspect. Up to this moment he had never considered them as symbols of sacrifice, and yet his history lessons had taught him that men had stolen to buy bread, had been hanged for stealing it. He suddenly pushed the plate away from him and stood up.

"You are right, Señora. I have no basis of judgment."

"Now you are angry," she murmured, and then, suddenly, she laughed. It was gay laughter filled with bubbling humor. "And I am not married. Bárcenas is my father, not my husband."

His heart gave a high leap, and in his head there were wild birds singing. He sat down again and offered her a cigarette from his case. She turned one between her fingers, then bent forward so that he could light it for her. "Why did you think he was my husband? Do we not look alike?"

"No," he shook his head doubtfully. "You have something he lacks. He seems so—so . . ." He paused, trying to find a word to express what he meant without offending her.

She supplied it. "Afraid?"

"I was going to say 'nervous.' "

She laughed again, and he wished she would never stop laughing, because, with laughter, she lost her remoteness and became a warm and vital woman.

"He is nervous, too," she admitted, and the mask slid back across her face.

She sat quietly, her hands folded in her lap. He noticed for the first time that her dress was a gray-green wool, plain to the point of severity. It was not fashionable, but it had a simplicity that made it right for her. The color heightened the honey tones of her flesh, and he knew that only a person learned in color would have dared put that olive green against her skin.

He said impulsively, "You painted the backdrops in the studio, and there was a miniature of a man with mustaches."

She kept her eyes on her clasped hands. "My father forgot he had left the miniature there. He looks at it often. I think he really likes to look at it." Her whole body began to shake, and the more she clenched her muscles to fight it, the more she trembled.

Domingo hastily poured hot coffee, knelt beside her, and slid one arm around her waist. With his other hand he pressed the cup against her chattering teeth. "Relax. You must relax. And drink slowly—slowly."

She obeyed him like an automaton. His encircling arm pressed her closer to him and for a single moment they were fused into one body, so that there was no separation between them, either of spirit or of flesh.

Then she sprang up and away from him. Her back pressed against the counter. Her arms stretched along its length. The lax body was at variance with the tense, expressionless face. He was still on his knees gazing up at her, his hands pressed around the cup.

"You must go," she whispered.

"But . . ."

58

"Please. And don't come back. Don't ever come back."

He rose and carefully set the cup on its saucer. After he picked up his hat from where it had fallen on the floor, he said slowly, "I must come back. How can I stay away?"

Slowly her head drooped forward. "Then I must leave."

"No." The decision in him surprised himself. "You will never leave, and I will come back."

She did not answer him. When he left, the picture of her standing there against the counter, her head bowed, went with him.

VII

The Vázquez de Anda house was very gay that afternoon. The sulpha had broken Cardito's fever, Brunhilda was home again, and don Agapito had left on the three o'clock plane to attend a bankers' convention in México City. For five days the family would be free of don Agapito's shadow. That alone, Domingo thought, was worth a celebration without all the added gladness.

Doña Otilia had been bustling about in the kitchen ever since she returned from church at five o'clock, where she had given thanks to the Blessed Virgin for saving her younger son.

Brunhilda spent the afternoon in her room resting from her journey; while Sofía rode back and forth from the house to the hospital, each time loaded with new instructions for Cardito's nurse. Domingo offered to perform this service, but Sofía told him rather cuttingly that women's instructions were too involved for the mind of man.

He did not like her riding alone so much with the new chauffeur: but he reasoned that Chapa's personal ambition to be a great real estate man would keep Sofía safer than any armed guard.

About six o'clock he wandered into the kitchen and teased doña Petra, the cook, who had come with doña Otilia from Veracruz when she moved to Monterrey as a bride.

He loved this kitchen. Its high ceiling and walls were washed in white, as was the chimney hood which came down over the long, tiled brasier. Little hooks had been screwed into the hood's plaster surface to hold cups and jugs from Guadalajara in such a fashion that the yellow pottery spelt out the word "Otilia," for all the world to see who was the mistress of the house. Other kitchens in Monterrey did not sport this magnificence. It was a custom that came from Michoacán. Doña Petra had a sister who lived in Michoacán, "And," said doña Petra, "if my sister can spell her name, then I can spell doña Otilia's."

The floor was unglazed red tile. Doña Petra was very strict with the kitchen maids, requiring that they get down on their knees and wash these tiles every day with stiff yellow brushes and soapy water. Early in the morning the girls could be heard at their scrubbing, the smell of strong soap invading both the great and small dining rooms.

A large black woodstove was a relic of old don Domingo's day, when it was not uncommon for fifty people to be entertained in the large dining room. There had been one banquet just after don Domingo returned from Germany of which doña Petra would often tell the Vázquez de Anda children. A hundred guests had been present, including handsome, dignified General Bernardo Reyes.

"It was in nineteen hundred and eleven," she would sigh, "just after Porfirio Diaz fled to Paris. All Monterrey was certain General Reyes would be the next president. Ay, he was a beautiful man. And it was a beautiful meal: twenty-one courses. The wine flowed like water. Your grandfather looked very grand with his German mustaches. You had been born, niño Domingo, but the rest of you were all in the future. I can remember how your mother blushed when your grandfather gave a toast to Germany and said that her first daughter was to be named for a Brunhilda he had known there."

"I was named for a goddess in an opera," Brunhilda pouted, but doña Petra sniffed knowingly, with a wink to the more precocious Domingo.

"Goddess or woman, what difference, you were named Brunhilda just the same. And General Reyes applauded, and all the people. Germany was much loved in Mexico in nineteen hundred and eleven. Well, that was a long time ago. It was the last great banquet held in this house."

"We have banquets now," Cardito always protested, then hid behind Domingo to escape a loving slap from doña Petra.

"Not as in those days. That was nineteen hundred and eleven. By nineteen hundred and fourteen General Reyes and your grandfather were dead. The Revolutionary general with the eyeglasses had captured the city, and there were soldiers quartered in this house. Can you remember them, niño Domingo?"

"I remember a man who used to set tequila bottles up on the gallery railing and shot the tops off without spilling a drop of liquor."

"If that's all you remember, the saints be praised."

"I can remember horses in the patios. . . ."

"Not the patios. The men stayed in the patios. The horses were kept in the formal parlor, and the top of your mother's French piano was used as a feeding bin. We of the family lived in the servants' quarters. Can you imagine your fine mother sleeping in the servants' quarters? Well, she did, and not a murmur of complaint did she ever make. Even your uncle Agapito must respect her for that. The woman he was married to at the time, God rest her soul in Paradise, made enough complaints to drive even your uncle Agapito crazy."

"I would like to have heard her," Domingo would say gleefully, promptly receiving a box on the ears from doña Petra for the sin of disrespect. But it was a gentle little slap in comparison with the spankings she administered if she found him flirting with the kitchen maids or stealing food from the icebox.

Remembering the old icebox, Domingo raised his brows in scorn at the fine new electrical machine which was the pride of doña Petra's heart. The old one had been a tremendous affair that opened from the top, so that the maids had to stand on a stool and go headforemost into its capacious insides in order to get out food or beer. The young Vázquez de Andas took malicious delight in catching the girls' heels and pushing them farther into the box than they had any intention of going. Muffled screams brought doña Petra with a flailing broom. She always said that when she reached Heaven and heard the angels scream she would automatically snatch up a broom, certain that the young Vázquez de Andas had followed her into the last retreat.

But the new box opened at the front, and Domingo privately decided, was not half so much fun.

61

A long table ran the length of the kitchen. On it were piled dishes filled with red and green chilis and small green tomatoes, boxes of garlic, strings of dried onions, and the baskets of *tortillas* which doña Petra herself patted out of finely ground cornmeal mash every morning. She heartily scorned the new custom of buying them from a *tortilla* woman.

Domingo took a paper thin *tortilla* out of the basket, rolled it up, and popped it into his mouth before doña Petra could snarl at him, "Hollow legs!" pushing him out of the way. Doña Otilia smiled at her older son while she measured rice on a small scale. All food in this house was portioned out daily in properly weighed amounts. Doña Otilia wore her pantry keys at her belt, and even the privileged doña Petra had to seek for her if an extra teaspoonful of flour was needed.

"Go away, Domingo," doña Petra snapped. "Can't you see that you are only in the way?"

"If you stay here," his mother said placidly, "there will not be enough food left for dinner. And don't forget, you are to go to Verónica Miranda's saint's day feast in an hour."

Domingo, who had forgotten all about it, grinned shamefacedly at her. He knew that his mother secretly harbored the thought that some day he would marry Verónica.

"Now go and see if Sofía has come back from the hospital."

He obediently went into the patio, to be halted by doña Petra near the fountain. "Eh, niño, one little moment."

As he turned to face her, she pulled her shawl tighter around her shoulders. At seventy she was as sturdy and agile as a woman of fifty. Her hair was black and glossy. Only the wrinkled skin betrayed her age. "What mischief are you up to now?"

"I, doña Petra? I don't know what you mean."

"And you so innocent! I've known you since the moment you were born. This is the second time you've had that look in your eyes. Who is she?"

"Doña Petra," he told her, amused, "you speak in riddles."

"Do I indeed? Perhaps you think I don't know about that pretty North American you were in love with ten years ago. And now you're in love again, praise the saints. When are you bringing her to call on your mother?"

Domingo stared moodily at the fountain. "Did I bring the North American girl to call on my mother?"

She shook her head at him but let him go without further protest.

Sofía had not yet returned, so he climbed the gallery stairs. As he passed his Uncle Lucio's door, it opened, and the little man's head popped out. Seeing that Domingo was alone, he opened the door wider and beckoned his nephew inside.

Don Lucia's room reflected all of his various interests. A miniature chemistry outfit was on its own table under the window. Another table was set up as an electrical workbench, while on yet another was laid out his carpenter's tools.

In place of pictures, his correspondence school diplomas were neatly framed on the walls, and his mandolin lay beside its case on the bed.

Don Lucio pushed some books off the only chair so that Domingo might sit down. "I want to ask you," he said importantly, "about this fellow, the Counselor Farías. What do you intend to do about him?"

"The Counselor Farías?" Domingo was puzzled. "Why should I do anything about him?"

"From what you told us, if he hadn't argued with the Rector, they might have called a doctor and gotten Cardito to the hospital sooner."

"I doubt it. You didn't meet the Rector."

"Hmmm." Don Lucio folded his hands behind his back and paced up and down the narrow space between his bed and the window. "Tell me about Farías, Domingo."

"There's nothing much to tell. He got a law degree through some miracle, set up a practice, failed at it, and finally persuaded the Governor to appoint him to the staff of the University. That's all I know, really."

"You certainly know more than that. Why does he hate Cardito?"

"I haven't the slightest idea unless. . . . Let me try and remember."

Out of the haze of the past three years a memory came into focus. Cardito had been secretary of the students' syndicate. That was three—no, four years ago. The son of an old enemy was in Farías' class, and Farías failed him. Cardito, knowing the true circumstances, ordered all of the students to go on strike until the boy was passed. Domingo vaguely remembered attending one of

63

the meetings and listening to Cardito's impassioned speeches larded with comments about government appointments. There was a strong demarcation in the school between men known as real professors and those called "the governor's friends." It had nothing to do with any governor personally but with the century old war between the University, which was not wealthy enough to support itself autonomously, and politics.

Domingo related as much as he knew of the case while don Lucio paced up and down. As he finished, the little man said, "He failed Cardito three times . . . deliberately kept him in the school of bachelors when he should have been in the law school. Why didn't the students go on strike for Cardito?"

"Cardito won't let them. He says it's a personal matter. He says he's going to force Farías to pass him."

Don Lucio came closer to Domingo. "Have you spoken to Farías?"

"No. It's Cardito's problem. I think he should fight it out himself."

"Does Agapito know about it?"

"Why should he? As long as the student strikes do not affect his bank, there's no need for him to be interested."

"Cardito is his nephew."

"A fact which I pray will not intrude too much upon his consciousness. I think he still sees Cardito as a ten-year-old child. May he forever continue to see him that way."

"Amen," don Lucio muttered. He struck his hands softly together. "But the matter is changed now, Domingo. Cardito can no longer take care of it himself. This fool Farías really almost killed him."

Domingo shook his head and rose. "I tell you it's Cardito's problem. The boy is twenty years old and must fight his own battles." Seeing his uncle frown, he added, "You think I'm being cruel, don't you?"

"Yes," don Lucio said slowly. "Or rather, let us phrase it that I think you are mistaken."

"I am not mistaken. I am simply tired of meddlers. It is a terrible thing to meddle in what is good. It is even worse to meddle in what is bad. When Cardito gets well, if he wants to go down and beat Farías to a pulp, I would be the first to shout 'Viva Cardito!' I will even pay his jail fine with pleasure. But I will not take care of his revenge for him. I am sorry, Uncle Lucio, but if you think about it for a while you will see I am right."

"I wonder," said don Lucio slowly, picking up his mandolin and fitting it carefully into its case. "Thank you for talking to me, Domingo. If any news comes of Cardito, I will be in don Primitivo's." His voice took on a casual tone and he carefully avoided looking at his nephew. "Did you know that don Primitivo was a good friend of the new commanding general of the military camp?"

"Of General Gil? What were they, old bullfighting comrades?"

"Do not be so cynical!" Don Lucio fitted his hat carefully on his round head and fastened his overcoat to the chin. "General Gil is a graduate of Chapultepec. He is of the Gil Treviño family from San Luis Potosí. Don Primitivo got his bullfight training on the ranch of General Gil's father."

Domingo pressed down on his lips to keep them from smiling, but he could not conceal the twinkle in his eyes. "Do not celebrate the general's arrival too much with don Primitivo. Remember that we are dining here at ten, and don't get too drunk."

"I never get drunk," Uncle Lucio told him with great dignity. He swished through the door like an angry turkey.

Domingo, much amused, went on to his own room. He lit the gas burner, then sat down in his comfortable armchair and stretched out his legs toward the flame. He decided that when Sofía came home for further instructions, he would return to the hospital with her after leaving Verónica's. Cardito, Sofía had reported several times that afternoon, was sleeping peacefully. The doctors seemed much relieved about his condition.

Domingo stretched his thin body and yawned. He had only to put out his hand to take any of several new books from the shelves. A shipment had arrived yesterday from Brentano's and this morning another from México City. Since don Agapito deplored the money Domingo spent so foolishly on books, he consequently bought more than he could really afford.

His searching fingers hesitated over a new volume by Mediz Bolio which had arrived in the México City shipment. Mediz Bolio was one of his favorite writers and this new book of Maya legends promised to be a great delight. But he knew that if he started it now, he would never reach Verónica's party, so he let his hand slide forward to a thin paper volume labeled *The Best Poems of the Best Mexican Poets*. His eyes wandered from page to page,

65

finding verses read long ago and long ago forgotten. Two lines from Salvador Diaz Mirón, which in the old days had always amused him, now leaped out at him:

> If you are ice, why, then am I not frozen?
> If I am fire, why are you not consumed?

and it occurred to him that the verses were no longer a matter of humor. He settled himself more comfortably in the chair and read the entire poem through:

> To sweeten for a little your indifference
> Turn on me your angel-borrowed eyes,
> And drown your death-pale fingers in my hair,
> In my dark and sorrow tumbled hair.
>
> But this is vanity, not consolation!
> We are separated by a world.
> If you are ice, why, then, am I not frozen
> If I am fire, why are you not consumed?
>
> Your graceful hand, slender and transparent,
> Rests too lightly on my slave-chained head.
> It is the glacial cup on flaming lava.
> It is the cup of snow on the volcano.

He had rejected poetry entirely after Doris left. The knife cut too deep. Then, with the turning of the years, with the dulling of pain, he had come back to it, but not to such sentimental verses as these. He preferred the mysticism of Ramón López Velarde, the modern sophistication of Xavier Villaurrutia. The older romantic lovers, who continually sang of broken hearted lovers and indifferent mistresses, had always amused him, possibly because he had never loved an indifferent woman.

Up to the time he met Doris he had divided all women into two types: the ones he might some day marry and the ones he would never think of marrying. Then Doris flamed to his flame, but he had been the one to turn away. The women he knew later were merely a searching after what he had rejected in Doris.

Verónica Miranda came the closest. She was a sweet, childlike creature whom he might have married had don Agapito not so completely approved of her. Domingo smiled wryly to himself. Like Sofía, he thought, I, too, have my small defiances.

Marriage to Verónica, he decided, however much it pleased

66

the family, would be very dull. Her conversational powers were limited, and she irritated rather than soothed him.

What was the strange elixir in human chemistry which caused an explosion when one pair of individuals met, yet had no effect at the meeting of another? Márgara possessed this elixir for him; Verónica did not. But did the flow of time dull such excitement?

Márgara belonged to a world he had never known. Her background, her thought processes were completely strange to him, whereas Verónica was a part of his own environment. With Doris he had met this same problem and had intellectually solved it. Better to solve the problem of Márgara immediately before he became so emotionally involved that no application of cold logic would be possible.

He sat quietly in the big chair, his head bowed, his long arms drooping toward the floor. The poetry book, forgotten, dropped from his hand. Against the curtain of his closed lids he fastened Márgara's image. What did he know of her, really? That the Indian blood was strong in her veins? That poverty had bathed her in its boiling stream, searing away true pride until only false pride remained? That much and no more. And yet she had rippled his blood as no woman had done since the days of Doris.

His left arm stirred, remembering the feel of her body against it. The chill of terror had been in her, and that terror had come into his arm. Even her hair, soft under his cheek, had vibrated with nerves, and all because of the painted picture of a man.

He tried to visualize the miniature. The light had been bad, and Bárcenas had snatched it away before it had been possible to really see it. During the brief glimpse, however, he had been struck by something faintly familiar about it . . . not as a man remembered, but as a picture remembered. Somewhere, some place, he had seen a picture of that man, and with it went a story which made the picture memorable.

The photograph, the studio, the mystery of Márgara. Was he in love with her? No, not really. It was merely a sexual attraction, an experiment in chemistry . . . Márgara. Márgara. . . .

As from a great distance he heard a scratching at the door. It sounded like a small kitten trying to get in, but there were no kittens in the house. Again came the scratching.

Domingo jerked free of his half doze and opened the door. A tear stained Serafina looked pleadingly up at him.

VIII

Shame jabbed him. His worry over Cardito's illness was no excuse to ignore this child. Nervous fingers were twisting and untwisting her apron, and the flesh had tightened on her face until the eyes were sunken in her skull.

She repeated her little sing-song phrase of begged forgiveness until he raised one hand to stop her.

"Nonsense, Serafina, you are not molesting me. And the niño Cardito is much better."

"You are sure, s'ñor Domingo?"

"I am going to a party in about an hour. Would I do that if . . ." He ended on a sharp curse as she swayed slightly and crumpled to the floor.

A bottle of smelling salts borrowed from doña Otilia's bed-room soon restored the girl to consciousness. She gave him a shamed smile, then realized that he was kneeling beside her. This shocked her servant's sense of propriety. Much against her protests, he maneuvered her into the large chair and pulled up a stool so that he could sit beside her.

"Ay, s'ñor Domingo, it isn't right that we should be here like this."

"Nonsense, Serafina. A sick person has more rights than the king of Spain."

"About that you would know more than I. But I'm not sick. I'm very well. Indeed, see how strong I am." She thrust out one arm and flexed it for him to feel her muscle.

He gravely circled it with his thumb and second finger. "Don't touch me, Death. I am trembling with fear."

"Now you are making fun of me . . ."

Catching his knee in his cupped palms, he relaxed into laugh-ter. "Does a rooster make fun of a newly hatched chick?" With a smile of his own he coaxed forth her shy smile. "Are you com-fortable?"

"Ay, yes."

"Good. Now cease to worry yourself. The niño is in good hands. In just a few weeks he'll be back with us again." He bent forward and peered into her eyes. "It would seem that you're the sick one, Serafina."

She sprang upright, but her weakness was still upon her, and he had to put out an arm to prevent her falling again to the floor. "You must not say such things, s'ñor Domingo."

He slid her back into the chair and held the smelling salts under her nose. After a few deep breaths the color returned to her cheeks and her skin changed from pale tan to warm toasted brown.

"I know a little of medicine," he told her, "and trying to lie to me is useless. You see, I would know you were lying."

She jerked her head aside, but he continued sternly, "You're going to have a baby, aren't you, Serafina?"

"Ay, s'ñor Domingo, to say such things . . ."

"Is it Cardito's?"

"Please, s'ñor . . ."

"Is it?"

"No! No!" This time her terror gave her a false strength, and she was on her feet facing him. They were so close together that he could feel her breath warming his cheek. Her eyes were round O's, and even the upthrust chin defied him.

Then a rapid knock at the door separated them as though they had been guilty of intimacy. Domingo breathed deeply to steady himself before he said, "Forward."

Sofía opened the door. Her glance stopped at the servant girl, and her mouth twitched in sudden comprehension. Serafina dropped a dignified curtsy and slipped silently out of the room.

Sofía raised and lowered expressive shoulders, casually dismissing the servant girl incident before Domingo could offer any explanation.

"Brunhilda refuses to go to Verónica's party. Our mother thinks that at least one of us should be represented."

"I was planning to go."

"Really?" She took a cigarette from its ornamental tin box and placidly waited for him to light it. As he did so he forced his hand not to tremble with irritation. Her cool superiority had always flicked the anger nerve in him. Sofía had a habit of calling a crumb with salt, supper. It was part of her Monterrey heritage, where a few misleading facts were often seasoned and spread out as a magnificent banquet of gossip.

Her deep contralto murmured, "I meant girls, not you, Dominguito. Since her highness prefers to rest, I shall have to go."

"I thought you liked Verónica."

"Should I?" She relaxed in his chair and blew a puff of smoke toward his face. "She's such a pretty little sheep. Tell me, does her wool tempt you?"

"Don't be vulgar, Sofía." He sat on the foot of his bed and lighted a cigarette for himself. "How is Cardito?"

"Sleeping, bless him. The doctor seems very pleased with him. Domingo . . ." She hesitated and critically examined the tip of one brown slipper. "What do you know of Jorge Palafox?"

"One of the banking family, I suppose. Why?"

"Uncle Agapito sent a note to Brunhilda. I read it." She lifted one shoulder at Domingo's expression of disgust. "Shocked, my brother? You should know by this time that I have no scruples if I want to discover something. You inherited our father's tender conscience. I didn't."

"Sofía, Sofía. You frighten me a little, I think."

"Why?"

"I don't know." He walked to the window. It was dark outside, and the street lamps threw pools of yellow light on the narrow sidewalk. A man pushing an ice-cream cart trotted past. He's not calling his wares, Domingo thought irrelevantly, he must be going home. Then his mind returned to Sofía. "If you ever wanted anything, really wanted it, I believe you'd get it if you had to damn the world."

"I have always believed in climbing the mountains even if I have to go on a burro."

"Since we're quoting proverbs this afternoon," he said curtly, "just remember, Sofía, that he who climbs a mountain often meets an avalanche."

She crushed her cigarette into a pottery tray. "An avalanche named Uncle Agapito?"

"N-no," he answered slowly, frowning at his own ineptitude to put into words what he was thinking. "Not precisely. I mean a sort of self-destruction . . . a loss of greatness within yourself."

She stretched like a tawny cat as she came to her feet. "Please don't grow philosophical with me, my brother. This afternoon my brain is too tired for argument. And you still haven't answered my question: What do you know of Jorge Palafox?"

"Why this interest in the Palafox?"

"Uncle Agapito took the trouble to write Brunhilda a note and tell her that he was bringing this person back with him from the Capital."

With this sentence Domingo could feel the air in the room change. Where there had been intense opposition between them, now there was a sudden bond of comradeship which always sprang into existence when the shadow of their common enemy touched them.

"Brunhilda and Uncle Agapito," he said thoughtfully. "I felt it this morning, Sofía. There is a secret understanding between those two, and I am afraid . . ."

"So am I," she whispered. They looked at each other, and their hands came together in a need of physical merging. Her voice deepened until the quality was more baritone than contralto. "The Palafox family is so very great. You remember. . . ." She mentioned the name of another great family's heir. Domingo could feel his flesh contract in distaste.

"Dope fiend," he said. "Degenerate. . . ."

"Do you think Uncle Agapito would care, if an alliance could be made with the Palafox?"

Domingo shook his head. "That is not what worries me," he continued. "Since this morning, I don't think Brunhilda would care, and that is worse."

"Ay, Domingo." Sofía jerked her hand from him and sat down again. Her palms rubbed against each other, as though she were trying to wash an inner horror from them. "It is fresh air this family needs, not the closed rooms of greatness. Brunhilda is such a stupid, grasping little fool. Do you love her, Domingo?"

"Do you?"

She gave a snort of disgust and lighted another cigarette. "I am younger than she—six full years younger—and yet there are times when I feel old enough to be her aged aunt. She is stupid and vain and selfish. I know that. I say to myself that she is not worth one moment's thought, and yet she is my sister. Yes, I love her."

He rested one knee on the stool and put a hand on either chair-arm. "Don't feel too bad, Sofía. I love her too, in the same way. And I am really older than she. Besides, we may be trying to take boiling water from a cold pool. How do we know who or what this Jorge Palafox may be?"

"You have friends. You could find out."

"I will. Before the young man arrives in Monterrey I will even know his brand of toothpaste. Does that satisfy you?"

She rested her fingers on his for a moment. Then her natural dislike of too close contact with anyone made her push him aside, so that she could stand and break free from him. "There are times, Domingo, when we do not always understand each other, but . . . but you are my brother, and if you are not always . . ." Her stumbling speech halted, then continued on a rush of sound. "I have few virtues, I know that. But loyalty is one of them. I mean that I would never tell anyone . . . I mean. . . ." With an angry snort at her inability to convey her thoughts, she jerked the door open and passed through to the gallery. This time her hesitation was physical. Without looking around at him, she said, "I meant what I said about new blood. We are too inbred, we old families, too proud of our grandeur. There is no shame in having been a servant. Honest labor wears its own dignity." This time the door closed with a bang of finality.

A secret spring of humor he did not even know he possessed began to bubble in him. He could not deny that Sofía had grounds for her belief that he was indulging in an affair with Serafina, and yet how little she knew her brother. Serafina fostered a tenderness in him, but nothing more.

As he automatically dressed for the party, he was aware for the first time that the feeling he had for Serafina equalled the feeling he possessed for Verónica. Both had that fragile helplessness one finds in all newborn things. And yet was Serafina so helpless? That flashing defiance had been coated with steel. But if she were really pregnant and Cardito, the father. . . . But, of course, Cardito was the father. Any other supposition was foolishness. Serafina's intense concentration on the boy answered that doubt. The real question was: did Cardito know the truth? And if he did, what was he intending to do about it? Surely he was not planning to marry the girl. . . . Yet he was impractical enough to attempt it.

Domingo frowned as he buttoned his shirt, pausing with one hand suspended in the air while he contemplated this possible development. The trick was to keep Serafina away from Cardito until suitable arrangements could be made. But what arrangements?

Slowly he finished dressing while he turned over plan after

plan in his mind, only to reject all of them. The great danger was
Uncle Agapito. If that great man ever found out the truth . . .

Ay, Serafina, Serafina, he thought, what am I to do about you?
And not only you, but Brunhilda? If Jorge Palafox is what I think
he may be, I must stop that wedding somehow. I stopped her once
before, and I'll do it again in spite of Uncle Agapito.

He shut his eyes tightly and wearily rubbed his forehead.
Strange. Until yesterday afternoon at five o'clock life had been
such a simple process of selling real estate and hating Uncle Agapito. Now, without warning, he was presented with a variety of
situations demanding definite attitudes. Was Shakespeare wrong?
Was there really something in the stars which influenced the destiny of man? On impulse he took an almanac from the bookcase
and discovered that February 3 was the thirty-fourth day since
January 1; that the year still had three hundred and thirty-one days
to run; that on the Aztec calendar the present year was I Tochtli,
corresponding to the day Xochitl (flower), third of the twentieth
Itzcalli (when plants take root). It was also the day dedicated to
a national observance of physical education and the feast day of
all those named Cosijoeza (king of Zaachila), Malinalli (the twisted
one), Blás, Ignacio, Celerino, Hipólito, Félix, Laurentino, Mili-
bella, and Verónica. On this day in 1814 a hero of the War of
Independence, Mariano Matamoros, was executed in Morelia,
Michoacán. The sun had risen at 7:11 and would set at 18:48.
There was also a brief essay on the cultivation of emotional power
in which Domingo was admonished to practise sincerity and not
to confound emotional equilibrium with frailty. "There is no
woman," the article told him, "who cannot acquire frailty. Let her
therefore guard herself with honesty. Artificiality is at no time
necessary to a woman's happiness. Everything can be summed up
in these words: Be natural."

All of this, Domingo felt, was interesting but not exactly
applicable to his own problems. He was tempted to copy the little
essay and take it around to Márgara so that he could watch the slow
smile break as she read it. But would she laugh at it? Perhaps to
her it might be a matter of serious consideration. What did he
really know of Márgara? If he were not very careful this woman
would soon become an obsession with him.

He tucked a pale blue handkerchief into the breast pocket of
his dark blue suit, stepped back and surveyed himself. Even Uncle

Agapito could find no fault with his sartorial splendor tonight. How nice that Uncle Agapito was in México City and thus spared the necessity of passing judgment on his nephew's appearance. Would Márgara think he looked nice? Of course his suit was blue while she had seemed to prefer green . . . that green dress so beautiful against her honey colored skin.

But he was going to Verónica's party, and blue was Verónica's favorite color. She always had something of blue on her, even if it were only a string of turquoise beads coiled about her throat. Better to please Verónica. She was his own kind. Yet Sofía was right. The Vázquez de Andas did need the fresh air of the strange, the unknown . . .

He picked up his hat and draped his overcoat over one arm. Perhaps doña Petra would spare him a cherished flower for his buttonhole. He went to the door and reached out his hand to switch off the light, then paused and glanced back at the leather handkerchief box on the dresser.

When he finally went downstairs he was whistling softly to himself. Sofía was in the vestibule, idly leafing through a new copy of the political weekly, *Mañana,* which had just arrived. A very quiet Serafina held his overcoat for him.

"Are you interested," Sofía asked lazily, "in knowing that the Governor of Veracruz has just dedicated a new hospital worth half a million . . . Domingo! What are you doing putting a green handkerchief with that blue suit?"

"I like it," Domingo said firmly. He retrieved his hat from Serafina, cocked it well down over one eye, and opened the door for Sofía. Through the aperture they could see the newly polished car with Matéo Chapa at the wheel. "After you, little sister."

She shook her head. "Let me warn you, Verónica detests green."

"I am sorry if it pains my family," Domingo said jauntily, following her across the sidewalk, "but I do not dress to please Verónica Miranda."

IX

The Miranda house also belonged to the old generation. It had been built in the early 1800's in the two-storied French style, with center door, and balconied windows. One of the ground floor windows to the left of the entry was bricked up. Although rarely mentioned, everyone who knew the story was secretly a little proud of it. To Monterrey it represented not only romance but also a cutting from the history that the South so jealously claimed as its own. "We may be the frontier," Monterrey said in effect, "but we too have our legends."

When they got out of the car, Sofía and Domingo automatically looked at the window. He could feel her sway toward him as though she were seeking to escape the blood on the sidewalk which had been washed away these eighty years.

They used the knocker to attract attention. There was an electric bell set in the stone facing, but don Agapito was the only person who used it. Electric buzzers did not belong to this house with its brooding tragedy. They were too new, too scientific, too remote from legend; whereas the knocker, a winged gargoyle fastened to an iron star, had come from seventeenth century Spain and was hammered to this carved door when the house was built. Generations of hands had stroked it, including the hand of the girl whose window had been sealed by her father. Who, then, save don Agapito, would not prefer the knocker to that modern implement, the bell?

A servant admitted the Vázquez de Andas and took their coats. From the rear of the house floated the buzzing of social chatter. While Sofía put a last film of powder on her nose, Domingo lazily examined the bricked aperture that once had been the door to the dead Graciela's bedchamber. No paint covered the brick, although the vestibule had been redecorated many times through the passing years, for the brick was a symbol, not of a girl's memory but of a broken-hearted man's self-punishment. Graciela Miranda's father believed to his death's day that he had murdered his daughter, and no one, not even the priest, could otherwise convince him.

As usual, whenever Domingo saw this door, the old story

flooded his mind. He had been told it so often as a child that the events seemed a part of his living memory: that he, too, had stood on Plaza Zaragoza that sunlit day in August, 1864 and watched General Castagny's French soldiers march in to take possession of the city.

At first Monterrey's citizens refused to walk the same streets as their French conqueror's but, as the proverb says, "the body can get used to anything but hunger," and soon crowds filled the streets again, eyes sliding curiously toward the blue uniforms and strange, sunburnt faces. One morning as Graciela Miranda returned from market, her servant trotting silently at her heels, one of the bags broke and tomatoes cascaded across the narrow sidewalk. A young lieutenant, who had followed her from the market, was glad of such an excuse to introduce himself. He was her enemy, but a courteous gesture must be met with courtesy. Every night after that the young Frenchman would come to Graciela's window, at first because he was lonely and she was pretty, but later, because he loved her. "Love," said the legend, "has little regard for nationality or circumstances."

What did they talk about as he stood at the window pressing inward against the bars? Of France? Of the long sea-journey? Of his gift of a brooch, the hinged cameo protecting his portrait? Then, on a moonless night, with only a distant street lamp to distinguish each from the other, she reached through the bars and pinned a jasmine blossom on his shoulder. The fragrance was almost too sweet. He dipped his head to kiss her fingers . . .

A shot cut the silence. There was a flash of light from a gun. The lieutenant's head jerked back, his knees curved flaccidly. He collapsed on the sidewalk. One high, clear scream came from Graciela. She rushed out to him, but he was dead before she reached him. That was the last time she ever left her room. Her father tried to explain to her that a French enemy was worth less than the life of a dog, but she seemed not to hear him. General Castagny, involved in retreat from Monterrey, had no time to punish the elder Miranda. The old man was left to the greater punishment of watching his daughter cut herself off from the world, her door opening only to admit food. For three years she sat in her room, her beauty fast disappearing as her hair turned white and her face thinned to the bone. Then finally came the time when the door no longer opened even for food, and so she died.

When she was buried, the cameo guarding the portrait and the red-stained faded jasmine were lowered into the earth with her. And the room that had been her sanctuary was sealed with brick.

A familiar tale, thought Domingo. There was such a room in Veracruz, another in Guanajuato, another in Torreón. There was even one in San Antonio, Texas, just as there were thousands of such rooms in the provinces of Spain. But the Miranda room belonged to Monterrey. To a Reinero that was enough to give it its own distinction amongst the romantic legends.

Sofía touched his arm. "Stop day dreaming, Domingo. Or has Verónica so enchanted you that you pass into a daze when you cross her threshold?"

He laughed at her words, and they crossed the patio to the high ceilinged parlor with its gilt Louis XVI furniture, and the tall wax image of the Sacred Heart which had been imported from Italy.

Verónica came to greet them, her black eyes softening as she looked at Domingo. He said, "You are even prettier than usual," as he bent over her hand. He thought, She's much too white. If she isn't careful, she will go into anemia. Then he turned to kiss her mother's hand.

The señora Miranda was a thin, nervous woman who represented Guatemala on the Pan American Round Table. She was also on the board of directors for a privately maintained orphanage and was president of the Monterrey Symphony Society. At the moment she was trying to organize a Little Theater and wanted Sofía to be treasurer.

"The great difficulty," she told Domingo, "is that people think I'm talking about marionettes. Simply because the word 'Little' is in the title does not presuppose I'm referring to dolls."

Domingo smiled, left Sofía to struggle against the temptation of handling money, and followed Verónica to the large table where her gifts were displayed. There were frothy lace fans, a silver picture frame, piles of embroidered handkerchiefs, a gold filagree rosary, and one book beautifuly bound in Russian morocco. The title, printed in English, said that this was an essay on various aspects of Hamlet. At the bottom of the page was the address of a small publishing firm in London. "I didn't know you were interested in Hamlet," he said.

She raised blue silk shoulders. "Is that what it's about? I don't like to read English. Your uncle Agapito gave it to me." Her fingers stroked the binding. "It's a beautiful book and will go very nicely with my new lamp."

The old proverb of a bad book in a good binding flashed across his mind. How typical of Uncle Agapito, to whom appearances were all that mattered, to give such a present. Which reminded him that he had not the remotest idea what his own family had given her. He should, of course, have made it his business to find out, but he had forgotten the feast day until his mother had reminded him of it this afternoon.

Verónica was saying, "Your presents were so lovely. Don't you like them?"

His eyes quickly scanned the table while he mumbled that he did like them very much. That, at least, was a safe phrase to use. She giggled a little and touched his arm. "They're on me, Domingo."

"Oh, I wondered . . ." He looked at her and saw them: yellow enameled daisies with sapphire hearts that dangled from her pierced ears. "I couldn't see them on the table. . . ."

"I thought you didn't really look at me when you came in. I've changed my hair, too."

The thick black hair was parted in the center and brought down with Madonna severity to a knot at the back of her neck. How much less artificial Márgara was, combed straight back with the fringe of curling tendrils at the hair-line. His hand unconsciously touched the green handkerchief in his breast pocket. Better not to think of Márgara, especially in this house where love had been made synonymous with death.

Don Jonás Miranda came up to them, followed by a servant with a tray of brandy filled glasses. "Eh, Domingo, this house is yours. Have a cup with us."

Domingo lifted the glass toward Verónica. "To your health, and to yours, don Jonás."

"I need it, for I grow older ever day. But not my daughter. . . ."

"I also age, Papá. Is not today my saint's day?"

"To me you will never be larger than this." He gestured a small space between his hands.

Domingo nodded with mock gravity. "Quite true, don Jonás.

For myself, I always see Verónica with her hair in pigtails and so proud of her school uniform."

Verónica thrust out her lower lip at them and stalked off to join some of her friends.

"Now we've angered her," don Jonás sighed. "But they will grow up. That is the tragedy." He thoughtfully inspected the bottom of his brandy glass. "What she needs, Domingo, is a husband old enough to realize that she is still a child in many ways . . . old enough to understand her."

This is dangerous ground, Domingo thought, and frantically glanced about for Sofía. But his sister was engulfed by a cluster of people who were all excitedly talking at the same time, each pitching his voice a little higher than his neighbor's in an effort to be heard.

Domingo said suavely, "My uncle Agapito was making the same comment the other afternoon. He has gone to the Capital to a bankers' convention."

"I'm glad you mentioned that. My brother Irineo is here. He wants to ask a favor of you in regard to Agapito." Sliding his arm through Domingo's, don Jonás drew him toward a group of men standing near the piano.

As they crossed the black and white tiled floor, Domingo felt a cozy warmth invade him. These were his people. He understood them; they understood him. Even as now, when don Jonás delicately suggested that he might push his courting of Verónica a bit faster, yet immediately retreated at Domingo's hesitation. There were no mysteries here, no phrases which had to be broken apart and examined before the truth was made clear. In this world individuals did not say they were one thing when in reality they were something else. Here the niches were labeled: engineer, real estate, doctor, banker. Some even carried double labels, as in the case of Irineo Miranda, such as lawyer-historian. But the important thing was that the label existed so that there was never any doubt as to the relationship of one to another. Even the Miranda legend had its own label of romance, and in those legends it was always the foreigner who was killed, the familiar one who sorrowed into death.

For a moment terror swept through him. The feeling of an unalterable destiny which had touched him in his bedroom returned. Was the Miranda legend but a forewarning of what his

79

own fate would be if he followed the exotic Márgara? Would she be destroyed and he left to mourn her in the closed room of his memory? Once again reason warned him that any relationship with Márgara would end in tragedy. Therefore, he was glad for the normality of this room, for the warm welcome of these men, the traditional embrace that Irineo Miranda gave him.

Although Irineo was ten years his senior, they were good friends with a common interest in the city they both loved. These other men loved it too. One was an engineer; another owned a large wholesale and retail grocery; another manufactured furniture. Those were their daily occupations. But on weekends and holidays they met in each other's homes and discussed what Zaragoza Plaza must have looked like in 1610, or the precise date when the old Hotel Hidalgo, next door to the Cathedral, was changed into the Casino Monterrey.

"The great trouble," Isaac Fuentes, the furniture manufacturer, told Domingo, "is the lack of documents. So much that we know is told to us by word of mouth. Someone remembers what his grandfather said, but how do we know that his memory is correct?"

"For folklore," the engineer murmured, "very interesting, but hardly the scientific approach to history."

"You have, of course, heard of the trunks of documents found in one of the vaults of Agapito's bank?" Irineo asked him,

Domingo grimaced and lifted another glass of brandy from a proffered tray. "I wondered why I was suddenly so popular."

"Eh, Domingo, you could be such a good historian," little don Wilfrido Vidal, the grocer, said. "You have such a cynical mind."

Everyone laughed and Irineo tapped Domingo's shoulder. "We hear that Agapito has ordered the papers to be burned as trash. Is there nothing you can do to save them?"

A slight frown creased Domingo's forehead. "That's strange. Uncle Agapito was saying the other night at dinner that he had ordered the papers to be turned over to the archives in the governor's palace for safe keeping."

"I told you," snapped don Wilfrido, "that my friend Agapito was not such a barbarian."

Isaac Fuentes gave a sigh of relief. "A story builds in the telling. You see why we prefer documents to memories."

Domingo was only half listening. It was true that don Agapito was his enemy, and yet such stories as these deeply offended him. He wondered if his family pride was really stronger than he thought. But Irineo was saying, "There is a new publication out that I want you to see. Your grandfather's picture is in it. Come into the library and let me show it to you."

As they passed Sofía, she called to him, "Don't forget, we must go to the hospital."

He nodded and told the story of Cardito's illness as they settled themselves in the library chairs. Don Wilfrido fussed angrily with his spectacles, which insisted on sliding down his nose. "That Counselor Farías. This is the end. We must speak to the governor about having him deposed."

"I don't know," protested the engineer. "Sometimes I think it is good for youth to be taught by at least one incompetent man. It teaches them to doubt—the true scientific approach."

"You and your science," Irineo muttered, not at the moment interested in the problems of the University. He thrust a magazine, bound in orange paper, into Domingo's hand. "The photographs come from the Casasola Archives. A graphic history of the revolution from nineteen hundred to nineteen hundred and forty. Really magnificent."

"Isn't it a rather thin copy?" Domingo asked hesitantly as he leafed through the illustrated pages.

"But, dear man, this is only one of the volumes. Number seven, do you see, covering June nineteen hundred and thirteen—January nineteen hundred and fourteen. Wonderful pictures. Wonderful."

"After all, the family Casasola," Isaac Fuentes said, "have been photographers for four generations. Their archives should be remarkable. They have photographed every newsworthy event since eighteen hundred and ninety-five."

Don Wilfrido flicked the magazine in Domingo's hand. "This isn't the right issue. Old don Domingo is in the first one that covers the Díaz regime. Where is the first one?"

Domingo's mouth jerked in irritation. There was something about these photographs that lighted up a memory and yet the memory itself was too nebulous for capture. But a copy with a gray cover was given him, and he had to make polite noises as he gravely examined the picture of his grandfather, very dignified in silk hat, cutaway coat, and striped trousers, standing with the German ambassador at a garden party during the festive week of the centennial in 1910.

"The last of the great celebrations," said Irineo with a touch of regret in his voice. "Do you remember the story of the daughter of the Spanish Ambassador, who thought she was coming to a country of barbarians?"

"And then," giggled don Wilfrido, "she had to send back to Paris for clothes in order to outshine Mexican society. . . ."

"Only to discover," complacently finished Isaac Fuentes, "that the Paris houses had sent designers to México City to prepare special wardrobes for the Centennial."

"The golden days," murmured the engineer, who had been a cadet at Chapultepec Military College. "They will never come again."

"And thank God for it," said Domingo with sudden violence.

The furniture manufacturer gave a barking laugh. "You speak from inexperience, Domingo, but me . . . well, my father was one of those who disappeared in Huerta's famous gray car. Under Díaz there would never have been a gray car."

"Yet Díaz wrote a telegram: 'Catch in the act: hang on the spot,'" said the engineer. "Huerta's gray car or Díaz' *rurales* . . . automobile or horse . . . they're both gone now, and, like, Domingo, I say, 'Thank God for it.' But ay, the golden days."

The words of the men swirled around Domingo, and he suddenly felt himself cut off from them. They were so much older than he. The names they spoke: Gonzalitos, Carranza, Dr. Velarde, Villa, Angeles, were only history-touched names to him, but to these men the names were labels for three-dimensional beings who moved in the shadow world of the past that was not his past.

He was glad to escape into the silence of the patio, where the chill air stung the inside of his nostrils. He thought for a few minutes about the strange flash of memory he had had when looking at the magazines. For some reason he associated those pictures with Márgara, and then he knew what it was: the miniature that had filled her with such terror had possessed a kinship with the Casasola photographs. The set of the stiff collar, the angle of the head, the combing of the hair . . . the same. Exactly the same.

Excitement stirred in him, made his heart beat faster. No wonder he thought he had recognized the painting in terms of

82

a photograph. Because, at some time, he had seen it as a photograph. True, that was the first time that the Casasola films had been gathered together as a collection, but all histories of the Great Revolution used illustrations from the famous files.

On impulse he turned toward the front door. He would send Mateo to buy him a series of the histories. Verónica's voice stopped him. She said softly behind him, "Dreaming alone in the patio, Domingo?"

He turned and looked at her. She had tossed a blue lace scarf over her black hair, and her white throat palely gleamed in the darkness.

"I was thinking of history, Verónica, and why men do the things they do."

"You are so wise, Domingo, always looking for reasons behind an action. For me, the action is enough. I don't even know myself why I do things."

"You are all heart, Verónica," he said gently. "And hearts are precious things. Do not let it break."

"It is my heart," she said.

He gazed at her with eyes very deep from an awakening awareness. Like Serafina, Verónica, too, had her steel curtain behind which she could hide. These soft, gentle creatures . . .

He felt embarrassed. She so fully expected him to propose, as did her family and his family, and yet, with Márgara in the background, how could he propose? His hand rose to the green handkerchief. Wasn't he really being a fool? A pale mask of a face glimpsed in a doorway . . . thirty minutes of conversation in a silent studio . . . was that enough to change a man's life, and not only his but Verónica's?

He said swiftly, "There are words that need speaking between you and me . . . private words."

As though she had been expecting this, she led the way into a small room, obviously a sewing room, with its baskets of mending and the machine piled with lengths of goods.

She shut the door and leaned against it, her skin white onyx against the dark wood.

"This would cause a scandal if anyone found us here."

He rested one hip on the edge of the long cutting table. "Then we must be quick about it. Our families expect us to marry. You know that."

"My father has spoken of it."

"But do you want to marry me? Think carefully, Verónica. Your whole life swings on the answer."

"You mean if I say yes, you will marry me?" She took a step toward him, her hands folded at her breast. Serafina had stood like this when talking about Cardito. He impatiently wished that he could get the Serafina resemblance out of his mind.

"It is only fair to tell you, Verónica, that I think I am in love with another woman."

She retreated against the door. Her lids drooped until her eyes were shielded from him. "You think so?" she murmured. "You don't really know? How can that be love, Domingo?"

He lit a cigarette to give himself time to arrange the proper wording of his answer. "You are very young, Verónica." Then, as he saw her impatient movement, "Please, I mean in experience, not years. I am so much older than you . . . fifteen years. There is a certain knowledge that comes from living."

"Does love need knowledge? Does it need anything but love?"

"It needs . . . intelligence." Watching her face, he knew that she did not understand him. To her, life was a matter of feeling, of likes and dislikes. This was a vain effort. He could never explain to her what he really meant.

"Fifteen years from you to me, Verónica. That is too long a time. You have just learned to play. I have forgotten how. . . ."

"Play? You mean like Tito?"

At his startled glance, she flushed and turned her head away from him. . . . "I have no time for fools," she said.

He whistled softly, then rose and went to her. His fingers laced into hers and for a moment they examined each other. "You are right, Verónica. I am a fool."

"I didn't mean it that way . . ."

"I know what you meant. But Tito is not a true stupid. He has a hard streak of practicality that will finally tell him the truth."

"I don't believe it. Brunhilda . . ."

"Will never marry Tito," he said firmly. "She came home this morning. She's changed, Verónica. Now she believes in hunting the hide that will give her the most shoe leather."

"Tito is so blind a worshiper . . ."

"Only to a certain point. When he realizes the truth, he'll be free of it fast enough."

She moved past him and sat in the straight chair, one arm across her lap, the other dangling at her side. He had seen portraits of fashion models sitting thus, but where they had posed, this was natural. For twenty years Verónica had been taught to sit, to stand, to move with grace, until the artificial had become a part of her nature. Sofía had it too, and Brunhilda, and all the girls he knew. That was why good money was paid to the nuns of the Sacred Heart, to the nuns of the Incarnate Word, so that society's young ladies could learn how to use their femininity to their best advantage. It was a part of their heritage, just as he himself was bound by the restrictions and regulations of his own inheritance. Whether it was right or wrong, they were all clamped into the same mold at birth, and the miracle to him was how any individual qualities escaped at all. And in that moment he knew that the mold which had fashioned him was a more effective barrier between himself and Márgara than any high wall. He took the green handkerchief from his pocket and twisted it around his fingers.

Verónica turned toward him. "You'll say I'm a fool, Domingo. I suppose I am. But I don't want to be second best. If Tito ever asked me to marry him, I'd have to say no. Brunhilda would always stand between us—the ghost of Brunhilda."

"That's a very foolish attitude, Verónica."

"It's mine, Domingo. With you, it's different. I like you very much. I would make you a good wife. You know that."

"Even if you thought I loved someone else?"

"You don't, Domingo. Thinking isn't enough. Love is a question of the heart, not the mind."

"Tito would always be between us. Every time I saw him . . ."

"And what about the woman?" Her nose wrinkled with laughter. "We should have a very interesting marriage. When are you going to speak to my father?"

"Verónica, this is a serious matter . . ."

She came to him and put her arms around his neck. "I am a wicked one," she said and pressed her mouth against his. Her lips were cool and fresh and tasted of violets. As his arms slipped around her, peace touched him. A quotation and a proverb leapfrogged across his mind. The proverb said, 'You never stop walking over a royal road or an old love,' but the quotation was from the Bible, 'As the hart panteth after the water brooks.'

He rested his chin against her forehead. She was as quiet in his arms as a young tree in the stillness of summer.

"Verónica, Verónica," he whispered, "we are two fools."

"You will ask Papá tonight?"

"No, I won't . . ."

"But you promised . . ."

"I didn't promise anything." He stuffed the green handkerchief into his pocket and led her back to the chair. After she was seated, he perched himself again on the edge of the sewing table. Her hands were still clasped in his, and he played with her fingers, taking each one gently between his own and folding them down into the palm. "When you were a little girl and broke your dolls, you'd never allow them to be mended. It had to be a new doll or nothing. Do you remember?"

"I don't understand what . . ."

"But don't you see, your doll named Tito has been broken, and now you want a new doll named Domingo. But dolls aren't people, Verónica. Suppose we were married and then, in a month or two, Brunhilda married someone else, and Tito were left free . . ."

"I wouldn't want him, Domingo, then or ever!"

"But suppose he fell in love with someone else? Would you want that?"

She tugged her hands away from him. "You mean, neither me nor Brunhilda?"

"Precisely. If Brunhilda's marriage freed him from Brunhilda, surely he wouldn't return to you, and you a married woman. He'd find another pasture in which to graze. He's a normal man . . . an everyday ordinary sort of man. What you want is marriage to one man and life-long adoration from another. But you can't have it."

"Aren't you making me out a bit of a fool?"

"Be honest with yourself, Verónica. And with me. Do you think I want that kind of marriage? Everywhere I went people would say, 'Ay, yes, he is the husband of Verónica Miranda. You know, the girl Tito Gómez is in love with.' Do you think I'd enjoy that?"

"Would people really say that?"

86

"Not only would they say it, you'd want them to say it. Verónica, you've grown up in a house shadowed by a tragic love. Your Great-aunt Graciela, who pined away in a sorrow filled room, is a heroine to you. No woman in your family has since been able to compete with the memory of Graciela Miranda. Now you feel that you have the opportunity to become a romantic heroine, and you don't mind sacrificing either Tito or me . . ."

She sprang up, her eyes flashing with fury. "How dare you say such things to me, Domingo Vázquez?"

"Because I've known you since you were in pigtails. Because I'm fond of you . . ."

"I'll thank you to leave this house and never speak to me again."

"You see? How could marriage between us ever work out?"

She came close to him, her lids blinking rapidly to keep back the tears. "I wouldn't marry you—I wouldn't marry you if you were—if you were your uncle Agapito!"

She swung on one heel and ran out of the room, her lace shawl catching on the door's hooked handle as she passed.

He lighted another cigarette, then carefully unfastened the lace. As he pulled it through his hands, the fragrance of violets came to him again. Doris had used violet scent. He took a deep breath of it, but there was no longer any pain attached to the memory. The proverb was wrong. One could stop walking over an old love, but not—and his hand touched the green handkerchief —until one met a new one.

He draped Verónica's scarf over his arm with tender fingers. He had hated to be cruel to her, but with the passing of days she would bounce into laughter again. She had very much the same sponge rubber quality that Brunhilda possessed. Their dark days were always summer showers, never hurricanes. Neither one knew the dark tempestuous moods of Márgara. At birth, Márgara had been older than Verónica was now. Or had she been? What did he know of Márgara really? There it was, the same tormenting question. One moment he was so sure, the next it was all doubt.

How nice it would be to slip away from this doubt into the old calm of inaction. This jumping bean process exhausted him. When would the lively worm die and leave him at peace again? But would he want peace? Was not the jumping bean better than simple vegetation?

87

Weary of his problem, he went in search of Sofía. It was not until he saw her looking at his arm that he noticed that everyone in the room was also looking at it. Puzzled, he glanced down and saw the blue lace draped there, mutely telling his world that he and Verónica had reached an understanding.

X

As the sharp realization of their conclusion struck him, he knew that he must act at once if he wanted to avoid a situation which, of its own momentum, would roll Verónica and himself down the road to marriage whether they wanted it or not.

His hesitation was so slight it was barely noticeable as he swung away from Sofía toward Verónica, his arm held out, his eyes steady on hers. "I found this in the patio," he said, and the finality in his tones surprised him. He knew by the expression that glinted behind her lids that she also recognized the finality. The coin had been tossed now, and there would never again be talk of marriage between himself and this slender, pale girl.

She took the scarf with lax fingers. Then something, a sort of fire, flashed in her eyes. Her voice took her words, warmed them, dipped them in intimacy. "How kind of you, Dominguito." Simple words, words of no account. It was the tone that tied the noose in them, slipped them around his throat, lashed him to her.

The señora Miranda heard the tone, recognized it, strode up to them, her face one smile. "Found it, Domingo," she teased, "or brought it after?"

He stared dazedly at Verónica, saw her white teeth flash in a smile that was not echoed in her eyes. "Domingo and I were talking, *mamacita*, of serious things. And on my saint's day." She added in a whisper, the smile broadening, "I will see you, Domingo, after church on Sunday . . . ?"

To meet after church: the privilege of engaged couples. He tried to break loose from her, to say, "No, no, no!" but don Jonás

88

had joined them now, putting his arm around Domingo's shoulder.

"A glass of cognac, my son. It is a fine time to celebrate. . . ." The briefest hiatus packed with meaning for everyone in the room, "Indeed, yes, to celebrate a saint's day, eh?"

No statement made, and yet all was said. In a brief moment he had stepped from one room of his life into another; but it was a curtained room, with the gauze too thick for him to perceive the image of his future. He felt suspended in time, watching dim shadows gather behind the curtains, and his hand unconsciously brushed his face in an effort to see clear.

Verónica, knowing him as well as he knew her, had taken the moment and turned it to suit her own purposes. How could he say now, "You are lying, Verónica. We want no marriage, you and I." But she wanted it, and she was demanding it of him. A moment ago he might have spoken. Now, he could not speak . . . not before this crowd of people. Later he would explain to the señora, to don Jonás. They would feel ashamed, and gossip would pound against them and against himself, but that was not his fault. Verónica was the devil. Good enough for her when the people pitied her for losing her man. But he would not marry her. He would not. Even Uncle Agapito could not force him to take this devil creature for wife.

His eyes told her what he was thinking, but she was laughing at him behind her own eyes. "If you dare," warned her eyes. "If you dare."

Tito grasped his arm, jerked at him. "Forgive me," the plump little man said to don Jonás, "but a matter of great importance. I must ask Domingo. . . ." He drew Domingo into a nearby corner. "I want to know about Brunhilda. Would it be proper for me to call this evening? I must see her."

Domingo, thankful to his friend for the timely interruption, felt a tinge of guilt at the realization that what he really wanted was to push Tito aside and rush out of this house, away from the trap Verónica had set for him. But his social training was too strong. The guests in the room held him to the rigid bonds of correct behavior. He had to guard against being too brusque. What was wrong with Tito that he should break his heart against the rock of Brunhilda with Verónica ripe to his hand? "Not tonight. You've heard about Cardito?"

"The world speaks." The little man swung in a waltz step

away from Domingo and back again. "I weep for the boy. But Brunhilda, tell me . . . she is more beautiful than ever?"

"Such eagerness!" Domingo shook his head impatiently. "Come tomorrow morning at eleven and see for yourself. . . ."

"We must go to the hospital," Sofía said, coming up to them. She bowed slightly to Tito. "Brunhilda asked for you this morning."

"Ay!" Even Tito's thick curly hair seemed to vibrate with his delight. "What did she say? Repeat to me her very words. . . ."

Wanting to hurt, Domingo murmured to Sofía. "So vulnerable. It is a pity to puncture this balloon. Better not to tell him the truth. Let him imagine that it was good, and we will keep the evil to ourselves."

He expected Sofía to enter into the game, to wink at him while telling Tito some obvious distortion of Brunhilda's words, but to his surprise she answered seriously. "Brunhilda asked how you were and what you were doing with your days."

"Did she now? She really showed interest?" There were pathetic overtones in Tito's eagerness.

"No, Tito." Sofía's voice was very gentle. "Not that much interest. I'm sorry."

The ecstasy disappeared to be replaced by a lowering of the lids, a drooping of the mouth. Even the line-thin mustache looked rejected. Then an attempted grin pulled back the lips, and the eyes tried to brighten. "Two years is a long time. Perhaps when we meet . . ."

Sofía brushed her fingers across his sleeve. "Don't hope too much, Tito. People change in two years."

People change in a day, in an hour, Domingo thought, watching his sister with puzzlement. This tenderness was as foreign to her as warmth from an iceberg. Is it lava flaming on the glacial cup, he wondered, or has Díaz Mirón drawn the picture true. Is she really the cup of snow on the volcano? Who is Sofía? Through all these years how could we, close brother and sister, be so remote from each other? Why is it that only now I see her with unbandaged eyes?

He slid his hand through her arm and felt her press it against her side before habit drew her away from him. She was saying goodnight to Tito, and Domingo patted his friend's shoulder before they went to make their adieux to their hosts.

The señora Miranda pressed his fingers warmly, while Verónica kissed Sofía's cheek. Then the girl turned shyly aside, lids lowered, even managing, somehow, to blush. Domingo's palm itched to slap her. Don Jonás gave Domingo a quick embrace, but at last brother and sister were safe in the darkness of the automobile, with Mateo's thick shoulders solid at the wheel. Domingo carefully pulled the lap robe across Sofía's slender hips before covering his own long legs. She said, "So, you have decided to marry that poor creature at last."

"Don't be a fool," he said violently. "That was a trick of Verónica's."

She bent forward, startled, then relaxed into laughter. "A most successful trick. Your face . . . so that was the meaning of your face. I took it for an expression of besotted love."

"Stop laughing!" he snapped at her, then lit a cigarette to calm the anger trembling in him. "I'm sorry, Sofía, but that kitten is not trapping me into marriage. I tell you . . ."

She shrugged and turned away from him, withdrew into herself, no longer interested. He wondered if she were thinking of Cardito.

"Don't worry," he told her. "The early breaking of the fever is a good sign. I'm quite sure he is out of danger."

"What?" She turned her head toward him with a puzzled gesture.

"I was speaking of Cardito."

"Ay, yes." He could almost see the image of Cardito slide from her.

By concentrating on Sofía, he was able to relegate his anger against Verónica to its proper place. The girl was a spoiled brat, and she needed a strong lesson in manners. Tomorrow he would go to see don Jonás and straighten out the whole situation.

Feeling free again, his usual calm returned, and he was ready to concentrate his attention on his sister. Sofía's interests were limited. He knew that it would not take long to find the key to her abstraction. Uncle Agapito, money, clothes, her family . . .

With his eyes fixed on the back of Mateo's head, Domingo said, "I asked a few questions about the Palafox. No one seemed to know much, although Irineo said he'd encountered him two or three times in Paris."

There was no response. He repeated his words, accenting the name slightly, and this time he felt her stir.

"Palafox? Who . . . oh. Very interesting," and then silence once more.

He checked Brunhilda and Jorge Palafox off his mental list. A reference to Tito's infatuation brought no response at all. He started to ask if she thought their Uncle Agapito would approve of her taking on the duties of Little Theater treasurer just as the car stopped at the signal light on the corner of Juárez and Padre Mier. Feeling a sudden need for his uncle's placid philosophy, he bent forward and tapped Mateo's shoulder. "Go around the block. Perhaps don Lucio also wants to visit the hospital."

Slamming the automobile door, he hurried into don Primitivo's saloon. As usual it was filled with a haze of tobacco smoke. The flavor of cooking sharpened with garlic perfumed the air. Knots of men called laughing greetings to him as he strode down the length of the bar to the kitchen section. There he found don Primitivo's brothers and a very young dishwasher.

Alonso, seeing him, gave a shout of relief. "Bless the saints you've come, Domingo. I've been trying to reach you on the telephone."

Nicanor, the younger brother, snorted and thrust a plate of steaming *tortillas* under Domingo's nose. He absently shook his head while he looked a question at both of them.

Alonso first wiped his hands on his apron, then rested them on the food ledge. "Do you know what those two fools have done, our brother and your uncle Lucio?"

"Don't tell me they have decided to enter politics again."

"Worse than that. There was a case of the black Christmas beer from Oaxaca left . . . just one case, mind you, and no more until next December."

"Drunk? And tonight of all nights. Primitivo belongs to you, but my uncle Lucio must be made sober again. Where is he?"

"At the military camp."

Domingo gulped and took a step backward. Anger swelled in him. This was one of the rare occasions when he did not love his Uncle Lucio.

"You don't understand," said Nicanor. "The beer was taken as a gift to General Gil."

"The new commander of this zone," added Alonso. "As you know, Primitivo trained on his father's ranch."

Domingo sighed with relief.

"Yes, I heard that, but I see no harm in this gesture. Indeed, I find it most commendable of our two beer drinkers to sacrifice the fine Oaxaca product to gratitude."

He found a dish of small chilis and carefully chose one. As he bit into its green fire, his anger disappeared to be replaced by his usual indulgent attitude toward his uncle.

"Commendable?" Alonso snorted. "They want to bribe General Gil. That's what they want to do."

"Why bribe him? What does the General possess that they do not have in greater luxury in this saloon?"

"Power," said the younger brother. He spoke with such finality that Domingo put down the half-eaten chili to stare at him in surprise.

"I don't understand you . . . either of you."

"The military zone is outside of the city laws. They plan to invite the Counselor Farías to the camp and beat him up. The gift of beer, plus family friendship, will make the General protect them, they think."

Domingo cursed vividly while the two brothers, glad that such responsibility had been shifted from their shoulders, returned placidly to their work. The miniature dishwasher giggled, but a glare from Alonso and a muttered "Doña Sansona" reduced him to the proper humility of a servant in the presence of his betters.

Yells from the outer room warned the brothers that the food supply was growing low. Both of them, with heavily loaded trays, left Domingo with affectionate pats on the arm to let him know that he possessed their sympathy.

Still cursing, he hurried to the sidewalk to wait for the car. Night had deepened the cold, and he had to stamp his feet to keep them warm. Pedestrians swirled around him, some pausing to wait for a bus, others to light cigarettes and exchange brief bits of the day's gossip. A few *conscriptos* passed, their shoulders straight in their khaki uniforms, the shaven heads under the narrow cloth caps proclaiming that they had only lately been inducted into the army. Busses, taxis, trucks and private automobiles made a long line of traffic as the signal light flashed from green to red and green again. But of the Vázquez de Anda car there was no sign.

Domingo understood that because of one-way traffic Mateo had to make a large circle in order to reach him. The car had doubtless passed just before he emerged from the saloon, and his own impatience was lengthening the seconds into minutes. His mind so told him, but his caution whispered that Sofía was alone at night with a chauffeur he hardly knew. What was to prevent Mateo from turning the car in the direction of the Guadalupe suburb on the highway to Reynosa? Out there was a certain house of entertainment. . . .

The image was so vivid that it was not until Sofía's voice said impatiently, "Are you going to stand there all night?" that he realized the car had slid silently up to the sidewalk in front of him. His legs were rubber as he collapsed on the seat beside her, and there was humble apology in the glance he directed at Mateo's rigid back.

Relief was so great in him that he found himself laughing a bit hysterically as he recounted the story of don Lucio, don Primitivo, and the Christmas beer. Sofía frowned and tapped her lips with one finger.

"What are you going to do about it?"

He slid forward on the seat and ordered Mateo to go to the military camp, then took her hand. "Eh, Sofía, what took you so long just now?"

"A tourist was driving the wrong way on Guerrero Street. It tied up traffic for a while."

They were passing along Bolívar Street. To their left they could see the Purisima plaza and the gray bulk of the Purisima Church. At night, Domingo decided, the church lost its monstrous swollen aspect. The gray curves faded into black shadows, acquiring a mysterious quality that was almost unearthly in its strangeness.

"There was a bad accident on this street last night," Mateo said, turning his face slightly toward them.

"This is news."

"A tourist had been up on the Bishop's Hill to look at the city lights. Instead of turning off onto Hidalgo, he tried to return down Bolívar. Of course there were pointing arrows on every corner to tell him he was driving the wrong way, but you know how tourists are."

"When was this?"

"About two this morning. He ran into a car coming home from New Laredo. Can you imagine, the tourist's car was not even dented, just a little scratched?"

"But the other car?"

"It turned over. The driver was killed, and one of the women had her arm broken."

"How terrible," Sofía whispered.

"No, niña, that was not the terrible thing." Mateo swung the automobile left for a block and then right again at the spot where Hidalgo Street becomes the Saltillo Road. Neither Domingo nor Sofía noticed that the chauffeur was disobeying orders by going to the hospital first.

"But what could be more terrible unless all of the people were killed?" Sofía protested.

"That the car which was obeying the law was punished for obeying it, while the law breaker was not even dented. That is not fair, niña. A man tries to do the best he can, and then, pouf, something on which he never counted: a cyclone for a farmer, a stray bullet for a pedestrian, a car out of place for a driver, or a woman for a man, and all the planning, all the life's work— destroyed in a moment."

Domingo chuckled. "You think a woman is as bad as a bullet, or a cyclone, or an unlawful car?"

"Worse, s'ñor . . . señor Domingo. You know that a cyclone will act in a certain manner, or a bullet, or even a car, but a woman . . . who but God knows what fancies a woman will get?"

Verónica, thought Domingo, and asked, "Does God always know?"

"I doubt it, s'ñor Domingo. I doubt it."

Mateo's cynicism amused Domingo, but he found himself in full agreement. Verónica's whim was fashioned in a mind that recognized no restraints save its own desire, and Márgara had certainly entered his life on the wings of a hurricane—had interrupted the smooth progress of his days to such an extent that marriage with Verónica was turned into an impossibility. But even as he thought this, he knew it was false reasoning. He and

Verónica could never have found a common meeting ground, even had Márgara never existed nor Tito cast his spell on the Miranda house. Somewhere, perhaps, a man was waiting for the dagger marked "Verónica" to pierce his heart, but that man was not named Domingo Vázquez de Anda.

As he thought of Verónica, the image of Serafina superimposed itself over the fading silhouette of the girl who was so like and yet so unlike her. There was a humble dignity in Serafina that Verónica lacked, a native grace that was at variance with Verónica's carefully fostered artificial naturalness. It was like comparing a real rose with the perfection of a wax one, but the real rose had life, the real rose had perfume.

The car turned into the half-moon driveway of the hospital and stopped at the double-width glass doors.

Sofía's voice possessed a biting edge as she said, "You told Mateo to take you to the military camp first."

"The hospital was closer," Mateo answered. His eyes met hers steadily before she allowed Domingo to hand her to the entrance steps. Entertained by this battle between Sofía's arrogance and Mateo's humble assurance, Domingo escorted her to the stairway that led to Cardito's room and then returned to the automobile.

Wanting to know more of this new servant, he sat in the front seat and launched on an intensive few minutes of questioning. Mateo, it developed, was the eldest of seven children. His father, a gardener at the Quinta Calderón, died in 1938, and since then Mateo, his three brothers, and the unmarried sister had worked harder than ever to augment the family income. "One of my sisters," he explained, "married a musician. He is a better cook than musician, but he has dreams. He plays the violin in a *mariachi*. Naturally he makes no money so they, too, must be supported. My mother cooks for some *gringos* in the Colonia Mirador."

Mateo had gone through the fifth grade in school, working mornings and evenings as a shoeshine boy. He had saved enough to buy a section of the Ancira Hotel corner, and this he had passed on to his brothers. It was now owned by his youngest brother, who was nine. The seventeen year old brother was helper to a mechanic's assistant in a garage on Doblado Street. "We are hoping that he will get into one of the large tourist garages where the tips are very good, but he still lacks the proper knowledge." His brother, aged twenty, was more fortunate. This one worked as a clerk in the grocery store of don Wilfrido Vidal and earned twenty pesos a week salary. "The difficulty," sighed Mateo, "is the bulls. My brother Manuel has a passion for the bulls. Already he has renamed himself Manolo and spends all of his free time and his money with the fighters."

"Don Wilfrido," Domingo said, "is also an enthusiast."

"A tragedy, s'ñor . . . señor Domingo, that my brother should ever have gone to work for such a man. Don Wilfrido is very good to him—that I do not deny, but he is too good. He lends Manuel books on the art, encourages him in this stupidity. Can you imagine a grocery clerk becoming a bullfighter?"

"The Sultan of Monterrey was a grocery clerk."

"Yes, señor, that is true. But Lorenzo the Magnificent had the genius. My brother Manuel—I refuse to call him Manolo— is a good grocery clerk and nothing more. Besides, it isn't practical."

"You mean an ambition is of no worth if it is not practical?"

"Precisely, señor. Examine the law of averages. Every year in the Republic there are three thousand young men who dream of becoming a great sword. They sacrifice their families, their jobs, their hopes of a decent future for this foolishness. Finally they arrive in the Capital. They haunt the impresarios' offices. And out of those three thousand, how many are chosen? 'Eh, you, Fulano. Rent a costume and go to Puebla to fight in a cuadrilla.' 'You, Mengano, here is a sword who needs a pick. Can you ride a horse?' So Fulano and Mengano, two out of three thousand, enter the ring. And what happens to these two? Do they become famous? Even the goats laugh when they pass by. They wander from *cuadrilla* to *cuadrilla*—never with name fighters. Ay, no! Just with the poor swords of the provinces, men who are still novices, who have never received the alternative to become true matadors. And in the end, our Fulano and Mengano —these two out of three thousand—what happens to them? Do they die gloriously on the horns of the black bull of pain? No such fate. They either fold up and die in a mendicant's hospital of tuberculosis, or they run a saloon like don Primitivo. Two out of three thousand. The law of averages. I tell this to my brother. You can't beat the law of averages, I tell him."

"And what does he say?"

"He says: Lorenzo Garza; Luís Procuna; Manolete. He says: Rudolfo Gaona; Belmonte. He says Armillita. Saints in Heaven, the superb Armilla. My brother Manual dreams that some day he will be a second Armillita!"

This sentence was produced in such tones of disgust that Domingo could not suppress his laughter. "Yet Fermín Espinosa, the great Armillita, was born in Saltillo. He breaks your law of averages. . . ."

"He does not, señor Domingo. Armillita comes of a family of fighters: his father, his brothers, especially his brother Juan. Armillita faced his first bull when he was thirteen, and even at that time he received an ovation. His period as a novice was marked with triumph. When he received his Mexican alternative, the plaza went insane over his performance. And when he received the Spanish alternative—Blessed Brother Michael, even the critics wept with joy. Armillita is stamped with genius. My brother is stamped with a grocer's talent."

"You have dreams too, Mateo . . ."

"I am a practical man. For me every peso contains one hundred centavos. I do not believe in dreaming them into existence. I believe in work, hard work, but work that I know how to do."

Here it is, thought Domingo, all of Uncle Agapito's philosophy —all of Monterrey's philosophy, rolled up in a paragraph. In a sentence really: "Every peso contains one hundred centavos." No room here for dreams, for a peso composed of eighty centavos, or even one hundred and twenty. Only the round, the practical number, one hundred.

Was he wrong to fight against such a philosophy? He glanced out of the side window and saw that they had turned off of Avenida Madero onto Cuauhtemoc Street, which extended its great length beyond the railroad station, the power plant, the brewery, the military camp, to cut straight north to Laredo and San Antonio, Texas. This street was really part of a dream. Somewhere an engineer had thought of a highway that began in Canada and ended in South America. Such a road was a very practical thing, bringing money to the towns, bringing tourists to the South. Before the highway there had been perhaps two thousand tourists a year. Now there were a million. Since tourists demanded luxury, commerce expanded. . . .

But this argument was on the wrong side of the ledger. Surely there were dreams, great dreams, which lacked practicality and yet were within themselves practical—not in terms of dollars and cents but simply because they gave so much of beauty, so much of consolation. He thought briefly of Beethoven, of his own patron, St. Dominic, of Rembrandt, men who had died in poverty but whose dreams had changed the world. He grimaced as he reflected that his Uncle Agapito would counter with the price of a Rembrandt canvas, a Beethoven manuscript, a Dominican convent.

The car stopped at the gates of the military camp, was passed by the guard, and then turned left to follow the avenue of palms to the general's private residence. Once more a guard stopped them, but they finally reached the house with the broad veranda where the commander of this important frontier military zone was lodged.

Domingo had come here often in the days of the famous General Aguilar, but this was a new general, and as he went up the steps he wondered what the man would be like. The doors to the wide entrance hall were open. In the rear a stairway rose to the second story. He hesitated, not knowing which way to go, when he heard a burst of laughter from the left. He tiptoed to the door and peered in. It was a dining room with a round center table. General Gil, a large-boned man with gray hair resting like a cap on his head, had his heels on the table, a bottle of the dark Christmas beer in his hand. Don Primitivo was hunched down in another chair, and don Lucio was sprawled forward, his chest flat on the table top, his head tilted sideways on his folded arms. They were listening to don Primitivo tell a story of the bullring.

"It was when Procuna came last year, my general. Tickets on the shade side were selling for eighty and a hundred pesos each. Me, I generally sit on the sun side, but don Agapito, may his soul dance on the devil's tail . . ."

"Amen," said don Lucio.

"Had two tickets sent to him as a gift. But he does not patronize the magnificent art. He believes in baseball."

"He owns part of the Monterrey club," don Lucio interrupted. "He has to believe in it."

"At any rate, he sent Lucio and myself the tickets, so we

99

went. Such a crowd, especially the women. That streak of white in Procuna's hair would draw a woman from a house of mourning. Right in front of us was seated a woman with a new fur coat . . ."

"Sealskin, my general," said don Lucio. "Very short thick hair."

"It must have been new, because the day was hot—it was December, and you know how hot it can get in December. Why else would she have worn it if it were not new? There she sat on the bench, near the low barrier that separates the shade from the sun side, all eager for that first glimpse of Procuna."

Don Lucio raised his head enough to swallow some beer. "Over on the sun side," he said, wiping his mouth with the back of his hand, "were some young devils with sacks filled with flour. They would swing these in their hands to get a good twist on the paper necks, and then they would throw them to burst on heads, against backs, anywhere it pleased them to aim. One of them saw this woman with her coat."

"You can imagine what happened when the sack burst, my general," don Primitivo continued. "The brown fur looked white-washed."

The General guffawed and took a deep draught from his bottle. "What did the creature do?"

"She took off the coat, folded it up and put it on the seat . . . all very slow, very quiet, then stood on the bench and stepped across to the sun side. The boy was stupid. He should have started running the moment she rose, but he was obviously an orphan and unused to the wrath of women. She gave him a slap that sounded like a firecracker. And then she really began to beat him."

"None of his friends could reach him to help," crowed don Lucio. "All the other victims on the sun side held them back. It was beautiful. Even the police kept out of it. I have never heard such shrieks. Finally the police felt a softening of the heart. They did not want the boy completely dead, so they took him off to jail for disturbing the peace. The woman returned to her seat. Ay, the people gave her a fine ovation!"

"It ruined the fight, of course. How could even Procuna compete against such a battle?" Don Primitivo sighed at this insult to a great art and consoled himself with more beer. "Lucio and

I went down the next morning to pay the boy's fine. I needed a dishwasher who would not break dishes. Now, whenever he looks as though he were about to break a dish I threaten him with the woman in the fur coat, whom I have named doña Sansona after that man of strength in the Bible."

"Is there such a woman's name?" the general chuckled.

"How should I know? But it is magic for keeping dishes unbroken. Eh, who's that in the doorway?"

Lucio peered toward the hall, then sprang up with a little cry of delight. "My good nephew Domingo. Come and have a glass of Christmas beer. It isn't iced, but I always say that the man who cannot drink warm beer has no head for liquor."

Domingo shook his head, then came in to be introduced to the General. The formalities finished, he explained that he had arrived to save the Counselor Farías from destruction.

"The plan is abandoned," said don Lucio. "Our friend, the General, has conceded that it is a good plan . . ."

"Excellent," murmured the General, with a wink at Domingo. "There is only one slight difficulty."

"Precisely," said don Primitivo. "Should we give this imbecile stature as a martyr, so that all the world could say, 'Have you heard of what happened to that poor man, the Counselor Farías?'"

"I have always contended," don Lucio insisted, "that a martyr should seek his own martyrdom. Me, I am not going to aid the Counselor Farías to achieve his. Do you not agree, Domingo?"

"Such a fate would make him the most popular man in Monterrey," Domingo gravely agreed. "And that we certainly do not want. I am going to the hospital now, Uncle Lucio. Will you go with me?"

"And me also." Don Primitivo pushed himself erect, contemplated the box of beer on the table, carefully lifted out four bottles, two of which he placed under each arm. Then, reasoning that this would keep him from bestowing the formal farewell embrace, he set them on the table and flung both arms about the General. "Son of my patron," he said, and brushed quick tears from his eyes with his sleeve. He took up the bottles again and trotted happily through the hall to the car, don Lucio speeding after him to help him, and himself to be helped in turn, down the steps.

The General grinned at Domingo. "Are you certain you won't taste this fine Christmas brew?"

"Thank you," said Domingo, "but the hour grows late." He held out his hand. "And thank you also, my General, for saving those two innocents from a wicked lawsuit for assault."

"Innocents," said the General. "A good word. I shall be sorry to see their generation disappear. We'll never have another that is so—innocent."

Domingo was pleased with this concept. He wondered why it had never occurred to him before that the children of México were passing, and in their place were coming the new adults represented by Mateo Chapa: the practical men who achieved their objectives without bothering with the nonsense of childish plans.

He shook hands again with the General, liking him and feeling just a little sorry for him. The strong personality of General Aguilar had dominated the northern frontier. To follow such a giant was, in the words of the last Aztecan emperor, hardly a couch of roses.

When he reached the automobile he discovered that don Primitivo had estranged Mateo by recognizing him as the brother of Manuel Chapa, who might, if the gods smiled, become a bullfighter. Mateo showed his disgust by sitting rigid as a cactus thorn, while don Primitivo jovially overflowed his section of the front seat. Don Lucio had curled up in the back and was already sound asleep.

"The hospital," Domingo said wearily, wondering if this time he would really get there.

XI

Family dinners at the Vázquez de Anda house were always something of a ritual. Don Rafael, while not a tyrant in the sense of don Agapito, was most meticulous in matters of etiquette, and demanded that his family observe certain customs to which he as a child had been subjected, and his father before him.

The dinner hour was set for nine on weekdays, at three in the afternoon on Sundays, and every child was expected to be standing behind his chair as the hour struck. The formal dining room was always used. Don Rafael sat at the head of the table, even when don Agapito was present. Doña Otilia stayed on one side near the foot, close to the kitchen door. On ordinary evenings, Domingo, as the oldest son, sat at the foot, but when honored guests were present he changed his place to the one facing his mother.

Tonight he made no comment when he saw that his napkin ring had been switched to the side, with the seat of honor reserved for Brunhilda.

While he waited for the family to gather, his eyes wandered around this room which had witnessed so many scenes of family triumph and disgrace. Over the door was a large ceramic plaque with the head of the Virgin in basrelief. Large armoirs of dark wood, one holding the family plate, the other wines and liquors, dominated two corners. Running the length of a wall was the carved chest where the silver and linen were stored. Keys for all of these cabinets swung at doña Otilia's belt, along with the kitchen keys. It was the table, however, which immediately attracted attention. Old don Domingo had brought it from Germany, and its dark wood had the sheen that comes only from years of patient polishing. Oblong in shape, the four corner legs were carved with hundreds of tiny figures: hunters, deer, boar, horses, and strange misshaped little men who were probably trolls. These figures had obviously enchanted the revolutionary soldiers, because there were deep cuts where unsuccessful attempts had been made to gouge them out. When there were more than ten guests, small tables were added to extend its length.

There were few such occasions now, the last having been the wedding supper in celebration of don Agapito's marriage to his third wife. For more intimate affairs, such as now, the crystal chandelier was turned off, and candles augmented the wall lights.

Doña Otilia had never become accustomed to the North American use of flowers as a centerpiece, although some of her friends, especially those who belonged to the Monterrey Garden

Club, were beginning to adopt the decoration. To doña Otilia, a table was a place for food, not useless ornament. However, her great love of flowers had resulted in tall iron stands which held pots of ferns and begonias, with caged canaries dangling from the top rings. There were moments when these canaries sang so loud that conversation was impossible. Then doña Otilia would ring her copper bell, and the downstairs maid would scurry in with cage covers, after which conversation would return to its normal pitch. When the meal was finished, doña Otilia removed the covers with a humble apology to each bird for the inconvenience it had suffered.

To her Veracruz soul, life without birds was impossible. In the afternoons she was often to be seen at her sewing, the birds, freed for an hour of exercise, darting about the room, now and then perching on her shoulders or her head. Every servant in the house had to come running when it was time to return them to their cages. There would be a swirl of activity, shouts interspersed by giggles, and doña Otilia placid as an island in the midst of raging waters. Domingo always suspicioned that she ordered these tempests so as to give the birds more exercise, because it was usually her own placid hand which reached into the air, caught a ball of feathers, and carefully replaced it in its accustomed home.

Tonight he noticed that the cage covers were in place before the meal. This meant that don Rafael had ordered an hour of uninterrupted speech. Florinda, the downstairs maid, was fluttering about the table, opening bottles of iced Coca-Cola, and seeing that there was a dish of green chilis at each plate. She never quite allowed her eyes to meet Domingo's, although he was aware that she was covertly watching him. He wondered if she, too, thought he was indulging in an affair with Serafina. He was tempted to sound her out on the subject, but had no chance, as Sofía, in her purple dinner dress strolled into the room.

"Where is our mother?" he asked her, fetching her an ashtray from the sideboard. He remembered that when he was Sofía's age, no unmarried girl would be seen smoking outside of her own bedroom, but in ten years customs change quickly, especially in a frontier city.

"She is dressing. Or rather she is helping our father to dress.

He is so proud of Brunhilda. I hope she does not disappoint him too much."

"You think she will?"

"She is Brunhilda."

The swinging door into the kitchen opened a fraction of an inch, and doña Petra's hand came through, beckoning to Domingo. When Sofía would have followed her brother, she was curtly told that her services were not needed, and Domingo found himself being led across the back patio to the cook's room in the servants' quarters.

"What is wrong, doña Petra?"

"As though you did not know," the old woman sniffed, and the tone, more than the implication, made him conclude that Serafina had fainted again. He found the girl stretched out on doña Petra's bed, her skin sallow against the blatant pink of the counterpane.

"You should be ashamed of yourself," the old woman muttered, then advanced to the bed, where she lifted Serafina's hand and gently began to stroke it.

Domingo opened his mouth to say something, then shut it again. He had no intention of involving Cardito, so he merely shrugged and accepted the responsibility. "Who else knows about this?" he asked, as he, too, bent over the girl.

"That fool of a Florinda has a nose for gossip. I don't think she suspects anything, but who could say?"

"Can you frighten her into silence?"

"I can try." Doña Petra's left eyebrow rose, the forehead wrinkling above it. "When you were eighteen you had more sense, niño Domingo. And I thought you were in love with a worthwhile woman at last."

He winked at her. "The main thing is to keep this knowledge from my mother. Are you sure that she . . . ?"

"That angel? This child would have to be more swollen than she is now to attract your mother's attention. But niña Sofía has a very noticing eye, and so does niña Brunhilda."

Doña Petra has never really liked Brunhilda, he mused, while he absently watched Serafina's face. What to do with this girl was a problem which had been nagging at him all evening, but he had not yet arrived at any definite conclusions. He heard doña Petra say, "If niña Sofía makes any remarks your father will be angry, niño. And I tremble to think of what don Agapito will say."

"Don't worry about Sofía. She already knows . . ."

"Does she now?"

"Not about the baby," he added too hastily. The moment the words were uttered he realized that he had definitely committed himself to all responsibility for Serafina. It was too late now to remedy the false impression. And even if it were not too late, what could he say? He knew doña Petra's talent for hardening suspicions into facts. Even if Cardito admitted the truth, if Serafina admitted it, if he himself insisted on it, she would never believe them. And as doña Petra thought, so thought doña Otilia. They had been together for so many years that each was a sounding board for the other.

Doña Petra sniffed. "In my day, fine young ladies only learned about such things after marriage. I tell you, niño, Sofía is too wise. If you're not careful, she'll get in trouble, too. You allow her too much freedom . . ."

"I am not our father, doña Petra . . ."

"You are her elder brother. Naturally you know more of her life than her father would. She's your responsibility . . ."

"Stop it!" He flung up an arm, then with an effort of will dominated his irritation. "For the last twenty-four hours it would seem that everything in this house is my responsibility. I want none of it."

"You have a responsibility now," said doña Petra grimly. She replaced Serafina's hand carefully on the bed beside the still figure. "What are you going to do about it?"

Florinda's voice called through the doorway, "S'ñor Domingo, the niña Sofía says that it lacks a few minutes of nine."

"Tell her that the niño Domingo will be there in a moment," doña Petra answered, then looked at Domingo. "Florinda will be in this room the moment my back is turned. And Serafina might talk when she recovers her senses. She is a wise girl, but she is very weak."

Domingo paced the narrow room. "The best thing to do is to send her home. See that Florinda stays in the dining room while I carry her to the car." He slid his arms under the lax figure. As he lifted her, he was aware of how very light she was. Like most Mexican men he preferred plumper women, but something about this fragile body touched a pool of tenderness in him.

He waited until doña Petra signaled him that the coast was clear, then crossed the back patio to the garage. After carefully settling Serafina in the car and covering her with a rug, he went to Mateo's room, where he found the chauffeur reading a book on salesmanship. He quickly explained that Serafina was ill and needed to be taken home. No expression changed in Mateo's blank stare as he asked for the girl's address. Domingo was shocked by the knowledge that he had no idea where Serafina lived. The last twenty-four hours had set up such a bond of personal relationship between them that the realization that he still knew very little about her was startling.

Promising to send the address by doña Petra, he hurried to the kitchen where the cook was making Florinda rearrange the fruit cups. He called doña Petra outside and told her what he wanted in a low voice. She gave him a curious glance. "There are times," she said fretfully, "when I do not understand you. That girl is nearly seven months gone with child . . ."

"Seven! Impossible. She—"

"Don't argue with me. You may get your doctoring out of books, but I have experience in such matters. The child laces to hide the swelling. Seven months, I can tell you, and during all of this time you've never once asked where she lived."

"I'm sorry, doña Petra, and the next time I get involved with a servant girl, I will ask your advice on every subject, I promise you. But now will you please tell Mateo where she lives? Or don't you know either?"

"She lives on Aramberri near the cemeteries. Perhaps the ghosts kept you away."

"Will you please go tell Mateo?"

He passed her angrily and went into the dining room. Florinda smiled at him, and one hand smoothed the dress over her knees, but he paid her no attention. He knew that she was consumed with curiosity as to what had happened to Serafina, but the servants were doña Petra's business. The old woman could cope with the girl much better than he could. As he opened the dining room door he looked back at Florinda. Her eyes widened slightly and a dimple creased one round cheek. It was only then that it occurred to him that she was flirting with him. A week ago he would have winked at her, but tonight he had had enough of pretty servants.

The clock set in the wall between the two patio windows was chiming the hour of nine as he slipped into place beside Sofía. Brunhilda was already standing behind her chair at the foot of the table.

"You are just in time," Sofía whispered in relief.

Brunhilda frowned at him. "On my homecoming night, Domingo, you might have tried to be more prompt."

Sofía hissed at her for silence as the patio door opened, and don Rafael, with doña Otilia on his arm, ceremoniously entered the room, followed by don Lucio.

Conversation, in spite of Brunhilda's presence, lacked its usual sparkle due to Cardito's absence. Doña Otilia insisted that a chair be set at his place, and now and then she would reach out and stroke it.

Domingo noticed that his father and mother would glance at him and then smile at each other, as though sharing a secret about him which pleased them. This worried him. He was afraid that the news of the Verónica engagement had already reached them, but as neither mentioned the subject, he as a dutiful son, could not.

When don Rafael tried to get Brunhilda to tell some of her New York experiences, she protested that conversation would give her no time for food.

"The food of our childhood," don Lucio sighed. "No matter how plain it is, no other food has ever quite the same familiar taste."

Brunhilda obviously agreed with him, because as course followed course, she ate with exaggerated appetite. After the fruit cup came broiled trout, then *sopa de aroz:* rice fried with tomatoes and onions and topped by thin strips of banana. This was followed by filet mignon wrapped in bacon with a mushroom sauce, and served on rum soaked toast. Next was the *frijol,* the fat brown bean of Mexico, first stewed, then fried and mashed, with melted cheese poured over the top. Flaky French bread was on the table, but Brunhilda's hand reached again and again toward the *tortilla* plate.

Don Rafael's brows rose slightly when Brunhilda asked for claret in place of Coca-Cola, but he made no comment as he nodded to doña Otilia. Domingo took the liquor cabinet key from his mother and fetched a bottle of the sour red wine. Doña Petra was called from the kitchen, to join in a toast of homecoming to the plump, pretty girl.

Then, after mango ice-cream and black coffee, they crossed the patio to the formal living room where the grand piano took up one entire wall.

"Now," said don Rafael, rubbing his hands complacently together, "you will play for us, eh, my daughter?"

"And I so full of food?" she protested lightly, collapsing in a Louis XVI armchair. Its gilded wood and cream upholstery suited her, Domingo thought. Her turquoise moiré dress, with its wide skirt and tiny waist, had a low bodice, daintily modest with an insert of shrimp-pink gauze that encircled the creamy throat with a narrow band of embroidered roses. This same embroidery, he noticed, was on the high heels of her turquoise moiré slippers. If asked, he wondered, will she say that Uncle Agapito also sent her the money for this dress?

He glanced sideways at Sofía, who was sitting beside doña Otilia on the loveseat. The slender line of her purple gown made her look too cold, too polished beside Brunhilda's femininity, yet, feature for feature, she far more resembled their mother than did any of the Vázquez de Anda children.

Doña Otilia's weight, which had come on her in her later years, had blunted the sharp lines of her figure, until now she was soft as a bed of petunias. These were her favorite flowers, and she preferred clothes in their magenta colors, although tonight she was dressed in gray, with amethyst brooch and earrings, and two amethyst studded combs in her gray hair. Her fine textured skin, magnolia white, retained the fresh resiliancy of youth, and her only wrinkles were the laughter lines at the corners of her eyes.

In contrast to her, don Rafael had grown thinner with the years. He possessed a tremendous amount of nervous energy which prevented his staying still very long at a time. "Chairs," doña Otilia often said, "were never intended for my husband." He had two passions, his home and music, and of these, Domingo sometimes thought, music predominated. The real estate business interested him not at all, but when Domingo had protested against entering the office, his father had called him in for a long talk. "At first I felt like you. Music dominated me. I thought that the world demanded my talent, but now I know that my talent was not great enough. As time passed I became more satisfied with this work, as you will become in time."

"I will never be satisfied," Domingo answered indignantly, but his father shook his head.

"You have not enough years to understand what I mean. But you will finally discover it for yourself."

Ten years had passed since that conversation, Domingo remembered, but the discovery of the truth behind his father's words was still seemingly in the future. Better not to think of medicine. Concentrate on Brunhilda. This was her night.

He intercepted one of his father's prowling movements and led the older man to a chair. "She won't play at all," he teased, "unless you settle yourself. How can she gain inspiration with you jumping about like a flea?"

Don Rafael laughed on a note of such gayety that all the others, with the exception of Brunhilda, smiled in sympathy. Domingo noticed that she seemed oddly nervous this evening, which was unlike her usual complacent manner. Her shrimp-pink handkerchief slid in and out between her fingers, and her eyes roamed the room like two brown birds seeking shelter. He wandered over to her and dropped his hand on her shoulder. "Can you not play for us now, Brunhilda?"

She jerked away from him, and jumped to her feet. "Stop nagging at me."

"Enough!" don Rafael's voice was sharp. "There will be no quarrelling tonight. . . ."

She moved impatiently toward the door, her handkerchief twisting and untwisting between her fingers. "I do not feel like playing. I don't want . . ."

The eagerness in don Rafael's face faded, then he bowed his head. so that the hurt was hidden. His voice was quiet as he said, "The temperament of an artist. How can we ordinary beings . . ."

"Stop it, Papá! Stop it!" Brunhilda's voice rose, gained a ragged edge. "Ay, why did Uncle Agapito have to go to México City today and leave me alone."

Domingo's brows drew together into a straight line. He glanced sideways and met Sofía's anxious eyes. The truth was plain to Sofía, he realized, even as it was to him. "How could you do this thing,

Brunhilda?" he asked, surprised that his voice should sound so harsh.

She whirled on him, a vivid awareness of his knowledge clear on her face. "So you have guessed the truth, my clever brother. My too clever brother."

"These are riddles, riddles," don Rafael protested.

It was doña Otilia whose voice cut the storm with a preemptory, "Brunhilda! Come here to me."

The girl walked sulkily to her mother, her head bowed, her hands clenched and hidden in the folds of her skirt.

"Fetch a chair for your sister, Domingo. Place it here in front of me."

He moved the chair forward, its delicate gilt lines feeling too fragile in his hands.

"Be seated, my daughter."

"Mother, there is no need—not tonight."

"When the occasion arises, there is always need. Rafael."

"I am at your shoulder, Otilia." The stooped tall man put his hand on his wife's arm.

Domingo, without thinking, had stepped into place behind Sofía, so that the family was lined up, the four of them, against Brunhilda. Don Lucio, as usual, sat quietly in the shadows, a part and yet not a part of the family group.

The girl's head rose, and defiance was in her. "Are all of you against me?" she asked in the tragic tones that she had employed for such occasions since she was a little girl.

Doña Otilia shrugged her plump shoulders. "We want fair answers to fair questions, Brunhilda. As your mother, I will ask the questions. As my daughter you will answer with truth."

Brunhilda looked up at her father, saw a quiet expressionless face. Domingo could sense the thoughts in her mind. When doña Otilia took command of a situation, it meant that the crisis was of truly great importance. Ordinarily she allowed the men, her husband and her sons, to dominate her world. But she had an instinct for the truly important, and when those moments came she was rock strong, the true matriarch. There is no need, Domingo thought, to appeal to our father, Brunhilda. As though she understood his advice, she dropped her head forward, her body tense.

"Did you study the piano in New York?"

"I tried." The voice was so low that Domingo had to strain to hear it.

"How long did you—try?"

For a moment the head stayed bowed, then came up with the wild impatience of a trapped animal. "I never asked to learn the piano. Never—not once. I have no talent. Anyone could have told you. . . ." Again her eyes, wide and frightened, went up to her father's face. "What good is technique without talent? Any good teacher could have told you the truth—the men here at the conservatory—but you didn't believe—no one believed—only uncle Agapito." The tears were coming now, the swift easy tears of a child.

"How long did you study in New York?"

"Two weeks." She was reduced to a whisper.

"Two weeks. You were gone two years. The letters you wrote . . ."

"I never lied to you. Did I ever mention lessons?"

"You implied that you were studying."

"Uncle Agapito said it would be easier for you to learn the truth later." Once more the voice rose. "That's what he said."

"Your uncle Agapito," doña Otilia repeated thoughtfully. She pressed her hand against her eyes, and in the manner familiar to her family, seemed to go away from them, so that the large, soft body was left, but the spirit was wandering through mazes along which they could not follow.

Domingo permitted himself a sideways glance at his father. The face was cold and set. He, too, had withdrawn into himself, rejecting reality as he so often did when faced with a difficult problem. Don Lucio, sitting in the shadows, was remote from this group. Sofía, too, was remote in her own way, a chiseled figure in her purple dress.

Reaching into himself, Domingo tried to determine his own reactions, but found himself as cold as Sofía. The initial shock, the first blazing realization that Brunhilda had stolen two years from them, had fed her father's hopes with tantalizing nothingness, consumed all of his feelings. Later, he would react emotionally, but now he felt cold, with ice where warmth should be.

Doña Otilia dropped her hand and looked at and past her eldest daughter. "As I understand it, your uncle Agapito was aware that you lacked a true talent when you left us, but he was willing for you to go so that you would learn . . . what? What was it he wanted you to learn?"

"The ways of the world," Brunhilda answered quietly. That space of silence had stiffened her also, and she was no longer afraid but slightly contemptuous of this innocence which had believed a lie for so long. The awareness of this in her attitude changed her image in Domingo's mind, so that she was no longer the soft kitten whom he had loved for so long, but a person he had never really liked, even as a child.

"Is Monterrey so small a place then that it is ignored by the world? Do men not live and die in Monterrey? Is there no passion here? No sorrow? No joy?"

"The world of fashion," Brunhilda answered. She preened herself a little, and her hands, no longer clenched, stroked the stiff material of her skirt. "Not the everyday world, but the world of culture, of importance."

"He sent you money for those clothes? He sent you enough money so that you could learn such an expensive lesson?"

"As much as I needed. He promised me that before I left. Uncle Agapito truly understands me."

"Do you understand yourself?".

"I know what I want."

"Marriage, is that what you want? A passport into this world of fashion?"

"He is bringing Jorge Palafox back with him from México City. We met in New York. He is interested in me. I would make him a good wife. The kind of a wife he needs."

These are words, Domingo thought. And being words, they must mean something. But such words coming from Brunhilda's mouth mean nothing. She is too stupid to have invented them for herself. Therefore they are Uncle Agapito's words.

With an effort, he pulled himself back into the scene, and consciously listened to his mother's voice saying, "It is a pity that this scene occurred while your Uncle Agapito was gone to México City. Undoubtedly he has a certain plan which we do not fully understand. Goodnight, Brunhilda."

The abrupt dismissal startled the girl. She half rose, then sank back into her chair. "You want me to say nothing else? But I have much to tell of my two years . . ."

"Better to tell it after we have talked with your uncle."

Brunhilda rose in one movement, like a dancer, artificial as Verónica, as Sofía. Domingo found himself absurdly wanting a few minutes with the natural grace of Serafina as relief from this stylized movement.

At the door Brunhilda paused, turned slightly to them. With her raised hand, her half turned head, she was a painting on a canvas, and not a woman at all. "I am sorry, Father," she said, and then, more passionately, "It was not good. You couldn't put in me something that was never there. It is not practical to . . ." She stopped, lacking the words to express what was in her mind.

She tries, Domingo thought pitifully. She tries to think. Then the door closed behind her, and they could hear her heels clicking across the tiles of the arcade. Don Rafael bent lower until his cheek was resting on the gray silk of doña Otilia's hair. Don Lucio moved his hand slightly, and the three of them, don Lucio, Domingo and Sofía, moved silently toward the hall.

"Leave those two together," said don Lucio. "Otilia knows how to heal the hurt. We three are only in the way."

Sofía made a sound half cry of pain, half cynical snort.

Domingo said swiftly, "Don't say anything, Sofía. What is in your mind is in our minds."

"Is it?" Sofía asked. "Are my two years in your mind? Two years for a world of fashion, of culture. What might I have done with two such years? Is that in your mind?"

"No," Domingo answered, who had been remembering two years of medicine withheld. "No, I'm sorry Sofía."

"Haven't we had enough of selfishness tonight?" don Lucio asked wistfully.

Sofía choked on a shrill laugh, whirled, and ran across the patio to her room. After a moment don Lucio followed her, and Domingo was left alone in the patio.

The night was dark. There was no moon nor even stars, only a faint fragrance of growing things. He shivered slightly as he thought of the seeds, dark in the earth, pulsing with life and waiting to send their tendrils up toward the sun. The trembling life, silent. and waiting in the darkness, to emerge and bloom, but as what? Did the seeds know the color and pattern of their flowers, or were they like human parents, who knew only that the flower was of their making, but with no control over the shaping and the destiny?

114

He heard his father's voice calling him, and he obediently returned to the music room. Don Rafael was sitting on the sofa beside his wife, the two of them holding hands.

"Domingo, Jonás Miranda called me this evening. He said you had declared yourself to Verónica."

Domingo half opened his lips to tell the truth, but before he could speak, his father said, "I am so glad, Domingo. Your mother and I—we are both so glad."

"We wanted to speak to you at supper," doña Otilia said with a gentle smile, "but we preferred to be alone with our oldest son."

Her smile, his father's pleasure, were twin knives cutting into Domingo. At any other time he would have told them the truth, but they had been hurt too much tonight. And the knives cut deeper as he realized that they were submerging their pain over Brunhilda in order to cast no shadow across his own happiness.

His father said with forced brightness, "I thought perhaps that Wilfrido Vidal and Irineo Miranda would be excellent choices to go and make the formal declaration. I know that it is an old fashioned habit, but I like it."

As though sensing a withdrawal in Domingo, doña Otilio said quickly, "It is very late for such important decisions. But we wanted you to know how pleased we are. How very pleased."

He went forward then, and kissed his mother's cheek, his father's hand, knowing as he did so that any decision he might have made was useless. Once, when he was very young, he was allowed to make decisions. He could say, "I do or do not want a dish of ice-cream," or he could say, "I do or do not want to go to the Alameda." Yes, in those days the decision was important, because eating ice-cream is important, and playing in the cool greenness of the Alameda, is important. But the little things: dedicating one's life to medicine, or getting married, these little things have no value. They are the decisions that other people make for you because they have no value. You walk through them like a ghost and they do not touch you, because they have no value. They are the substance of your life and they have no value. Your life has no value. You are a dream being dreamed by someone else, and you have no value. Calderón wrote:

> Life is a dream
> And dreams are dreams.

But he never said, not once, who did the dreaming. And perhaps the dreamer was God, and perhaps the dreamer was a spirit forged from the substance of the Family. The Germans thought that about the State. They said that the State was a spirit forged from the substance of the people. Somebody had called the German idea Metapolitics. Perhaps there was a Metafamilia, and he was trapped in the substance and was one with the substance, and therefore he, as Domingo, as the man Domingo, as the aching desire Domingo, had no value.

The wind blew, and he turned with the wind. His uncle Agapito was the wind, and his father was the wind, and Márgara was a wind. . . . Márgara, Márgara, my heart breaks for you, Márgara, I love you, Mágara, but my love has no value because I am going to marry Verónica Miranda, and it makes no difference because I have no value. None of us have any value. Listen, Domingo has no value. Sofía has no value. Cardito has no value. Brunhilda has no value. I, valueless, have been forced into this marriage because of Brunhilda, valueless. And I, valueless, can no longer love because I cannot hate. I should hate Brunhilda, but I do not hate her. How can I hate her, the poor stupid, the poor grasping stupid? To hate is to have value, and I have no value. I have nothing but marriage to Verónica, amen.

XII

For the next several days Domingo rose in the mornings, he ate, he slept, he visited Cardito at the hospital, he kept the real-estate office open and he tried to see Verónica. He knew that it was useless to speak with her parents until he had seen her and tried to reason with her, but she made herself inaccessible by going to Linares to visit an aunt.

He could, of course, telephone her or go to Linares, but such actions would be interpreted as love-longing, and he wanted to add no fuel to the gossip fire that was already burning too brightly for comfort.

And he was worried about his father. Although don Rafael

made two visits to the office, he returned home almost immediately to stay near his wife. A broken dream, Domingo knew, could give far more pain than a broken limb, and the last of don Rafael's musical ambition had been crumbled by Brunhilda. For this hurt, doña Otilia was both doctor and nurse. He felt lost in a dark ocean if he were not near her.

So the full weight of the office descended on Domingo. His secretary was efficient, but she could not be expected to make important decisions. It was more necessary for Domingo to be in the office than out in the car. Realizing this, on Thursday Mateo asked for the opportunity to sell.

Domingo relaxed in his chair and examined the young man. The shabby blue suit was badly cut, the shirt was too pink, and the boxtoed button shoes were more yellow than brown. But he was immaculate. In spite of working with the car, his fingernails were clean, and his hair was not too slick with grease.

"Sit down, Mateo. I want to talk to you for a few minutes."

Domingo saw the muscles flex in Mateo's broad shoulders as he pulled the heavy leather chair across the black and white tiled floor. In the days of don Porfirio, this office had been the dining room of a mansion on Hidalgo Street, with various other mansions at the intersection where Morelos runs into Hidalgo and becomes one with it. After the Great Revolution, commerce had flowed up Morelos and overflowed into Hidalgo, and when the great Central Market was built, the resisting families retreated to the more fashionable sections further west, leaving their houses to be converted into business buildings.

These old families knew how to build. Their architects had not yet succumbed to the lure of the New York apartment. This room, instead of being a tiny cubicle, was fifteen feet square with an eighteen foot ceiling. Two long windows, masked with individual balconies, hung out over the street, and for eleven months of the year the crash and clang of traffic invaded the office. Since this was the cold month of February, the windows were kept shut. The sounds of traffic were only a muted snarl.

Both Mateo and Domingo were so used to the clamoring claxons, the shrill calls of street vendors, the hum of pedestrian speech, that both were subconsciously bothered by having it muted, although neither was aware of what it was that disturbed him.

Naturally, at this moment they were more than usually nervous, Domingo because of what he must put in tactful words, Mateo because this was his longed-for opportunity.

With elbows propped on the chairarms and his hands clasped in front of him, Domingo began slowly to speak of the type of clients who came to the Vázquez de Anda office. "You have seen a few. Most of them have money. One out of five really knows what he wants. The rest—well, they have money. You understand?"

"The new rich," said Mateo. "They're hunting for fine corners. Real gentlemen corners."

"Precisely. They are willing to spend, but they want true value . . ."

"I know values, s'ñor . . . señor Domingo."

"I don't mean values in terms of pesos, but values in terms of living. They must always feel that you are showing them the best, that you know what the best really is."

Mateo flushed, turned his head aside. Domingo grimmaced with distaste in his mind, yet he knew the words had been necessary. It was only fair that Mateo should understand why he could not be allowed to show the houses on the Vázquez de Anda lists. The new rich were sensitive to class distinctions. They wanted a gentleman's house, chosen by a gentleman, and it gave them a secret satisfaction to do business with a gentleman. For one thing, Domingo thought, they're convinced we're poor business men. As a class we have the reputation of being poor business men. And no matter how much we charge them, they are perfectly certain that they would have paid twice as much to one of their own kind. Which is stupid.

Mateo said humbly, "I was thinking perhaps you had other clients, men with not too much money to spend . . . as in the new *colonia*."

"The new *colonia* is an experiment. We've never handled that type of development before. I don't know that I like it. It is an idea of my Uncle Agapito. My father has enthusiasm, but I don't know. . . ."

Something in the tilt of Mateo's head attracted his attention. It was an oddly familiar gesture, and then Domingo remembered that Tito often sat that way with his head on one side, like a bird listening. Substitute Tito's round face for Mateo's round face, and where would the difference be then? Tito's body was plump, while Mateo's was solidly muscular, but both were about the same height, and both had the same unawareness of movement. Tito, of course, spent more on one suit than Mateo earned in a year. . . .

Domingo suddenly pulled open the bottom desk drawer and took out a cash box. "I'm going to make an office investment in you," he said. "If it doesn't pay off, well, we'll put it down to bad judgment."

Mateo's face brightened. "You mean you're going to give me a chance, señor Domingo . . . ?"

Busy at the telephone Domingo said, "You'll have to learn a few things that will seem stupid to you . . ." and then into the instrument, "Florinda, tell the niña Sofía I want to speak to her." He reached for a cigarette. Mateo hastily fumbled with the desk lighter.

Domingo frowned in reproof. "Lesson number one is never to move too fast. Keep steady, keep slow." And then into the telephone, "Eh, Sofía, I want you to do a favor for me. Come to the office, and bring a tablecloth, silver and some dishes, as though for a restaurant lunch. Get a taxi. The office will pay for it." After he hung up, while Mateo fetched their hats, he told the secretary that when the señorita Sofía arrived to ask her to please wait, then led the way to the street.

Two hours later, Mateo, in a new suit, new shirt, new shoes and a new haircut, was sitting at the map table in Domingo's office, while Sofía taught the chauffeur how to order a meal, and eat it after he got it.

Domingo had gone into his father's adjoining office to work, but the door was open. Now and then he would glance up at the sound of Sofía's voice saying, "No, Mateo, don't stick out your little fingers," or, "Bring the food up to your mouth, don't go down to your plate." Her patience astonished her brother. He had thought that after an hour or two she would get bored, and remember an improvised appointment at the dressmaker or the beauty shop. But four hours passed, and there was no tinge of impatience in her tone as she repeated instructions over and over. Finally she came to the door and said, "I think we should have a real test. Also, I am hungry. It's three o'clock. Let's make Mateo take us to the Arcos."

Domingo shrugged and got his hat. He watched with interest as he noticed Mateo holding Sofía's coat, the way he handled her purse and gloves. Only the quick, sideways glance betrayed that these small courtesies had been part of the lessons.

Then they were in the car and headed out Cuauhtémoc Street toward the military camp where the Arcos was located. This restaurant boasted a mixed clientel of customers ranging from farmers to Monterrey's best. Tourists from the nearby motor courts also ate there. The food was excellent, but its chief attraction was that its doors did not close from six in the morning until midnight.

When they got out of the car, Sofía said, "Remember, we're clients and you're taking us to lunch. Act like a client, Domingo."

Domingo grinned and entered into the spirit of the game. He wondered how Mateo was going to act under the strain of sitting down to eat with his employers. As though sensing this, Mateo halted at the door, but Sofía touched his arm. "Remember what I told you, Mateo. If you just remember that . . ."

Domingo looked at her with some amazement. There was the faintest touch of pink under her clear skin, and the almond shaped eyes, with the thick curly lashes, were shy. There had been a note almost of pleading in her voice. Domingo could not associate this attitude with the aloof Sofía he knew so well. True, she had changed since Brunhilda's arrival, not in great ways but in little ones. Almost it seemed as though the two sisters were trading places, so that the formally cold Sofía was warming into softness; the warm Brunhilda chilling into steel.

Venetian blinds were drawn over the restaurant windows. The large room was dim and quiet. A pair of young lovers were at one table. A farmer, his family and two servants, were at another. A few men's voices floated at intervals from the bar, secluded around a corner. There were no other customers. Domingo was glad of this for Mateo's sake.

At table, the choosing of which Mateo managed very well, shyness finally enveloped the chauffeur. He ordered, but it was a stumbling, stuttering business. When the waiter left them, Sofía said, "Don't worry, Mateo. You need practice. In a month you'll look back at this moment and laugh."

"But, niña . . ."

"Señorita, Mateo. I'm a client, remember?"

"Yes, señorita. I—it's very difficult. So much to remember. The trouble is," he added frankly, "I don't understand why this—all of this—is so important."

Domingo and Sofía laughed. Sofía said, "My father has sold more real estate over a luncheon table than out in the car. Isn't that right, Domingo?"

"Perhaps," said Mateo doggedly. "But to me it's not practical."

"Who wants to be practical?" Sofía asked mischievously.

Mateo launched on the wings of his philosophy.

During the rest of the meal, Domingo relaxed while his sister and the chauffeur argued. It's interesting, Domingo thought, when Mateo's talking about something he knows, a light turns on inside of him. Sofía is clever. She knows how to switch on the light. I thought that this would be a dull strained lunch, but it isn't. When he talks like that he has a sort of inner poise. Someday, perhaps, I may be working for him, because his heart's in this business and mine isn't.

Sofía was interested in the restaurant lights: fluorescent tubes twisted into the shapes of guitars, and stapled to the long walls. Domingo was amazed when Mateo gave them a slightly technical lecture on the theory of fluorescent lights, especially for use in factories.

Before he realized the implications of his question, Domingo asked, "But how did you learn all that?"

Mateo answered agreeably enough that he had been interested in it as a point of architecture, but the damage was done. His servant shyness enveloped him again, and he refused to be drawn into further discussions.

That Sofía was furious with him, Domingo knew, and he was irritated with himself. He had not meant to sound superior over Mateo's lack of cultural background. He would have asked the same question of Tito, of Cardito, and they would have posed before him with the little arrogance of their hidden knowledge. Mateo could not pose. Where they stood firm against the wall of their education, he had nothing at his back but the bleak spaces of his inquiring mind.

Domingo tried to put Mateo at ease again by giving a spirited description of General Gil and the Christmas beer. But the chauffeur was all servant now. The smile was dutiful. The blunt, square-fingered hands trembled slightly as they moved above the silver.

Assurance returned for a brief moment when he paid the bill. This was dealing with money, and money he knew how to handle. He objected to the size of the tip that Domingo insisted on leaving, but Sofía said, "Remember, Mateo, Monterrey is Domingo's home, but Monterrey's spirit is not in his blood."

Mateo said seriously, "I have heard the jokes, niñ—señorita, but I think they are stupid. There is a difference between a careful man and a stingy man."

Domingo hoped that he would go on talking. He did not. He lapsed into silence, and, without instructions, drove Sofía home before taking Domingo to the office.

As Sofía stepped out of the car she turned and looked at Mateo, the eyes heavy behind the almond lids. Words trembled against her lips, but she only murmured, "Until later," and went into the house.

Domingo made no comment. He was suddenly very tired. These days had been a strain on him, and now, without warning, he was tired. The strain has been released, he thought. Already I've accepted Mateo as a salesman, and now that I've shifted the pressure from myself to him, I'm tired.

Is this a wise thing I'm doing? Sofía seems to think it is. Or is she only being agreeable because she understands my strain? I want to shut my eyes and go to sleep. No, I don't want that, either. I really want to go and talk to Márgara, but I mustn't do that until after I've seen Verónica. No difference. I want to talk to Márgara. I'm tired, I want to talk to Márgara.

Then they were at the office, where they found a client waiting for them. He was a man in his early fifties, small boned, with a mustache that was too big for his face. His name, he said, twisting his hat nervously, was Palma, Simón Palma, and he jerked out his explanation as though he were cutting off the words with scissors. Having made a good deal of money in Saltillo, the capital of the neighboring state, he wanted to give his daughter, soon to marry a Monterrey boy, a fine house for a wedding present.

It was not in Domingo's mind to turn over a client so soon to Mateo, but the lassitude which had touched him in the car was now even heavier on him. When Mateo calmly began showing Palma a map of the city, with comments on desirable features for this section or that one, Domingo was frankly glad to release himself of the responsibility and leave it all to the chauffeur.

Sitting in his office, he could hear Mateo's comments, and, through the angle formed by the door, watch Palma's reactions. The man seemed much less nervous with Mateo, more sure of himself. Perhaps that was not such a good thing. Many men bought lots they did not want because Domingo's superiority made them too nervous to say no. Well, he thought, it has started now. I've put this thing in motion. The only way I can stop it is to fire Mateo, and I don't want to do that. Domingo shuddered when he contemplated what his uncle Agapito would say, then dismissed the whole matter from his mind as he glanced through his correspondence. Attached to it was a telephone notice that Tito had called to remind him that on Saturday they were to go and see the Bárcenas' proofs, and that the señor Gomez had a most elegant idea concerning them.

Domingo detached it from the other papers, held it between his fingers. He folded it until it was capsule size, then carefully unfolded it and rubbed the creases with his fingers. Márgara, he thought. Márgara. Her name filled his mind. Then the word disappeared, and her image came in its place, until she was all there, clear to him. The office receded and there was nothing but Márgara.

He could see her, the gold of her skin, the green of her dress, the black of her hair. He could smell her perfume, and feel the smoothness of her.

Then she seemed to flow toward him and enter into him, and become a part of him. Yet she did not warm him. He felt bone cold, and the lassitude was a weight that pressed him, heavy, to the desk.

Late that night, too tired to sleep, Domingo relaxed on his bed and stared at the ceiling. It was set in molded plates of tin, with fruit and flower designs embossed on each square, then painted white. The radiance from his lamp touched a few squares with cream leaving the rest in shadow.

When he was a small boy his nurse had told him that if he counted every stem, every leaf, by the time he reached number twenty-five he would be asleep. So awed by her, so certain that everything she told him was truer than truth, he had never been able to count as high as twenty before he drifted off.

Sometimes, especially the first nights after returning home from New York, when he had been in revolt against domination of all kinds, he had stubbornly refused to attempt to count them, but in the end he always did, and he always went to sleep. Now he was thankful for this device. He had no desire to stay awake, remembering his father's frozen face, his mother's quiet, expressionless voice. But most of all he did not want to remember how much he disliked Brunhilda, nor Sofía's plaintive cry, "What might I have done with two such years?" and don Lucio's, "Haven't we had enough of selfishness?"

Domingo fixed his eyes on a curling grape tendril and stolidly began to count, "One—two" then, like a bird swooping, his attention shifted to his uncle Agapito. How carefully all of them had skirted the image of that man. Even doña Otilia had merely commented that Agapito might have clarified the issue. No word of complaint against him from anyone. For two days, no word of complaint from don Rafael, who had twice been thwarted in his musical ambitions by the stern elder brother . . . the coldly successful elder brother.

With the fascinated attention of a painter, Domingo began to fashion the image of his uncle. The narrow feet in the well-shined shoes, brown, usually, because don Agapito loved this deepening shade of gold. The thin ankles attached to the medium-sized legs, clad in the tweeds that he affected, brown with small flecks of red, the tweeds that were especially imported from Scotland.

In Domingo's imagination, his uncle was sitting behind his desk at the bank, his head and shoulders outlined against light filtered through Venetian blinds. The right shoulder was raised, to allow his hand to rest in his coat pocket, and held in the fingers of the left hand was the inevitable cigarette. "He keeps his right hand hidden," whispered Monterrey gossip, "so that what he gives with the left, he can steal back with the right."

But such gossip was never spoken to don Agapito's face, because his personal charm was greater than gossip. It was said that no man had ever met him who did not instantly like him, nor left him without hating him.

At sixty-five he had the youth and vitality of a man of forty. He loved athletics, especially polo and frontón, and this exercise kept his body trimmed down beyond even the hint of a tiny paunch. Age had slightly loosened the muscles of his throat, so that there was a suggestion of a double chin, seen only when he tilted his head too far forward. His crisp black hair receded just enough to give the impression of a scholar's high forehead, and the only lines in his face were the two deep indentions between his thick brows, and the calipers from slender nostrils to the wide, well-shaped mouth. A thick mustache, trimmed in English style, formed a V on his long upper lip. His skin, normally ruddy, had been tanned to the color of cane syrup, and it glowed with health, just as he himself glowed with it.

Having been well all of his life, he could not understand sickness in anyone else, and there was no quicker way to lose one's job in the bank than to offer the alibi of illness. For this reason he was constantly warring with the banker's syndicate, and it was a mystery to Domingo, as well as the rest of Monterrey, as to how don Agapito was able to keep an adequate staff. Yet, oddly enough, the people who worked for him liked him, and could not be stolen away into other industries. Since don Agapito, if he wanted a man, hired him, regardless of any inconvenience to the man's employer, it was extremely irritating not to be able, in turn, to hire anyone away from him.

He called his bank, "My home," and his employees, "My family," and he had the gift of exacting a loyalty which he seemingly did nothing to repay.

Domingo, coldly examining this portrait, tried to remember when he had first come to hate his uncle Agapito, and could not. His earliest memories were filled with terror of this man, who punctiliously came to dinner twice a week. Since he never chose regular nights, but only such nights as suited his convenience, the house was in a constant turmoil, each morning greeted with, "Will today be free?" Each night ending with, "He came," or "How wonderful, he did not come."

When Domingo was twenty-six he discovered a subject on which the all-wise Agapito professed ignorance. Up to that time Domingo had taken it for granted that his uncle would never admit ignorance on any subject, whatsoever, and it was refreshing to know that children were an enigma to the great man.

Remembering the day he had discovered this, Domingo smiled slightly to himself. It had been Cardito's tenth feast day, and Domingo had been summoned to the sacred bank for consultation about a suitable present. There had been a strange hesitancy in don Agapito's manner which had puzzled the younger man, until he realized that his uncle was actually concerned with whether Cardito would like the present or not.

"I know so little of children," he kept repeating. "You understand, Domingo? They should have things educational, I think, do you not agree? Toys are stupid things. Perhaps he would like a toy. You think he would like a toy? A train, perhaps, or a baseball? Something not too expensive. Children break things. It is foolish to spend money on something that is easily broken. A book, of course, would be most educational."

Back and forth had gone the argument, not with Domingo but with himself, and in the end he had decided on Alamán's *Historia de México*, all eight volumes, beautifully bound in Spanish leather. At the presentation, Cardito, who had been praying nightly for a bicycle, burst into tears and ran upstairs. For this disrespect he had been restricted to his room by don Rafael, but doña Petra had cooked all of his favorite dishes, and Domingo sold some of his own books in order to get enough money for the precious wheel.

Recalling the incident now, Domingo remembered that Sofía had also donated toward the bicycle, but that Brunhilda had refused to contribute, contending that if Cardito had possessed any sense, he would have told his uncle what he had wanted in the first place.

"I wanted some gold earrings and I got them. Cardito is a fool."

Sofía and doña Petra had both fussed at Domingo. "When he asked you what to get for the boy, why didn't you tell him?"

"But I did tell him. 'A bicycle would be nice,' I kept repeating, but he had his mind fixed on something educational."

" 'A bicycle would be nice,' " doña Petra mimicked in disdain, and Sofía said cuttingly, "The trouble with you, Domingo, is that you don't know how to assert yourself."

Angry at such disrespect from women, he took himself off to the village of Santa Catarina, where Tía Nicanora, his nurse, lived. She soothed his ruffled feathers, restored the ego proper to a young man of twenty-six, fed him burnt milk candy, and sent him home.

But the realization that don Agapito was not infallible did more to reconcile Domingo to staying in the real-estate office than anything else. Since then he had managed to have few quarrels with his uncle. Now it was no quarrel, but a great and overmastering hatred which gave Domingo moments of physical trembling, leaving him exhausted on his bed.

"What right gives him such dictatorship?" he repeated drearily to himself. "We all knew Brunhilda had no talent, but what are two years against our father's hope? He wanted it so much—two little years for something our father wanted so much. What right did he have to take those two years away from our father?"

The fact that Brunhilda was also involved in that stealing did not greatly concern Domingo. He knew that his sister lacked the capacity to understand what she had done; but don Agapito knew, he understood perfectly, yet he had done it deliberately. For a whim? Or to prove once more that his was the iron hand of the Vázquez still?

Domingo impatiently threw back the covers, lit the gas, paced up and down the room. The night sounds of Monterrey drifted through the windows: the pattering steps of a factory worker returning home from a late shift; tourist automobiles en route to the hotels after the long trek from México City; the low voices of the watchmen who guarded nearby valuable properties, exchanging gossip. And over all, the silent thrum-thrum-thrum that was no sound but a pulsing—the heart beat of a factory-filled city in the quiet stretches of the night.

He lit cigarettes and ground them out after a few puffs. Perhaps if he read a little . . . His bookshelves were divided into two sections: English on one side, Spanish on the other. His eyes slid across the English titles, but he did not want to bother with the barrier of the language. At the moment he wanted an opiate, not an exercise of the intellect.

The new volume of Mediz Bolio's Maya legends was very tempting, but tonight he wanted something treasured, something well remembered, so he chose instead the same author's *Land of the Pheasant and the Deer*. As he leafed through the pages, absently admiring the colorful designs of the Mayan painter, Miguel Tzab, his roving eye glanced at a paragraph, passed on, then, startled, returned to it:

You poor creature. The Xtabay is the woman you desire in all women, and that you have never yet encountered. Ay, if you should see her appear one night in front of you.

Márgara, he thought. Márgara. And went on reading:

If you do see her, she will be as beautiful as you never imagined a woman could be beautiful. You think of a lovely woman as being like a shaft of moonlight that passes between the leaves. But she is lovelier than that.

The virgin that this morning consumed with love your nights and days, now will be less for you than a dead leaf powdered in the wind of your memory, and you will want never to hear more of her. Because when you have seen the Xtabay, it seems as though you are meeting life for the first time. You poor creature.

Ah, you will pursue the Xtabay, and she will escape you like a bird flying. You will never find her, and you will never return. No one has ever returned from following the Xtabay. And all who have seen her follow her. Where are they that they do not return? No one knows. There are those who go armed with courage, and those who go armed with cunning, who set out to search for her. But she does not appear to such as these. Only to the young and strong who walk alone thinking of love does she appear. Because this one must follow her without ceasing.

There is only one talisman that will serve against her. A man must pluck a hair from her head, and then she will follow like a slave, and he will be her master, and command her to obey, and she will obey. But who is such a man? Where is he?

Hunt for her if you have faith; and find her if you have strength.

The Xtabay, Domingo thought, the demon woman, the woman without mercy, the eternal Circe, Márgara; and for a moment it seemed as though it made no difference where she led him, so long as she did lead him away from this engulfing whirlpool that tossed him in and out so that there was never any rest for him.

What difference did it make if he were never freed from her, if he were never able to capture the talismanic lock of hair? The enchantment was escape and that was what really mattered. He wondered cynically why all of the pity in the legends was for the poor captives: the swine of Circe's isle, the pale young knight of Keats, the lover plunging through the forest after the phantom Xtabay. All the pity was for them, and yet they had never spoken. Perhaps they preferred their enchantment, perhaps they mourned for it when some righteous Ulysses returned them to the world of men.

A cautious scratching at the door distracted him. It was Sofía doubtless, come to talk over her private worries, and he did not want to talk about them. At the moment he wanted only to release himself into the land of Márgara, but politeness forced him to open the door. He was startled to see Mateo, overcoat pulled over pajamas, eyes bleary with sleep.

"What the devil . . ."

"Please, señor Domingo, I didn't want to come and wake you, but there's a boy downstairs who demands to speak with you."

"At this hour?"

"I told him to go away. I even threatened him with the police, but he started to cry, señor Domingo. I think he is in great trouble."

"Where is he?"

"I left him in the kitchen patio . . ."

"Devil take you, Mateo! By this time he has entered the lower part of the house and stolen all the silverware. You should be smart enough not to be taken in by such a trick!" Domingo was angry, but not too angry to notice with detached amusement that Mateo was not flustered by his anger.

"He will not steal anything, señor Domingo. I put the dog-chain on his wrist and fastened him to the garage door."

Domingo grinned in spite of irritation, slid into his dressing gown, and followed the chauffeur down the stairs to the back of the house.

The kitchen patio was a large enclosed space, which had originally been a corral for horses, chickens, a few pigs and a cow. Now cement had been laid over its moist earth, a broad-brimmed pool set in the center for the washing of clothes, and the animal stalls had been converted into a garage. Tall wooden gates opened on Matamoros Street, so that the car did not have to be driven through the patios. This was an improvement put in by Sofía whose practical mind decided that any house a block deep should have the privilege of using both streets.

Mateo, walking a little in front of Domingo, went up to a sniveling boy crouched against the garage door. Above his head, a light in a tin shade cast a radiance about them, leaving the rest of the patio in darkness. When the chauffeur unfastened the chain, the boy shot forth a stream of profanity. Mateo's hand snapped up, sent the boy tumbling head over heels toward the pool.

"Here is the señor Domingo. If you really have something to say to him, I will be much surprised."

"Prepare. yourself then!" The boy hitched himself sideways toward Domingo. "And fill your ears with wax. My message is private."

"How, private?" Domingo demanded. Some of these street urchins were as fast as a striking cobra with a razor blade. He did not relish having a slashed cheek or throat to provide escape for the boy.

The boy hung his head sullenly. "I won't talk in front of him."

"The impudence of him," Mateo marveled.

Domingo said sharply, "If you have a message, spit it out. I don't like secrets at three o'clock in the morning."

"She said I wasn't to talk . . ."

"She? What she?"

"Serafina."

"Ay." Mateo's syllable had hardly more than a breath. Without looking at Domingo, he strolled into the garage, and they could hear him puttering about with the car, opening and shutting doors, opening the hood. The amount of noise was to cover the delicacy of retreat, and Domingo had to bite down on his lower lip to keep from laughing. So Mateo, too, thought him involved in the Serafina affair. The logic was flawless: it was only the premise that was wrong.

"What about Serafina?" he asked the question quickly to keep his frayed nerves under control.

"She wants to talk to you."

"Indeed? At this hour? Tell her to forget her ideas, and if I can find time in the morning . . ."

"You must come now."

Domingo jerked in surprise at the commanding tone. As though realizing that now was the moment to speak the boy chattered, "Indeed, I tried to make her wait until morning—she is my cousin—but she was so pale, as though she were dead." The rigid tone broke, and he began to cry, wiping his eyes with the back of one hand.

On impulse Domingo motioned the boy into the circle of light. The thin body had betrayed the age, and it was a child who was quivering there.

"How old are you?"

"Twelve, s'ñor Domingo."

"You say you are Serafina's cousin?"

"Jaime Lozano, at your orders."

"What has happened to Serafina?"

"She wouldn't tell me. Earlier this evening my uncle—her father, you understand, who is famous for his drinking—came home after a week's absence for a grand drunk, and he was still very drunk. He was surprised to see her at home, and then she told him that she was with child. They went into the kitchen and shut the door, and he began to shout and yell, it was terrible, and Serafina began to scream. My father does not like to interfere between a man and his daughter, but we have a sick neighbor, and such yelling is not good for sickness. All the people in the block started to complain, so finally my father went in and chased my uncle away with a stick. It was just in time, too, because someone had fetched a policeman."

Domingo sucked in his breath. If the man were taken to jail, scandal would break with a vengeance. "Was your uncle arrested?"

"No, s'ñor, he got away. The policeman was angry at not finding anybody. He wanted to put Serafina in jail for making such a racket, but my father persuaded him to leave. Then in the middle of the night Serafina woke me up and told me to come and fetch you. I told her I could not fetch a young gentleman like you on such an errand, but she began to cry, and looked so dead, I was frightened."

Domingo knew that the wise young eyes that had seen so much of living were contemplating him with detached cynicism. The story of the rich young man and the poor maiden was very old. It had been retold so often through the million years of humanity that this telling needed no footnotes or explanations. And because of its very commonplaceness, Domingo was suddenly, and for no reason, ashamed. He could not decide whether he was ashamed because of the story, or because of the age in this child's eyes.

"Wait here with Mateo. I'll have to go and put on some clothes." He turned toward the front of the house, then glanced back over his shoulder, a puzzled frown pulling his brows together. "Are you sure it was me she wanted you to fetch? She mentioned no other name?"

" 'Go to the Vázquez de Anda house,' she told me, 'and fetch the s'ñor Domingo.' Those were her very words."

With a brief nod, Domingo hurried off to his room. While he dressed he tried to reason through to Serafina's sending for him, and at such an hour. Surely if she had wanted protection, it would have been more reasonable for her to send for doña Petra. The other servants were terrified of the cook, but they never hesitated to go to her with their little problems. The Serafina that he had drawn in his mind would have gone to doña Petra for aid. How far, then, was the real Serafina from what he had imagined her to be?

Having worked his problem through to this point, he pulled on his overcoat, and tiptoed down the stairs. He thought he saw Sofía's door open slightly and then close, but that was doubtless imagination. If the noise disturbed her, she would have come out on the gallery to investigate. Sofía had courage in her, and refused to cower in bed as Brunhilda often did at fancied monsters.

"She knows it's I," Domingo thought, "and she probably reasons I'm going off to visit a woman. Well, I am, and to the devil with her ideas."

When he reached the kitchen patio, Mateo had already taken the car out. Fully dressed, he was standing by it, one hand firmly clenched in the boy's collar.

"Holding this young one is like trying to possess a fish slithering through the water," he said dryly.

"No need for you to come, Mateo. I should have told you."

"I know the way to the house. You do not."

"The boy can tell me."

"This one? What does he know of traffic rules?"

"Rules at three in the morning? And I know them."

Mateo shrugged, pushed the boy into the back seat, opened the door on the driver's side.

"The señor Palma wants to view houses at nine."

As Domingo settled himself behind the wheel he said impulsively, "The señor Palma is your client. You show him the houses."

The joy that flashed across Mateo's eyes was instantly veiled. "Thank you, s'ñor—señor." He opened the tall gates, and Domingo let the car roll forward of its own momentum, afraid lest the starting engine would waken doña Petra. Voices, he knew, never disturbed her, but Domingo had learned early in life that the sound of any mechanical device brought her to instant awareness.

Once the car was in the street, he turned his head to call to Mateo to borrow an extra car from don Agapito's wife in case he hadn't returned by nine. Mateo waved his hand in answer, and the tall gates swung shut, but not before Domingo received the impression that a woman in white was standing near the pool. It was imagination, of course, but the impression had been very strong. A paragraph from the account of the Xtabay came into his mind, "You should see her, dressed all in white, poised above the earth. Behold her long hair, black and shining. Twist it about your hands, and comb it with the leaves of the *ramón;* and see her feet, like two small birds flying close to the ground."

The Xtabay, thought Domingo. Tonight, wherever I look I see the Xtabay, and I wish that this car were turned toward Márgara and not toward Serafina.

XIII

The boy Jaime directed Domingo to a door on Arramberi West. From the sidewalk rose a single wall, pierced by the doors of seven different dwellings. This wall was dark in the night, and Domingo did not know whether the place he entered was differentiated from its fellows by color, or if it were a part of a continuous single shade.

Not that such a consideration bothered him. He was more interested in discovering that the front room was a carpenter's shop, and that Serafina's uncle was no ordinary carpenter, as was her father, but a *maestro.*

"The father of Serafina," Jaime whispered, "could also be a *maestro.* He has talent, that one—more than my father, really, but he is a drunkard." All of the resignation of his class was in his youthful voice, and Domingo had to repress a cold shudder. It was monstrous to him that this child could be so wise.

Jaime left him alone in the shop. "If we wake the family there will be much scandal. Better to stay here."

Domingo devoutly agreed with him, and wandered about the room, his shoes making sibilant sounds on the wood shavings. Enough light from the corner street lamp filtered through the iron barred windows·to outline the furniture still in construction; bedsteads, coffee tables, straight chairs, a dining room table. His hand brushed a finished chair, and he felt the soft pile of velvet. He mischievously made a bet with himself that the shade would be purple, and snapped his lighter. The color was chrome yellow. He shrugged and blew out the light, then hesitated, his hand still lifted, at the sound of something dragging in the passageway. The door opened, and Jaime entered, propelling Serafina in front of him. She was bent over like an old woman, one arm pressing against her swollen stomach.

Domingo instantly reacted to her pain. He strode across the floor, and slipped his arm about her waist. "Eh, Serafina, eh little one," he murmured.

As though her strength, now that she had found the longed for land, had been expended in a sea of pain, she collapsed against him. Jaime tried to hold her erect, but his arms were too fragile to the task, and Domingo felt her entire weight dangle limply within his embrace.

"Leave her alone," he whispered fiercely to Jaime, suddenly jealous that anyone else should contribute strength to her weakness. He turned her slightly so that he could lift her, carried her to the velour covered chair, and sat down with her cradled on his knees.

"Now, Serafina, are you too weak to talk to me?"

"Take me away, s'ñor Domingo, please. Ayyy . . ." the moan caught in her throat, and she trembled against him. Márgara had also trembled in the circle of his arm, but hers had been a trembling of a terrified spirit. This was the trembling of a tortured body.

"Be still, my bird," he whispered. "Jaime says your father beat you this evening . . ."

"Next time he will kill me, s'ñor Domingo. What am I to do?"

"You can't stay here," he agreed, and frowned in perplexity. Where could he take her? At home doña Petra would care for

134

her without question, but gossip from the other servants would circle Monterrey. At the moment, with the problem of Brunhilda to be worked out, scandal would never do. And Cardito was too sick in the hospital to be bothered with such details.

What then? Where in all his world could he take her, where she would be cared for, and the secret of the Vázquez de Andas kept? Of course a secret was no secret where a family was involved. Her father, her uncle knew the truth, and this small, too wise Jaime.

She moved her head against his shoulder like an animal trying to burrow into greater comfort. "You are so kind to help me, s'ñor Domingo. and it is none of your affair."

"Is it not, Serafina? And why not?"

"Just because I work in your house—and I such a wicked girl . . ."

Jaime moved closer to them, tugged at Domingo's coat. "What I say is, the boy should be forced to marry her. Just because he works in a hotel—and what hotel, shouts everybody? But does she answer? She's a stubborn one. Let her be beaten, I say, and good enough for her."

"You leave my boy out of this," she whispered harshly. "Because the s'ñor Domingo is kind is no reason to burden him with too much. I told you he would come, didn't I?"

"And a fine job it was to make him come. That driver of cars chaining me to the door like an animal . . ."

"Stop bickering!" Domingo's sharp voice silenced them. Unconsciously he had gathered Serafina closer into his arms as he realized they shared a secret common to only the two of them.

The cynicism he had seen in Jaime's eyes was not the awareness of Domingo himself as Serafina's man, but simply the acceptance of the realities of life. It was more logical to this family that Serafina should be courted by a bellboy from one of the hotels, than that she should have attracted the attention of one of the Vázquez de Anda, and such logic they were willing to accept against even a suspicion of the truth.

It came to Domingo with a brief shock that for all he knew it might be the real truth. He had only his own suspicions, the memory of her devotion to Cardito, to tell him that Cardito was the father. Perhaps he was sitting here at four o'clock in the morning concerning himself with the pretty little love of a bellboy. What mattered such an affair to Domingo Vázquez de Anda?

Unfortunately he had been too closely brushed by this affair that was no affair of his. Servants in his own house, Mateo and doña Petra, were convinced that he was responsible for Serafina's child, and even his sister, Sofía, thought that he had played the cavalier with the girl.

Why, then, should he involve himself further? If she were nothing to Cardito, then she was no responsibility of Domingo's. His arms loosened at the thought. He was greatly tempted to set her gently on the floor and walk out of this house.

Then a cold nose brushed against his cheek, and her voice said plaintively, "It hurts so much—so much."

He tilted his head so that he could look down at her. In the light from the street lamp he could see her thin face, with the pointed chin and the weak, childish mouth. Her black hair was brushed straight back and twin red bows fastened the plaites at either ear.

A week ago he might have walked off and left her, but since the night of Cardito's drunken sleep, a companionship had sprung up between the two of them, so that to desert her now would be like deserting any helpless thing that trusted him. And the fact that she was in pain chained him tighter than anything else. This he had been born for, to stop pain when he could, and, his mind told him, leave her he might, but her pain he could not leave.

Where to take her? Where in all of Monterrey was there refuge for her? The only human being he might have trusted her with was Márgara, but Márgara was the Xtabay, the woman vanishing in the green jungle depths, not a nurse to cradle helplessness.

At the thought of a nurse, he raised his head. There was one person; his old nurse in Santa Catarina. The girl would feel safe with a woman of her own kind, and he knew from experience that Tía Nicanora could be trusted with any secret.

"Bring a coat for your cousin," he whispered to Jaime.

The boy snorted with derision. "Is she a fine lady? A shawl is good enough . . ."

"I said fetch a coat."

The boy grumbled, but slid out of the room in obedience. Domingo lowered Serafina to the floor with gentle care. "I am

136

going to take you to my old nurse in Santa Catarina. She is a good woman, and has forgotten how to ask questions."

She hung suspended between his hands, hardly hearing him, aware, he knew, only of the immensity of her pain. Once she had transferred her problem to him, she was no longer concerned with it, but entirely with the whirlpool of which she was the quivering center.

Jaime materialized at his elbow, a cheap, belted coat dangling over one arm. "This belongs to my sister. She will beat me in the morning for stealing it."

"It will be returned to you before then. Sleep in here so that you can take it from me."

"As you say, s'ñor Domingo. Please," and the voice deepened and became a man's voice, "where do you take my cousin?"

At first Domingo hesitated to answer, but the boy's head was high with dignity, and there was nothing ridiculous in his attitude of a man protecting his own.

"To Santa Catarina, to the home of an honest woman, doña Nicanora. Widow of Llano."

Jaime muttered the name over several times. Domingo was as certain as though the boy had spoken, that he would catch a bus to Santa Catarina the next morning. Impulsively he put his hand in his pocket and drew out a peso bill. "Here, this will pay your bus fare to visit Serafina. She will be lonesome without you."

At once the man disappeared, and it was a child who grinned gleeful thanks at him. Jaime, completely satisfied now that Serafina was in safe hands, opened the door and Domingo carried her to the car. The coat was grotesquely large for her, but its bulk provided warmth, and he wrapped her in the lap robe until only her heart-shaped face was visible.

"I wish I had cushions, Serafina."

"You are too kind," she whispered. "Indeed I am comfortable. And I have much shame for being such a bother to you."

Domingo did not answer, but turned south on Victoriano Carranza. This street that was wide as a boulevard tempted him to stay on it until he reached Hidalgo. At this hour in the morning there was no traffic, and surely . . . then the memory of Mateo's story of another accident on a one-way street deterred

him. With a sigh he obeyed the law, and turned west on Bolívar.

Mateo's philosophic comments about the accident returned
to his memory. It was true. A woman would come into a man's
life and without warning it would change into a strange and
different pattern. Verónica of the strong will was trying to change
it, and Márgara—indeed, she was the Xtabay and there would
nevermore be rest for him anywhere.

Of course, in the stories enchantment was a sharp sword that
cut the victim off from contact with all former life; but in the
real world, the victim had to continue in his ordinary fashion,
doing the things he had to do: eating, sleeping and working in
an office, and what person looking at him could say, "He is crazed
with love for the Xtabay?"

Lost in his private fairy tale, he was not aware that they
were passing the hospital until Serafina said, "That is the place
where the niño Cardito is sick?"

"The same."

"He will get well?"

"Of course. The danger is past now."

"He is in pain?"

"No. He is asleep."

"How beautiful sleep is," she whispered. "I haven't slept for
a long time."

He did not answer, but settled down to his driving. Santa
Catarina was the first town after leaving Monterrey for Saltillo.
Here the mark of tourists could be seen only in a few highway
saloons. This was the turning spot to reach the Huasteca cañon,
that great gash in the side of the Sierra Madre range. It was on
the guided tours of Monterrey, and many a boy with his burro
had earned as high as a peso a photograph, posing with his animal against the backdrop of mountains.

But the town of Santa Catarina was as remote from tourists
as though it had been completely off of the Saltillo highway map.
No tourists ever walked through the narrow dirt packed streets,
nor paused to admire the gaily painted houses.

A few guides would point to one house on the plaza, the bust
of a man perched on its front wall. They would patter a small
tale about this being the hiding spot during the French invasion
of the Honorable Benito Juárez. As most of the tourists had never

heard of Juárez, it made little impression. It never occurred to them to go and look at the house with the strange bas-reliefs of Spanish cavalier heads above the doors and windows, nor to realize that if this same Benito Juárez had not been so carefully sheltered here, the entire history of the North American continent might have been changed. For with Juárez' victory over the French-sponsored Maximilian, the United States did not have to go to war with France.

Domingo had often thought of this when on some Sunday afternoons following a visit with Tía Nicanora, he would sit lazily in the sunshine on the plaza, watching the tourists exclaim over the yellow painted grace of the small church with its single rock tower. The Juárez house was on the same side as the church, half a block from the highway, but no one ever exclaimed over it, nor felt the fluttering wings of history enfold them as they passed it by.

Yet, at the same time, he was thankful that the tourists paid it no attention. There were no concessions to sell reminder ashtrays, and cheap photographs of Juárez. It was as free of the economic whirlpool as it had been in the early days of 1864, with Sherman's march to the sea not yet begun, and Louis Napoleon still dreaming of an Empire to rival Sixteenth Century Spain's.

There were moments when Domingo could almost see the small stolid Indian figure, in frock coat and tall silk hat, come through the west door to indulge in a brief saunter in the sunlight. Was he remembering the day he had released all of his daughter's caged birds with the cry, "What good is liberty unless you possess it?" Perhaps he had wandered over to sit on this plaza, on this same bench, and Domingo, to whom history was not a series of words in a book but a human document, would jump to his feet and stride off to his car, with the absurd impression that for a moment he had intruded on the solitude of a tragic and great man.

This, then, was the Santa Catarina, the village that was suspended in time, fruit of the past not yet ripe in the present, to which Domingo was driving Serafina.

He wondered how she would like it there, and if she had ever visited it. As the car crossed the flour mill bridge, she turned her head slightly, "Is it much farther?"

"About fifteen minutes." Remembering suddenly that he had

some brandy in the glove compartment, he slowed to a stop by the road, took out the bottle and poured a little in the cup that formed the bottle's stopper.

"Drink this."

At the first whiff of the liquor she drew back. "Please, s'ñor Domingo, no . . ."

"Nonsense. Pretend it is medicine and gulp it down."

She lifted her face, and a half smile dented her cheeks with dimples. "I cannot even hold the cup, you have me wrapped so tight."

He laughed and tilted it against her lips. "There, a good gulp of it. Don't cough it all away!"

She sputtered and giggled at the same time. "It makes me feel—warm. But I don't like it."

"You're not supposed to like medicine. That's against the rules."

This time she actually laughed. "You say such funny things, s'ñor Domingo."

"As funny as Cardito?" He held his breath. He had to know the truth, and though he felt that it was a terrible thing to trap her into an admission she did not want to make, it was necessary to any future plans to know for certain if the child were really Cardito's.

Caught in a spasm of pain she swayed forward a little.

Instantly he bent over her, his hands gentle as he held her. "Is it still a great pain, Serafina? Be strong—only a little longer, and then we will have a doctor and comfort."

"It doesn't matter how much pain, s'ñor Domingo, as long as you do not leave me."

"How can I leave you? Are we not trapped together in this automobile, part way to Santa Catarina? What do you expect me to do? Open a door and throw you out on the road?"

"Ay, no!" She laughed again and relaxed against the seat cushions. As he started the car she looked upward at the stars, which emerged for a brief moment before hiding once more in the approaching dawn.

"Have you ever thought, s'ñor Domingo, about those stars up there?"

"What kind of thoughts?"

"I don't know. In these last few months I have not always

slept well, and sometimes, through the window, I could see the stars. The way they shimmer . . . do you know what a telegraph machine is, s'ñor Domingo?"

"I don't know what you mean by one, Serafina."

"My cousin Jaime works at the post office, in the telegraph department. He says they have a machine that sends messages with little dots and dashes instead of words."

"And you think the glimmering of the stars are spelled out messages?"

"Perhaps. Perhaps it is the saints trying to talk to us, and we too stupid to understand. Do you think that could be, s'ñor Domingo?"

"The only trouble is that if you look at them through a telescope, Serafina, they do not glimmer at all. They are as solid as—well, as this earth."

He wondered helplessly what he would answer if she asked him to describe the physical nature of the universe, but she did not.

"Telescopes," she repeated thoughtfully, and then, "telescopes are well enough for the rich people like yourself, but for a poor girl like me, I think the idea of the saint's telegraph machine is better. Tell me, s'ñor Domingo, do you go much to the movies?"

He did not want to stop the flow of words that had seemingly been released by the brandy, so, instead of intruding himself on the answer, he merely asked, "Do you?"

"No, not often. My aunt goes every afternoon. At four o'clock she goes to the movie, and she comes home at eight exhausted with crying because the poor hero is dead. Me, I think that is foolishness. 'Listen,' I say to my aunt, 'why weep for the dead? It is the living who need your tears.' My aunt says I am a hard, cruel girl. Do you think I am hard and cruel, s'ñor Domingo?"

"Can a flower be hard and cruel?"

"Some flowers kill. A friend of my aunt has a flower that traps flies. I don't like trapped things!"

He could feel her shudder, and he grinned in the darkness. "I am afraid, Serafina, that you are the kind of a woman who breeds the kind of hero that gets killed."

She said sulkily, "Now you are making fun of me."

"Indeed I am not, Serafina. I am only comparing you to the

mothers of men like Hidalgo, and Morelos, and Ignacio Mina, heroes who preferred to die rather than surrender their liberty."

She was silent again, and it was a long time before she said, "My father says I must give up my baby to the nuns."

"Is that what you think would be right?"

"Listen, you know I told you about the stars. Well, I asked them one night if I should give up my baby. I thought if I recognized they were speaking, the least they could do was answer me."

"Did they?"

"I don't know. But I began to get strange thoughts. I thought: Why should this baby suffer for something he could not help? I am sure the nuns are very good, but it is not the same as growing up with one's real mother, is it?"

"No, Serafina, it is never the same."

"Precisely. Well, the child is mine. I am responsible for it. One must be practical about these things."

Domingo repressed a shudder. "Don't use the word 'practical,' Serafina. At the moment it is not a word I love."

"Love or no love, s'ñor Domingo, food is food and duty is duty, and we must have one and perform the other, or there is no peace anywhere in the world."

As she spoke these words, the car emerged from the corridor of giant *aguacate* trees, and they reached Santa Catarina's plaza just as dawn thrust its shoulders above the line of the mountains.

Tía Nicanora's corner house was on a side street. Most of these houses were known to the town by the names of the owners, but Tía's was labeled the "House of the Tassels," because her pension from the Vázquez de Andas enabled her to paint it every year, and she had a fancy for tasseled adornment. At the moment it was stained an over-all pale lavender, with a roof band of deep purple. This band was hemmed with a line of bright pink tassels, large ones on the corners, small ones forming scallops across the front and single side. Her house was attached on the east to another house painted orange yellow.

The front door was guarded on either side by two medium-sized windows, the ornamental ironwork belled out at the bottom so that she could sit on the sill in comfort and look up and down the streets without the necessity of trying to thrust her head through the bars.

It was, in that of doña Nicanora's opinion (and that of her neighbors) the most elegant house on the street. She told Sofía, just after the new paint job was completed in October, that next time she would have the decorations repeated because the tassels added such distinction.

This was extremely pleasing to Sofía who had worked out the design, and she refused to be abashed by Cardito's criticism that he thought the house looked pretentious; as though Tía were putting on airs about her pension. When Domingo casually explained that there are periods in life when pretension is good for the soul, Cardito flew into one of his quick rages and went off to sulk because he was being criticized for the helplessness of youth.

Cardito's quick temper was a matter of grave concern to Domingo, who was always afraid the boy would cross don Agapito at an unfavorable moment. In the case of Serafina, that temper worried him more than ever. Cardito was so unpredictable Domingo could not even begin to guess what the boy would do when informed that he had become possessed of an illegitimate son.

If he thinks we are against it, Domingo mused, he is very apt to run off to the nearest civil judge and marry the girl, which would be disastrous to his whole future.

The very thought of Cardito married to Serafina made Domingo fastidiously shrink aside. Yet there also was mixed up in his attitude another emotion which he could not clearly define. Even while he knocked at Tía Nicanora's door, he was aware of this emotion—feeling, rather, because it was not big enough to be called an emotion, and it worried him.

It was beginning to dawn upon him that he did not want Cardito to marry Serafina, not for Cardito's sake, but for Serafina's. "Anyone would think," he muttered crossly to himself, "that I have adopted the girl—this paternal interest that I have in her welfare. And I still do not know if Cardito is the father. I am three times a fool, as Tía will presently inform me, and if I had any sense I would have never involved myself in this from the beginning."

The door, painted pink to match the tassels, swung open and

Tía, eyes narrowed with sleep, peered out at him. Her small, round, toothless face was split from side to side by the line of her mouth. Her nose and chin seemed to meet so that her head gave the impression of two hoops, one fitting at right angles into the other. Her white hair, tightly drawn into two wisps of plaites, dangled to her shoulders.

She wore a man's bathrobe, which Domingo vaguely recognized as his own, over a long white flannel gown. Once she had been a fairly tall woman, but age had shrunken her until now she did not stand as high as Domingo's shoulder.

When she saw who it was, delight shone from her small black eyes, and she gave a shrill little cry. "My Dominguito! But what is it, at this hour? Has that uncle of yours turned you out of the house?"

"My uncle has nothing to do with this, Tía. I have a girl here who must be protected."

She scurried around to make an extra bed when Domingo carried Serafina into the house, then without comment directed him to the doctor's house, who lived on the other side of the plaza. "Look for the hanging lantern and the oleander bush near the door. You can't miss it."

She was right. It was the only such door on the street. Domingo waited impatiently while the doctor, a pompous stout man, dressed himself.

As they hurried to the House of Tassels, the doctor said coldly, "You understand that I am a man of ethics. I will do nothing to help this girl lose her baby. . . ."

In spite of his hurry Domingo came to a full stop. His eyes blazed with anger as he said between locked teeth, "Did I make such a request of you?"

"No, but many young men from the city think we town doctors do not know right from wrong."

"Right and wrong have nothing to do with this. The girl is in great pain. She was badly beaten by her father. . . ."

"Hmm," said the doctor, continuing his dignified pace, "indeed?"

"And if it gives you any moral satisfaction, she is not my mistress!"

"My dear young man," the doctor told him firmly, "it is not my place to inquire into such relationships. But let me tell you,

144

the number of young men who take a paternal interest in servant girls is amazing."

Domingo clenched his teeth tighter together, and strode toward the house so fast that at frequent intervals he had to wait for the doctor to catch up with him. Anger was boiling in him, and his half formulated thoughts were mostly concerned with cursing this knowing man, and all the other young men who had made him so knowledgeable.

While the doctor, whose name was Mancini, was examining Serafina, Domingo told Tía Nicanora as much of the story as he knew.

"Hmm," murmured the old woman, rising to turn off the electric light as the dawn whitewashed the black sky. "You don't really know that Cardito is the father. And yet you are still interested in her?"

"Tía, the girl is a homeless kitten. How could I desert her when her need was so great?"

"As long as the girl remains a helpless kitten that is all very well, but the moment she turns into a woman you make a trip to visit your cousins in Veracruz."

The strain under which he had been laboring for so many hours broke, and he sank into a cane rocker, hysterical with laughter. Tía said nothing but let him exhaust himself, fetching him a small glass of pale yellow liquor at the end of it. "This *tequila* is not the fine kind you drink in Monterrey, but it has more bite to it. And here's lemon and salt."

He put his tongue to the salt, drained the *tequila* at one gulp, and then sat back to suck on the lemon.

"You feel better, eh?"

"Well enough. What kind of a doctor is this Mancini?"

"A good doctor, but rough. His great-grandfather was an Italian in Maximilian's army. The French left him behind when they retreated."

"After all, Tía, this doctor is hardly responsible for the politics of his great-grandfather."

"Maybe not, but I was ten years old when the French marched out of Santa Catarina, and I remember Mancini going from house to house begging no one to betray him to the Mexicans. Such cowardice, but what can you expect from an artist?"

"What kind of an artist?" Domingo was not really interested, but Tía's voice was a sound that helped to cover the moans from the bedroom.

"He molded little figures from clay. Some of the images for the *Nacimiento* were broken, and he made new ones. It was only a matter of common courtesy not to betray him, but no one ever respected him again, because of his cowardice, not even his wife. He married the daughter of don Idelfonso who built the drugstore on the Plaza."

"From artist to scientist in four generations. Well, why not? Doctors use their hands just as much as artists . . ." A shrill scream from Serafina brought him to his feet. "What is he doing to her?"

"Calm yourself. If she is strong enough to scream like that, she is all right. Take another glass of *tequila*."

"She is—having the child?" He could feel his hands twitch, his heart pump faster at the mounting desire to rush into that room and relieve Serafina's pain. And with the desire came a dull pain of his own because he lacked medical knowledge— because it was Mancini who possessed the skill and not himself.

Domingo was dimly aware that Tía had crossed to the bedroom, had opened the door and peered in. Now he heard her say, "No. I think Mancini is turning the child. I'm not sure . . . I can't tell. But she is not in birth pangs."

The window's iron bar felt cool against his hot forehead. He could see people emerging from their houses. Domingo jerked his head and crossed to the window. Children were shooing ducks and donkeys into the streets from their nightly imprisonment in the patios. Domingo's car was a great attraction, and one small creature, a strip of pink bedspread wrapped around him in lieu of trousers, had clambered into the front seat. Before Domingo could reach the car, the little boy encountered the horn. A small palm pressed down, and sound exploded, the echo flung back and forth by the houses and finally tossed to the mountains which returned it as though it were a ball.

Domingo lifted the child to the sidewalk, and was promptly chastized by a pair of round black eyes in an even rounder brown face. He felt as though he had been guilty of major cruelty by depriving this morsel of a magnificent toy. He was spared further humiliation by the emergence of Dr. Mancini, who snarled so that the child fled as though chased by devils.

146

"Eh," said the doctor, climbing into the car, "you can drive me home now."

"She—she's going to be all right?"

"I am a man, not God. In my opinion she will be all right."

Domingo looked fearfully at the man. Did he really know his profession? Was he competent enough to . . . ? He said quickly, "Tía said something about turning the child . . ."

Mancini shrugged. "Under the beating she doubtless fell, and the child was lodged out of position. It was necessary to . . ." he checked his words with that secretive air common to some doctors. "Men should learn never to beat pregnant women, but . . ." Mancini's right hand rose with a fatalistic gesture. "If nature were permitted to go her own way, there would be no need of doctors. Perhaps I should not complain."

There was something in the man's attitude, a cold-blooded acceptance of human suffering, that repelled Domingo. It reminded him too much of tales he had heard since childhood of the infamous Dr. Velarde, evil genius of Huerta's regime. He said curtly, "I shall only be a moment," and returned to the house.

When he said he wanted to tell Serafina goodbye, Tía shook her head. "Mancini gave her something to put her to sleep. Don't worry so, niño Domingo. These girls may look frail but they have an endurance that would put even your strength to shame." Her voice took on a commanding note which reminded him of her authority over his childhood days as she added, "For your sake I will take care of her, but there is no more need to concern yourself with her. Of course Mancini costs money, and there is the matter of her food, but you can always send that in a letter."

He pulled her to him in a quick embrace to hide the smile in his own eyes. She was clever, this woman fox, but age had dulled her methods, and he knew that she was trying to separate him from Serafina before the girl gained too much of a hold upon him. He was glad he had not included Márgara in his confession. To a person who has never entered the enchanted land, the fascination of the Xtabay can have no meaning.

After emptying his pockets of all the money he had with him, he took the doctor home, silently enduring a lecture on the tragedy of young men who concerned themselves too much with the luxuries of life, and not enough with the necessities.

Thankful to be rid of Mancini, Domingo drove the car at

high speed back to Monterrey, pausing only long enough to thrust the borrowed coat through the window into a sleepy Jaime's hand.

At home he found Mateo sitting on the sidewalk waiting to open the gates for him.

As he got out of the car, he scolded the chauffeur for such solicitude. "Better for you to have gotten some sleep. A man needs all his wits about him to make a sale of property."

"Not so much wits," Mateo muttered, "as incentive."

"You should have enough incentive. I've never known a man with more ambition."

Mateo turned aside, and it was difficult for Domingo to hear the next words. "There are many kinds of incentives, señor."

"As you say, Mateo, but I am too sleepy for a philosophic discussion. Goodnight. Or should I say, goodmorning."

As he reached the patio stairs, he heard Mateo hurry up behind him. "The little Serafina. She is all right? Forgive me for asking, señor, but when I took her home, she seemed such a helpless creature."

"She is all right now. Thank you for asking, Mateo."

"To you, señor."

Domingo was glad to escape to the privacy of his bed. As he pulled up the covers a sudden idea startled him into momentary wakefulness. Could Mateo be Serafina's lover? His great ambition to rise in the world would prevent his wanting to marry a servant girl, and yet he might be snaring two birds with one net, by working for the Vázquez de Andas. He could thus enter the field of real estate, and be near his woman at the same time. A hazy memory of Mateo's words floated through Domingo's mind. "A man tries to do the best he can, and then, pouf, something on which he never counted—a woman for a man, and all the planning destroyed in a moment."

It would be difficult enough for a man of Mateo's background to climb the social ladder, but to attempt to drag a servant wife with him would be courting certain defeat.

Domingo realized that he had small basis for such a presumption. Yet Mateo had stayed awake to hear the news. What beside anxiety would have kept him from the three best sleeping hours of the night?

Sleep was stronger than cogitation. The feathery darkness that enclosed Domingo was punctuated with strange dreams. He seemed to be running across a vast sandy plain, a knife in his hand, eternally pursuing a figure that part of the time was Mateo, and part of the time a ghost-like woman dressed in white with heavy black braids. Now and again he would stumble to his knees, but he always hung on to the knife. The knife was important. He needed it to cut the life from Mateo and the hair from the woman. But each time he reached the fleeting figure, the sand would give way under his feet, and he would plunge into a vast underground lake, the water rippling about his face, seeming to murmur over and over, 'Serafina, Serafina.' His parched mouth eagerly gulped the cool water, and then once more, tortured with thirst, he would be plunging across the plain, the knife tight in his hand, still pursuing the mocking figure in the distance, that was not the woman, and was not Mateo, but was some evil of which he was deathly afraid.

Domingo awoke and glanced at his watch. It was ten o'clock. He thought vaguely, "I hope Mateo makes the sale," turned over and went back to sleep again. After that there were no more dreams. He did not wake again until three in the afternoon.

The memory of his nightmare was so vivid that he cursed himself for having read Mediz Bolio's book at all, but, he admitted wryly to himself, legends were a weakness of his. He had a large collection of México's folk tales, and now he was trapped in his own hobby, because the idea of the Xtabay had taken complete possession of his imagination. He remembered again the vivid image he retained of a woman in white standing near the patio pool just as he drove away to Serafina's.

In the midst of washing his teeth, he paused, the toothbrush suspended in mid air. Bit by bit he fitted together the mosaic of memory: Mateo had been standing partly behind one of the tall wooden gates, pushing it shut to join the other which was already in position. Thus, Domingo considered, his own angle of vision had been narrow, as Mateo's body filled the space between the two doors. The tin shade on the garage light had kept the radius of illumination very small. The woman was in the shadows by the pool, and he would not have noticed her had it not been for her white robes, pale against the darkness.

If she were human, she would necessarily have to be a member of the household, and he had distinctly received an impression of height: a tall, thin creature. This crossed the too short Florinda and the too plump Brunhilda off the list, leaving only Sofía.

Thoughtfully, Domingo finished washing his teeth, and slid into the bathtub. This tub was installed in 1910. Originally of the curled edge type, the sides had been blocked with Puebla tile of crushed raspberry color, as a final concession to Brunhilda's protests that the bathroom was hideous. She had cried for weeks because the men in the house firmly refused to replace the tub with one of the modern square types. Domingo, don Lucio, and don Rafael might have given in to her, but it was Cardito who held out against her. "A man likes a tub he can stretch in," he snorted indignantly.

Domingo, with his hands laced beneath his head, and the water rippling about his nose, was, as always, thankful for Cardito's stubbornness. Now he stretched himself luxuriously while he considered Sofía's being the woman in the patio.

He remembered that when he descended the patio steps he had thought her door opened and closed. She must have followed him to discover why he was leaving, although such curiosity was unlike her. Nevertheless, the idea of the woman being Sofía was much more probable than ghost or hallucination.

Lucky, he grinned to himself, that it was Mateo and not doña Petra who was closing the gates, or Sofía would have received the well-known lecture on curiosity in young women. Of course, doña Petra's lectures lacked the fine cutting edge of Tía Nicanora's. Thinking of Tía, he wondered how Serafina was progressing today. He'd have to get a check cashed at the bank, and take some money out to Santa Catarina. He might also take a bag of groceries, although what a girl like Serafina enjoyed eating was a theory beyond his conjecture.

He had also to visit Cardito at the hospital, as well as find out how Mateo had progressed with the real-estate sale. Also, the thought hit him with the force of a physical blow, today was Friday. Verónica was coming home from Linares. And Verónica he had to see. That was imperative.

So much to do and so little time to do it in. He glanced at his watch and was shocked to find it was already nearly four o'clock.

Dressed at last, he hurried down the stairs to the kitchen. Doña Petra told him that doña Otilia had gone to the hospital with Brunhilda, but that Sofía was in the library. As the old woman put some eggs with chili sauce in front of him, she patted his shoulder. "Don't worry too much about niña Brunhilda. She is made of rubber, that girl, and knows how to bounce to safety, as we both well know."

It was the first time in several years that the cook had referred to Brunhilda's youthful escapade, when she had eloped to Laredo with the son of an *Arabe* shopkeeper. It was one of the great family secrets, known only to don Rafael, doña Otilia, doña Petra and Domingo.

The boy, whose name was Oscar Danigrís, knowing that the International bridge did not open in those days until nine, came for Brunhilda at four A. M., while the rest of the household was deep in slumber. This allowed them five hours to drive the one hundred and sixty miles to the border town. They went slowly, Brunhilda later insisted virtuously, and Oscar was exceedingly careful while descending the Mamulique, that engineering cut in space, where the road drops one mile straight down a mountain side.

Luckily one of the bridge officers, who knew Brunhilda, was worried by the young couple's arrogant answers to his questions. He had been acquainted with the Vázquez de Andas for a long time, and was quite certain they would never let a girl of their house drive alone to the States with a boy hardly older than herself.

The family was at breakfast when the telephone summoned Domingo. Since Brunhilda always slept late, no one had noticed her absence. Domingo thought his friend was playing an elaborate practical joke until he went upstairs to investigate. Leaving doña Petra on guard, so that Sofía would not wander into her sister's room by accident, Domingo drove to Laredo in a little over two hours, and, he grimly told Brunhilda, he did not descend the Mamulique with any care at all.

She had cried and screamed and flatly refused to go home, but Oscar, frightened by Domingo, meekly agreed that elopement was more romantic in theory than in practice.

Oscar's father, don Zénon Danigrís, was as angry as don Rafael. Strangely enough, their mutual anger drew the two men together. It was not uncommon for them to wander into don Primitivo's for a glass of evening beer.

Oscar had been packed off to the States immediately, to the

care of an uncle who owned a small drygoods store in Ohio, where he displayed an amazing gift for organization. The Danny Grey chain of women's clothing stores that laced the middle west was the result of his talent. Don Zenón said Oscar was married now, had four children and money in the bank.

When Brunhilda was told, she said venomously, "He is fat, I know he is fat, and sticky with money." Then, with a grand gesture of forgiveness she added to Domingo, "Lucky you caught me that day. Can you imagine me as the wife of a man who deals in cheap clothes for women?"

Doña Petra's words brought this remark back to Domingo. "You know," he told the old woman gravely, "I have always regretted that they did not manage to pass the border. If they had, Tuesday night would never have happened, and my father would have been spared much pain."

"But he would have shed tears over Brunhilda's marriage." Doña Petra shrugged fatalistic shoulders. "One kind of pain or another kind of pain, it all adds up to the same thing: pain."

Domingo sighed in agreement, finished his meal, and went off in search of Sofía.

She was sitting curled up on the sofa, absorbed in a book. Knowing Sofía, he was not at all surprised to see that she was reading Fábila's *Five Centuries of Agrarian Legislation in Mexico*.

It was not until he thrust a package of cigarettes under her nose that she became aware of him. She daintily covered a yawn with her fingers before accepting the small offering. As he held his lighter for her, he noticed that there were dark circles under her eyes, and that her skin had that glazed look it always possessed when she had gone without sleep.

"Lack of sleep is not becoming to you," he told her with brutal candor.

She shrugged and toyed with the pages of her book, too polite to intimate that he had disturbed her reading, yet obviously hoping that he would go away and leave her alone.

As usual with Domingo when he had not gotten his sleep at his accustomed hours, he was irritable. Without tact or cautious preamble he said curtly, "I do not approve of you wandering about the patios at three in the morning in your night clothes, especially with Mateo to see you."

Her eyes flashed, then were hidden under lowered lids. "And

where did you receive the impression that I was up at such an hour? Perhaps you were gossiping about your sister with Mateo?"

"I saw you."

This time she lowered her whole head, but her voice was steady. "How interesting. And where did you see me?"

"By the patio pool just before I drove off."

"Ah, and what were you doing driving off at—what was the hour you said, three in the morning?"

"It is not my actions that I am discussing, but yours." He ground out his cigarette with the frustrated sensation that she had put him on the defensive, when she herself should be humbly promising to mend her ways. "Doña Petra told me that I should look after you better. She thinks you are too wise for your age . . ."

"In what way?" Her head was up now, and he could see laughter behind the mask of her face. This infuriated him, and his temper took full control of his caution.

"I think perhaps she may be right. If it was you by the pool . . ."

"Ay, now there is doubt. A moment ago you were all sureness."

"It could have been no one else but you. Or do you think I saw a ghost?"

She came to her feet in the same fluid motion common to Brunhilda and Verónica. "This house is said to have ghosts. If I had a brother of a decent mind, he would take it for granted that it was a ghost, and not his sister in her night clothes."

When he attempted to interrupt, her voice flowed smoothly onward, not pausing for his comments. "And what should I be doing in the patio at such an hour I would like to know? Spying on you, perhaps? You think I am a spy? I knew you were going out, I heard you go down the stairs. But I do not have the curiosity of our precious Brunhilda. You are a man after all. If you want to pay a visit at such an hour that is none of my affair. I do not concern myself with what you do. I know that Serafina is sick, and you, all trembling with terror for your pretty girl, must rush off in the night to find out how she is . . ."

"I will not have you say such things . . ."

"You think I don't know that she is going to have a child? Any fool with eyes could have seen that a month ago . . ."

"Keep your mouth shut!" He was white with rage and she was equally pale.

"I will not! You coming in here so moral to insult me, and you panting after your woman. . . ."

His hand reached out blindly and caught her shoulder, gave her a hard shake, then released her so that she fell against one corner of the sofa.

"I will not have you speak so of Serafina. Do you hear me? Never mention her name to me again."

Still trembling with rage he slammed out of the room, found his hat and overcoat and left the house. With his hands deep in his pockets he strode west on Padre Mier toward don Wilfrido's grocery store. He was so angry that at first there was nothing in his mind but the red glare of anger. Then the cold wind blowing against his heated face, and the exercise exhausting the excess energy in his blood, he slowly returned to normal.

It was not until he had crossed Zaragoza Street, and was passing his uncle Agapito's bank, that it occurred to him that he had not been angry so much at Sofía as at himself. The fact that his anger existed had further angered him and he had taken it out on his sister.

He knocked at the bank's side door. A clerk, recognizing him, admitted him, and agreeably went off to cash his check although business hours had ended before he had even awakened.

While he waited, he mentally apologized to Sofía. If it had been Brunhilda, he would really have been worried. Brunhilda knew only one law: her own desires. If she had to cross convention to get what she wanted, then a snap of her fingers to the scandal involved. But Sofía was as proper as a porcelain statue, and he had been a stupid fool to suspect for even a moment that she would parade before a manservant in her night clothes.

Free of his anger, Domingo went to don Wilfrido's. This store, like don Primitivo's saloon, was a sort of club. In the morning most of the women from the American colony came in to do their buying, and English was the accepted language. But in the late afternoon the bullfight devotees gathered to discuss the various fighters and exchange views on the aesthetics of the art.

This afternoon was no exception. There were only one or two customers on the ground floor, but floating down from the balcony, where don Wilfrido kept his desk so that from time to time he could survey his little world, came the monotonous rhythm of men's voices.

A clerk, recognizing Domingo, bustled forward with a smile. "Don Wilfrido will be glad to see you. If you will just take the stairs . . ."

"I come on business." Domingo gravely explained that he wanted a basket of groceries to take to his nurse in the country.

The clerk helpfully pulled down cans of tomatoes, peas, and corn, but Domingo shook his head. "She can get those in Santa Catarina. That bottle there, what is it?"

The clerk replied doubtfully, "Red caviar, señor. I do not think your nurse would like it."

In his imagination, Domingo visualized Serafina exclaiming over fish roe, the shade of burnt sienna. Even if she did not like the taste, the color would enchant her. "Give me two bottles," he said firmly, "and olives, and smoked salmon, and fruit pastes, several kinds of fruit pastes: guayaba, mango, peach, pear. And chocolate . . . you have good chocolate?"

"The best," the clerk admitted, his voice intimating politely that Domingo might say this basket was for his nurse, but a man was welcome to his own opinion. "Black chocolate from the interior, some flavored with cinnamon, some with vanilla."

"Put in both. And a box of candy, a large box. Make it two boxes."

Familiar tones from the balcony told Domingo that Irineo Miranda was visiting don Wilfrido. This would be a good chance to learn if Verónica were back in town . . . no, better not to ask. The teasing from the men would be insupportable.

"Where is the telephone . . . not the one in don Wilfrido's office."

The clerk did not allow so much as a flicker of a smile to touch his lips. He pointed to a small booth near the balcony steps.

As he moved toward it, don Wilfrido, leaning over the balcony railing, waved to him, shouted, "Come up and meet a promising young bullfighter."

Domingo answered that he had to telephone first, and went into the booth. A servant's voice answered the distant buzzing, said regretfully that the niña Verónica had gone to the Hotel Ancira to meet the señorita Brunhilda. He replaced the instrument, half relieved that Verónica was in town, half annoyed that he could not see her immediately.

As he climbed the steps to the balcony, he realized that don

Wilfrido's bullfighter must be Mateo's brother Manuel, renamed Manolo.

Don Wilfrido had furnished the balcony more as a lounge than an office, although an old-fashioned roll-top desk stood against one wall. Irineo Miranda was seated on the sofa, Isaac Fuentes, the furniture manufacturer, was stretched out in a large chair, and Néstor Cortés, the engineer, had draped himself on another. The four cronies, who spent most of their free hours together discussing history and/or bullfighting, were beaming at the boy standing near don Wilfrido by the balcony rail.

Manolo had the body of a bullfighter Domingo thought as the introductions were made. He was slender as a rapier, and all his movements were made from the waist.

"I've heard of you," Domingo said agreeably. "Your brother Mateo is my chauffeur."

Manolo's shoulders rose and sank. "He does not approve of me, my brother. He says my soul belongs to the grocery business."

Don Wilfrido shouted with laughter. "And so it should during working hours. Off with you, little one. Tilt your lance at the grain sacks."

The boy's exit was as elegant as that of a bullfighter already acclaimed, and don Isaac nodded in approval. "He has the arrogance. Without the arrogance, what is a fighter?"

"The demi-gods," Domingo said distastefully. "To watch them in the arena, yes, that is true pleasure. But acting as a mirror to reflect their golden arrogance—that does not amuse me."

"Their golden arrogance," don Isaac repeated dreamily. "But of course. Everything in the arena is golden, even the blood, the golden blood. Everything steals its color from the sun. The golden sand—the golden sheen of sequins on the torero's shoulder. . . ."

"All but one thing," said don Wilfrido. "The bull is black— black as pain, black as all tragedy, black as death."

"Night and day," said the Engineer. "That is the basic story of the arena. The eternal battle of the sun against the shadow of night . . ."

Knowing that these rhapsodies might continue for an hour, Domingo said hastily, "Don Wilfrido, forgive me—but those magazines you showed me the other night—the one with my grandfather's picture . . ."

156

"The Casasola collection? Yes? You would like a copy? Perhaps I have another . . ."

"Do you have the set? All of them?"

"Eh?" said Irineo, "is it possible that the lover is turning historian? Can it be that you wish to impress Verónica with the dignity of your ancestors?"

All of the men laughed as the color swept across Domingo's face. He knew that they were mistaking his anger for embarrassment, and he was even more strongly determined to have a firm and definite talk with Verónica.

Don Wilfrido pulled papers, letters, and copies of bullfight magazines from the choked interior of his desk. "I have them all here someplace. But your grandfather appears only in one issue. . . ."

"Is is not my grandfather's picture I am hunting. I saw a miniature the other day. . . a painting, but I believe it was copied from a photograph. The man was most familiar. I've been trying to identify him. . . ."

Their historical enthusiasm sniffed like dogs at a bone. "A miniature of someone in the Casasola collection?" Irineo demanded.

"Could it be General Angeles?" Néstor Cortés asked eagerly. Having studied under the General at Chapultepec, he worshipped the sound of Angeles' name.

"No," Domingo frowned, "I would have known the handsome Angeles. But the miniature was not of a handsome man. He was rather, well, mediocre looking."

The questions came very fast. Had the man been with Carranza, with Villa, with Obregón? Domingo flung up his hands in exasperation. "I don't know, I tell you. I'm not sure that he would even be prominent enough to be included in such a collection as this." Under the barrage of their curious eyes he added lamely, "I have—private reasons—for wanting to identify him."

Irineo Miranda nodded kindly. "We will help you. But if you just knew the period it would be so much easier. Wilfrido, you take the magazines to the fall of Díaz. Isaac, take the two Madero years. I will take Huerta, and Néstor, you can have the rest."

"But I will have to look myself," Domingo protested. "None of you saw the miniature. . . ."

The men smiled at each other. Don Wilfrido said kindly,

"Most of these pictures are of men you would have recognized immediately. Those we can discount. The rest we will show you. It is a simple method."

Domingo, who had wanted to take the magazines into a corner and study them for himself, could only bow with courtesy. For a moment there was silence, then don Isaac said, "Is it this one?"

After a quick glance, Domingo shook his head. "The man was not in uniform."

"That makes no difference," said Néstor Cortés. "I have an autographed picture—signed with his own hand, mind you—of General Angeles, and he is not in uniform. You are sure it was not Angeles?"

"Quite sure," said Domingo wearily.

Again there was silence, then Néstor said, "Is this the man?" But before Domingo could look at the picture he shook his head with disgust. "Ay, that's Obregón with his arm still on."

"Do you know how they found that arm on the battlefield?" don Wilfrido, who had been a Carranza man, chuckled. "Someone walked over the field holding out a hundred peso bill, and Obregón's arm leaped right up and grabbed it."

"I deny that story," said Irineo Miranda hotly, putting down his magazine to free his hands for argument gestures. "I was an Obregón man, and he never loved money that much."

"Ho!" snorted Néstor, who had followed his beloved General Angeles north to fight under Villa. "And what of the pretty pesos that passed under the counter in nineteen hundred and fourteen, eh, when Obregón ruled the capital?"

"There was not a hundred peso bill in the Republic," Irineo shouted triumphantly. "That devil Huerta and his followers had taken every bill of any value out of the country with them."

As the argument grew more furious, Domingo cautiously picked up Irineo's copy and began hunting through it. Afraid that such discourtesy would offend these men, he had to keep one eye on them and the other on the page, and so he almost missed the photograph. It was not the one he remembered. That had been a single portrait. This one showed a group of men, some in uniform, some in civilian clothes, bearing huge funeral wreaths of white daisies and ferns. Under it was written, "The President of the Republic, General Victoriano Huerta, arriving to present his offering in front of the tomb of don Benito Juárez in San Fernando." Directly behind the bald-headed president was the figure of a stout man with a round, expressionless face partly obscured by a drooping black mustache. There was no doubt about it. This was the same man.

He tugged at Irineo's sleeve, excitement overcoming his sense of good manners.

"This is the man. I am sure of it. Who is he?"

"I think that's . . . eh, isn't this . . . ?"

Don Wilfrido took the picture and held it closer to his eyes with one hand while with the other he lifted his spectacles free of his nose. "Undoubtedly," he said. "Yes, indeed."

Domingo gave a snort of disgust. "Very clear, very scientific."

The Engineer laughed and took the magazine. "They pretend they know everyone, but their ignorance stands on the pit of the abyss." He rubbed his thumbnail down his cheek. "Hmm . . . this is . . ."

"Make way, shoe, here comes your shoestring," snorted Isaac Fuentes, gently lifting the magazine out of the Engineer's hands. The moment he saw the picture his lips pressed tightly together. "I dream of that face sometimes," he said, and tossed the copy on the sofa.

"I told you," insisted don Wilfrido. "Isn't that whom I said, Irineo?"

"Undoubtedly, friend Wilfrido. I said the same."

"When you no longer wish to keep it a secret . . ." Domingo suggested with irritated amusement. He knew, as did all of them, that the furniture manufacturer was the only one who could put a name to that round face.

"He's Fernando Velarde," Fuentes said with a cold edge to his voice. "Once he owned a gray car that was very convenient to Huerta."

Domingo whistled softly through his teeth. "I've heard my uncle Lucio discuss him with don Primitivo. Wasn't he a bull-fighter at one time in his career?"

"What an insult to the bull!" snapped don Wilfrido. "It was his henchman, the malodorous Ratkiller, who was a veterinarian attached to the bullring. Velarde himself was a genius of medicine . . ."

"Who practised vivisection on his enemies," said don Isaac. "He cut out the tongue of Ruperto Martínez."

"I've never quite believed that tale," Irineo said slowly.

"Do you not?" snapped Isaac Fuentes. "Read the newspapers of the period. One of them said that he wore the black gown of an inquisitor."

The Engineer raised his hands in protest. "Peace, friend, peace. We have one great fault in Mexico: all of our heroes are without stain, and all of our villains are blacker than the blackest devil in Hell. Those news accounts, I've read them, mind you, appeared after the fall of Huerta when he and his cabinet were nicknamed Sathanas, Lucifer, and all the other Princes of Darkness."

"I suppose," Fuentes said hotly, "that you would even deny the existence of the gray car . . ."

"That I would not. Nor that this doctor was an evil man. But I do not believe that he cut out the tongue of Ruperto Martínez, nor the heart of Federico Navarro, nor chopped off the ears of Enrique Ortiz. I think that he served Huerta, and killed where he was told to kill, but always as a doctor, not as a monster."

"At any rate, he's dead," Irineo said placatingly, trying to calm don Isaac's growing anger. "He died in exile in Brooklyn."

This attracted Domingo's fancy. "Why Brooklyn?"

"Why any place, when a man's in exile? Besides, Brooklyn has a certain charm for exiles. Santa Anna stayed there, and Juárez. . ."

"Juárez rolled cigars in New Orleans, not Brooklyn," said don Wilfrido.

This began a heated argument which Domingo was thankful to escape. He picked up his grocery order from the clerk and went out on the street where he whistled for a taxi. On the way home he thought about the miniature in connection with Márgara. If she had painted it, then she had truly caught the cold, expressionless face, evident even in the photograph. Fernando Velarde, Huerta's evil genius . . . no wonder Márgara had shuddered at her father's hatred of this man.

But what had Velarde done to Bárcenas to cause such hate? Domingo decided to question don Primitivo about the dead exile. Irineo Miranda and the others might be historians with a passion for the scientific approach, but to don Primitivo history was the product of living men and women, who changed the progress of the country through greed or penuriousness, love or fear.

The saloon proprietor was not interested in documents. "Many a man has been hanged because the judge had a stomach-ache and wanted to finish the trial in a hurry," said don Primitivo. "Didn't a man get executed right here in Monterrey because he overslept? He was a Federal, and during the night a surprise attack by the Revolutionists captured the plaza. The Federal general had no time to send out messages to all his officers to evacuate the city; so this pretty captain, full of good liquor, slept through the retreat, woke up the next morning, leisurely dressed in full uniform, and strolled along Zaragoza Street to headquarters. He went six blocks before some astonished Revolutionary soldiers realized they had a fine Federal rooster in their net. But the captain was a brave one. When Gonzalitos, his glasses shining on his nose, said, 'Of course I must execute you,' this rooster answered, 'If I were in your place I would do the same.' Then he asked permission to arrange his own funeral. My good friend Pascual Ascona, the same Ascona who has a funeral parlor on Juárez Street, took care of the details. Pascual says that at the execution they let him command the firing squad as a tribute to such bravery. And they fired true, I can tell you, to save him pain. There was no need for the shot of grace to put him out of torment. Pascual said he'd never seen a deader Federal."

Don Primitivo, Domingo thought, as he paid off the taxi and went into the house, might not be scientific about Velarde, but he would supply plenty of human interest.

Domingo left the groceries with doña Petra. She examined them, sniffed at the contents, but made no comment. He wanted to get the car from Mateo in order to go to Santa Catarina. Mateo, doña Petra said, had returned doña Otilia to the house, and had taken Sofía to the hospital only a few minutes after Domingo had left. Where he might be now was beyond conjecture, although she thought he might be at SYR's. "You know how Brunhilda likes ice cream, and naturally Sofía would take her to SYR's."

If he went to SYR's, Domingo calculated, he would undoubtedly find Verónica with his sisters. At the moment he desired conversation with Verónica above everything else.

"I'll go there, doña Petra. And if Mateo should come home, tell him to wait here until I call."

"Very well. And, niño . . . ."

"Yes, doña Petra?"

"Fish eggs are not good for expectant women. Nor chocolate, nor all of these fruit pastes. . . ."

He said crossly, "You leave that package alone, doña Petra."

She shrugged. An expression of infinite sadness came into her eyes. She murmured, almost too low for him to hear, "I'm sorry, so very sorry."

For a moment he was tempted to tell her the truth, but he knew she would never believe the truth—that she would think he was taking the coward's way of trying to shift responsibility. And it seemed to him that a new strength of responsibility came into him, and strengthened him, so that he was no longer the old vascillating Domingo, but a new man, with the weight of Serafina's future in his hands, and beyond that the weight of an entity not yet fully formed but still in the process of forming, secret still as to male or female. What lives would that entity, yet unborn, touch and change because of being born? Already, not yet owner of its own blood, its own breath, it had thrown the veil of its influence over this house and the house of Serafina.

Through it all Cardito slept in the hospital, as yet untouched, but soon to be touched. Cardito, sleeping, his child-head heavy on the pillow, child no longer but a man grown, with a child of his making forming slowly in the womb of darkness.

But Cardito's future was also in the womb-darkness, and the child could mold that future, dwarf it, destroy it before its birth. Only Domingo stood between that child and its destructive force. He clenched his hands, raised them to his forehead. "I must choose right," he thought, "whatever happens, I must choose right."

XIV

A taxi took him to SYR's, the great drygoods store which stands on the corner of Zaragoza and Morelos. It was late on Friday afternoon, nearly seven o'clock, and he knew that he would find his sisters in the basement soda-bar. Now that tourists had so completely absorbed the hotels and Sanborn's, most of Monterrey's younger set went to SYR's, where tourists seldom found their way, to consume vast quantities of banana splits (called here The Three Marys), and sundaes, and to pass on one scrap of gossip in return for another.

The subterranean room was very pleasant with its lattice screens over which were trained artificial vines and flowers never created by God or Burbank. The booths were filled with laughing groups of young men and women, and in one of them he saw his sisters with the faithful Tito. Verónica was not with them, but surely Brunhilda could tell him where to find her.

Tito said happily, "I ordered a Three Marys for you when I saw you on the stairs."

"I don't see how you can endure them." Brunhilda daintily sipped at a cup of steaming coffee.

"At least one a day," said Sofía. "And when he's worried he eats two. How many does this make for you today, Domingo?"

Tito, happy at the chance of sitting beside Brunhilda, grinned teasingly. "What weighs your spirits now, friend? Your engagement to Verónica?"

"I am not engaged to her," Domingo said. "Rumors do not make a truth."

Brunhilda laughed delightedly at the game of pretence in love. The teasing, the lovers' shy reluctance, how well this affair followed the ancient pattern. Domingo was sick of it, and humbly thanked Sofía with his eyes, because, although her mouth quirked at the corners, she did not allow the smile to dent her cheeks.

The waitress brought the order, pointing out that she had added an extra scoop of ice cream for the señor Domingo. Brunhilda flung up one hand and pretended to hide her eyes. "It makes me ill just to look at it."

"Really?" he examined the dish carefully. There were four mounds of ice cream, a small sliver of fruit on top of each proclaiming its flavor: pineapple, banana, mango, and strawberry. Over two of the mounds had been poured pineapple syrup, over the other two, cherry, and all of this was held together by long slices of bananas.

Domingo opened his mouth, popped some mango ice cream into it, tasted it, and then nodded. "Very good," he said condescendingly. "Not so good, perhaps, as at other times, but it will do."

"He remembers yesterday's masterpiece," Tito confided. "The one at Sanborn's had whipcream on it. . . ."

Brunhilda gave a little scream. "But you are making me ill, Tito."

"Whipcream," Domingo agreed, "is a barbarous *gringo* custom with which you should be fully familiar, Brunhilda. . . ."

"Not even in the States," she assured him. And then, her eyes gleaming, "Guess where Tito took us this afternoon, Domingo?"

He bent sideways and sniffed at Sofía. "I thought I detected the odor of stale beer. So pious, you three, with your disdain of my simple pleasures, while you spend the afternoon lapping free beer at the brewery."

"Oh, Tito didn't take us to the brewery," Brunhilda told him in her candid way. "Mateo gave us the beer."

Domingo, startled, glanced around at Sofía. "Mateo gave it to you!"

She shrugged and took out a cigarette, bent gracefully across the narrow table toward Tito's lighter. "After we left the hospital Mateo wanted to show us the new *colonia* . . ."

"It was your idea really, Sofía," the literal Brunhilda said.

"Was it?" Sofía asked indifferently. "At any rate, I've never really seen it. Since it is named for me, naturally I'm interested. She turned her body slightly, so that she was facing Domingo more than the two across the table. "Mateo showed it very well. He almost persuaded Brunhilda to acquire a snug corner for herself."

Tito snatched at the words, grinned at Brunhilda. "I'll buy you a corner—any corner you say."

She hid a yawn with graceful fingers. "Don't be tiresome, Tito. Domingo, you should have been there to hear Sofía lecture on the proper details to interest clients."

"Sofía lecture?" Was his younger sister continually to jab him with these small daggers of surprise?

"A very complete lecture," Brunhilda said. Her tone deepened, took on the contralto quality of Sofía's as she mimicked. " 'Now these lots, Mateo, will be offered to people of moderate means. What they are looking for are bargains. Here it is better to stress how much they get for so little money.' Most instructive. Neither she nor our humble chauffeur cared how bored I was. And I was bored. Bored, bored, bored!"

"I'm sorry, Brunhilda," Sofía murmured. "I didn't think . . ."

"Of course not, why should you?" Her hand rose in a sweeping gesture. "The world of finance is so completely your world. I can understand why you've never married. Your heart is shaped like a silver peso."

Sofía thrust her cigarette into the ashtray and extinguished it with a vicious turn. Even Tito was aware of the hostile atmosphere, and said quickly, "Where did you get the beer? Does your colony have beer pumped into the lots, Domingo?"

Brunhilda gave her trilling laugh. "Of course not, my fat idiot. There are no houses—nothing but empty fields and one sidewalk drink stand. That is where Mateo bought the beer, in celebration, he said, of selling a lot this morning. And," she added to Domingo, "that is where I telephoned Tito to meet us at the Hotel Ancira and amuse us for an hour."

Domingo, in spite of being curious as to which lot Mateo had sold, said on cue, "And did he?"

"It was simply enchanting. I've had my photograph taken . . ."

Flinching as though a match had been applied to his nerve ends, Domingo said sharply to Tito, "You took them to Bárcenas!"

"It is an amusing place," Sofía said.

Tito frowned at his friend's anger. Brunhilda, also was looking curiously at him. Conscious of their regard, Domingo pushed the half-consumed plate of ice cream from him, and made small rings of moisture on the table-top with the bottom of his water glass, the anger in him more snow than flame. Bárcenas, to him, was synonymous with Márgara. A criticism of the one was a criticism of the other. To go to that studio for amusement, as one goes to watch animals feeding at the Alameda. . . .

He pushed his anger down, forced himself to say quietly, "I can understand that you might find it amusing. However I should not think that—" Not Márgara. He must not say Márgara. ". . . that Bárcenas enjoyed your mirth."

"Oh, Domingo," Brunhilda protested, "don't be so class conscious. You're always afraid of upsetting the feelings of those below. And truly, Domingo, they are just as insensitive as we are. I learned that in the States. They bark at you and you bark at them and that's all there is to it."

"Brunhilda's world is so simple," Sofía murmured. "I wish mine were as simple."

Brunhilda wrinkled her nose. "Now you're getting intricate,

Sofía. You know I can't understand you when you get intricate."

Domingo was determined to keep Brunhilda's flea-like mind still long enough to discover what had happened at the studio. Tito, he knew, would neglect the important details, and Sofía had probably already forgotten them. "But what did you do at the studio?"

"We had our pictures taken. Very stiff, and I'm sure no expression at all. I can't wait to see mine, and as for Verónica's . . ."

"Verónica!" Domingo shouted. At Brunhilda's horrified gasp he managed to lower his voice, noticing as he did so that people at nearby tables turned to stare curiously at him. "Did Verónica go too?"

"Certainly. It was all a part of Tito's plan . . ."

"Plan? Tito, have you lost your senses . . ."

"Domingo," Sofía whispered, "stop shouting. Anyone would think you had a special interest in that studio."

"Be quiet, Sofía. If this is a part of your advertising scheme, Tito . . ."

"And a very excellent scheme it is," the fat little man protested, his eyes sparkling with injured pride.

"Bárcenas doesn't want a magnificent studio. He's perfectly happy where he is. . . ."

It was Sofía who came to Tito's defense. "How do you know that? Every man wants success. And Tito has genius as an advertiser. His whole plan is extremely clever."

"I think so, too," said Brunhilda, giving Tito's arm a quick pat. He looked at her with the eyes of a petted mongrel, and Domingo was suddenly ashamed for this love that was naked and unashamed. "Tito explained to us that if Sofía, Verónica and I had our pictures taken there, the studio would become a fad. Other girls from above would go, and the girls from below would follow. Before Bárcenas knows it, he'll have all of Monterrey storming his doors to be photographed."

"You know how Brunhilda adores having her picture taken," Sofía said. "She enjoyed the idea so much that she insisted on Verónica joining us."

"I loved it," said Verónica at Domingo's elbow. He jerked at the sound of her voice, and then slid out of his seat to stand and take her outstretched fingers. Under his lids he knew that acquaintances at the various tables were watching the little scene while

166

murmuring amongst themselves that the rumor of the Miranda-Vázquez engagement was undoubtedly true.

Verónica dropped some parcels on the leather seat, and slid in beside Sofía. "I detest shopping. Domingo, I want coffee, please."

He resented the proprietory note in her voice, but obediently crossed the room to the service counter. Late customers were jamming the small tables and booths, so, to relieve the waitress, he remained at the counter for the cup.

He could still feel his anger, like a lump of ice, pressing against his stomach, nauseating him. How dared Tito take those butterfly girls, those pretty simulacrae of girls, all wax and surface feelings, to parade their charming comedy in front of Márgara? Their names had gone down in the order book: Brunhilda Vázquez de Anda; Sofía Vázquez de Anda, and Márgara would think, perhaps, that he had known they were coming, that he had been willing for them to come, to smother laughter behind their pointed fingers, and point at photographs and brightly say, "But how charming—how primitive." Yes, primitive was a good word. A good art word. A meaningless word sweet on the lips of meaningless people.

His hands, deep in his pockets, clenched tightly. He looked across the room at them, and detested them: Brunhilda and Verónica in their furs, their smart little hats, weighted with flowers, tilted forward over their brows. Sofía wore no hat, unless that gigantic rose balanced on top of her upswept gleaming curls counted as such. She had taken off her cloth coat, and was slimly elegant in dark blue with bands of pale blue, white and coral at the throat. Looking at Sofía, he felt a little better. Of the three, she would not have laughed, would not have made superior fun. From the eminence of her cool detachment, she might have rejected the studio, but she would never have ridiculed it.

Grateful for his younger sister, he carefully balanced the cup of coffee across the gossip-buzzing room, grinning automatically at acquaintances without really seeing their faces. Tito had captured a chair for him, and he sat down at the end of the table, facing the wall, Tito on his left, Verónica on his right.

Verónica, taking the cup, smiled at him. "Tito says you missed seeing the woman when you two were there."

"I don't want to talk about her," Brunhilda pouted. "She frightened me."

Tito said wisely, "Any woman who doesn't talk frightens Brunhilda."

"Don't be a stupid. It's just, I don't know . . . the way she looked at me."

Domingo wanted to hurt. He said coldly, "Perhaps she didn't like you."

"Not like Brunhilda!" For Tito such a thought was incomprehensible.

"Brunhilda's human," Sofía drawled. "Some people like her, some people don't."

Tito said seriously, "I like her enough to make up for all the people in the world."

Domingo looked around at Verónica to see how she was accepting this obvious love-making on the part of a man she herself loved. To his surprise, she was looking at himself, but the moment his eyes met hers, her lids swiftly lowered, so that he could not read the expression behind them. She stirred the sugar in the bottom of her cup, and said diffidently, "I thought the woman very interesting. As a type I mean. She recognized your name, Domingo."

He caught his breath, held it for a moment. When he released it he could feel it blowing against his lower lip. "You mean my name entered into the conversation?"

Brunhilda giggled. "You really should have been there, my brother. When we entered Tito had to pound and pound to get anyone to come out at all. Then this woman came in, and looked at us, but just with her eyes, you understand. Not with her face. There was no expression on her face at all. It was like a mask. Tito told her we wanted our pictures made, and then she called the man. He took us into that funny studio."

"I thought she had stayed in the other room," Verónica said, "but when I turned around, there she was, standing in the archway, looking at us."

"Sofía insisted on that ocean background," Brunhilda interrupted, irritated at losing the center of attention. "I thought the garden was more—well, interesting. But Sofía said she wanted the ocean."

Domingo took a sip of water to relax the tightness in his throat. "Which one did you choose, Verónica?"

Brunhilda answered quickly, "She wouldn't. She just looked

at the woman and said, 'You choose.' Then the woman said, 'For what purpose is the picture . . . ?' "

"As though she didn't guess," said Sofía on a deep note. "She knew we were there to amuse ourselves. She has intelligence, that one."

"Stop interrupting me, Sofía. Anyway, my brother, I didn't know what nonsense Verónica might speak, so I said, very quickly, 'As an engagement present to her fiancé. And I want you to make it very nice, because it's for my brother.' "

This is it, thought Domingo. This is what I've been dreading. He was surprised to see the steadiness of his hand as he lifted the water glass, but the next moment he noticed that everything around him had dulled a little, as though the air had thickened. Verónica's voice was no longer bell-clear as she said, "That was when she mentioned that she had heard of you. She said that they would be very careful of my photograph. It surprised me, because as she said it I had the strangest impression. . . ."

"Oh, you're always getting impressions, Verónica," Brunhilda protested.

"I can't help it. I got one this afternoon. I had the impression she—she didn't approve of you, Domingo."

"Such frankness," sighed Sofía. "Everyone not approving of everyone else this afternoon. And it's late. And we'd better go home."

While the men were gathering up the girls' packages, Tito said, "Don't forget that we see my proofs tomorrow noon, Domingo."

"You don't need me for that."

"But I do. I can always judge other people's pictures, but never my own. Perhaps we can go to don Primitivo's for lunch afterwards."

Domingo half nodded. He knew that the next time he saw Márgara, he wanted to see her alone, not with Tito dancing attendance at his heels.

When they emerged on the sidewalk, Tito waved his hand to Mateo who was leaning against the building wall, his arms folded, waiting for them. At the signal, the chauffeur turned and hurried to get the car. Watching the stocky figure disappear into the crowd, Domingo also wanted to lose himself in the flowing dance of traffic.

Then Verónica's hand came to rest on his arm. He moved

slightly away from her so that the contact was broken, but nevertheless, her touch had drawn him back into the world of reality.

"I must talk to you," he said under his breath, and she nodded.

When Mateo stopped the car in front of them, she said, "My house is so close. Will you walk me home, Domingo? Give these luxurious ones my packages. No need for us to carry them."

Tito pretended to sink under the weight of the small parcels. "Such women. Always spending money. Should we not make them carry these heavy trifles?" he demanded of Brunhilda.

She giggled, said lightly, "Better not if they have value, or these two cooing doves will leave them, forgotten, on a bench somewhere. Sofía, why are you getting in the front seat?"

"Why not?" Sofía asked, settling herself next to Mateo. "Poor Tito has few pleasures. Sitting in solitary grandeur with you should not be denied him."

Before Brunhilda could form an appropriate retort, Sofía beckoned Domingo to her, whispered, "Don't tell Verónica about Serafina. Believe me, Domingo, she'd rather not know."

"Secrets," Brunhilda said petulantly. "You have no right to have secrets from me."

"If you knew it," Sofía retorted, "then it would be no secret. Drive us to the señorita's house, Mateo." The car started off, Tito yelling at them through the traffic's clamor. "We will leave word that you are safe with Domingo, Verónica, so that your parents will not worry."

She waved her hand to him, then slid it once more through Domingo's arm.

He had paid no attention to this little waterfall of conversation, being too intent on Sofía's advice. I've never really appreciated my sister, he thought, and wished that through the years they might have had the same feeling of friendship that possessed them now.

"I love Monterrey at night," Verónica said. "This long street, like a lazy serpent, and the neon lights glowing."

He nodded. They strolled toward Zaragoza Plaza. The street lights glistened from sidewalks and building walls. Their slow-moving feet carried them past an ornately carved corner building, and they were in the open square of the plaza. The Plaza Zaragoza. Monterrey's *Plaza de Armas*. It was this plaza that was the city. In time of war, the enemy might fight to that ornate corner, but if this plaza held, then the city held. On one side were the arches of the city hall, and that could fall; on the other was the upthrust tower of the Cathedral, and that could fall. But so long as the plaza held, the enemy could not send the boasting message: "We have taken the plaza. Monterrey is ours."

Three times that message had been sent: one to Washington, one to Maximilian, one to Huerta. And three times the city won it back again, once by peace treaty, twice by force of battle. And yet, in the quiet of night, with the moon trapped between cantle and pommel of Saddle Mountain, the plaza was merely a large hollow square with trees growing in the center; orange trees, pecans, a few scattered palms. Long iron benches lined both sides of the cement walk, and here people were sitting: young lovers; mothers with children; old men discussing the dreams they had almost forgotten.

Domingo and Verónica found a bench near one of the fountains, not too close to a light standard to invite curious glances, nor yet so far that the darkness prevented their seeing each other's faces.

He turned so that he could face her, but she did not turn to him. Her arms were folded across her breasts, and she stared straight in front of her, breathing in rapid little puffs as though she had been running. She laughed tremulously and said, "It is stupid, but I am afraid. I know you want to scold me, and I don't want you to scold me."

"I'm not going to scold you," he said. The lassitude he had felt yesterday was suddenly upon him again. After that brief talk with doña Petra in the kitchen he had felt strong, but now he was once more tired. "Have I ever scolded you?"

"No, but there must always be a first time."

"Not tonight. I am too tired."

"I am sorry, Domingo," she whispered. "Truly, I am sorry. It was just that you had made me so angry. I wanted to hit out at you. Do you believe me?"

"Yes," he said. "I knew that you were trying to get even with me, like a child getting even with a playmate."

He could see the tenseness go out of her. "I am very like a child," she said seriously. "Sometimes I amaze myself with my childishness. But I did not want to hurt you. I love you, Domingo."

"Tuesday," he said, "you loved Tito."

"Did I?" she turned her head toward him, and he saw mischief bubbling in her. "It was you who said I loved him, not me . . ."

This shocked him into stiffness. "Saints in Heaven, Verónica, you said . . ."

"I know what I said. The moment you were all sympathy over my heart breaking for Tito, I could not help myself. And," she admitted, "I hoped you would be jealous. When you were not, it made me angrier than ever."

"Verónica, what are you saying to me?"

"Only the truth, Domingo. Didn't you know it when I kissed you?"

"This time," he said grimly, "I shall leap to no conclusions. This time you must put what you mean in clear words. . . ."

"I am not ashamed of them." She moved closer to him on the bench. Her violet perfume enclosed him in a fragile box of fragrance. "I love you. There has never been anyone else."

The violet fragrance was too strong. He felt smothered by it. "You are a romantic child with a dream you've built . . ."

"I am not," she persisted, moving still closer until he could feel the weight of her against his arm. "You are the romantic one, not I." Then harshly, "That Bárcenas woman. I could kill her."

He jerked away from her, jumped to his feet. "Don't be a fool, Verónica."

"She's the woman you said you thought you were in love with . . ."

"Verónica, I will not discuss this . . ."

"But I want to discuss it." Her voice lashed at him. "The truth was there when Brunhilda told her we two were engaged. There was a mask on her face, but I smelt her feelings. Oh, yes, very satisfied, very sure of herself."

"You are inventing these words . . ."

"I am not. You know I am not." She was standing beside him, clinging to his arm with both of her hands. "Every woman who has ever looked at you . . . I've always known how they felt." She was silent while a man passed them, then she sat down again on the bench. "We are making a spectacle of ourselves."

He sat beside her. He was so tired that he could not make his mind behave. Thoughts were a jumble, and there was nothing clear to him. He bent forward until his arms rested on his knees.

"Verónica," he said wearily, "I love that woman with my bones. Her name is a song in my blood."

She was silent for so long he raised himself and faced her. Now that he had spoken he felt weak from released strain. Realizing that she was not going to speak, he took her hand as a doctor takes the hand of a patient. "Verónica, a girl I once knew told me that every girl must sometimes experience a breaking heart. It is a sort of growing up for girls, and men, too, I guess. I wish I could have saved you from it. You think I'm cruel, but so is a surgeon cruel. A lie would have been kinder at the moment, but not in the end."

"Don't," she whispered. "Don't say anything."

He nodded, and leaned against the curved arm of the bench. A shine boy hurried past, wheeled back toward him, then shrugged as Domingo shook his head. Disturbed in its sleep, a bird in one of the trees chirped angrily a few times. A tourist couple, arm in arm, paused to look at the fountain. Their North American voices made soft murmurs like water rippling over stones. After they walked on, Verónica said quietly, "You want your freedom? You want me to tell my parents and your parents that my intimations were lies?"

"Yes, Verónica. I'd rather it came from you."

"And if I refuse . . ."

"Refuse?" His incredulity was so plain that she laughed dryly.

"Yes, Domingo. If I refuse to speak, what will you do then?"

"I don't know," he said blankly. "Such a thing had never occurred to me—that you could be so stubborn. Surely, Verónica . . ."

"I love you, Domingo. I want to marry you. I want everyone to say, 'There walks the wife of Domingo Vázquez de Anda.' "

His lips twisted with impatience. "Marriage isn't a toy to be bought in the market, Verónica. It's my life and your life with death at the end of it."

"I know what it means. And I think you love me."

"Verónica . . ."

"Please. Listen to me. When you came back from the States, you were in love with a *gringa,* weren't you? Be honest with me, Domingo."

"Yes, Verónica, I was."

"That was ten years ago. I was ten years old. I loved you so much I was sick with jealousy of that *gringa*. Every morning I thought, perhaps today he will fetch Sofía and me to school in place of the chauffeur. And you often did, Domingo. Perhaps you sensed that I worshipped you, and you needed worship from somebody, even a ten-year-old girl." Her voice broke a little, then steadied. "When I went to San Antonio, you came with my father to see me graduate. You brought me a bouquet of white roses."

"I went to see Brunhilda graduate, too, and Sofía."

"You didn't take them to the senior class dance. But you took me."

"They had so many boys begging to take them . . ."

"Do you think there were no boys begging me?"

"I didn't mean that."

"You took me because you wanted to take me, and you didn't want to take them. You took me, and you enjoyed it. You laughed all evening, and at the end you said you hadn't had such a good time in years. Didn't you say that?"

"I suppose I did. . . ."

"On the night of my debut, here in this Casino, you danced the first dance with me . . ."

"It was the privilege of an old friend . . ."

"Was it the privilege of an old friend to forbid me dancing more than twice with Fidel Carvajal?"

"Yes, it was. Gossip starts easily, as both of us know well this night. If you had danced too much with him, you would have been engaged to him before the year was out."

She laughed on a small triumphant note. "Why did you care if I married Fidel Carvajal? He is a nice boy. His family has money . . ."

"He's a stupid fool. You deserve better than Fidel . . ."

"You didn't want me to marry Fidel. You didn't want me to marry anybody. Now you're so sure of me that even my poor little taunts about Tito do not disturb you. If I could cut you out of my heart, I would. Just to punish you, I would." The tears came. She fumbled blindly in her purse for a handkerchief. He took his own from his breast pocket and slipped it into her fingers. A pain within him answered her pain, and for a moment he was tempted to put his arm around her shoulder, draw her to him, comfort her. But he kept himself rigid beside her.

"When two people have known each other as long as you

and I," he said, "there are always gentle memories between them. We have had a good friendship. I am sorry that it has had to end like this."

She blew her nose with a businesslike air. "It's not ended, Domingo," she said quietly. "You are older than I, but I think in this I am wiser than you."

He said, "You refuse to make any effort to stop the gossip?"

"Yes, Domingo. You can make a scandal of it if you like. You can stay away from my house, and not come near me in public. All of these things you can do, because you're a man. But I shall tell my father, and yours too, that you asked me to marry you the other night, and that I accepted."

"That's a lie, Verónica."

"They'll believe me, because they want to believe me. My family and yours want this marriage. And I want it. And I will marry you, Domingo. Not this year, perhaps, nor next. But someday in that Cathedral I will marry you. You said that woman was in your blood and bone. But blood thins, and bones grow old."

The tension in her body, the upward thrust of her chin, the finality in her voice, told him that she meant what she said. From this moment she was his enemy, fighting with every weapon, honest or dishonest, to hold him prisoner. To his surprise, he found in himself a grudging respect for her.

An only child, she had never been thwarted in any desire. It was the thwarting, he realized, and not the desire that had turned her into this fighting creature. Given time, he could find the key that would unlock the steel box of her resolve, but he had so little time. Don Agapito would be home on Monday. Hearing the gossip, he would try to hound Domingo straight into this marriage which had been so long desired. And Domingo was not yet ready for revolution against his uncle. There was don Rafael to be considered, already fragile with pain over Brunhilda. Domingo's doctor-instinct told him that his earlier reasoning had been correct: a little added pain would scarcely be felt. But it also told him he had not reasoned deep enough, for too much pain in a single dose could kill. Nevertheless, he was certain of one thing: he had no intention of being the victim of Verónica's selfishness.

From Friday to Monday—Domingo sighed and rose. "I'll

take you home now, Verónica. But let me repeat it: I am not going to marry you."

"In that Cathedral," Verónica said calmly. "And I shall have ten bridesmaids dressed in yellow."

XV

The lounge in the Casino was almost empty. Domingo had never particularly liked this marble space, although the broad staircase was beautiful on dance nights, when women in varicolored dresses trailed up it to the ballroom on the second floor.

During the week, however, only a few scattered tables were occupied, generally by tourists, the women looking suitably impressed, while their husbands beamed with pride at having obtained cards to this most exclusive of all the city clubs. Membership was determined by social position. Nevertheless, in the last few years some of the new rich had invaded the sacred precincts, so sacred that the club had no name beyond that of the Casino, which means the Club.

Domingo, in common with most of his friends, had been a member for years. He went to the Saturday night dances—on the roof in summer, in the supper-room in winter. And he attended all the major dances; the Fifth of May, the Sixteenth of September, New Year's Eve. These things he did, not because he particularly wanted to, but because they were a part of his life pattern. But to use the Casino as a lounging room did not interest him. The members who did offered him little in the way of companionship. When he wanted good talk, he went to don Primitivo's. Also, the beer was better.

Tito had said to meet him at the Casino at noon, and Tito was invariably late, so Domingo strolled into the adjoining billiard room to watch a game between Irineo Miranda and Néstor Cortés.

"Such industry," he murmured, perching on the arm of a chair, "and in the mornings. Is there no honest work waiting in your offices?"

176

Irineo grinned while he carefully rubbed chalk on the end of his cue. "Did the Engineer and I ever make any pretense at honesty?"

"Not during my memory," Domingo admitted in mock sorrow, while ordering a round of drinks from a hovering waiter. "Tell me, Engineer, since you are an expert, can billiards be learned from a book?"

"I never heard of it," Cortés said. "Are you ambitious to write such a book?"

"No. My uncle Lucio is taking a correspondence course in it."

"Ay," said the two men in chorus and smiled at Domingo.

"I must take him on for a game," said Cortés. "Perhaps the book will have taught him a trick or two of which I know nothing."

"Speaking of tricks," Irineo said, "I hear your chauffeur pulled a clever trick yesterday morning. Is it true he sold that lot on the Bishop's Hill where only an eagle would be fool enough to build its nest?"

"Yes," Domingo admitted. "I'll bring the contracts to your office this afternoon, if it's convenient."

"That's the best of being a lawyer," Cortés said. "You know all the business in town. Be sure and tell the purchaser what a good engineer I am. He'll need an engineer to build a house on that spot."

Irineo pushed a counter along the wire. "How did your chauffeur get rid of it? Your father was telling me some days ago that he always counted that lot off as pure loss."

"Mateo's outside with the car, and it makes a good story if you'd like to hear it," Domingo said lazily.

A waiter was promptly dispatched to fetch the chauffeur, and in a few moments Mateo, in his new clothes, came into the room. Since Thursday, Domingo decided, the stocky young man had gained poise. If he were flustered by the elegance of these rooms, it did not show. At Domingo's nod he sat in a nearby chair. Irineo perched on the edge of the billiard table, and Cortés rested his weight on his cue stick.

"We hear you worked a miracle yesterday," Irineo said kindly. Then, as the waiter entered with the drinks he said, "Fetch another for this young man. We have a miracle to celebrate."

The waiter's eyes were supercilious as he went out. Domingo thought, he knows Mateo's a chauffeur, and he's much too vain to wait on a servant. Then he saw that Mateo was watching him. That's the trouble with those from below, Domingo thought. They have no assurance. He's proven that he's a better salesman than either my father or myself. It's a pity he doesn't have more of his brother's arrogance.

"By the way," he said aloud to Mateo, "I forgot to tell you. I met your brother yesterday." And to the others, "Don Wilfrido's bullfighter is Mateo's brother."

The Engineer examined the chauffeur with frank curiosity. "Is it possible?" he marveled. "There is no resemblance at all."

"But there is," Irineo said. "In Manolo it's arrogance, but in Mateo . . ." he shook his head, frowned, "I can't name it. Self-assurance, I suppose, is the word I want."

Domingo was irritated. They had no right to discuss Mateo as though he were an object without feeling or sensitivity. He was pleased that these frank comments were not making the chauffeur nervous. The waiter returned with the new drink, and Mateo took it from the tray in a manner that would have made Sofía proud of her pupil.

Irineo raised his glass. "To the miracle."

The Engineer smiled and nodded and Domingo raised his own glass. Mateo sat quietly watching them, waiting for them to take the first sip, and then he also drank a little of the brandy. Domingo winked at him, and a faint smile curved the chauffeur's lip corners.

"It was not such a miracle," he said easily, leaning back in his chair and crossing his knees. "Palma wanted to buy, so I took him to the Bishop's Hill first. There was much discussion about the view. Then I took him to those lots behind the military camp."

"Those small hemmed-in lots?" Irineo shouted with laughter.

"The same. Every time Palma wanted to say 'No' I showed him a new lot. You can sell anything if you don't let them say 'No.' Then I took him to the Arcos and bought him his dinner," he raised his eyebrows at Domingo. "By that time it was dark enough to take him back to the Bishop's Hill. The lights from the city were extremely beautiful. That completed the sale." He shrugged and drained his brandy glass.

Irineo and Cortés liked the story. They congratulated Mateo, and Domingo because of Mateo. When they wanted to order another round of drinks, Mateo stood up.

"If you will excuse me," he said, and after a nod from Domingo, he walked out of the room.

"Now he looks like his brother," Cortés said. "From the back —that walk—it's a true bullfighter's walk."

"Don't tell Mateo," Domingo begged. "He detests bullfighters. For him they are not practical."

"Yes," Irineo said slowly, "I can understand that. I wonder how long it will be before he becomes a member of this Casino? Would you like to bet, Engineer?"

Cortés was startled. "Bah, you are crazy, Counselor."

"Do you think I am crazy, Domingo?"

"I know you are not," Domingo said. "Fifteen years, do you think?"

"Ten," Irineo said. "He has the bit in his teeth now. Soon he will begin to trade property. And in ten years all we stupid ones will discover we have traded the whole city to him in return for some nice lots on top of Saddle Mountain."

"I don't believe it," Cortés protested, a little shocked. "The man's a servant."

"That man's no servant," Irineo said. "Didn't you notice the way he sat in his chair? He was on a level with us in that moment, and he knew it. That's why he left when he did. He's had luck, so far, and he knows enough not to push it. As yet he's not ready to be on level with us. He still has things to learn, but when he learns them—well, I for one will vote for his entry to this club, and I am sure the rest of you will, too."

"Including my uncle Agapito?" Domingo inspected the contents of his glass before he drained it.

Irineo rubbed his chin with his thumb. "Especially Agapito. He has enough force in himself to recognize it in others."

"I don't know," the Engineer said doubtfully. "All this change ... I can't understand it."

Irineo Miranda lazily pushed two balls across the table's green felt. "As a historian, it worries me a little. We have grown too fast in our social order. From feudalism to socialism in one step with no middle ground to cushion us. We old ones from the past, we don't know how to stand aside. These young ones from the future, they push against us, wrap themselves like vines around our trunks. We try to fight, but what good is fighting? The vines always win in the end, and the trunks die."

"I don't understand it," Cortés said. "In the days of don Porfirio, everything was so simple. There were the men above and the men below, and no stepping from one class to another."

"We were all very proud," Irineo admitted, "and just a little stupid, don't you think? We never seemed to remember in our pride that the man who led us was an Indian from Oaxaca. All of us above knelt to one who had come up from below. I have some portraits of don Porfirio serving under Juárez. This chauffeur has the same muscular body, the same strong jaw. . . ."

Domingo laughed politely. "You are not trying to say that Mateo will ever be the iron man of Mexico?"

"I don't know," Irineo said. "Calles had the same build, and he was a rural school teacher from Sonora. These stocky, firm-jawed men frighten me a little, I can tell you."

Domingo understood what the lawyer meant. It was not really Mateo himself who was so frightening, but rather the fact of Mateo. To the Lawyer, to the Engineer, even, in a measure to himself, the world they had known was tumbling around them, and it was the Mateos who were causing the earthquake. These men from nowhere were taking over the ruins and building a new world out of them—a world in which such families as the Vázquez de Andas, the Mirandas, the Cortés' had no place. The really clever men adjusted themselves to the changes, but for many there was no bending, only breakage. And it was not that they did not approve of bending. It was simply that they did not know how.

Tito came in, bringing with him his bubbling good humor. He told the story of the photographs with much delight, adding, "Domingo does not approve of my scheme."

Domingo shrugged, knowing that anything he might say would be useless.

"I plan to use it as a test case," Tito told the two older men. "The pictures are really very bad, but I believe that advertising —the correct psychological approach—could sell anything. Once I have Bárcenas established as a fad then I can go to the really big men who have something worthwhile to sell, and use Bárcenas to prove my methods." He rubbed his hands delightedly together. "It means that I get my own agency."

"A fad," Domingo repeated coldly. "And after the fad passes, what happens to Bárcenas then?"

"Oh, that." Tito shrugged plump shoulders. "He'll have made more money in two months than he'd make in a year in that place where he is now. Why should he complain?" He turned back to the Engineer and the Lawyer. "Is it not an admirable scheme?"

"I think," Irineo told him dryly, "that you should go in partnership with Domingo's chauffeur. Two such geniuses of salesmanship should surely form a partnership."

Tito swung around toward Domingo. "Is it true that Mateo really sold that lot?"

"It's true," Domingo agreed. "And there is rich cream on the jest. Palma advised me this morning to fire Mateo."

"Ah," Irineo sighed in relief. "It is good to know that the young man is not truly perfect. But," he added, puzzled, "how did you ever resell him the lot, Domingo? Because it is sold, isn't it? You spoke of my drawing up the contract."

"Ay, yes, it is sold. But I didn't resell it. No, Irineo, Mateo is smarter than even you give him credit for being. You see, he knew that the lot has fame as a worthless building proposition, and that Palma would hear about it afterwards and be furious. In fact he might refuse to buy. So he prepared for it."

They were all three watching him, and he chuckled at his own pride in Mateo's methods. "Palma said that Mateo begged him not to buy the lot, because only very clever planning could produce a house on it. In fact Mateo convinced Palma that the mere building of the house would make him famous in Monterrey. And it undoubtedly will." On impulse, he asked, "How did you hear the news so quickly, Irineo?"

"My chauffeur told me."

"And you, Tito?"

"I heard it from a taxi driver."

Domingo snapped his fingers with delight. "I thought so. There's a chauffeur's bar on Cuauhtémoc Street. Mateo kept his promise of making Palma famous. By this morning every soul in Monterrey knows that little man's name."

"Umm," said Tito thoughtfully, "very interesting." He lapsed into silence while the Lawyer and Cortés demanded more details from Domingo.

Tito was still silent when the two young men got in the car to be taken to the Bárcenas studio. He sat in his corner and fixed his eyes on the back of Mateo's head, an expression of intense concentration on his face.

Domingo was glad of the silence, because it left him free to anticipate his meeting with Márgara. Several times during the past week he had been tempted to climb the steps to the picture gallery, but he had not gone.

It seemed incredible to his well ordered mind that he could be in love with a woman he had seen only twice, and one of those times a mere glimpsing in the doorway. Yet last night he had told Verónica that he loved Márgara, and he knew that it was true. I am a fool, he thought. If I were wise I would know that marriage to Verónica would round my life into a perfect circle, most suitable to my family and my place in society. But I am a fool, and I prefer the enchantress to the patient Griselda.

He stretched himself a little and took a deep breath of the crisp air, tainted with the odor of frying onions, of gasoline, of dust, of women's perfumes.

His battle with Verónica had killed the lassitude in him, and he felt buoyant as a ball on water. He admitted honestly to himself that his vanity had been touched by Verónica's determination to marry him; but he was certain that she did not really love him nor anyone.

When a man has been an eligible bachelor for a long time in a city like Monterrey, he quickly learns the rules of the game called "Trapping a Husband." The sideways glances, the softening of the voice, the gentle prods from parents and interested relatives were all a part of the game. Verónica knew the rules as well as he, and exactly how to play them. Many of her friends were getting married, friends who, in their way, had also tried to snare Domingo. It pleased Verónica's vanity to think that she could trap him, and having trapped, hold him against any wild efforts to escape. She is so young, he thought pityingly, so sure of herself. And I must not underrate her cleverness. For her to discover my relationship to Márgara was a very clever thing. From one clue she added the column and got the right answer. And tricked me into admitting it. It will need cleverness to fight her, and strength of will. But I will not marry her, he thought with a grim determination that both pleased and astonished him.

Bárcenas' studio was as lacking in personality as it had been the first day Domingo and Tito found it. Once more the room was empty, and Tito had to rap on the counter to attract attention.

Domingo said, "Perhaps you should make Bárcenas' indifference part of the legend you are building around him," in order to keep Tito from noticing his prowling nervousness.

Just beyond those curtains was Márgara. He could feel his heart fluttering so fast that it was difficult to breathe.

Tito said grimly, "I will have to speak to him about this." He shouted, "Bárcenas. Where are you, man? Bárcenas!"

The curtains parted and Márgara came through. She wore a green coat fastened high about her neck, and a black lace shawl over her smooth black hair. She seemed so beautiful to Domingo that the studio faded from his consciousness and he was lost amongst the feathery vines, the scarlet flowers, in the enchanted jungle of the Xtabay.

Then Márgara bowed her head in greeting, and the spell was broken.

"I came to see my proofs," Tito said petulantly.

She bent and took an envelope from beneath the counter, spread the lavender proof sheets for Tito's inspection. There was no expression on her mask-like face. Domingo felt cut off from her, as though he were a ghost to her, a phantom she could not see.

Tito said over his shoulder, "Come and look at these, Domingo. Which do you think the most suitable?"

Domingo moved slowly to the counter, but he did not take his eyes from Márgara's face until he was so close to her he could smell her faint woman fragrance. And still she did not look at him.

Then he glanced down at the proofs. They were all equally bad. Whatever Bárcenas had been in his past life, Domingo thought, photographer was not his title. The lighting was too flat, so that Tito's round face had a stiff, pasteboard expression. Sparkle was lacking in the eyes, vitality in the flesh.

"They are all the same," Domingo commented indifferently. "I can see little choice."

"This one, I think?" Tito pointed to the most wooden of the poses. "And that one?"

"If you like."

"But which one should be tinted?" Tito asked, and Domingo heard a malicious overtone that was a copy of Brunhilda at her most devilish. My sister is not a good influence for this poor creature, Domingo thought. He looked at Márgara. "Since the señorita is to do the coloring, perhaps she should be the one to choose."

Still she did not look at him. Her voice was as deep and melodic as he remembered it. "The señor's first choice would be best, I think."

She doesn't care, Domingo thought. She knows that all of this is a joke, and she hates us both for it.

"Very well," Tito shrugged. "That one, then. Bárcenas promised them to me on Monday."

"They will be ready," she said.

Tito grinned and lit a cigarette. "And the proofs for the señoritas?"

Márgara, Domingo thought. Look at me, Márgara. You know I had nothing to do with that.

She took a card from a file and examined it. "Their proofs will be ready on Monday with your finished pictures."

Tito rubbed his palms together. "If they are as good as mine, señorita, soon your father will have to move to a new studio you will have so many customers."

Her lids shadowed her eyes, and her carved face betrayed nothing. The desire to touch her was so strong in Domingo that he had to keep his hands deep in his pockets.

"We are very happy here, señor," she told Tito. "We ask little of success. And now, señor, if you will forgive me—I was just going out."

Tito said, "I think I will have good news for your father on Wednesday." He bounced toward the door, swinging toward it and away with his little waltzing steps.

Domingo did not move, still staring at Márgara. She must look at me, she must know I'm here, he thought, and tried to force his will on hers so that she would glance toward him, but she did not. She stood there quietly, gathering the proofs together and putting them back in the envelope. At Tito's impatient call, he had to follow his friend. At the door he turned. She had vanished behind the curtains, and the room was empty again—empty and silent.

"That woman is a strange one," Tito said as they went down the stairs. "But fascinating. Very fascinating." He ran a finger along the thin line of his mustache. "She could enchant a man if there were life in her. But she is too much a statue—too quiet."

Domingo did not answer him.

Mateo had found a parking place almost in front of the studio. Tito bounced into the car's back seat, his mind already busy with something else. "Mateo," he said importantly, "take me to don Primitivo's. There is an idea being born in my mind, and I want you . . ."

"Tito," Domingo said. And more loudly, "Tito!"

"Don't bother me, friend. I am thinking."

"Then think by yourself. I have private business."

Tito's face drooped with sadness. "Always you have business, and I with such a wonderful idea."

In spite of his preoccupation, Domingo had to laugh. "Is it I you want to talk to, friend, or Mateo?"

Tito puffed out his lips and wrinkled his nose. "It's Mateo. But if you go, you take him with you. And the idea is truly magnificent. You see, I thought that . . ."

"Peace," Domingo said quickly. "And take Mateo. I won't need him before three."

"You are certain?" The delighted relief on Tito's face made Domingo shake his head in mock reproval.

"Tito, Tito, how can I be sure whether it is me you love or the things that belong to me? My sister, my business, and now my servant. No matter. Take him, and I put my blessings on you."

He stepped away from the car, smiled at Mateo, who nodded and winked at him, and the car slid into the line of traffic. That wink, that smile, had come from a friendly equal, not a servant. Domingo remembered Irineo Miranda's comments, and shrugged. The world progresses, he thought, and I must hunt a new chauffeur.

Lighting a cigarette, he leaned against the building wall, patiently waiting. Márgara should come downstairs in a few moments, and he preferred speaking to her on the street rather than in the cold seclusion of the studio. Here, the presence of passing people would force her to listen to his explanation, while upstairs she could refuse even to see him.

His cigarette burned steadily with a pale gray ash. Still she did not come. But patience was strong in him, and he did not mind waiting. The flow of people around him interested him, and he watched them with pleasure: the shine boys, the street vendors, the beggars, the hurrying business men and the chattering housewives. A boy on a bicycle passed, balancing a tremendous bread basket on his head. An ice-cream salesman pushing his cart paused with a hopeful expression, then took off his hat and rubbed his head with a bandana handkerchief when Domingo said he wanted none.

"The trouble is," the vendor sighed, "that no one wants to buy ice cream in February. July is a good month, and August, but not February. If my wife were not so lazy, she could make *tacos* for me to sell—hot fragrant *tacos*. But she is so lazy. Are you married, señor?"

Domingo shook his head.

The man gave a long sigh. "Then take my advice, señor. Don't choose a woman who sews with a silver needle." He started pushing his cart, his shrill vendor's cry cutting through the traffic's uproar.

A woman selling lottery lists thrust her wares under Domingo's nose. The long yellow, blue, green, and pink tickets fluttered in the air.

"There will be a great drawing," she confided, "on the first of March. Already I am selling tickets. One complete ticket for a hundred pesos, señor. Last year a Monterrey man won two million pesos. Perhaps this city will have such luck again, eh?" She laughed, her lips rolling back from her pink gums to show a gaping line of teeth. Domingo lazily examined one of the pink tickets. "No such luck for me," he assured her, "but I will buy one of these. The drawing is next month, eh?"

"Yes, señor. A grand prize of two thousand pesos. You do not want a whole ticket?"

"No. I never win the lottery. I'll take a half ticket."

She sniffed in sorrow. "This Monterrey, never spending money. Me, I am from Saltillo, and there the sale of tickets is magnificent, but magnificent."

"Why bother with Monterrey then?" he asked curiously.

She flung out both hands in resignation, the tickets fluttering in the small breeze. "All the money is here, señor. What can a woman do?"

He said consolingly, "No matter. There are two things in which all Mexicans have faith: peace in the cemetery, and wealth from the lottery."

She nodded and passed on, chanting the traditional song of the lottery vendor. Domingo folded his purchase and was sliding it into his wallet as Márgara came through the door.

Seeing him, she paused, and started to retreat toward the stairs, but he snatched off his hat and looked at her so humbly that her lids lowered, and she turned toward the post office.

He thrust his wallet into his pocket, wrapped his fingers around her arm, just above the elbow. She made no effort to free herself, but suffered his hand as a prisoner suffers the chain. When they paused at a street intersection, he said, "I know what you are thinking, Márgara, but I heard nothing of the girls' visit until it was over. Will you believe that?"

She did not answer until they had crossed the street. "Because I did know that I am speaking to you now. Believe me, señor . . ."

"My name is Domingo. I told you on Tuesday . . ."

"We said a great deal Tuesday that should never have been spoken." She began to walk so rapidly that he had to lengthen his stride to keep up with her. "I told you then that any further speech between us was useless."

"But you must listen to me, Márgara. My sister told you that I was engaged to Verónica Miranda. She thought she was telling you the truth, but it was not the truth."

"Indeed, what difference can it make to me to whom you are engaged?" She looked around at him, and his heart leaped at the expression of sadness in her eyes.

"Márgara," he whispered, "you have only to look in your mirror—but that's no good, because you don't look to me the way you look to yourself or to anyone else."

"Precisely." She stopped and faced him. "For some reason

187

you have manufactured a new me in your imagination, and I'm not like that at all."

"I know what you are like. Men have repeated legends about you in the shadows of campfires. . . ."

"You see?" She flung out her hands and started walking again. "You are turning me into a fairy tale."

"To a man enchanted, the Xtabay is not a fairy tale."

"Whatever the Xtabay may be," she commented with a shrug.

He caught his breath, and his grip on her arm made her slow to his slowness. From the beginning he had sensed Bárcenas lied about his background and here was the proof of it. He shook her a little, and her eyes were puzzled. She dipped her body away from him, trying to break free of him.

"Let me go," she said. "People are staring at us. And why are you looking at me so strangely?"

Domingo was confident that once he had pierced her father's masquerade Márgara would admit him to her full confidence. In the story of the Xtabay he had found his weapon. Actually, he perceived, it was a double weapon, the word itself being the knife that would cut the lock of hair from the woman of magic.

Her lips parted slightly, and her eyes were grave and questioning. "What are you thinking, that you look at me so?"

"Márgara, the Xtabay is peculiar to Yucatán. Anyone who has ever lived there would know it."

She stood still, flung back her head. The long line of the throat formed a curve to the chin, and the face was carved from pale wood. He kept his gaze intent on that face, and neither noticed the pedestrians swarming about them, drawing away from them to give them room, leaving them as an island in the midst of busy traffic.

"So you have guessed it," she said. Fury mounted in her. "True, we are not of Yucatán. But what difference does it make to you where we have lived or what is our past?"

"Because I love you," he said steadily. "Because I want to marry you."

She started walking again. "You are a fool. What of the señorita Miranda?"

He told her what had happened at the party, and she listened without comment. Then he told her about Brunhilda's shattering blow to don Rafael's dream, and the pleasure don Rafael had taken in Domingo's rumored engagement. And finally he told her what Verónica had said on Zaragoza Plaza. By this time they had reached the plaza in front of the pink granite expanse of the Governor's Palace. She turned and followed the path that bisected the plaza to the statue of Juárez, and sat down by it. A few poinsettias were still in bloom, and the roses sprayed the air with heavy fragrance. It was one of those sun drenched days that come sometimes in February with color everywhere: the glossy green of orange trees, the rose-pink columns of the Palace, the terra-cotta houses, and in the east the placid bulk of Saddle Mountain darkly blue against the paler blue sky.

But to Domingo the only color was in the green clothes, the gold skin of the woman beside him.

"Perhaps Verónica is right," Márgara said. "Perhaps you are really in love with her."

"Do you believe that?"

"No—yes—I don't know what to believe."

Her hands were clasping each other tightly in her lap. He covered them with his hand. "I love you, Márgara. That you must believe."

She shook her head, tightly compressing her lips.

"That is a foolish thing. How can you be in love with me? How can any man be in love with me?"

His fingers tightened on hers. "But Dr. Velarde is dead. How can he harm you if he is dead?"

She whirled toward him like an animal, and this time there was no mask on her face, only fear, a deep bone fear. Her lips trembled until it was difficult for him to understand what she said.

"What do you know of—that man?"

He moved closer to her, and still holding her hands, he slid the other arm along the back of the bench. He said gently, "Don't be afraid, Márgara. You're with me, my beautiful. How can fear touch you when you are with me?"

"I asked you: what do you know of that man?" Her voice was sharp edged, insistent.

"I recognized the miniature—I located another picture of him."

"Where? Where did you find another picture?"

189

"In the Casasola collection."

"Ay, yes. The Casasola collection." She relaxed and put her elbow on the bench arm, then rested her face against her hand. "They were such good photographers."

"I don't know what your father had to do with Velarde, but Velarde's dead."

She raised her face from her hands, and her lips curved in the ghost of a smile. "Dead? Yes, he's dead. So many are dead. So many."

"Velarde's evil days reached their climax thirty years ago—before you were born."

"I will be forty in September," she said. "I remember him very well." She gave a little snort of laughter. "I remember all of them: The Ratkiller, General Angeles, Huerta, and Dr. Velarde. I remember them very well."

"Márgara, these men are dead. They only touched the fringes of our world. What they did was evil, but we can't help that, and we should not be asked to pay for their evil."

"I told you Tuesday that you had no right to judge. You in your safe world so calmly judging! What do you know of fear? The animals in the fields know more of fear than you. The animals have their caves of refuge. The bull in the arena, facing the sword of death, finds one spot where it believes itself safe. For the first time in thirty years my father has found a place of refuge in this city of money. Here there is progress. Here there are eyes to the future, not languishing memories of the past. Here he felt safe. And now there is no more safety. . . ." Tears trembled on her lashes, glistened in the sun.

"Márgara, no one knows of this but me. Believe me, you are still safe . . ."

"If you found it so easily, others can find it."

"But how, if you keep the miniature hidden . . ."

"The Casasola collection is very complete. My father's picture is in it. To hate sharpened eyes, the resemblance would not be difficult to find."

"Hate?" Domingo said angrily. "But I love you, Márgara."

"Verónica Miranda hates me . . ."

"Now you are searching out trouble. Verónica is a stupid little girl . . ."

"She is a clever little girl. Already she hates me. I could

smell the hate in her yesterday. And if she were clever enough to guess there was anything between you and me, she will hunt her weapon, and she will find it."

"I don't believe it. How could she ever associate you and your father with any person in the Casasola collection?"

"I don't know. But I can't take the risk. My father and I must leave Monterrey tonight."

"But why, Márgara? Why must you run away and hide?"

"I can't tell you. Please," she looked up at him, her eyes pleading, "let me go." He knew that it was not freedom from him at this moment she was asking, but freedom for all the future. He pulled her closer to him. "You love me, too, don't you, Márgara?"

Her eyes dilated until they were black sequins flat against the whites. Then they softened, became remote, withdrawn. She no longer saw his face, but only the face in her mind. "As long as my father lives there can be no love for me. And afterward, perhaps no love either."

"That is foolishness, Márgara."

"No, it is not. And that is why we must go away."

"Márgara, will you listen to me with common sense?" He must break this terror, so that she could reason clearly. "At the moment you are frightened. You can think only of escape. But if you leave here, where will you go?"

"I don't know. Mazatlán, perhaps—no, we've been to Mazatlán. Tampico—I don't know."

"They have the Casasola collection in Tampico, in Mazatlán. Wherever Mexicans gather together in a group you will find copies of it. Even if you went to San Antonio, or Denver, Los Angeles, or New York, there would still be copies of the Casasola collection. Every man who ever fought in the Revolution wants to own that series."

"Yes," she admitted, "that's true, I suppose."

"And if it would serve to identify you here, it would identify you any place."

"Yes. Yes, it would."

"But I am here in Monterrey. Here, my family has a certain influence. I can protect you."

She laughed without humor. "You don't know what you are promising."

"If I can promise it without even knowing who your father is, surely you can accept my protection."

She turned her hands, until his hand was imprisoned in hers. "I wish I could tell you who he is. Everything would be so simple if I could do that. But I can't."

"Don't worry, Márgara." He brushed her hair back from her face. She smiled at him, the tears trapped behind her lids.

"I must go now," she said. "I must have time to think."

"But you won't leave Monterrey?"

"No. You are right. There comes a time when running is no longer valid."

They rose together, and his hand clung to hers, did not want to leave hers. Then she was hurrying away from him, toward the white modernity of the postoffice. The green arrow of her body made the legend of the Xtabay even more realistic. Mediz Bolio had written:

> Ah, you will pursue the Xtabay, and she will escape you like a bird flying. You will never find her. . . .

XVI

Domingo spent Saturday night and all of Sunday in Santa Catarina. He knew that if he remained in Monterrey his family and the Mirandas would expect him to dance attendance upon Verónica, and he had no intention of fanning engagement gossip until he could have a conversation with his father. The only reason he put the interview off at all was because he wanted his father to recover from the blow dealt him by Brunhilda. Yet the passing days seemed to do nothing to strengthen the old man. Every noon, swathed in blankets, he sat in the patio, trying to absorb a little heat from the sun. Doña Otilia, sitting near him, would busily crochet an endless series of doilies, now and then smiling at her husband. Then, when he laid down for his siesta, she would go to the hospital with Brunhilda or Sofía, to sit by Cardito's bed and crochet more doilies.

The road to Santa Catarina led past the hospital. Saturday evening Domingo parked his car on the curve of the half-moon entrance drive, then paused on the steps to look across the valley. Although it was only five-thirty, the winter twilight was closing its arms about the earth, so that this section of the city, resting against the side of the Bishop's Hill, seemed to be enclosed in gray pearl.

Ordinarily Domingo loved this hour that was neither dark nor light but partook of both. There was a melancholy streak in his nature which responded to it. Some lines from Rubén Darío floated through his memory:

> In the twilight, gray and sad,
> I saw the velvet sea.
> The sky profound with pain, I saw.

There was another verse that hovered on the rim of his mind, but when he clutched at it, it slipped away from him, even as Márgara had slipped away.

In front of him the roses oppressed him suddenly. Even the colors of the houses across the road were dull and lifeless in the gray air, and the great wall of mountains in the distance hunched their shoulders against the sky. Mountain . . . that was the line. Something about the voice of the mountain. He almost had the quotation, then it slipped away again. With an exclamation of disgust, he whirled and ran up the steps.

He found his mother sitting in Cardito's room. The boy was asleep, his hair tousled, five days' growth of beard on his face. Domingo bent over his young brother for a moment, his heart warm with love for the boy who was not so much brother as son to him.

Then he went across to his mother, and after kissing her cheek, gravely examined her crocheting. He could feel her eyes watching him, but he kept his head turned slightly from her. "Where is Brunhilda?" he whispered.

She answered in a low voice, "Stop whispering, Domingo. You should know by this time that a full orchestra could not waken Cardito from sleep. Brunhilda has gone down the hall to gossip with some friends."

"Someone else is sick?" he asked blankly, and she chuckled at him.

"Can friends not be in a hospital without illness? No, my oldest, these are Brunhilda's friends who came to inquire about Cardito. She hasn't seen them for two years . . ." her voice trailed into silence at mention of the time, and her needle recommenced its eager consumption of crochet thread.

"Sit down, Domingo. I want to speak to you."

"I can stay only a moment, Mother."

"For that moment, then."

He relaxed on a chair in front of her, snatched at the crochet ball as it slid from her lap, and began pressing it between his hands.

He worshipped his mother, but she had always been as remote as a saint worshipped in a church. When he was small it was Tía Nicanora who spanked him, nursed him through the measles, told him stories of heroes when he was frightened in the dark. His mother was merely the lovely lady who acted as advocate between himself and the stern discipline of his father.

In the evenings he was washed and brushed and taken to her room for a visit. She asked him gentle questions about his small world, to which he gave the proper answers supplied by Tía Nicanora. Doña Otilia was sick a great deal, and he was always warned never to disturb her.

He was aware that in the houses of those below, fathers stopped work for two hours at noon so that they could play with their children, while mothers would not consider leaving their babies with nurses or neighbors while they went to market or out for an evening's fun.

Knowing this, it never occurred to him to resent his own restricted life or envy those luckier children. They belonged to the world below, and he to the world above. In each the cultural pattern was too static for anyone, especially a little boy, to consider changing it.

He was four when Brunhilda was born. Between that time and the year he was ten, his mother spent most of her time lying on a couch. Those were the years of the Great Revolution, and the entire period was chaotic in his memory. His father was gone a great deal, and doña Petra and Tía Nicanora between them kept the house in a constant uproar with their terror of all soldiers, whether Federal or Revolutionary. Through all of this, Domingo's mother went her placid way, so that somehow he identified her with the idea of safety. As long as she was in the house, nothing could hurt himself or Brunhilda.

When he was ten, Sofía was born. Every morning Tía Nicanora took him and the small butterball Brunhilda to church where they prayed that this new baby would live. Domingo knew vaguely that there had been other babies who had not lived. He decided that this new child was extremely important to the happiness of his mother, and he prayed devotedly, not only at mass, but also at odd moments through the day. And Sofía lived.

For two years he felt as though Sofía were his personal contribution to the family. Then another baby was born, and all of his prayers were of no avail. Nor were his prayers for the next one. By the time he was fifteen, when Cardito shrieked his way into the world, Domingo was entering upon that period when the mind of youth is questioning the mind of God. He decided not to pray and await the result. And Cardito lived.

Four children alive, four children dead. The scales were balanced. The doubt of his own contribution toward Sofía's life made him withdraw from her, but Cardito was none of his doing. Cardito started life with only the aid of his own vitality. Cardito was an individual. Cardito was a boy.

Domingo, used to a world of women, was so thankful for Cardito's existence he did not much care whether the boy were the result of God's miracle or Nature's law of survival. The fifteen years between them placed him more in the role of a father. What Tía Nicanora had been to Domingo, Domingo was in turn to his younger brother.

And through the center of this emotional upheaval had floated the quiet figure of doña Otilia, the one certainty in a chaotic world.

Looking at her now, Domingo wondered what type of mind existed behind that face, capable of hysteria over small crises, placidity over big ones. There had been no overtones of disappointment in her voice when she mentioned Brunhilda's name. Seemingly she harbored no resentment for the pain the girl had inflicted on her family.

My mother is an angel, Domingo thought suddenly. A true angel.

On impulse he bent forward and kissed the plump hand that was holding the flashing needle.

195

She smiled at him; patted his head with her other hand.

"I want to ask you about Verónica."

"Mother, there is no time . . ."

"Only one question. Is it truly in your mind to marry her?"

He liked the feel of the crochet ball in his fingers. The thread felt silky and solid, yet when he pressed inward, it thrust back against his palm like rubber. The problem of Verónica was much like this ball. He could lie to his mother, and the problem could snap back against him. Or he could tell her the truth, and perhaps the problem would unwind, form itself into a pattern, even as the doily under doña Otilia's busy fingers.

The lie, of course, was easier, because she wanted him to marry Verónica, but his new strength, strengthened more by his love for Márgara, would not let him lie. Also, it would be easier if she broke the news to don Rafael. The old man could stand the blow better if it came from her.

He said, "No, mother." Then he told her of the party, and what Verónica had said to him on the plaza.

Her sigh was so faint he barely caught it. "I am glad. She is not the girl for you."

"But I thought you wanted me to marry her." He looked at her with surprise. As usual he found himself lost in the maze of his mother's mind.

"Verónica is a good girl," she said gently, then chuckled. The crochet needle flashed in the shaded light. "She came to see me this morning. She asked if I thought she should marry you."

Verónica, he thought, you child of surprises.

"And what did you answer?"

"I told her that my son's life was his own, that I did not dictate to him."

"That was kind of you, mother."

"Very kind, considering that she didn't believe me." Doña Otilia grunted and changed her position a little. He noticed that, intent though she was upon her conversation with him, she flicked frequent glances toward the bed where Cardito was sleeping.

He asked, puzzled, "But why shouldn't she believe you?"

"Domingo." After speaking his name, she paused. Her hands became quiet in her lap, and she bent toward him. "Have I tried in these last years to dominate you—demand explanations of you?"

"No, you have not," he admitted frankly.

196

She nodded as though pleased, and resumed her crocheting. "That is good. With the oldest son it is so difficult. There is never another child like the oldest son. The others, you love them, you watch over them, but the oldest son. . . ."

She pursed her lips, and there was silence while she worked.

He watched her intently, wondering what she was trying to tell him.

She said, "You bring your children into the world, and you watch them grow—not up, but away. They grow away from you, every year is a step farther away. Finally they are grown, and they are people, and you are a person, and there is a wide field between you as there is between you and all the people of the world. You try to bridge that field with love, but unless they also build toward you, it is no good."

"I don't know what you mean."

"You see? I am standing in my field, and you are standing in yours, and I can't reach you, Domingo. I can't reach you."

"But I love you, mother. You know that."

"Of course. But your bridge is higher than mine, because you are my oldest son. You were the first, you see. You stole something from me that the others never had a chance to steal."

"Stole what, mother?"

"I can't tell you. That is the price of living alone in your private field. There is no way for me to tell you." She turned her head slightly, and looked at Cardito. "I wonder. Cardito has been more your son than your brother. Perhaps he stole from you the thing that should have been saved for your eldest son. Ay, don't bother talking to me, Domingo. I am an old woman wandering with words."

Domingo, looking at Cardito, divined his mother's meaning. Individually, he loved his family, but it was as though they were digits in a list of numbers which, added together, were summed up in Cardito. All of his love for his family flowered in his love for Cardito, and if it came to a decision between his own happiness and Cardito's, or between Cardito's and his sisters, or even his parents, there was no question: Cardito would have to come first.

And this was what his mother felt for him, Domingo, the oldest son. He bowed his head in a flash of shame, because he discerned her loneliness. She was stretching out her hand to him across the open field, but the distance was too great. Years ago he might have crossed to meet her, but not now. The space between was wide, and he had lost the talent for building bridges. He had lived too long alone in his secret world.

He said humbly, "I thank you for this speech, mother."

She took a handkerchief from her lavender crepe sleeve and wiped her eyes. "It was foolishness. Pay it no attention. There is one thing more. When you greatly love a person, sometimes you can injure them with an act of love, even when you think you are helping them." She looked directly at Cardito. "You only succeed in destroying yourself."

"I will remember," he answered gravely, and kissed her cheek.

Shyness now built a wall between them. Doña Otilia murmured, "Your single moment is more than devoured."

Accepting this as dismissal, he crossed the room and shifted Cardito's head to a more comfortable position on the pillow. A few minutes later he was headed for Santa Catarina.

It was not until the car had passed into open country that it occurred to him that his mother knew about Serafina. This realization was so overwhelming that he had to stop the car while he stared unseeingly past the mountains to the darkening sky beyond.

She must naturally have been concerned over Serafina's illness, and wormed the truth of the girl's pregnancy from doña Petra. Of all those who knew him best: Sofía, doña Petra, even Tía Nicanora, his mother was the only one who had recognized that the true father was Cardito.

Domingo seemed to see his mother standing beside him. Swiftly, she grew to gigantic proportions, until she was taller than the mountains, and her head pressed against the stars. "Your bridge is higher than mine," she had told him, but it was not true. It was hers that was the higher. Although he could never hope to reach her, she could bend down to him, the pigmy. Yet she did not bend. She stayed aloof, watching him fight his battles, giving him nothing but the sense of her nearness and love.

If she knew about Serafina, the chances were very good that she knew also about Doris. From that battle, too, she had stayed aloof, letting him fight it out alone, when she might so easily have interfered and softened him with her pity into a morose, embittered man.

Now she was telling him not to interfere with Cardito's life. As though a rind peeled back from his memory, a statement of doña Otilia's returned to him. It was after the bicycle episode. The wheel had just been delivered to the house, and Domingo invited her to view it before presenting it to a woebegone Cardito. He had expected her to exclaim over it, but she had not. She merely smiled at him and said, "Your heart is too good, Domingo. Life does not always repay disappointments with such rich rewards."

After all these years, the awareness that he, who had always tried to make Cardito fight his own battles, was actually the greatest barrier to the boy's true independence was not a pleasant medicine. It tasted bitter as quinine. He rested his head against the coolness of the plastic steering wheel to try and calm the whirling storm in his brain. Thus released, his subconscious, obeying his previous command, gravely presented him with the lost lines from Rubén Darío's poem:

> The horn of the horizon
> Bursts into sound.
> It is the vibration of mountains.
> It is the rude chant
> Flung by a lion against the wind.

In spite of himself he began to laugh at remembering such lines in this moment of turmoil. At the moment he was no better than the lion trying to stop the wind by yelling at it.

With an effort he started the car, and drove toward Santa Catarina, the majestic ranges of the Sierra Madres flowing past him on either side.

XVII

On Monday afternoon, Domingo, in his uncle's car, drove to the airport to meet don Agapito, who was returning on the three o'clock plane from México City. And bringing with him Jorge Palafox.

So far Domingo had been able to learn very little about this man who would doubtless soon be his brother-in-law. The family name possessed such glamour that those who had met young Palafox had, Domingo decided, been so enchanted by the name they had not really seen the man himself.

But if he were like certain other young men of great family, Domingo thought, Brunhilda would not marry him if she had to be shut up in a convent. Don Agapito could not be trusted in the matter, nor could Brunhilda. To them, also, the name meant glamour. They were not really capable of judging.

Domingo felt briefly sorry for Tecla, don Agapito's wife. Jorge Palafox was to stay at her house. That morning she had come to doña Otilia and wept copious tears in the study. All of the flowers in her patio were withered, her cook had left her that morning to attend a sick relative, the plumbing would not work in the guest bathroom, and her sister in Saltillo was expecting a baby at any minute. When the milkman delivered a bottle of sour cream, she could accept nothing more, and she had driven to doña Otilia's to be petted and provided with the luxury of an audience for her tears.

Doña Otilia called Domingo in for a conference. About the sister in Saltillo they could do nothing, but the other problems were solved with little difficulty. Doña Petra agreed to lend herself as cook. Mateo was dispatched to fix the plumbing, carrying with him some of doña Otilia's finest plants and two bottles of cream.

Mateo telephoned at noon to say that the plumbing was in good condition. Don Agapito had stuffed the faucets to keep possible leaks from staining the porcelain. "Although," Mateo said, "I don't see how the stains could show. The porcelain is black, with brass fixtures, and a stained glass window over the tub. It is most elegant."

"My uncle Agapito," Domingo said grimly, "is a careful man. He does not believe in taking chances."

Mateo's voice sounded puzzled. "Señor Domingo, if the sun is shining, and one is taking a bath in this tub—well, the water in the black tub would be black, eh? And the sun would send colors down from the window. . . . What I mean to ask, señor Domingo, is how does one know when one gets one's self clean?"

Domingo grinned at the telephone. "Isn't that a problem we should leave for the señor Palafox to solve?"

He could hear Mateo clicking his teeth together in drum rhythm, a habit he had when thinking deeply about something.

"You know that house on the Calle Washington, señor Domingo— the one with the dark green bathroom?"

"Yes."

"I think we should put a stained glass window in it. A peacock, perhaps, in a garden scene."

"We are selling houses, Mateo, not decorating them."

"That house has been on the books for three years. People buy houses for strange reasons. And this is an elegant bathroom— very elegant."

"I'll think about it," Domingo had promised. He was trying to keep his promise now as don Agapito's chauffeur slipped the car through the traffic on Juárez Street. But he had other things to worry him beside the selling of houses.

What would don Agapito say when he learned that Domingo had no intention of marrying Verónica, and every intention of marrying Márgara Bárcenas? Thus crossed in one of his major desires, don Agapito would doubtless hound him out of Monterrey.

Domingo tried to cleanse his mind by concentrating on the passing scene. They were nearing the Juárez Street market. Its blue expanse squatted like a brooding hen over an entire block. This was the market where dishes were sold, and pots and pans. Here could be bought violins, birdcages, straw hats and rope-soled shoes. A bookstall sometimes yielded rich treasure, and in the music section, old records, long out of print, could be found. Few vegetables and little meat were sold here, but there was the pungent odor of dried onions, of garlic, of strange herbs used in making home medicines.

It was a good market. Domingo loved its scented, cool interior. Every city in México had such a market, but this was Monterrey's own, and Domingo loved it because it was Monterrey's, and Monterrey was his city.

It would not be pleasant to leave this laughing, raucous town. For himself, if he stayed, he could outlive the scandal, provided any man dared give him a job after don Agapito had turned against him. But it would be too awkward a position in which to place his family, too much grief for his parents, too much gossip for his sisters.

To marry Márgara meant giving up his city. Then he thought of Márgara, green and gold in the sunlight, and he knew that he loved her even more than he loved his city.

At that moment the true fear touched him. Márgara had a secret to hide. Like most women she doubtless exaggerated its importance, but nevertheless the mere thought of its discovery filled her with terror. What would don Agapito's enmity mean to Márgara? Her secret was bound up in some manner with Dr. Velarde. Of all the men in the Great Revolution, the one man don Agapito most despised was Dr. Velarde. Huerta's doctor was reported to have cut out the tongue of Ruperto Martínez, and don Agapito had been don Ruperto's *compadre,* godfather to the eldest Martínez boy, the one who had been killed fighting the Fascists in Spain.

Domingo cupped his chin in his hand and thought intensely for a few minutes. Dr. Velarde was dead, but for some reason Márgara was still afraid of him—so afraid that the mere mention of his name made her run to cover like a rabbit frightened by the scent of a fox. Bárcenas, then, must have been connected with Velarde. But how? In what capacity?

Let that go for a moment. The important thing was Bárcenas in the present, not Bárcenas in the past. If he had been connected with Velarde, he had no business in Monterrey or any place in México, because all of that group had either been executed or exiled. If Bárcenas were arrested he might have to face a death sentence. Men like don Agapito and the Huerta regime hater, Isaac Fuentes, did not easily forget. They had tremendous influence, the influence of the wealthiest city in the Republic.

Domingo drew a shuddering breath. Until he knew definitely who Bárcenas really was, he must do nothing, in any way, to draw don Agapito's attention to the photographer. He knew his uncle's methods. Once marriage to Márgara was stated, don Agapito would hire detectives to discover her background. No scandal must touch the Vázquez de Anda name. And no act of Domingo's could stop him.

"We are early," the chauffeur said, parking the car in front of the airport's white building. "Eh, señor Domingo, I said we were early."

Domingo blinked his eyes, feeling as though he were recovering consciousness after a deep trance. "Yes," he muttered. "I'm glad. I will go in and wait."

He could feel his legs trembling as he stepped to the ground. When he crossed the curved driveway to the restaurant, he made an inarticulate prayer of thanksgiving to his patron, St. Dominic. He had grazed Márgara's destruction so very close. When he left home, he had been determined to state his course of action to don Agapito, and to the devil with the consequences. But now he knew that such action would prove disastrous.

The tiny restaurant was empty, and only one waiter was on duty. He recognized Domingo, grinned at him, and produced a bottle of icy beer. "Ten minutes early," he said complacently.

Domingo nodded, not really hearing him, because a new fear had touched him. What of Verónica? He had admitted to her that he loved Márgara. And Verónica had no conscience when her desires were thwarted. She might conceive the idea of trying to bribe Márgara to leave Monterrey. And to get the bribe money she would have to go to don Agapito. Domingo gulped down his beer and called for another bottle.

"Five more minutes," the waiter said.

"What?" Domingo looked at him blankly.

"The plane is due in five minutes." The waiter rubbed the top of the gleaming table with his cloth. "There is a newspaper photographer in the waiting room. He says that it is rumored Jorge Palafox is returning from México with your uncle."

"Well?" At the moment Domingo was not interested in Jorge Palafox.

"I was just thinking, señor Domingo. Here is the photographer to take a picture of a man because he belongs to the family Palafox. Yesterday, Calles' daughter arrived on this same plane. No one was here to greet her but her brother. No photographers, no reporters, nothing. And yet in the old days, when her father was president, saints in heaven, it was all she could do to get through the crowds."

"Her father is dead. They are all dead, the leaders of the Great Revolution."

"It doesn't matter. Calles is a great name, too. Why is a Palafox more important than a Calles?"

Domingo said viciously, "The Palafox name has a golden sound —the tinkle of money in a bank. What is even a President of the Republic against the tinkle of money in a bank?"

The waiter raised both hands, shrugged. "Me, I am a Monterrey man. My father says that in the old days we had no such reputation. What has happened to us?"

"Progress," Domingo answered, then raised his head at the distant humming of the plane. "Progress, with wings fastened to it."

He threw some money down and went through the waiting room to the open area that was railed off from the landing field. The plane was a blue insect in the distance. Here comes my enemy, Domingo thought. Once I might have fought him, but I was too much a coward. Now I have the courage, but I am trapped without weapons.

A camera slipped into his line of vision, and he heard the photographer say excitedly, "Be a good friend to me. Help me get a picture of Palafox before don Agapito breaks my camera."

Domingo laughed dryly. "Photograph them together and my uncle will buy you the most magnificent camera in the Republic." After a moment he added, "If you come to the office tomorrow morning, I will buy you a drink."

"Such generosity," the photographer said suspiciously. "What do you want for it?"

"You've already given it to me," Domingo told him. The photographer had opened a door in his mind.

Glamour plus a great fortune was on that plane. The Palafox history was embroidered with the romance Verónica craved. A careful word to don Jonás, a proper presentation to Verónica, the correct handling of Palafox, and any thought of Verónica's marriage to Domingo would evaporate from the Miranda minds.

Domingo had no pity for Brunhilda's dreams. She had possessed none for her family's. Against Márgara's safety, Brunhilda's desire amounted to nothing. As for don Agapito, disappointment would be such a sickness in him, Domingo could marry a thousand Márgaras, without the old man showing any interest in the matter. Once the marriage was consummated, don Agapito would protect anyone, including the infamous Dr. Velarde, to prevent scandal touching the Vázquez de Andas.

Domingo thought briefly of taking Márgara to Saltillo tomorrow, marrying her, and then announcing the news to his family. This idea slid from his mind as quickly as it appeared. Elopements belonged to the world below, not to the world above.

Marriage to Márgara meant the civil ceremony at nine, and mass in the cathedral at eleven, not a coldly legal performance in a Saltillo judge's office.

The best plan was to focus don Agapito's attention so strongly on Palafox, he would have no time for his nephew's affairs.

Domingo smiled and advanced to meet the plane.

Jorge Palafox was thirty-six years old, slenderly distinguished, with a long narrow face, a proud, high bridged nose, an English mustache outlining a sensitive mouth. But it was his eyes that attracted immediate attention. The lids, too long for the eyeballs, were hooded like a hawk's. His hair was so smoothly black it was startling to notice how blue his eyes were behind those hooded lids.

His Spanish was faintly tinged with an accent that came from speaking French as a child. His mother Jeanne was the second daughter of the Comte de St. Aubert. There were many marriages between French and Mexican families in the eighties and nineties.

The Palafox had given one viceroy to México, one to Perú. In the Revolution of 1810, they retired to Spain, but returned in time to support Iturbide during his single year of empire. Next they hitched their fortune to Santa Anna's star, shielded their faces in horror at the mention of democratic Juárez, and welcomed the Hapsburg Maximilian with open arms. The Palafox heir accompanied Carlota to Paris; later preferred Parisian exile to Mexican Republicanism. Ten years after Díaz came to power, the Palafox returned once more, bringing French gold with them. Joining the *Científicos,* the small group of men who believed that government was a science, the people an experiment in chemistry, the Palafox helped rule México's destiny for twenty years.

Then came December, 1910. Díaz, an old man, weakened by power into stubbornness, insisted on supporting Ramón Corral as vice president. Corral was the Republic's most unpopular man. The people hated him, threw mud at his carriage, tore down his election posters. But Díaz still believed his will was greater than the people's.

Sebastián Palafox saw the handwriting on the wall. The days of Díaz were finished, and with him the days of the Terrazas of Chihuahua, the Reyes of Monterrey; the Palafoxes of México; all the great families. Their carved work was soon to be destroyed. The sound of axes and hammers was growing.

Transferring his bank account to Paris, Santiago Palafox took his French wife home. On January 12, 1911, she gave birth to young Jorge, lived long enough to smile at him, and then slipped away into death.

The only son of a wealthy, indulgent father who never re-married, Jorge's growing body delighted in athletics, and he had a magic hand with horses. From the time he was nineteen, women were cherries ripe to his plucking. When he was twenty-three he married Diane Fentris, an English girl. One year later Jorge waited at Croyden for a plane that never arrived. His father and his wife were lost together in the Channel.

During 1935, Jorge traveled, mostly in China and India. Then he went to Egypt and nearly broke his leg in a tumble down a pyramid. A fellow traveler laughed at his accident. "Why, climbing these pyramids is child's play compared to your own Mexican pyramids at Teotihuacán. You should be able to run up these like one of your mountain goats."

Jorge saw no reason to tell this man that although he traveled on a Mexican passport, México itself he had never seen. He had visited the States and Central America, but the jungle lands, the desert wastes, the plateaus and mountain ranges of his own country were unknown to him.

Within a month he landed in Veracruz. On the train going to México City a man told him, "I envy few men anything, but this I do envy: a man's first glimpse of the City. I was born there, grew up there, but to a stranger coming upon it, no matter how well prepared, it must seem a very miracle of a City."

To Jorge it was a miracle. Rio de Janeiro was more beautiful, Paris more captivating, London more mysterious, New York more brilliant, but this was his own city. His family had walked these streets for three centuries. One avenue was named for his grand-father, the viceroy. Every tree in the Alameda, which one of his ancestors had helped to plan, whispered secrets to him. Each colonial building seemed to recognize him, murmur little greetings to him. And he, who for a year had been completely alone, was now no longer alone. The City caressed him, soothed his troubled spirit, brought him peace.

He bought a house in Chapultepec Heights, and reopened acquaintance with old friends of his father's. His polo was good enough to elect him to the national team, and he played against old team-mates in Argentina, in Brazil, in Chile, not as in the old days, as Jorge Palafox, but as a representative of México. After twenty-five years he had found his country, and he delighted in it. In his bedroom a candle burned perpetually before a lithograph of the brown-skinned Virgin of Guadalupe. No woman could compete with her for charm.

But, as he later told Domingo, something was still lacking. He found safety in his country, delight in his city, but he was not contented. His father's friends were not his friends. His mind and theirs did not meet in true companionship.

He started traveling again, fishing off Mazatlán, hunting wildcats near Tampico, exploring Maya ruins in Yucatán and Oaxaca, but the restlessness stayed with him.

Once more he returned to the Capital, decided to try business, turned his money into the traditional channel of his family: banking.

On a business trip to New York, a relative by marriage introduced him to her house guest, Brunhilda Vázquez de Anda. Her plump prettiness, her bubbling humor, her childish ways amused him. He began to wonder if he should marry again. He knew that he could never love another woman as he had loved his first wife, but the love of twenty-three is not the love of thirty-six, and Brunhilda was a charming playmate.

When he returned to México City, he met her uncle Agapito. The man's force, his great personal charm fascinated Jorge. And more than that, don Agapito's description of Monterrey, the famous "Stingy City" intrigued him. Don Agapito was so certain of his city's industrial future, of her power as one of the key cities on the great highway that soon would stretch from Canada to Brazil.

"To a man who loves beauty," don Agapito said, "Monterrey is not beautiful. But to a man who loves power, she is magnificent."

"I must see your city," Jorge told him, and the result was this invitation.

The first man he met in Monterrey was Domingo Vázquez de Anda.

At first Domingo could not decide whether he liked Jorge Palafox. The man's smooth elegance both interested and repelled him. There was a preciousness about him that Domingo did not quite like. He seemed so completely a person of his own environment that it was impossible to visualize him in any other. When he was relaxed in a chair, a cigarette held loosely between his fingers, he was more an illustration in a smart magazine than a living man.

At don Agapito's request, Domingo introduced Jorge to the Casino and the Country Club. They played golf, they played tennis, and in the late afternoons they took Brunhilda and Sofía to drink cocktails in the lounge at Sanborn's, in the Mexican Room at the Hotel Ancira.

Don Agapito arranged for Jorge to meet the industrial giants of Monterrey. At late luncheons he listened to don Roberto Sada, to don Jesús Barrera, to don Mariano Hernandez, to all the men who guided Monterrey's destiny, discussing their city and their city's future. Domingo began to notice that Jorge did little talking himself. He had a trick of listening, so that he seemed to be the center of conversation without contributing particularly to it.

On Thursday night they went to the opera. This opera, *La Traviata*, was a pet scheme of the señora Miranda's. As chairman of the Monterrey Symphony Society she would decide, at periodic intervals, that the time had come when Monterrey needed cultural music.

Her plans for the Little Theatre meeting with what she called "Obstinate refusal" from everyone (the girls refused to act anything but sympathetic roles; the boys, fearful of offstage fiancées, would not interpret romantic lovers), she was determined that Monterrey should have a dramatic offering whether it was wanted or not. A clever advance agent heard of her, and the result was the presentation of the señorita Ofelia Mabel (accented on the last syllable) as Violetta in the musical version of *Camille*.

When approached by the señora Miranda, don Agapito, delighted at the rumors of Domingo's attentions to Verónica, subscribed to a box. The Vázquez de Andas, the Mirandas, and Jorge Palafox shared it. Domingo thanked St. Dominic that don Agapito hated opera, for don Agapito's eyes were keen, and he would have known immediately that matters were not smooth between his nephew and Verónica.

Domingo had to admit that she looked very lovely tonight in blue lace, with a necklace of sapphires that once belonged to the romantically dead Graciela. Brunhilda was in pink satin with a square neckline and long sleeves. Few women in Monterrey would have the courage to indulge in such severity, with no prettiness to soften it and make it feminine. Domingo wondered if don Agapito had paid for that dress also, and glanced at Jorge Palafox, an illustration in white tie and tails.

Jorge was watching Sofía. In honor of the occasion she had put on her best evening dress, oyster white at the shoulders, shading, by imperceptible degrees, to dark brown at the hem. Domingo remembered watching her dye the chiffon, cut it out and make it. She had found a string of topazes in her mother's jewel box, and doña Otilia had brushed the black hair to gleaming smoothness, then threaded the yellow stones through the thick curls.

Sofía was sitting in front of Domingo, bending forward a little to watch the people enter the auditorium. Once she borrowed her mother's opera glasses and made a quick survey of the gallery. Then she turned and smiled at Domingo, offered him the glasses.

"There is doña Petra in the front row upstairs, and Florinda is with her."

Domingo glanced up. "Mateo is sitting just behind them."

"Is he?" she asked indifferently, and leaned to one side to wave to a friend in an opposite box.

"Who is Mateo?" Jorge Palafox asked suddenly.

Domingo, surprised at this interest, told him briefly of the chauffeur and his talent for selling real estate.

Jorge, still looking at Sofía, said, "I must talk to him. Perhaps I should buy some real estate."

Domingo frowned, puzzled by an overtone he did not quite understand in Jorge's voice, then forgot it as he answered some question of the señora Miranda's.

The señora was indulging in a wellbred tantrum. Don Jonás and don Agapito had discovered at the last moment that they had important business to discuss. They were prostrate with shame, but they could not attend the opera. No, the business could not wait until morning. It had to do with an oil lease, and the leaser was leaving Monterrey early the next day. Both she and Tecla were well aware that their husbands were playing a game of billiards in the Casino at this same moment, but where Tecla was resigned, the señora was furious. Doña Otilia thought it all very funny, and felt a little proud, because don Rafael had enough courage to say that he loved music too much to hear it murdered by the señorita Ofelia Mabel (with accent on the last syllable).

Don Lucio, therefore, represented the older generation of men. His evening clothes, which he had bought twenty years ago when he was a taller and plumper man, did not so much clothe as enfold him. He wore an expression of such resigned patience that Domingo could not look at him for fear of laughing.

Brunhilda tapped Domingo on one knee. "Did you give the servants money for tickets?"

"No," Domingo confessed, feeling a little ashamed. "I meant to say something to Mateo, but I forgot it."

"Then where did they get the money? Those first gallery seats are expensive."

"I bought them," Jorge said. "I hope you don't mind."

Domingo and Brunhilda stared at him in amazement. Sofía also glanced around at him. His tanned skin showed a line of red at the cheekbones. "Doña Petra asked me what an opera was. I thought it was easier for her to come and see for herself than to explain it."

"How kind of you," Brunhilda murmured, fluttering her lashes at him.

Verónica said, "I doubt if she'll be any the wiser when she leaves. As for Mateo and Florinda—their food is cinema, not opera."

Sofía's nostrils flared with anger. "They will probably enjoy this performance more than we do, Verónica. They will if it has any real music in it."

"Stop being so defensive about servants," Verónica snapped. "The last week if one mentions a servant breathes, you are ready to make a speech. You should join the servant's syndicate."

The lowering of the house lights prevented the argument from growing stronger.

Domingo bent forward in the darkness and put his hand on Sofía's shoulder. "You are very beautiful tonight," he murmured in her ear. She laid her cheek against his hand for a moment, then straightened as the orchestra began the overture. He smiled fondly at her. Could Sofía's new softness, he wondered, be a defense against Brunhilda's selfishness? Sofía is beautiful. Even Jorge Palafox, accustomed to beautiful women, sees it.

He felt a weight on his knee, and stiffened as he realized that it was Verónica's hand touching him in the darkness. He gently took her hand and returned it to her lap, then whispered to her through the clash of music, "Behave yourself."

She whispered back, "Ten bridesmaids, dressed in yellow. I chose the pattern for their dresses this morning."

When Verdi wrote *La Traviata,* he indicated that the setting was Paris in the 1840's. The señorita Ofelia Mabel, deciding that a universal work could be presented in any period, chose México City in 1910. Since she was quite short and stout, she was under the impression that the form fitting clothes of 1910 were more becoming to her than the full skirts of the '40's.

Therefore the curtain rose on a typical *diner galant,* long tables covered with skimpy cloths, paper napkins folded arrow-shape and thrust upright in glasses, and bottles of beer scattered around with the Carta Blanca label prominently displayed to the audience, since Carta Blanca beer was a product of Monterrey's famous brewery.

As the actors wandered on stage, laughing and chattering amongst themselves, Domingo could feel Jorge Palafox stiffen. Costumes ranged from modern evening gowns, through uniforms of Balkan splendor, to a medieval page.

The orchestra ceased playing, since none of these people were singing. Instead they chattered gayly in Spanish, until a burst of music heralded Violetta's regal entrance. The señorita Mabel wanted her voice to shine like a jewel, so she was very careful to have no competition. She permitted Alfredo, her lover, to sing, but no one else. All the others, Alfredo's father; Aninna, the confidant; the dandified Viscount, the ponderous solemn doctor, spoke their Spanish lines with passion, almost with abandon, using the broad gesture, the hand clutching at the heart. The moment they stepped forward for a scene, the music in the pit stopped, and the musicians relaxed for a brief rest until the principals should again need their services. Italian was sung, of course, but the transition from Spanish to Italian was so smooth that the audience never noticed it. Also, the señora Miranda told her startled guests during the first intermission, no one has ever been able to understand a singer's words. Much better to have part of it spoken. That way the audience had no difficulty in understanding the tragedy.

Jorge Palafox, smoking a between-the-acts cigarette with Domingo, was enchanted. "I have never seen anything like it. The voices are of no consequence—they can be ignored. But the speaking parts! And those beer bottles! It is really magnificent."

Domingo laughed, but he shook his head in protest. For some reason he could not explain, Jorge's attitude irritated him. He sounds like a tourist, Domingo thought, and then hastily smothered the idea. One did not compare one's friends to tourists. "Monterrey is not always this naïve," he said. "This theater has been host to Heifitz, Argentina, Levine. The great actor, Fernando Soler was here last November with his company. It was excellent."

"Ay," said Jorge, "to have such artists is good. But to find such a production of *Traviata* in a city of this size. I have seen *Traviata* in Paris, in Milán, in Buenos Aires. The finest voices, the most magnificent productions, and I was bored. I do not enjoy opera, you understand. I came tonight expecting to be bored." His teeth flashed whitely beneath the line of his mustache as he laughed. "I can assure you I am not bored. The performance enchants me. The audience enchants me. I tell you, man, I think I am beginning to love your city."

A tourist speech, the imp in Domingo's mind repeated.

The three gongs rang for the third act, and they returned to their seats.

It was an act charged with drama. The doctor warned Violetta that she would soon die, and left alone she wept over the cruel whims of fate. Alfredo, filled with remorse, came to comfort her. Before the audience's enchanted eyes she grew stronger, danced about the stage, her one hundred and seventy pounds making the scenery tremble. Alfredo's father entered, remorseful that he had divided two lovers for so long. He said so, in Spanish, very loudly, with much beating of his breast. The doctor came in, and the maid. For a few minutes every one was extremely sad. Then the orchestra conductor tapped his stand loudly with his baton, the musicians put down their instruments, and the cast settled themselves on convenient chairs.

There was a long pause. People looked curiously at each other. What was going to happen now?

Jorge wanted to know what was wrong.

Don Lucio said, "Perhaps they are tired and desire a short rest."

At that moment a small man in ill-fitting evening clothes walked out on the stage. One arm clutched a violin to him. In the other hand he carried a metal music stand. He made no speech, paid no attention to either audience or opera troupe. After putting up the stand, he set some music on it, opened his first selection, placed his violin under his chin, and with many flourishes of the bow, began Augustín Lara's popular melody, "Farolito," the Street Lamp. He was a bad violinist, but he had an instinct for tempos, and when he finished the house shook with applause.

Domingo recognized Mateo's voice shouting from the gallery, "I Carry My Forty-Five." This choice pleased the audience, and they yelled in unison.

The violinist smiled, held up his hand, searched among his sheets of music. When he found the piece, he beamed as though he had won a victory, and he played it with such vigor that Domingo privately wondered why the violin did not shake to pieces.

Someone started singing the chorus:

> I carry my forty-five
> With which to kill traitors. . . .

The words were picked up by others, and soon everyone was singing. When the violinist gave them a final chord more songs were demanded, and he played on for nearly forty-five minutes.

"Marvelous," Jorge Palafox repeated over and over.

Stop it, Domingo thought with aggravation. It is not marvelous. It is natural. The man wants to play, he plays. The people want to sing, they sing. There is nothing "marvelous" about it.

The little man finally came to the end of his repertoire. He smiled, bowed, picked up his music stand and trotted out. The audience kept on applauding. He made three bows, then waved his hand to the conductor. The performers took their places with self-conscious little pats at their costumes, the musicians started the finale, and the opera, which had once, in Verdi's mind, been titled *La Traviata* came to its tragic close.

Palafox snatched up the señora Miranda's hand and kissed it. "I have never had an evening of such enchantment in the theater. Never."

She smiled flutteringly at him, then looked around at the others with a helpless raising of the eyebrows. Verónica muttered, "I thought it was stupid." Brunhilda caught her arm, and pressed it with such force that Domingo could later see the finger marks.

"Very quaint," Brunhilda said firmly. "But I can assure you that the Symphony Society brings us also Heifitz, Ezio Pinza, doesn't it, señora?"

Doña Otilia said placidly, "If we enjoy it, what difference does it make how insignificant the performance? This will make an amusing story for your father, Brunhilda."

The girl smiled, chattered nervously as they made their way slowly through the crowd, bowing to acquaintances. Don Lucio, muttering to Domingo that he was going to don Primitivo's, was swallowed up in the crowd. As they neared the door, Verónica touched Domingo's arm, murmured, "There to the right. Isn't that Tito?"

But before he could glance that way Brunhilda poked him in the back. "Domingo, look to the left, quickly, the woman in the green coat."

It was the mention of the color that snapped his head around. There were two men standing between himself and Márgara. For a fraction of a second no one was there, not the men, not his family, not Verónica, no one but himself and the green and gold that was Márgara. Then Brunhilda spoke again and he was sucked from the airy heights into the foyer, and Márgara passed through the door.

"That was the woman from Bárcenas' studio . . . the one you missed seeing when you went with Tito. Remember, we told you about her?"

"I remember," he said, looking around at Verónica. Her mouth was twisted into the semblance of a smile, but her eyes were stormy with jealousy.

"Where did you say Tito was?" he asked coldly, and she shrugged as she answered, "I thought I saw him on the right. Perhaps I was mistaken."

They had to wait a few minutes on the sidewalk for Mateo. Tecla wanted the Mirandas to go with her in her car, but Jorge Palafox decided to stay with Domingo. Perhaps they could join don Agapito in a late drink at the Casino? Brunhilda was delighted with this arrangement. There was triumph in her as she allowed Jorge to hand her into the car beside her mother. Then Sofía entered, and this left the front seat to be shared by Mateo, Domingo and Jorge.

When the car, with the aid of much honking from automobiles in the rear, finally joined the line of traffic, Brunhilda said petulantly, "It was a charming interlude but what was the reason for the violinist?"

Domingo thought, Why does she work so hard to impress

Palafox? She didn't really think it charming. Brunhilda hates anything that is out of pattern. She is truly the most conservative of us all, my poor flutter-brained Brunhilda.

"How I enjoyed that man," Jorge said. "Does anyone know who he was?"

"My brother-in-law," Mateo said. And to Domingo, "I told you about him—the musician who married my sister."

"But why did he play, and at such a point in the opera?" Brunhilda persisted.

"The management thought the opera was too sad," Mateo told her. "The management thought there should be a little interlude of laughter before the heroine died. Too much tragedy, the management thought, is not good for anyone."

"A magnificent idea," Jorge Palafox said, the laughter deep in his voice. "I wish more managements were of the same opinion."

"But why did they hire such a bad violinist?" Brunhilda demanded.

Sofía stirred beside her, said coldly, "And who gives you leave to judge what is good and what is bad? The audience liked him, and I liked him. I liked him very much indeed. Much better than the opera. Much better."

After a pause Mateo said, "I will tell my brother-in-law what you said, niña Sofía. He will be pleased. Tonight was a night of triumph for him. He will be very pleased."

"I am glad he had such a success," said doña Otilia gently, then curved the conversation into other lines.

Domingo, taking no part in the new chatter, was glad that Sofía had defended the little violinist. Sitting so close to Mateo, he had felt the chauffeur's reaction to Brunhilda's thoughtlessness. My sister is like a wasp stinging, he thought. She hurts everyone she touches, and I don't think she means to hurt. She is merely selfish, just as Verónica is selfish."

Remembering Verónica's flash of jealousy tonight, he was frightened. If she lashes out at me in public where Uncle Agapito can hear her, what will I do? What in God's name will I do?

Mateo stopped the car in front of the house, and Jorge Palafox said goodnight to the women. He kissed doña Otilia's fingers and shook hands with Brunhilda. But he did not touch Sofía. He bowed to her, very formally, and she as formally returned his bow.

When he and Domingo were in the car again, Domingo asked

Mateo where don Agapito might be. Before Mateo could answer, Palafox said:

"He is at the Casino. He told me he was going there. But is there nowhere else to buy a drink but at the Casino or the Ancira? In all Monterrey is there no place where a man can go and have man's talk?"

After a moment's hesitation, Domingo said, "Take us to don Primitivo's, Mateo. After that, you can go to bed. We'll get a taxi when we're ready."

Don Primitivo's was, as usual at this late hour, filled with customers. The great man greeted them jovially, and led them to a table where don Lucio was consuming a plate of broiled kid.

Jorge Palafox sniffed it, decided that he also wanted a plate of it. "Can you imagine," he demanded of don Primitivo, "I never tasted true Mexican cooking until I was twenty-five? I have much time to make up."

Don Primitivo nodded solemnly. "We must correct that," he said.

Domingo said he wanted only an *aguacate* sandwich and a glass of beer. He said he had respect for his stomach, and did not want young goats chasing him through nightmares.

"My nephew," don Lucio explained to Jorge Palafox, "is an old man, a very old man. Now don Primitivo and I are still infants. We do not have to watch our diet."

Jorge, his mouth full of the succulent meat, grinned at him. As soon as he swallowed, he said, "I hear you collect correspondence courses."

Don Lucio dipped a tortilla in chili sauce. "Has my brother Agapito been telling you tales of me?"

"He only told me about the courses. I was much interested. That is the way I was educated, you know."

The men looked at him curiously. Jorge said, "My father had strange ideas of education. All day I went to school, but at night I had to take correspondence courses in finance, government. I've taken about fifteen such courses. Believe me, friend, I understand what patience, what industry, what self-discipline such a course demands."

Don Lucio pushed his chair back, folded his arms, and stared at the young man. Don Primitivo wiped the top of the table with his cloth. "Did you take any courses in Mexican history?"

"Three or four. I can't remember."

"Did you ever hear of a song called, 'Farewell, Mamá Carlota'?"

"Riva Palacios wrote it, didn't he?"

"The same," don Primitivo said ponderously. "General Riva Palacios. Do you know how he wrote it?"

Palafox frowned, pulled at his ear lobe. "There was a story— I'm not quite clear about it—something to do with an envelope."

"Ahhh," said don Primitivo. He took a deep breath and hitched his trousers higher around his fat waist. Don Lucio took a complacent sip of beer.

Knowing that the time for the telling of the story had come, Domingo slipped quietly away from the table and went out on the street. It's all right, he thought. They like him. And he likes them. After a while they will sing together, and he will have a very fine time. Monterrey has captured him this night. If he stays here and marries Brunhilda, in time he will inherit my uncle Agapito's bank, and the Palafox name will bring luster to my city.

He walked quickly through the chilly streets to warm his blood. He remembered his plan to trip Jorge Palafox into marriage with Verónica. Everything about the man, his distinction, his personal charm, his money, his great name, was true bait for a Monterrey girl. But during these past days Domingo had come to know and respect Jorge Palafox. True, there was a flavor about him that was not quite Mexican, but the man was worth more than Verónica, worth more than Brunhilda. Domingo could not bring himself to aid in the trapping of Palafox in order to free himself. No, not even to free Márgara.

He lifted his face up to the star-spangled vastness of the sky. Had not such planning stamped him with the chief vice of the Vázquez de Andas, which was to try and move human beings as though they were problems in chess rather than free born individuals? Was he so vain that he might casually plan: I shall make myself free to marry Márgara by trapping Jorge Palafox into marriage with Verónica? That would have been don Agapito's way, but it was not Domingo's.

He sat on a ledge thrust out by a corner of a building and watched the moon flirting with a nearby star. It was a full moon tonight and he could see the rabbit in it, squatting on its little haunches, its long ears tilted forward better to hear the voice of the Fair God. The old legend Tía Nicanora had told him as a child returned to him:

"There was this little boy, very selfish, very wicked. His name was Hualpa, and he killed small animals, not for food but for sport. Because he was so strong, so arrogant, the other boys who lived in his village thought him very grand, and all the things he did, they did. Then came the great feast of the Fair God. The village went on pilgrimage to the Temple in the City, but Hualpa would not go. He was so proud he said that he was equal to the Fair God, and would carry no fruits or vegetables to the Temple's altar. 'The War God is my god,' he cried, 'this god of the fields and streams, this god of small beasts and birds, this gentle peaceful god is not for me.'

"The other boys were frightened by such blasphemy. His mother wept, and his father also. But Hualpa laughed, and ran away into the forests, and killed a rabbit because it gave him pleasure to see the tiny creature die.

"As he went home that evening, swinging the dead rabbit by its ears, he saw an old woman crouched by the road that led into the deserted village; for, mind you, everyone in the village except Hualpa had gone to the festival. This old woman was weeping because she was hungry. She begged the rabbit of Hualpa that she might eat. He laughed at her and told her she was a weak thing, not worth staying alive. 'No one,' he said, 'should be alive but the strong and proud. Die then if you are too weak to find food for yourself.' He tossed the rabbit up on the roof of the house where she could not reach it, put his hands on his hips, flung back his head, and laughed at the old woman who was too weak to live.

"The old woman said nothing. She merely looked at him. But he felt a grinding pain in his bones. He felt his ears stretch longer and longer. He felt his hands turn into paws. He felt himself shrink smaller and smaller, until every blade of grass widened to the size of a tree trunk, and every tree trunk widened to the size of a house, and every house widened beyond the reach of his eyesight. He tried to cry out, but there was only a squeak in his throat. He tried to run, but he found himself leaping in great bounds. At last he encountered a stream. He was afraid to peer into it, but he had to peer into it. Then he knew that what he had feared was really true. He had changed into a rabbit.

"During the next year the arrogance, the pride of strength,

218

was washed out of him. The boys he had taught so well were always trying to trap him. The larger animals were constantly on his trail to kill and eat him. Then, on the eve of the Fair God's festival, his own father attempted to catch him and take him as an offering to the Temple. He escaped, but he sat by the stream and added his tears to the water. He knew then that even the smallest beast has the right to the peace of freedom.

"As the twilight darkened he thought perhaps, if he went humbly to the Temple, the Fair God might take pity upon him and change him back into a boy. He started off on the long journey to the city and the festival.

"Many people were on the road, but they did not notice the tiny creature. The road was long, his legs were short, and after a while he grew very tired. He paused to rest, his heart pumping for fear someone would see him and trap him, now that he was too tired to evade them. But no one was near except an old beggar, crouching in a ditch.

"From time to time the old man would call out, 'I am so hungry. Aid me or I will die.' But none of the marching pilgrims heard him. Or if they did, they paid him no attention.

"Hualpa looked at the beggar for a long time. Once in the proud days he had refused an old woman food. Now he had no food to offer. He thought of the Fair God, so grand in the temple. In his tiredness he knew that the God had so many creatures to watch over that the problems of one rabbit were of no account. He crept closer to the old beggar. Pushing his nose against the beggar's hand, he remembered that the very young and the very old can hear the voices of the animals.

" 'Old man,' he whispered, 'eat me to cure your hunger.'

" 'Do you know what you are giving?' the old man asked. 'It is your life you are giving.'

"Hualpa shivered in his rabbit's form. 'Tomorrow the boys will kill me for sport, or a pilgrim will kill me for food. They are clever, and I am no longer clever. They will know how to trap me. Better for you to eat me, than for them to have me for sport.'

" 'Where is the arrogance, where is the pride?' the old man asked. 'Is this a true humility?'

"Hualpa, the rabbit, wanted to answer him, but he was afraid. The skin of the old man had begun to shine until it seemed the night was as bright as the sun-cradled day. He grew then, taller than the distant Temple, taller than the clouds. The stars were a necklace on his breast. Hualpa, crouching close to the earth, was gently lifted on one giant palm, drawn up to the face that was broader than the earth, whiter than the tender blossoms of the *yuca*. Trembling on that palm, Hualpa could see the eyes that were as blue as feathers from a peacock's tail, the hair that was yellow as cantalope meat. And Hualpa knew that this was the Fair God, and that he should be afraid, but he was not afraid. The love in the face that was broader than the earth, strengthened him, and he was not afraid.

"Then the Fair God spoke and his voice was louder than the wind in a tempest, louder than the crash of thunder, and sweet as a birdsong. 'You have truly learned your lesson, my tiny servant, and so I am going to set you in the moon. Then all who see you sitting in the moon will remember your lesson; they will remember that when they harm my children they do even greater harm to themselves.'

"That is why, on clear nights, when the moon is full, we can see Hualpa sitting there to remind us to love all things, not with arrogance, but with humility."

Domingo smiled up at the rabbit. The clear air of childhood had washed his mind clean of selfish plans. Feeling much better, he walked slowly home thinking of Márgara.

XVIII

The next morning Domingo went to a small bookshop on the Avenida Madero and bought a complete series of the Casasola collection. He realized that he was doubtless adding a fifth foot to the cat, but he could not help it. Márgara's terror of discovery was so very great that he was afraid to take a step in any direction unless he knew exactly what was waiting at the end of the chosen path.

In his imagination, don Agapito was a shadow looming over Márgara, threatening to cut her away forever from the sun, and that shadows had to be converted into smoke, blown away by the wind that was Domingo.

220

Taking the magazines back to the office, he sat down at his desk and took a magnifying glass from the drawer. Picture after picture he examined, even the shadowy heads in the background. He refused to be sidetracked by interesting glimpses of General Reyes, of don Santiago Palafox, of his own grandfather. At the moment he was concerned only with the man Bárcenas. Márgara had stated definitely that his picture was in this collection. Domingo leaned back and tried to visualize Bárcenas, not as he was now, but as he must have been twenty years ago. A fuller face, perhaps, a heavy mustache of the period, hair thicker and black. There was no resembling portrait in Volume I. He was certain, now that the photographer had not been prominent in the early Díaz period.

The second volume reviewed the 1910 presidential campaign, and the centennial celebration of México as a Republic. There was a report of the Díaz-Taft meeting at El Paso, and of Henry Lane Wilson's arrival in Mexico City as the new ambassador from the United States. But there was not one figure, bare-headed, in derby, silk hat or helmet that might in any way be identified with Bárcenas.

The third volume, covering October, 1910, to May 25, 1911, showed a large photograph of Santiago Palafox with an interview stating why he was sailing for France. His rejection of Ramón Corral was emphasized. That interview had been given to the newspapers in December, 1910. Doubtless, Domingo thought, government officials, re-reading it in 1936, decided that Santiago Palafox could not be considered a traitor to the Mexican people, and that young Jorge might therefore be permitted to return to his own country. The resemblance between Jorge and his father was remarkable. Jorge might almost be Santiago Palafox reproduced in a new generation.

There was still no sign of Bárcenas.

Afraid that such intense concentration would make him miss the picture he so much wanted to find, Domingo left word with his secretary that he could be found at Sanborn's.

He sat in the beautiful, glass covered patio of the famous restaurant, drinking coffee he hardly tasted. Tito found him there and slid into the booth across from him.

"Friend," the plump young man said dolefully, after ordering a strawberry tart, "I want you to speak to Mateo for me. He has confidence in your judgment. You should be able to persuade him."

Domingo, flicking his mind aside from the problem of Márgara, stared with puzzled eyes at his friend.

"What are you talking about?"

"I want Mateo to come into my advertising agency with me, but he insists he wants to sell real estate."

"Are you serious, Tito?"

A change came over the plump face. It was no longer laughing and young, but drawn and tired.

"Everyone makes fun of me, I know that. I am a man of little importance . . ."

"I didn't mean . . ."

"I know." Tito fitted a cigarette into his amber holder, made a small ceremony of lighting it. "I am thirty-seven years old, and I have been with the newspaper for fifteen years. I am head of their advertising department, that's true, but what does it mean? A small salary—so small I have difficulty saving anything out of it. My father is not well, I must help support my family, I must dress elegantly because that is important to my business. And now I want to get married. All of our friends, Domingo, have homes and children. When a man is thirty-seven, he needs such things."

Domingo nodded gravely. "True words, friend."

"It is a good newspaper. It pays me the highest salary it can. Sometimes the thought of opening an agency, of taking the chance of failure frightens me. That is why I conceived this Bárcenas idea. . . ."

When Domingo started to speak, Tito held up his hand.

"I know you are angry with me about it—that you think me heartless and cruel, but I can't understand your point of view." He paused while the waitress put the tart in front of him. Laying his cigarette on the ashtray, he picked up a spoon. He took up a scoop of whipcream, examined it, put it back on the plate.

"The Bárcenas idea is not a thing that came into my mind in sudden inspiration. I had been considering it for a long time. If I could just find a business, I thought, a business of little worth, that would become a success, not of itself but because of my advertising. If I could do that, then large firms would have trust in me. I searched this city for months, hunting such a business. I know

222

every shop on the Avenida Madero, even the fruit stands out by the Smelter."

"But you never spoke of this, Tito."

"It meant too much to me. And I had to do something to keep from thinking about Brunhilda."

"Tito, she's . . ."

"I know, she's in love with Jorge Palafox. I'm a fool for keeping hope, I suppose." He pushed his mouth into the semblance of a grin, and poked at the tart with his spoon.

Domingo wanted to say to him, "You lucky fool, she's not good enough for you," but he said nothing.

Tito said, "When I saw Bárcenas' studio, saw the kind of pictures he made, I knew that he was what I had been hunting so long. And it's not a cruel thing I've done to him, Domingo. I'm turning him into a success . . ."

"A success with money, is that what you mean?"

Tito shook his head in exasperation. "Domingo, I don't understand you. We have been friends for many years, and now for this coldness to come between us. . . . And for what reason? Did you expect me to say to Bárcenas, 'My good man, you are a failure because your work is no good. Never mind, I will make you a success anyway.' Would you have liked someone coming to you in such a lordly manner? Isn't my way the best way?"

Domingo rubbed his forehead with his hand. "It's a matter of values, Tito. Success to you means money and nothing else. Perhaps Bárcenas puts another value on success."

Tito laughed without humor. "What right have you to judge what success means to me, Domingo?"

"None," Domingo told him. "I'm sorry, Tito."

"It makes no difference. I just don't want you to be angry with me any more."

"I'm not angry, Tito."

"That is good." His flesh took on life again, and the twinkle returned to his eyes. He put a large spoonful of cream in his mouth, obviously enjoying it. "And you will speak to Mateo? It means so much to me."

Domingo rested his folded elbows on the table top. "Have you thought what it would mean to take a servant into partnership? His brother works as a clerk in don Wilfrido's grocery store. His mother is a cook, his brother-in-law a street musician."

Tito said seriously, "When we were little and played at soldiers, who did you always want to be?"

"Pancho Villa," Domingo admitted laughing, "but that means nothing. The world of make-believe is not the world of reality."

"You measure the frog by the size of his voice. If he sings loud enough, who cares how small he is?"

"I suppose you're right," Domingo admitted, putting some bills on the waiting check.

"Business is not concerned with social position. When you sell a house, do you bother to inquire if the purchaser was born to his money or made it?"

Domingo flung up one hand. "Peace, friend. Just say that I am conservative, and let it go at that."

"And you will speak to Mateo?"

"I will speak to him."

He kept his promise. As soon as he returned to the office, he called Mateo in and told him what Tito had said. The chauffeur examined the tip of his new shoe, saying nothing until Domingo had finished.

After a moment he said, "I like the señor Ti—the señor Gómez. He is a good soul."

"You could make much money, the two of you. It is a fine opportunity."

"Yes," Mateo admitted. "I understand that."

"What is wrong, Mateo? Something has been troubling you for days."

The chauffeur's teeth began clicking their usual drum rolls. "Señor Domingo, do you know why I want to sell real estate?"

"You are a practical man. You say so yourself. And there is money in real estate."

"Yes, but it's something more than that. My people have never owned land. They were artisans, my father's people being weavers of blankets, and my mother's were potters. They always worked in factories, lived in rented rooms. But me, when I was a little boy, my father took me one day to Santa Catarina. I saw a man plowing a field. There he stood, with the earth around him, and nothing between himself and the sky. He put seeds in the earth and they grew. My father took me back again, later, he and the man were *compadres*, and I saw the corn that the man

224

had planted. It was like being God, to put something in the earth and command it to grow, and it grew."

Domingo nodded understandingly. Mateo bent toward him. "To own ground. I could think of nothing more wonderful than owning a piece of ground. I've never forgotten that day."

Domingo's hand brushed the pile of Casasola magazines. On the cover of volume three was a group of horsemen riding across a sandy waste, with a fence gleaming palely through dust in the background.

"Not all ground is fertile, Mateo."

"I am a practical man, señor Domingo. I learned that lesson when I grew up. In fact I saved my money for years and bought a little farm on the Laredo Highway near Cienega de Flores. Nothing grew there but rocks and cactus. I finally had to sell it to an owner of goats. That was when I learned that no matter how worthless the land, it has value for someone. To discover that value, and then to link it to a purchaser's necessity—that is a game, an exciting game. I like it."

"Is that why you sold Palma that worthless lot on the Bishop's Hill?"

"Ay, that." Mateo grinned briefly. "To him it was not worthless. He had need of it. You should have heard him talking about his daughter. He wanted, so much, for her to be proud of him. Conquering that lot will make her proud of him, make her proud of the house he built for her. And I did not lie to him, señor Domingo. I explained every difficulty to him."

"You explained them so well he thought you were a poor salesman."

"I did not sell him the lot, señor Domingo. His own pride sold it to him."

"With help from you," Domingo commented dryly.

Mateo dismissed the Palma sale with a brief shrug. "But now you understand, señor, why I cannot join the señor Gómez in his agency. He sells little spaces of paper. How can I get enthusiastic about little spaces of—" he paused, stared dreamily at the wall. "You think he is a good advertising man?"

"The best in the city."

"Señor Domingo, did you know that the Green Arrow bus line intends to put in a bus that will start at the Smelter, run west on Avenida Madero to the City Hospital, then turn south on J.E. Gonzalez until it reaches Hidalgo?"

"I have heard it mentioned."

"J.E. Gonzalez is undeveloped territory. A colony out there, houses already built, modest houses, not mansions as on the Bishop's Hill."

He pulled his chair up to the desk, snatched a pencil and began to sketch on a scratchpad. "The bus line would mean that no one needed a car in order to live there. And in the summer it is so cool! The wind is trapped between the mountains and the Bishop's Hill. It sweeps through that section every evening. Any man who bought land there would have all his Monterrey friends visiting him every evening from April until November. He would never be lonely. Roses could be planted to turn it into a second Chapultepec Heights. . . ."

"Just a moment," Domingo said, frowning. He took a city map from his desk drawer and unfolded it. "I thought so. The tracks to México City cut across the section."

"The wealthy would rather endure heat than the noise of the trains. That's why we can buy land there at a cheap enough price to make a modest colony worthwhile."

Domingo doubtfully shook his head. "I don't know. We have never dealt with anything but money property. This new Santa Sofía colony of ours has worried me for that reason. . . ."

"Precisely," Mateo said firmly. "And do you know why? It is not a location for homes. I drove the niña Sofía out there the other afternoon and took a good look at it. She was enthusiastic, but me, I don't think so."

"The señorita Brunhilda said that you almost convinced her that she should buy a corner."

"The señorita . . ." Mateo's eyes were blank for a moment, then the lids quickly lowered. "Yes, of course, the señorita Brunhilda. I was merely trying out the sound of the words on her to see if they would work. But I could not get the proper intonation. Deep in my mind I knew it was no good. I am glad you have never put any houses on it. It is not a place for houses. Too much sun, and it's in an air pocket. In July and August it would be impossible to live there unless the houses were air-conditioned."

Domingo nodded, trying to visualize the development in his mind. "I think you've put your finger on it. That's what has been worrying me. But it is a pet project of my uncle Agapito. He would not like me getting rid of the development." He did not add that at the moment he did not want to antagonize his uncle in any manner, but the thought was there, vivid in his mind.

Mateo flung up his hand in horror. "Who wants to get rid of it? Tell me, señor Domingo, when don Agapito suggested this land, did he suggest it for homes?"

Domingo tried to remember the original conversation. "I don't think so. Some man died and the ground was taken in by the bank. I don't remember that part of it. My uncle Agapito insisted that it was an excellent buy, so we acquired it."

"Ay," Mateo murmured, "I did not think that don Agapito would make a mistake like that. Señor Domingo, let me consider it for a few days. I have an idea, but I am not sure that I am right. How much was paid for it?"

"I told you we got it very cheap—twenty thousand pesos."

"If I can sell that land for a good profit, will you let me start work on the Gonzalez Road development?"

Domingo picked up a pencil, tapped its rubber on the desk top. "I would have to discuss it with my father, but—I think I can promise you. Yes."

A light seemed to turn on inside of Mateo's head and shine through his skin. "Will it be all right if I discuss it with the señor Gómez?"

This surprised Domingo. "Why with him?"

"It will need most careful advertising, señor. Very careful. No man must be allowed to think he is buying cheap land. He must believe that he is more fortunate than his brother in acquiring such magnificence at so little cost. You say the señor Gómez is the best advertising man in the city. It will take a genius to convince Monterrey people that a summer breeze is worth money."

Domingo, listening to Mateo, suddenly realized that the old comfortable days of this office were finished. He did not know if he was sad or happy, but there was one thing he did know: Mateo's sale to Palma had already marked him as one of the younger men to be watched. If he left this office, another real-estate firm would hire him within the hour. And Mateo would go up to success, while the Vázquez de Anda office rocked along at its usual slow pace, making just enough money to support four people.

Don Rafael could no longer be counted upon. He had said at breakfast that he was tired of business, that he wanted a long rest. It was Domingo's responsibility now, and this was his moment to decide for success or failure.

Cardito would never come into this office. He lacked the temperament for it, and the ambition. If Domingo himself took the step he planned, and married Márgara, no client would dare to buy from him for fear of don Agapito's anger.

But here stood Mateo, ambitious, practical, and in love with the power of land. Years might pass before another such salesman appeared. And he was loyal. Whatever happened to Domingo, he would watch over don Rafael's interests.

It was not a question of choice, really, Domingo thought. It was the candid admission that Mateo was worth more to this office than himself.

He walked past Mateo to the outer office, picked up his hat and said to the secretary, "Move my things into my father's office. And fix up mine for . . ." he hesitated over the title for the space of one heart beat, "the señor Chapa." He said in an aside to Mateo, "What is your mother's name?"

"Castro," Mateo whispered, his eyes wide with disbelief.

"Get some cards printed with Mateo Chapa Castro on them." Domingo refused to look at Mateo, kept his eyes steady on the secretary's startled face. She had a broad face, and the expression of amazement was very plain. He added brusquely, "If anyone from my house telephones for the señor Chapa's services, tell them that the señor Chapa is otherwise engaged."

He shut the door carefully behind him. He did not bother to wonder over what his uncle Agapito would say.

The rest of Friday afternoon and most of Saturday, Domingo devoted to the Casasola collection. It would have been much easier to take the magazines to Márgara and say frankly, "Show me your father's picture. Tell me who he is, so that I can protect you against my uncle Agapito." His instinct, however, told him that if he ever did that, Márgara, instead of admitting the truth, would vanish with her father from Monterrey and he would never see her again.

She said she was forty. During the Huerta year, from February, 1913, to July, 1914, she must have been about seven. Thirty-six years is a long time to be afraid. No, he could expect no aid from Márgara, who distrusted even a flower's shadow.

The Casasola collection yielded interesting fruit. Ruling a page down the center, Domingo wrote on one side the names of the men who might have been confederates of Velarde's; on the other the names of his victims. Among the confederates he put down Francisco Cárdenas, Madero's murderer; and the notorious Ratkiller, ex-veterinarian. The victims (alleged) included Ruperto Martínez, whose tongue had been cut out; Enrique Ortiz, whose ears had been chopped off, and Federico Navarro, whose heart was torn out in a saturnalian replica of an Aztec sacrificial ceremony. So far as he could tell there was no proof that any of these outrages had been committed. The Casasola editors admitted that the stories were based on reports of revenge-mad people who bitterly hated Huerta, and Huerta's followers.

The only story which might have been true was that of Ruperto Martínez. It was so notorious that, it was said, Huerta's followers had turned against their fellow and forced Huerta to exile Velarde.

Disregarding truth or fiction, every single name on the victim list represented men who were dead. Bárcenas, complete with ears and tongue and heart, was very much alive.

On the confederate side of the ledger, two names only were credible, and those two, Cárdenas and the Ratkiller, were reported to have been executed after Huerta's fall. It could be that one or both of them escaped, and for political reasons news of the escapes were suppressed. Cárdenas, broad-faced, narrow eyed, heavily mustached, very cocky in a magnificent, silver-encrusted charro costume that was the uniform of the Rurales; and the Ratkiller, insignificant looking, his eyes humble, frightened (the picture was taken after his imprisonment), his chin shielded by the sarape that wrapped his tiny body . . . neither of these men bore the slightest resemblance to Bárcenas; but a constant diet of terror for thirty-six years can change a man beyond all recognition.

Of one thing Domingo was certain: nowhere in the collection was there a single photograph that might be recognized as

Bárcenas. Márgara had said that her father's picture was there. Well, if he could not find it, neither could don Agapito.

Domingo felt much relieved by this knowledge. Exposure, he knew now, could come only from an organized prying into Bárcenas' past, following the thread from town to town until finally the heart of the labyrinth was reached. He did not doubt for a minute that don Agapito would order such prying if it were necessary. The trick was to keep it from becoming necessary.

He finished dressing for the Saturday night supper dance at the Casino, and smiled at his reflection as he tucked a green handkerchief into the breast pocket of his dark gray suit. Then, after consideration, he substituted a white one instead. Verónica's eyes were sharp, her jealousy strong. It was stupid to deliberately antagonize her.

When he went downstairs, doña Otilia called him into the study. "Your father told me that you have taken Mateo into the firm."

"I thought it was best, Mother."

"He seemed pleased by it. He thinks Mateo has a true future."

"I'm glad," Domingo told her. "Perhaps now, free of responsibility, he will get well."

She nodded and patted his arm. "The girls are waiting for you. Have a good time tonight."

He bent and kissed her plump fingers, then joined the girls in the car. Mateo had found a new chauffeur for them, a quiet, middle-aged man. Brunhilda said that he admitted to the possession of a wife and five children. "I'm not concerned with his home life, but whether he can drive," Domingo said, bending forward to watch the man manipulate the car.

"Mateo would not have sent a man who could not," Sofía said.

"Well, if Mateo chose him . . ." Domingo began.

Brunhilda snapped. "There is no doubt of it. Mateo is in all ways wonderful! How has that man so enchanted the two of you? Anyone would think you were his proud professors!"

Domingo and Sofía, remembering the office lessons, chuckled softly together. The car stopped at the Miranda house and Domingo went in to fetch Verónica. She looked very pretty in a simple blue wool frock, some blue flowers fastened in her hair.

As he held her coat for her, he said, "Are you going to behave tonight, Verónica?"

She looked sideways up at him, smiling faintly, "That depends upon you, Dominguito."

"I think I am getting a little tired of this game, Verónica."

There was a note in his voice she had never heard before, and she was solemn as they went out to the car.

The winter Saturday night dances at the Casino were always held in the supper room across the hall from the ballroom.

Brunhilda, sulking because Domingo told her Tito Gómez had been added to the party, swept into the room ahead of them. She wore gray, embroidered with silver cord, and Domingo thought she looked like an angry little dove. How essentially selfish she is, he thought. She invited Verónica to keep me occupied, and it means nothing to her if Sofía sits alone all evening so long as her flirtation with Jorge is not disturbed. Tito will upset that flirtation, and now she will deliberately try to make everyone very miserable. Why couldn't she have been more like Sofía?

His younger sister was in her favorite shade of golden brown. It was the same dress, Domingo remembered, that she had worn to the train to meet Brunhilda. That was two weeks ago. Since that morning his whole world had changed. Two short weeks to change a life.

Tonight, however, he refused to be philosophical. He followed the girls to their table, where Tito Gómez and Jorge Palafox were waiting for them. Brunhilda pouted through most of supper, because, in the various maneuverings for position, Tito to stay near Brunhilda, Verónica to remain by Domingo, Jorge Palafox sat between Sofía and Verónica.

Her pouting did not seem to affect Jorge, who was looking about him with much interest. There was one table of tourists. It was easy to distinguish them, because the women wore the only hats in the room.

As far as the other tables were concerned, it was more like a banquet in a private house than a public gathering. All of these people had gone to school together, made their first communions together, in their own generations. They had been in each other's weddings, were godparents to each other's children. This was the family of Monterrey sitting around to enjoy itself on Saturday night.

Sofía leaned across the table to Domingo. "The third violinist in the orchestra is Mateo's brother-in-law. He got the job because of the performance Thursday night."

Domingo turned in his chair to look at the small stage at the end of the room. "It must pay him a fair salary. Perhaps he can support himself and his wife now."

"Perhaps. The difficulty is that the moment he gets a job he goes out and gets drunk to celebrate, and enjoys the celebration so much that he stays drunk until he loses the job. At least that's what Mateo says."

"Mateo says, Mateo says!" Brunhilda mimicked viciously. "I am tired of what Mateo says!"

"Mateo is very smart," Tito protested. "Did you speak to him about the agency, Domingo?"

Brunhilda slapped the table with her palm. "I will not hear any more of Mateo." Then, as the music started, "I want to dance." She said this, looking straight at Jorge, but he did not see her because he was looking at Sofía.

"If the señorita will be so kind," he murmured.

Sofía seemed startled, but she smiled and rose. As she passed Domingo she raised her eyebrows in mute inquiry, and he allowed his shoulders to rise in a slight shrug.

Tito was already standing by Brunhilda's chair, his eyes pleading with her. After a moment she pushed back her chair and stalked toward the circle of dancers. When she turned to face Tito, her eyes were stormy, and her mouth tightly closed.

"I do not imagine that Tito will enjoy this dance," Domingo said lazily, lighting a cigarette.

Verónica flushed. "Aren't you going to dance with me?"

"No, my pretty, I'm not."

"You mean I have to sit here in this chair all evening?" she demanded indignantly.

He said quietly, "I know you love to dance, Verónica, but if you want to dance this evening, you will have to choose either Tito or Jorge Palafox."

"They won't ask me to dance."

"It's your own fault then for intimating that we are engaged."

Rage sparkled in her. "Sometimes, Domingo, I think I hate you."

"Good. Then you won't want to marry me. And you can return the pattern for the bridesmaid's dresses."

"Certainly. That's what you want me to do, so that you can go to the arms of your mask-faced woman . . ."

He controlled a flash of anger. "That's not a very pleasant thing to say, Verónica."

"I don't feel very pleasant at the moment." She lifted her head, forced a smile as the others returned to the table.

"It is not a bad orchestra," Jorge said, holding Sofía's chair for her.

"I think it's a horrid orchestra," Brunhilda sniffed.

"Of course after Ciro's or the New York orchestras . . ." Tito began apologetically.

Jorge shook his head. "It's strange. I've been all over the Republic, but this is the first time I've ever had occasion to visit a small city Casino . . ."

Tito gasped in outraged astonishment. "Monterrey is not a small city. We have two hundred and fifty thousand inhabitants . . ."

"Forgive me. I only meant . . ." Jorge looked around with such concern in his eyes that Domingo laughed softly. Poor creature, he thought, can you never escape the tourist's attitude? He said, "Tito misunderstood you for a moment. We know what you mean. Continue."

"Yes. One goes to night clubs, to private dance clubs, but this is different. There's a warmth here, a friendliness. The señorita Sofía knew everyone on the floor."

"I should," Sofía agreed pleasantly. "Their families and my family have been friends for two or three generations."

"I am making some rather interesting discoveries about myself," Jorge said. "I think my trouble has been that I have always lived in cities that were too large. Do you think that could be it, señorita?" He smiled directly at Verónica. She flushed and bit her lip in confusion, because she had not been listening to him.

"I—I suppose so," she murmured helplessly.

No, Domingo thought. That is not your trouble, Jorge. You simply have not lived in México long enough.

233

The music started again, and Jorge, still looking at Verónica, rose and bowed. "If the señorita would honor me."

Brunhilda opened her mouth to protest that engaged couples never dance with anyone else, not even relatives. Domingo, divining her words, gave her a well placed kick on the ankles. "Verónica is an excellent dancer," he said smoothly. "It is always a pleasure to dance with her."

Verónica touched her forehead, said frantically, "I—have a headache."

"Nonsense," he said to Jorge. "She is merely shy. I've known her since she was a little girl, and she's very shy with strangers."

"But, Domingo . . ." Brunhilda began in an amazed tone.

Sofía said quickly, "You should dance with the señor Palafox, Verónica. He is really a magnificent dancer. Not a jumping flea, like Tito. Come and jump me around the floor, Tito." She thrust her hand through his arm, and led him out to the floor while he was still turning from side to side in an effort to explain Mexican etiquette to Jorge Palafox. Domingo half lifted Brunhilda to the dance floor. Verónica, without open rudeness, could not keep Palafox waiting any longer. With a self-conscious tilt of her head, she slipped into his arms for a waltz.

Brunhilda swayed away from Domingo, glared at him. "Have you lost your mind? What makes you want to embarrass Verónica like that? It will be all over town by morning. Look at everyone staring at her now."

"Brunhilda," he said quietly, "if you minded your own business more and other people's less, you'd be much happier."

"Jorge Palafox is my business. This is the second dance and he hasn't asked me yet."

"Perhaps he's shy."

"Nonsense. It takes the bravery of a lion to ask Sofía to dance. And then you force him on Verónica." Tears flooded her eyes. "Have you no feelings for me—none at all? And my heart breaking?"

He danced her into the hall. "Go fix your face," he told her with brotherly frankness. "When you cry you look like a hag. If you threw yourself less at Palafox you might make him more eager. Why don't you devote yourself to Tito tonight? That might make Palafox jealous." And give the poor Tito a few hours of happiness, he thought as Brunhilda stalked away from him.

The rest of the evening passed without incident. Tito was so enthralled by Brunhilda's kindness that his obvious happiness threw a haze of joy over the table. Jorge danced with Brunhilda twice, with Verónica twice, and the rest of the evening with Sofía. During an intermission Domingo took Tito outside and gained his promise to dance a few times with Verónica. "Enough gossip has been spread about our engagement. Help me out like a good friend."

Tito said doubtfully, "I don't want anyone to say that I am trying to separate you two."

"Does not all the world know of your devotion to Brunhilda? I ask this special favor of you as a friend . . ."

"Well, all right. But if don Agapito gets mad at me . . ."

"Leave my uncle Agapito to me."

In the supper room, Tito bowed to Verónica as though he expected her to bite him in return. But the girl, seeming to realize that tonight's triumph belonged to Domingo, followed him to the dance floor without a word. Feeling compassion for Brunhilda, Domingo swept Sofía away before Jorge could make a gesture.

Sofía said softly, warningly, "Verónica hates you tonight, Domingo."

"I had to do something, Sofía. She has made up her mind to marry me. And you know how stubborn Verónica is about something she wants."

"Uncle Agapito is on her side."

"That's the difficulty," Domingo admitted with a sigh.

They swung in and out amongst the other dancers. The floor was so large they did not have to confine themselves to tiny steps, and their bodies twisted and turned with the freedom of ice-skaters.

"Don't worry," Sofía reassured him softly. "There is always an answer to every problem."

He lifted his eyebrows cynically. "I wish life were as simple as a problem in mathematics."

She looked over his shoulder, her eyes dreamy and soft. "I'm very happy tonight, Domingo. Don't spoil it for me. Please don't spoil it."

He drew her closer to him. So our Sofía is in love at last, he thought. And Palafox certainly seems interested. Poor Brunhilda. Poor baby-wasp Brunhilda. But what a colossal joke on our uncle Agapito. To think he spread so much honey on Brunhilda only to have the fly trapped in the lily chalice of Sofía.

"Be happy, Sofía," he whispered softly. "Be happy enough for both of us."

"I will," she answered. "Oh, Domingo, I will. I will."

XIX

If Domingo had really been courting Verónica, he would have waited outside the Cathedral on Sunday morning until she emerged from twelve o'clock Mass, and then walked around Zaragoza Plaza with her.

Instead, he took the car and went to Santa Catarina, where Tía Nicanora and Serafina greeted him with little cries of delight. The girl had never lived in a village, and the village life fascinated her. She had many stories to tell him about the people: the meat vendor, the woman who kept chickens, and the woman who kept ducks. She told about them all with a little air of discovery, as though they had never existed until she saw them, and then they came, fully bloomed, into existence.

Sunday was a good day, the sun yellow and rich. It was warm enough to sit in the patio at the back of the house in the shade of a tall, thickly leaved *aguacate* tree which was already beginning to put out white blossoms, tiny as a baby's fingernail, yielding a pleasant perfume that mingled with the scent of damp earth, of growing things, of the innumerable fragrances of the country. Chickens scratched in the dust around their feet, and when Serafina held a handful of corn down to them, they pecked it from her fingers. She chortled with pleasure, her face fuller now, and soft with pregnancy.

"It seems impossible," she told Domingo, "to think that so many people live in places I've never heard of. All these people living in the world, all these animals, and I never knew they existed."

"Doesn't your aunt keep chickens?"

"Ay, yes, chickens and birds . . . now you're laughing at me, s'ñor Domingo. You know what I mean. But tell me, what has been happening in Monterrey?"

She accepted his news of Mateo with a slight shrug. "That one, he will be a great man some day. It is in his face." Mateo, Domingo realized, had never been in Serafina's world. She saw people only in relationship to herself, and Mateo had been a shadow beyond the range of her horizon.

When he spoke of Cardito, her eyes softened, but they were the eyes of memory. He wondered if the door of Cardito had already closed in her mind. She was entirely consumed now by the thought of her child, swearing that she could feel it kicking inside of her, wonderfully alive.

Every morning, early, she went to church to talk to the saints, especially to Santa Catarina, patron of the town. "I think I will name my child for the blessed saint, she has been so kind to me."

The child, Domingo thought. The ribbon of the child's existence stretched backwards in his imagination, through the line that was Serafina, into the oblivion from which had come Serafina's people; and through the line of Cardito to a rocky castle in Asturias where the first records of the Vázquez de Andas began. But before that, when the Romans built bridges and roads across that mountain region, and left the imprint of their language on the *Bable* of the people, what Roman legionnaire might not have contributed his blood?

The tape unwound, passing through the Phoenicians who had furled their sails in the seaports of Asturias to the savages who left their paintings on the walls of caves. And before them, the darkness and the sea . . . the sea alive with the life that would pass through all the centuries to come to rest for a brief moment in the child that was Cardito's.

"How fortunate Cardito is," Domingo murmured, caught in his fantasy.

Serafina drooped her head, said nothing. But the gesture spoke, as did her hand that went to the swollen line of the child, pressing it gently. Her Indian blood showed, then, in the patient resignation of her body, in her attitude, more than in the high curve of cheekbone or the shortness of the thigh.

Where did she get that Indian blood? Nuevo León was a

creole state. The early Indians, found here by the Spaniards, had been fierce warriors, nomads, without a settled culture, jealous of their grazing lands. To have peace, the Spaniards tried first to form treaties, but knowing the treaties meant slavery, the Indians fought and died. When there were no more left to serve, the Spanish overlords imported slaves from the south. Perhaps on Serafina's bone there was stamped the memory of Cortés' entrance to México City; of Moctezuma's litter with the coverlet woven from hummingbird's feathers. In her might still remain echoes of the poet emperor, greatest of the Aztecans, who, like David, came from the fields to sit on the throne and there compose psalms to God.

Had one of her people been born in a small boat, tossed by storm winds from island to island and finally across the Pacific to the Mexican shore? Or had he been born in the great migration that began in Siberia and ended by the lake that was now no lake, but México City? Did the slant of her eyes come from Tartar warrior or gentle voiced Samoan?

However the passage through generations, it all began in the sea, the restless, never silent sea. For a moment Domingo had a vision of a huge oval, that began in the sea, its two lines stretching wide apart, then meeting again in the child that was visible only through its pressure against the curtain of Serafina's flesh.

On impulse Domingo caught up her hand and kissed it. She seemed to sense that he meant nothing by it save the gesture of a man toward the Mother-Woman. This instinctive understanding in Serafina no longer surprised Domingo. He accepted it as a segment of the girl who had, in a way, withdrawn herself from the world into the shell of her own body, even as a nun withdraws to the cloister.

When he drove home that night he knew that Serafina had found her peace, while he still had his to find.

Monday, Domingo worked very hard at the office. Mateo rented two small houses, and located a contractor who agreed to put a stained glass window in the green bathroom for a moderate sum. When Domingo signed the contract he said teasingly, "If that window sells the house, Mateo, I'll buy you a dinner at the Ancira."

"About that I am not worried," Mateo said indifferently, but he paused at the door before he went out. "Would it be convenient to have a small bottle of water analyzed? It should not cost very much."

Domingo was startled. "Why a bottle of water?"

Mateo lifted his shoulders. "We have such good water. Strangers coming here from places where the water is not so good—if we had an analysis to show them it would be very valuable. Also many industries depend on good water. . . ." He said the last sentence shyly, almost as though he expected Domingo to understand his meaning.

Domingo, reaching for the buzzing telephone, shook his head in pretended resignation. "Mateo, you have ceased to astonish me. Have the water analyzed by all means." And then into the telephone, "Well? Oh, it is you, Tito."

Tito said that Bárcenas had not finished the pictures, but would deliver them that night at don Primitivo's, where it might be fun, Tito thought, to get Bárcenas a little drunk on beer before breaking the news of his coming success to him. Domingo hesitated before agreeing to join the gathering; then decided that, in order to protect Márgara's interests, it might be better if he were there.

After Tito hung up, Domingo thought several times of telephoning Márgara, but merely hearing her voice was not enough. He wanted to be close to her, to smell her perfume, to put his hands on her shoulders, to rest his face against her cheek. He pushed the thought of Márgara from him, and savagely plunged into the pool of documents that awaited his decision.

For some reason, don Primitivo's was always quiet on Monday evenings. Perhaps the gayety of weekends had something to do with it. At any rate there were no strangers in the saloon when Domingo entered it in search of Tito.

He saw the young man at a table with Jorge Palafox, don Lucio and don Primitivo. They were listening to a group of *mariachis* chanting dolefully of a deserted ranch, where even the flowers were withered and the birds flew no more.

As the song reached its tragic close, Jorge Palafox sighed and took a sip of beer.

239

"G. K. Chesterton," he said, "wrote a poem about the mad Irish." He quoted lazily:

> For all their wars are merry
> And all their songs are sad.

Don Lucio translated it for don Primitivo, who shrugged. "And what have the Irish to do with us?"

"Our songs are so very sad," Domingo explained, "and our wars so very gay."

"Me," said Tito, "I want the *cante hondo*, the sad gypsy song that breaks the heart."

Jorge Palafox, his elbow resting on the table, his cheek against his hand, dreamily repeated García Lorca's lines:

> The weeping of the guitar begins.
> It is useless to silence it.
> Its crying is a monotone,
> Like the crying of water,
> Like the crying of wind
> Over snow.
> It is impossible to silence it.
> It weeps for distant things.

His voice ceased, but the tone was caught by the guitarist. His fingers rippled over the strings, and there was the sound of tears in the air. The violin was silent and the flute. They knew that the *cante hondo* belonged to the guitar, spoke with its voice and the voice of the singer.

Jorge Palafox lifted the melody into words:

> This love I have
> Is nailed so deep
> That when I most desire to speak,
> The words cannot escape.

"Olé," said don Lucio softly. "Olé."

For Domingo, the air grew thick, rippled as water on a glass, and through the waves he saw the flash of earrings, the sheen of combs; he smelt the roses and carnations, and watched the gleam of brown skin against the deep blue, the violent purple, the pale pink of silk-fringed shawls. The tremulous light from the camp-fire thrust back the shadows, and revealed the woman, her carved face masked by her long black hair. But her eyes were visible, the pain-filled eyes that could no longer weep, that could find expression only in song. . . .

He flung out his arm, thrust a glass from the table. As it smashed, the music—trapped on a thin, high note—paused.

"I'm sorry," he muttered, "but the *cante hondo*—it breaks the heart."

Tito, his face framed by his hands, whispered,

> It is the afternoon without tomorrow,
> It is the first bird dead upon the branch.
> Oh, guitar!
> Heart, wounded
> By the five swords.

Domingo pounded upon the table with his clenched fist. "This is Monterrey, not Spain. This is laughter, not tears."

"This is the olive tree that has never been bombed," Jorge Palafox said, and into the memories of all of them swept the images of men they had known and loved who had died under the guns in Spain. Follower of Franco or the Loyalists, it made no difference, the men were dead, and Spain, the sweet, rich wine of Spain, was bitter on the tongue.

"The devil take you, Tito," Domingo said violently. "Why must you trap us in these orgies of sadness?"

"I am sad," Tito said. In his eyes was the reflection of Brunhilda.

Domingo shook his fist at the musicians. "Are we Spaniards, that we weep for Spain? We are the tinkle of silver, the shrill cry of the street vendor. Yesterday, I bought a lottery ticket. Tomorrow I may win, or I may lose. Who cares? The past died with yesterday. We are the frontier and if we stretch out our hands, we can touch the future. Give us the ballad of Monterrey."

The violinist winked at the flutist, who played a laughing little trill. The guitarist joined in, then tossed the words at their ears:

> I was born in San Luisito,
> In the shade of Saddle Mountain. . . .

Don Lucio's hand rose and fell in rhythm. In a moment his cracked voice joined the chorus, then Domingo started to sing, and Tito's high tenor took its place in the harmony. As though waiting to prove how thin their voices sounded without his, don

Primitivo's bass came booming in to join them. From the kitchen, don Primitivo's brothers shouted the three-toned yell of the cowboy, clapping their hands in rhythm to the tune. After a moment Jorge joined shyly in the shouting, not quite sure, but attempting to be part of the group, like a foreigner trying to please. They all shouted together as the song ended, and then everyone, including the musicians, shook hands to show how proud they were, each of the other.

Don Primitivo's two brothers brought some more beer, and added themselves to the party.

"Ay," said don Primitivo on a deep breath, "it is good to sing. Music is a true magnificence."

"It breaks the heart," Tito repeated, sad again . . .

"What is wrong with you, Tito?" Domingo demanded, worried by his friend's despondency.

Jorge Palafox lifted his hand to his mouth, whispered behind it, "He wanted to call on Brunhilda tonight, but she told him she was tired of always seeing his face in front of her."

"Ay, Tito, what you need," don Primitivo decided, "is a man's song, a song that measures a woman's worth in sarcasm, not in tender phrases. Here, musicians, play, 'Farewell, Mamá Carlota.' . . ."

The guitarist, who had been expecting this request all evening, glanced resignedly at his companions. The violinist sniffed and started the melody, while the flute came in with an obligato.

Don Primitivo flung back his head and flung the words with full force at the ceiling:

Farewell, Mamá Carlota.
Farewell, my tender love.

Domingo was facing the swinging entrance doors. Just before the song started, he saw Bárcenas enter, a flat package clutched in his hand, and pause hesitantly near the long bar.

With a muttered excuse to his companions, Domingo went toward him. Out of his studio, Bárcenas lacked his cold self-assurance, was oddly childlike standing there, as though the world were too vast for him, and he were afraid in it.

Then Domingo saw his eyes widen, the package fall to the floor unheeded. He clutched at his collar, tore it loose. His jaw tightened, and his lips, half-open, quivered away from his teeth.

With a piercing, fear-ridden scream, he whirled and fled through the doors into the street. Domingo, shocked at such terror, dashed after him.

"Bárcenas!" he yelled. "Bárcenas!"

The photographer did not hear him. His hands were tight over his ears, and he was rushing into the middle of the street, unaware of cars or busses, intent on only one thing, escape.

Angry drivers, angry because they were frightened, honked furiously at him, but he paid them no attention. Hesitating only a second, Domingo plunged into the traffic after him. His long legs and his youth carried him faster than the trembling photographer. He was able to thrust out one arm, catch the man by the back of the coat collar and jerk him to safety on the sidewalk.

A truck driver leaned out and yelled at him, but Domingo paid no heed. A policeman was blowing his shrill whistle at the corner, and the stalled traffic, still raucous with the sound of horns, started forward again. Bárcenas twisted in Domingo's hands, hit at his chest with clenched fists.

He was trying to say something, but his fear-locked jaws would permit nothing but low animal sounds. Domingo looked at him in horror. He could stand the suffering no longer. A quick upper-jab slumped the man into insensibility.

Hailing a taxi, Domingo took Bárcenas to the studio on Zaragoza Street. As he lifted the unconscious man out of the car, the driver said cynically, "Drunk this early. Ay, well, some men have all the luck."

Domingo did not answer. He thrust his money through the window, then slinging Bárcenas over his shoulder, carried him upstairs.

The gallery was dark. There was no light showing around the rim of the studio door. Domingo pounded on it, was about to put Bárcenas down in order to search him for keys, when Márgara opened the door.

Her eyes widened slightly, but she said nothing, merely stepped to one side, indicating the curtained arch behind the counter with a gesture of her hand.

He found a small room with a campbed in it, a table with a cupboard of dishes suspended over it. In one corner was a gas burner and an icebox. He dumped Bárcenas on the bed then turned to face her. His heart leaped at the sight of her, tense, quiet, remote.

She said without inflection, "He is drunk?"

"No, my beautiful. Terrified."

She took a step toward him, one hand extended, the other at her throat. He caught the outstretched hand, drew her closer to him. "It's all right. Do not worry. It was nothing serious." And he told her all about it.

She passed her tongue over her dry lips. "But why—what happened? What terrified him?"

"I don't know," he admitted, leaning closer to her to smell the perfume of her hair. "In the taxi I tried to solve the puzzle. He must have seen something—or recognized someone."

She caught his coat lapels, gave them a little shake. "But whom? Who was there?"

"Now stop frightening yourself," he ordered. He put his arm around her, led her into the main studio. "The saloon was almost empty. In fact no one was there but Tito Gómez, my Uncle Lucio, Jorge. . . ." He paused, remembering Jorge's amazing resemblance to his father. "Márgara!" He caught her arms, held her away from him. "Is your father afraid of Santiago Palafox?"

"Palafox?" she whispered.

"He was an enemy of Ramón Corral's. You remember, the man Díaz insisted on running for vice-president."

"I remember Corral. No—" she twitched away from him, sat on the sofa, "I don't remember Palafox. Just his name. They are all names!"

Domingo sat down by her, put his arm around her. "Márgara, you've got to tell me what it is. How can I help you if I don't know?"

She turned, took his face in her hands, her eyes serious, intent. "Don't you understand? I don't want you to help me."

"But, Márgara . . ."

"Please. I don't want it to touch you. I don't want anything to touch you."

He bent toward her, toward the red lips, trembling and soft. Then his mouth closed down on hers, absorbed hers. The terror disappeared and there was nothing between them but his love for her, and her love for him.

When he finally released her, she dropped against the sofa, her eyes shut. With an inarticulate sound, he put his head in her lap. He could feel her hand on his hair, stroking it.

244

"I love you so much. Please, Márgara, help me. I love you so much."

She bent over him, and her breath fanned his cheek. "This is so wrong, Domingo." Seeing his eyes, she put her palm on his lids, hid them. "I must never love anyone."

"But you love me."

From the darkness beyond her palm he finally heard her say, "Yes, I love you."

He tried to straighten, but she surrounded him with her body, would not let him see her face.

"Please, Domingo. There can be nothing so long as my father lives, and after that. . . . No, he's stained me with his terror. I am black with it. I shall be black with it until I die."

"Nothing," he protested, "nothing that he did can touch us."

"Ay, yes it can. It touched us before we were ever born. When he was a young man, brilliant in school, the wall between us was built."

"I want you, Márgara. I want you."

She bent until her face was pressed against his hair. "Don't say it, Domingo. What is the good of hopeless wishing?"

His arms freed themselves of her, then gathered her closer to him. This time it was she who was the prisoner. He could feel her struggling to breathe, and yet when he loosened his arms, she crept closer to him, clung to him. Her head dropped back, and she whispered, "My bones—they are made of water, my bones." His lips followed the curve of the throat to the chin, then brushed upward to the cheek, across the fluttering lids and down to the mouth.

The great clock of the Cathedral boomed, but they did not hear it. Bárcenas moaned a little as he passed from unconsciousness into the deep sleep of exhaustion, but they did not hear that either. All they heard was their own blood pounding in their ears. All they knew was the texture of their own desire.

Time passed as a dream sequence for Domingo in which he seemed to be two persons; the real man who loved Márgara, and the shadow man who moved amongst his friends and family.

This sensation of being and not-being did not disturb him. In the sixteenth century Calderón de la Barca had, through his plays, indoctrinated the Spanish mind with dream philosophy:

That all life is a dream
And even dreams are merely dreams.

Domingo, who had for so many years lived in a semi-private world, now made the complete transition with no difficulty.

In the past two weeks he had glimpsed his family as individuals, but that was during the period of his awakening love for Márgara. Now that the love was clarified, complete, his family slid back into their original veiled positions.

He was aware that Sofía was attractive to Jorge Palafox, but he was not conscious of it. He knew that Mateo took Jorge out for hours in the car, but he had no curiosity about where they went or what they discussed. Tito's ambitions, his love for Brunhilda, were to be admired or pitied, but in a detached manner, as he would feel admiration or pity for don Juan in the October Tenorio play.

Márgara filled his consciousness, and what did not touch her could not affect him. She was constantly in his thoughts. When he was not with her, he had no existence. When he was with her, he held the stars in his hand.

Meeting her presented its difficulties. Bárcenas, connecting Domingo with his terror, refused him entrance to the studio. Márgara telephoned the office and told Domingo that the mere mention of his name sent Bárcenas cowering into a corner with his hands over his ears. Luckily the photographer usually went to bed early, so that they could meet after nine. Domingo would drive slowly down Zaragoza Street, and Márgara would dart across the sidewalk and into the car.

But then they had no place to go. Domingo was so well known in Monterrey that any restaurant they might visit was certain to number among its customers at least two or three acquaintances. He had an inflexible rule: no rumor of his hours with Márgara must reach don Agapito.

Once they drove up to the Bishop's Palace and looked out over the city lights which spread like a great fan below them. They played a little game of identifying the pale blue cross on the Cathedral, the green and red neon sign on Morelos Street, the vast oblong of clear yellow that was the military camp. Saddle Mountain loomed to the east, flames from factory furnaces silhouetting it against the sky. Far to the north was the pale twinkle of the

246

small town of Cienega de Flores, and beyond its horizon lay Laredo and the States.

Domingo pulled Márgara closer to him, rested his cheek on her hair. "I'll take you to the States some day," he told her.

She murmured, "Denver, Los Angeles, New York."

"You know them?"

"I've been there. My father took me once to the top of a tall building in New York and we looked at the lights. They made my heart ache, they were so beautiful. But the lights went up and down, up to the sky and down to the earth, and they frightened me a little."

"How could that be?"

"Because behind every light was a room, and in every room was a person, and all those people, suspended between heaven and earth, they frightened me."

"But you are not frightened now?" he asked, breathing deeply of her fragrance.

"No, because these lights are spread out, and the sky has its place, and the earth has its place, and no one is trying to climb from one to the other. These lights are not in rooms but on streets, so that you cannot count the lights and say, 'Every light is a person.' Here I can feel like myself, Márgara, not like an insignificance of whom the lights know nothing, and do not care to know anything."

He told her what Serafina had said of the village not seeming to exist until she saw it, and Márgara nodded. He could feel her moving against his shoulder. "I read someplace about a tree not existing until you looked at it. Sometimes I wonder, does anyone ever see me? Do I exist, Domingo?"

"I see you."

"I know. But until you came, did I exist?"

"No," he said. "I dreamed you and you came alive. You had no life until I saw you. You are all mine, and before me, there was nothing." He tilted her head back, kissed her mouth, her lids, the delicate convolutions of her ears. He unfastened the pins that bound her hair, and held the heavy coil in his hands. It seemed to have a life of its own, and it curled itself about his hand. He gently separated the strands until they formed a thick web.

"You gave me eyes and a mouth and ears, and now you are giving me hair," she said teasingly.

247

He took a small gold knife from his pocket, snipped off a lock. "The talisman against the Xtabay," he said. "It is written in the legend: 'A man must pluck a hair from her head, and then she will follow like a slave, and he will be her master, and command her to obey, and she will obey.' "

She shook her hair free from him, held it out like a shawl. She parted it, flung the two thick ropes about his neck, held the ends tight with her hands. "The talisman itself shall bind you to me," she said joyously. "You must cut all my hair before you can be really free."

He slid the back of his fingers along the smooth curve of her cheek. "Márgara," he said. "Márgara."

Her mouth rose to his. Then a light flared around them, and a tourist car drew up beside theirs. They could hear a guide's voice droning in heavily accented English, "To the left, please, the green lights. They are the brewery."

Márgara slid to her corner of the seat, bent low, her hands catching her hair, twisting it into place. Domingo started the car, backed with violence, swung it around. The squat bulkiness of the Bishop's Palace, Monterrey's only remaining colonial building, flung the echoes of the car back at him as he drove down the narrow road that curved like a lizard's tail around the hill.

He said harshly, "Everywhere we go! Can there be no privacy for us any place?"

She said, "It's no good, Domingo. I told you from the first— it's no good."

He turned at the foot of the hill toward Hidalgo Street in obedience to the order of the one-way street arrow. When they reached Hidalgo, he jammed on the brakes. "Márgara, if we go east on this street we will reach your father's studio, but if we go west. . . ."

"Well?"

"To the west is Saltillo, Márgara."

"Saltillo?" she repeated, puzzled.

"I seldom go to Saltillo. Few people know me there."

"But, Domingo, we can't . . ."

"Why not? I love you, Márgara. I—it is as though we were married. In your heart you know that."

"I know . . . I do know . . . but Saltillo . . ."

"Next Saturday—we could leave in the afternoon, come back Sunday morning. Please, Márgara."

"My father. What can I tell my father?" She shook her head from side to side.

"Listen, Márgara, the cathedral in Saltillo—it is the most beautiful on the frontier."

She said slowly, "I could tell him I wanted to go and do a little painting. He lets me go, sometimes, to do a little painting."

"Márgara, will you come?"

She raised his hand to her lips. Her deep voice lightened, purred with music. "What did you say of the talisman, 'She will follow like a slave . . .'?"

"Not like a slave, Márgara," he said seriously. "I love you, and you must come to me of your own will."

"There is no will in me but your will. Only in obeying your will is there any happiness for me. With you I will go to Saltillo, or to Cienega de Flores, or to a house in Villa Guadalupe. It makes no difference. When I am with you, I am. When I am without you, I am not. Take me to Saltillo, Domingo. Promise me that you will take me to Saltillo."

On Saturday they went to Saltillo. They went late in the afternoon. It was after five when the car freed itself of Santa Catarina, and moved through the ranges of the Sierra Madres to the capital city of the neighboring state of Coahuila.

History rode with them along that road. One steep decent was known as the "Lowness of Carvajal," in memory of the Jew who had been granted the Tragic Square by Phillip II, a tract of land that extended from Tampico to San Antonio, Texas. But México, in 1578, was six months journey from Spain. The Spaniards already in possession refused to recognize Carvajal's overlordship. Instead, because he was a Jew, they turned him over to the Inquisition in México City, and he was burned at the stake, he and his son . . . the two most famous victims burned in the Alameda.

Domingo and Márgara, however, rode through the Lowness with no thought for the tragic ghost that guarded it. They watched the sunset turn the distant mountains into flaming volcanoes. They pretended to reach out their arms and touch the mountains that guarded them on either side.

249

"Not like mountains at all," Márgara said dreamily. "There are no rocks in them. They are frozen crystal."

It was true. They lacked the granulated quality of rock, and were more like opaque glass—gray glass—molded into the shape of mountains.

"Not crystal," Domingo protested. "Water—frozen water."

"No, no. They are not cold like ice."

"The frozen water of the sea," Domingo insisted. "When the seas left this land, some of the water loved it and refused to leave. God froze the water into mountains to stay until the ocean should come again."

"Yes," Márgara whispered, pleased with the fancy, "they are remembering the sea—the cool green depths, the water lapping around them and over them, protecting them . . ." She rested her head against the back cushions. "I wish the waters would come now, and cover them and us, so that we two could be together always in the green depths of the sea."

"We are together," Domingo said. "That is all that matters. We are together. Say it, Márgara."

"That is all that matters. We are together."

He held out his arm, and she moved into its circle. She clung to his hand like a child.

Neither noticed that the car was traveling a slow twenty kilometers an hour. The Saltillo valley had opened its arms to them, and they were lost in the enchanted vastness, the blue arch of heaven stained with the orange, the red, the violet of the dying sun. Then the twilight faded into darkness that stayed black for an hour, until the moon rose. It was a giant moon, a golden plate that by some alchemy spread a silver cobweb over the valley. The mountains were no longer mountains but jagged shapes cut from black paper and pasted against the sky.

The beauty of the scene clamped Domingo and Márgara in a magic circle. They knew afterwards that they must have passed through the town of Ramos Arrispe, but they could not remember it. The moon had blinded them. They saw nothing but each other's faces stenciled in silver against a deeper silver.

The yellow streetlamps of Saltillo's narrow streets thrust away the moonlight. The monotonous rows of houses, oblong and flush with the blocks, gave an impression of a village instead of the important capital it really was.

At this hour the market was silent. Few people sat on the benches of its plaza, or circled the statue of the poet, Manuel Acuña. A marble angel, supporting the sad, young spirit with one arm, spread tender wings above him to protect him from the cruelty of the world. Márgara touched Domingo's arm. He stopped the car for a moment so that she could look at the statue.

"His love hurt him so very much," she whispered. "I memorized a little of 'The Nocturne' once, when I had need of it." Her voice deepened, leveled into the monotone of Spanish poetry:

> Farewell, sweet mouth,
> Farewell, dear mirror eyes,
> Where I shall never see my face again . . .
> I love you still.
>
> My bird, when your wings tire,
> Return to my arm's safety.
> The candle is on the altar,
> The door is open. . . .
>
> At night I dream
> We two are joined forever,
> Forever in love,
> We two in one soul, in one breast.
>
> Once there was hope.
> Now the chasm lies between us.
> Farewell for the last time
> Love of my love.
>
> Light of my clouds,
> Perfume of my flowers,
> My poet's lute,
> My youth,
> Farewell.

Domingo listened to the familiar lines but hardly heard them, black jealousy in him. When she finished speaking he asked savagely, "There's been another man—someone else you loved?"

She turned with a quick gesture of negation. "You are my love —believe that."

"Another man . . ."

"Has there never been another woman for you?"

The jealousy closed its ears to her words. When Circe's lovers, he thought, were first changed into swine, the sight of other earth-grubbers must have been a greater pain than the fact of the enchantment. He said, "The thought of a man touching you . . . kissing you. . . ."

She bent forward, rested her cheek against his hand, clenched on the steering wheel. "When I was a young girl I dreamed of you. Somewhere, I thought, there is a man who will not pity me. Self-pity is a terrible thing, Domingo. It can be cured in only one way: by pitying someone else. Then I read 'The Nocturne' and felt pity for Acuña. I had to feel that pity to keep from weeping for myself."

He could feel her breath against his hand. The jealousy faded to grayness, disappeared. He lifted her into his arms. "Ay, Márgara, you understand. I love you so much. . . ."

Her voice trembled a little. "All the other women who have loved you—who have had a part of your love. I have been jealous, too."

He laughed with the joy of her, started the car, turning it with the one-way traffic, stopping finally in front of a hotel.

She stared at the neo-Spanish lines of the building, shook her head. "I wish it might have been the old Coahuila."

He glanced at her with surprise. "You remember that old hotel?"

Her head drooped, revealing the softness of her neck between hairline and collar. "When I was very small my father brought me here. We stopped at the Coahuila. In those days it was the only hotel. Tourists had not yet discovered Saltillo. The rooms were so large, and the bathroom—the tub was lost in it."

She laughed and turned toward him, her face no longer a mask, but the living face of a woman who can remember pleasant things. "It was winter and there was no hot water. Finally the chambermaid brought a tiny pan of it. My father asked her how we could bathe in that little pan, and she said, 'But it is winter, señor. Who wants to bathe in winter?' " The joy faded; the mask returned as she said, "We left the next day."

Something about the rigidity of her body made him realize that this spurt of talking was meant to hold him to the car, prevent his entering to register. He could glimpse the reasoning in her mind: once he had registered, they were constrained to the adventure.

He dropped his hand over her two clasped ones. "Do you want to return to Monterrey? It's what you desire that matters."

She was still for so long he wondered if she had slid down the tunnels of her memories through which he could not follow her. Finally her fingers turned convulsively, clutched his. "I want to stay here with you."

He nodded, and went across the street. When he returned with the bellboy, she was smoking, and the glowing tip illumined her face slightly as she took deep inhalations of the smoke.

He sent the boy off with the bags, then got in the car to park it in the garage. As he started the engine she asked, "How did you register?"

"Does it matter?"

"Please. I want to know."

He chuckled softly. "When I picked up the pen I realized for the first time that I couldn't use my own name. My mind went blank. Nothing occurred to me. Then I thought of the angel guarding Acuña so I wrote down Angeles, Felipe Angeles."

The street lamp revealed her widened eyes, her trembling mouth. "The great Angeles from the Revolution! He was shot." Her fingers gripped his arm. "It is an omen, Domingo."

To stop the rising tide of her fear he said sharply, "Don't be foolish, Márgara. All men must die. Just pray that the desk clerk does not remember his Revolutionary history."

"Of course he'll remember. Angeles was one of the great four. They were called the Four Musketeers."

"Nonsense. The clerk is young. That history is thirty years old."

She said, not hearing him, "Obregón was Porthos. Big, blundering Porthos; Carranza, but naturally, the sly Aramis. The flashing, roistering D'Artagnan—who but Pancho Villa? And as for Athos, the delicate, the wise, the handsome, lovable Athos—there could be only one, Athos, Felipe Angeles."

"You sound like the Engineer Nestor Cortés," he told her, laughing gently at her, trying to quiet her. "He worshipped Angeles."

"I have good cause to remember Angeles," she said. "He used to bring me little cakes in Paris." Then she hid her face with her hands. He caught her wrists, pulled her hands down to her waist. "That was thirty years ago. The past is finished, Márgara. For us the past began when we first met. Remember that."

The garage attendant came up to them, looked curiously at them. Domingo said, not loudly but clearly, to snare Márgara's attention. "The man wants me to back into that stall. Why don't you get out here?"

She obeyed with the quiet manner that was so much a part of her, and stood watching him maneuver the car into place, then lock it. When he took her arm to help her across the street, he saw that she was calm again, that the terror in the car was conquered.

They walked sedately into the hotel, she a bit in advance. They might have been any married couple going into a hotel after a long trip.

Domingo found their room without difficulty. He stepped around her, his leather heels clicking against the tile of the patio arcade, unlocked the door.

The room was large and brilliantly lighted. In one corner was a double bed covered with a white material that gleamed like satin. The window beside the bed was so large it covered almost the entire wall, but its heavy drapes prevented any chance of peeping eyes. The dresser, the desk, the night table, were carved walnut.

The bellboy had put her overnight bag on top of the dresser. She went to it now and opened it. Sensing the shyness in her, he slipped his arms about her waist. They looked at their reflections in the glass. Because of his height her head came to the level of his shoulder. He rested his chin on the soft hair. "You're just tall enough," he said. "Very convenient."

There was a quiet pride of each other in their eyes, and they smiled at their reflections. He tilted her head back and kissed her lips.

They went into the dining room, completely deserted by tourists at this late hour. It was a long pleasant room, with window-doors that opened on both the front and back patios. Although Spanish in design, raftered ceilings, slanting fireplace, and carved chairs, it had a family feeling about it, with the small square tables and shining tiled floor.

The solitary waiter possessed a friendly face. As he pulled out Márgara's chair, he said in English, "Be seated, please."

"Do we look like tourists then?" Domingo asked in Spanish. He rejected the chair across the table from her, where he would have sat with reserved politeness if they had really been married. Instead he sat catercornered to her, so that they could be closer together.

The waiter grinned. "You know how it is, señor. So many tourists. One gets the habit." He handed Domingo a menu, suggested the vermicelli soup, filet dipped in rum, *aguacate* salad.

Domingo frowned, shook his head. "No filet. Chicken and rice, I think, with almond sauce. And wine—you have the good white wine of Santo Tomás?"

"For gentlemen who know wine, señor. Naturally."

Domingo handed him the menu, but looked at Márgara. "Bring us a bottle then." As the waiter went into the kitchen he said softly, "Are you happy, Márgara?"

"I was just thinking—this is the first time I've been in such a fine restaurant since. . . ." Her eyes evaded his. She picked up a spoon, pushed it into the cloth. "Once in New York my father took me to a very famous night club. All the waiters knew Spanish, of course, because of the wealthy Argentinians. Our waiter was a Mexican from Celaya. My father ordered the white wine of Santo Tomás, and the waiter drank a small glass with us. It made my father so happy, he cried all the way home in the taxicab. To think that a Mexican drank wine with him. . . ."

"Márgara!" he said sharply. "You must promise me . . ."

"I'm sorry." She tossed the spoon aside, took a deep breath, forced a smile into her eyes. "It's merely that one memory always leads to another. Tell me about you, Domingo, all about you. All the things you've loved, and all the things you've wanted. Don't leave out anything. Give me your past for a gift."

He talked steadily through the rest of the meal, and if most of his stories concerned Cardito, he was not aware of it. His love for his younger brother was so deep that only his love for Márgara cut deeper. The tempestuous child came alive for her, his dark moods, his temper, his stubbornness, but most of all, his courage. Cardito was not afraid of anything, Domingo assured her, not even of don Agapito. If he wanted to do a thing he did it, regardless of the consequences. When Cardito was thirteen, a cousin of the same age had died in México City. The mother had written and asked to keep Cardito for a year. Everyone thought that a year in

255

the Capital would be good for Cardito, but not Cardito. He disappeared for three days. When he was finally located acting as a waiter in a Saltillo restaurant, Domingo and doña Otilia joined forces against the family to keep the boy at home. Luckily his cleverness in getting a job had pleased don Agapito, so the México visit was declined.

"Such courage," Domingo said with pride. "And in a boy of thirteen."

Márgara, finished with her meal, propped her elbows on the table, rested her chin on her palms. "And you—what did you do when you were thirteen?"

His eyes smiled at her. "Was I ever thirteen? Was I ever any age before I met you?"

The answer pleased her. He could read the pleasure in her face, that was relaxed now from its carved stiffness into the beauty of a woman who loves and is loved.

He paid the bill and they went into the patio. Both were shy of the silent room, so they went out of the hotel for a brief stroll, her left arm tightly clasped in his right one, their hands palm to palm.

The city's main plaza was deserted at this hour, although the Casino was shining with lights. They could hear the music for the Saturday night dance. It pleased them to feel aloof from the dancers in a private world of their own, to which no one but themselves had the key.

The great bulk of the Cathedral rose in front of them, the towers, high above the lamplight, sheathed in moon silver.

Márgara shivered, held tighter to Domingo's hand. "It's so old," she whispered. "It remembers so much. I wonder what it thinks of us, we pitiful pygmies?"

Domingo tilted his head back, followed the line of the major tower to its crown of carved stone. "I don't think it sees us," he said slowly. "It's beauty is so timeless, that our time must pass too fast for it."

"You mean we're like a spinning pinwheel, the blades going so fast they're invisible?"

"Yes. We can see the Cathedral, but it can't see us. All it can see is the face of God."

"Yes," Márgara said. "Yes, I like that."

A chill wind whipped around them, forced them to continue

their circle of the plaza. They spoke little, savoring the pleasure of each other's nearness. All the time their feet were carrying them back to the hotel, to that quiet room.

She stood in the center of the room, her hands folded at her throat. He could not see himself in her eyes. She was thinking, doubtless, of other hotels, where she had stayed with her father in that strange past that was not his past. He was jealous of her memories, and immediately was ashamed of his jealousy.

He reached out and flicked the light switch. The moonlight could not penetrate the heavy drapes at the window, and darkness, thick impenetrable darkness, shrouded them. He heard her gasp, speak his name on a frightened note.

"I am here," he said. His hand touched her shoulder, slid to her waist.

The fear note deepened. "Always be near me in the darkness. Promise me, Domingo. Promise me."

"Always," he promised. "Always, my Márgara."

Later, much later, he heard her say, "Felipe Angeles," sleep deadening her voice.

As the knife of jealousy cut deep, the knowledge came to him that of all the men who had passed through her world, it was Angeles who dominated. At seven, she had given her heart to that tall, beautiful man, just as the child Verónica had given her heart into Domingo's keeping.

His arms closed about her. She stirred, woke under the fierce insistence of his mouth.

"You are mine," he said harshly. "Tell me you are all mine, Márgara."

Her hands pulled his face down to her shoulder. He could hear her murmur soothing little words. As his cheek turned against the softness of her flesh, a sentence from the legend mocked him: "You will follow the Xtabay, and you will never find her, you poor creature."

The next time he woke, the glowing face of his watch told him that outside it must be dawn, but the thick curtains permitted only darkness inside the room.

His left arm felt lifeless under the weight of Márgara's head.

He pulled it gently away from her, massaged it until the prickling assured him circulation had started again.

Her voice spoke out of the silence, "I have been thinking. Will there always be a shield between us . . . my father, your family . . . ?"

His arm, fully alive now, dropped across her. He could feel her twisting toward him.

"There is nothing between us, Márgara. You are me. I am you."

"I wonder," she said thoughtfully. Then her mouth was demanding his.

Through the song of his desire, he heard her say, "I ask too much. Why must I always ask too much?"

"This is happiness, Márgara."

"Yes, Domingo. This is true happiness."

In the morning the sun slashed across the city and the broad sweeping valley. Already March was nudging February, trying to push the coldness back, so that the long warm days could come again.

They laughed a great deal, turned on the car radio, sang with the announcers the rhyming commercials that were hitched to the tunes of "Anchors Aweigh" and "Jingle Bells." It seemed to both of them that the journey passed with such quickness, they did not finish their farewells to Saltillo before they found themselves in Monterrey.

She insisted that he let her out at the hospital. "I'll go home on the bus. The streets are empty of traffic at this hour on Sunday, and we might be recognized. Also, I'm sure you want to see your brother."

When he tried to argue, he watched her face set in the closed, masked lines. Rather than be left with the memory of the mask, he agreed. He stood and watched her walk down the road to the bus, her suitcase swinging in her hand, her body moving with a new arrogance. Then he went inside the quiet building.

He found a telephone message waiting for him. Don Jonás wanted to see him at his earliest convenience.

XX

Domingo glanced at his watch. It was a quarter of twelve. That meant Verónica was entering the Cathedral for noon Mass. The señora Miranda would be in the kitchen, measuring out food for three o'clock dinner, and there would be no one to disturb his conversation with don Jonás. This was undoubtedly the best hour for a visit.

A flash of his old distaste for unpleasant scenes momentarily chained him, but he shrugged it off. It was doubtful that Verónica had told her father the truth, so don Jonás probably wanted to know when Domingo intended to make the formal declaration. The interview would need delicate handling, because Domingo had no intention of committing himself to any specific date. The moment don Rafael was strong enough to stand the shock, he would completely free himself of the Miranda entanglement.

He parked his car in the Ancira Hotel garage, exchanged a few pleasantries about tourists with the garage manager, and walked to the Miranda house.

The day that had started so brilliantly with sun, was now dulled by clouds. A cold wind whipped Domingo's overcoat around his legs. Since tourists ignored this narrow street there were no curio vendors on it. A street of homes, there was no reason for business traffic, and because it was so cold, there were no pedestrians. The clicking of his heels was the only sound, and he felt alone, deserted, completely ignored by the shuttered, iron-barred houses.

He paid no attention to the Miranda's famous window. A man as thoroughly in love as himself had no use for the tragic tales of other lovers. Knowing that the Miranda rooms would be cold, he did not surrender his coat to the servant, and followed the woman across the patio to the same small sewing room where he and Verónica had held their conversation three weeks before.

"Forgive this room," don Jonás said after a pleasant greeting, "but it is the only warm spot in the house. There is the kitchen, of course, but so much activity. I am exhausted just watching such activity."

He poured a small glass of brandy for Domingo, took one

himself. "At times I say to myself, how is it possible that we humans can be such a nuisance to ourselves? In the matter of food, for example. We need a cook, a kitchen maid, a girl to serve the table—three servants, and for what? A meal that our ancestors ate with their fingers in a cave."

Domingo, who had often heard don Jonás on this subject, smiled politely and sipped the brandy, determined that his host should open the important conversation himself. For fifteen minutes don Jonás discussed civilization and its by-products, but finally the stem wound down, nervousness came into his manner. He drummed his fingers on the table, took hurried sips of a brandy he ordinarily absorbed as slowly as possible. His chair would hold him for a moment. Then he would leap up, stride rapidly about the room, play with the material piled on the sewing machine, come to perch again on the chair, his voice trilling all the while through words that meant nothing to himself nor to Domingo.

Finally he paused, drew a deep breath, and said, "My dear son —I call you that because I have known you since you were a small boy. . . ." He hesitated, and Domingo bowed his head.

A very good opening, Domingo thought. Three more phrases of this order, and he can ask me when I intend a formal proposal. How can I tell him the truth without wounding his pride too much? Verónica's deviltry is really to blame for all this. A selfish woman is worse than a plague of locusts for causing trouble.

Don Jonás took another sip of brandy. "The world progresses in some ways. In other ways there is no progression at all. The difficulty, of course, is in adjustment."

He's off again, Domingo thought, lazily crossing one knee over the other. It's a pity, he was beginning quite well. It would be kinder, of course, to help him out, but how can I tactfully say, "I am not going to marry Verónica?"

Don Jonás said, "When I was a young man—when my father was a young man—it is a very old story. I want you to know I understand such things."

Domingo blinked at him. Was it possible don Jonás understood the situation, was trying to open an easy retreat that would hurt the pride of neither family?

"I appreciate your understanding, don Jonás." Domingo felt a surge of affection for the nervous little man. How kind he was, how good. "Young girls often indulge in romantic fancies. . . ."

"You explain that to me, in this house? Can you comprehend what it is like to live with a great legend, especially when your daughter is romantically inclined? There is no imagining what may come of it. Why, Verónica may stick a knife in you and another in herself if she hears of it. I tell you, she is a very romantic girl, my daughter."

The warmth in Domingo was replaced by a cold shiver of apprehension. He carefully set his brandy glass down on the table, then looked around at Miranda. "Stick a knife in me? What are you saying, don Jonás?"

"Women, my dear son, are the devil. They get notions, especially when they are jealous."

Jealous, Domingo thought dully. So, it was out. Verónica had told her father about Márgara. And once don Agapito got hold of it. . . . Perhaps, while Márgara and he were in Saltillo, don Agapito's mill had started to grind. He said through dry lips, "My uncle Agapito . . ."

"No, no, no. So far our good Agapito knows nothing. Our great one has so much to worry him, I could not see the need of adding an extra worry. I made the man promise. I don't trust him, but the lure of money is strong enough to bind him, for a while at any rate."

Man—Bárcenas. It was Bárcenas who had found out the truth. The photographer, insane with terror, needing money to escape, went to the quickest source. But how had he connected don Jonás with Domingo?

Gossip of the Miranda engagement, of course, was all over town. But why to don Jonás? Why not to Domingo himself? Or to don Rafael?

Domingo's fingers felt cold against his hot forehead. He pressed his temples trying to clear his muddled thoughts. "If you could begin at the beginning, don Jonás. I am all confused . . ."

"Of course, my son. Believe me, I have been confused since last night. Women are the devil. You never know what they are going to do. The girls from above stick knives in you, the girls from below feed you *toloache*. How we men ever survive to the age of forty is one of nature's miracles. I was fortunate. No one ever wanted to feed me *toloache*. But a classmate—a fine, brilliant boy—you know the family, the Morales O'Briens from Caydereta —that ranch girl fed him *toloache*. What could he do? He had to tell her he was finished with her when his marriage to the Stéfano girl was announced. That ranch devil put *toloache* in his coffee. He still lives out on the ranch. I go to see him now and then, take him a few toys. He loves small automobiles, the type you wind with a key. They say his mentality is that of a five-year-old child. Very sad. Such a brilliant boy."

Domingo kept his eyes shut, allowed these senseless words to spray around him until he felt don Jonás' hand shaking his shoulder.

"Saints in Heaven, you're not sleepy, are you? That's one of the symptoms. How is your appetite? Do you eat much more than usual? Do you laugh without reason? You haven't laughed since you came in the room. Perhaps it's not very advanced . . ."

Jerking away from Miranda, Domingo stood up. "Calm yourself, don Jonás. Do you think I've been fed *toloache?*"

"My son, jealousy is the devil's arrow. No one knows where it will strike."

"Who, in God's name, would be jealous enough of me to feed me *toloache?*"

Don Jonás slowly took off his glasses, peered at Domingo from beneath heavy brows. "Serafina."

Feeling as though his legs were fashioned from crumpled paper, Domingo groped for his chair, sat in it. For some reason his eyes would not focus, and he concentrated on trying to see the brandy decanter. After a moment, he poured himself a stiff drink, gulped it down. An old proverb popped into his mind, "The greatest danger is the danger a man fears least." In his great concern over Márgara, his relationship with Serafina had never entered his mind.

He said as quietly as he could manage, "You say a man came to see you about Serafina?"

"Yes. A drunken, loud mouthed creature named Lozano, Pancho Lozano, who called himself her father. It seems the girl disappeared from home about a week ago. He still has not found her. . . ." Domingo's mind flashed with relief, she's still safe. Then he listened carefully to don Jonás, who was saying, "He beat the truth of you out of a nephew. Lozano hunted for you but couldn't find you, so he went to see your father."

"Ay, God."

"But you know how your father is. Rafael simply called the

man a liar and kicked him out of the house. So then he came to me. He really wanted to go to Agapito . . ."

"I can imagine that he did."

"But I think he lacked the courage. He came to me. Lozano wants money, Domingo."

"The whole thing is preposterous."

"Not if Verónica hears about it. She has a very jealous nature, that girl. And growing up in the shadow of a romantic legend has not helped her any. Sometimes Verónica frightens me."

"She frightens me," Domingo assured him. He rubbed his palms together, trying frantically to think of some solution to this new problem. He said harshly, "I didn't even know Serafina had a father until two weeks ago."

Don Jonás answered him from the depths of experience. "They always have fathers, or mothers, which is worse. I met a mother once. Sometimes I have nightmares about her."

Domingo tried to sort the pertinent facts from don Jonás' rambling statements. If Lozano had courage enough to visit don Rafael and don Jonás, his cupidity would make him overcome any cowardice in seeing don Agapito. That meant a family scene of terrific proportions, but it also meant . . .

Domingo raised his head, his eyes blinking with rising hope. "Naturally, don Jonás, you could not expect . . . I mean about Verónica."

Don Jonás patted his shoulder, handed him a glass of brandy. "Calm yourself, my son. Calm yourself. Me, I was a gay rooster when I was young, and my father before me. I would not want my daughter married to anyone less than a true man. This fellow wants money. I say, give him a little money and a great fright. The only true danger is for the story to reach Verónica's ears."

The hope glimmered and died. Domingo cursed his family's intimacy with the Mirandas. He thought with envy of a friend's father-in-law who had pretended such anger at losing his daughter that he refused to speak to the young couple until the first child was born. Since everyone concerned knew the anger was mere pretence, it worked out very satisfactorily for all concerned, keeping the first year of married life free of parental domination, and turned the baby's baptism into a love feast of high order.

Unfortunately, Domingo thought, both the Vázquez and the Mirandas had set their hearts on this marriage since Verónica's

263

sixteenth birthday. It would be stupid for don Jonás to turn against his most desired prospective son-in-law.

"I must have time to think," Domingo muttered. "The unexpected situation . . ."

"Naturally. But whatever course of action we pursue, Verónica is the one to consider. I want to attend a wedding, not a funeral."

Domingo's lips turned up in what he hoped was a grin, as he shook hands and walked to the door. He had consumed four brandies too quickly in too short a space of time, and his feet would not go where he wanted them to go. As he fumbled at the doorknob, don Jonás said cheerfully, "I want it all settled by Wednesday night. I want to feel really happy by Wednesday night."

"Wednesday?" Domingo asked blankly.

"Didn't your father tell you? Wednesday night my brother Irineo and don Wilfrido Vidal are coming to ask me to give Verónica to you in marriage. Your father and Agapito thought Wednesday would be very fine. And so do I It will be a fine marriage, Domingo. We are all most happy about it.'"

There was one flower blooming in the patio, the bell shaped Cup of Gold with lavender stamens rising from the lily chalice. Domingo snapped the head from the thick stem and crushed the petals in his fist as he left the house. He felt the need to destroy something, and this golden flower reminded him of Verónica's taunt. "Ten bridesmaids," she had said, "dressed in yellow."

He knew that if he went home, don Rafael would be waiting for him to give an explanation of the Serafina affair—an explanation he was not yet ready to make.

On the other hand his father might be asleep, and what Domingo needed was the seclusion of his bedroom where he could think the problem through in peace. He went into the Ancira lobby, paused to shake hands with the old woman who managed a precarious living through the sale of fine drawnwork. She had been a friend of his since childhood, and it never occurred to him not to stop and inquire after her health.

At this hour the blue tiled lobby was filled with travelers: business men for Torreón, Guadalajara, México City; and tourists, en route north or south. He threaded his way through the groups, hailed by various acquaintances. He could feel his face smiling, hear his voice speaking the correct words, but his mind was intent on the desk telephone.

He was finally allowed to reach it, and after a brief argument with central (who thought it absurd that anyone should want to use a telephone at one o'clock on Sunday, when the world and its wife was indulging in the Alameda Promenade) he finally reached his mother.

She said, "I want to talk to you, Domingo."

"I know. I've just come from don Jonás. Where is my father?"

"Asleep. This has been a great shock to him."

He pulled the phone closer to his mouth to guard his words from gossip hungry ears in the crowd. "But if we keep him from speaking to my uncle Agapito . . ."

"You know how your father is. He telephoned Agapito last night."

A wave of dizziness swept over Domingo, forced him to lean against the long desk. "I was hoping. . . ."

His mother's practical tones sounded remote.

"Agapito has been over here all morning waiting for you. I convinced him he should take Jorge Palafox and Brunhilda for a ride around the Alameda."

"Where is Sofía?"

"I sent her to the hospital to stay with Cardito. This is the best time for you to come home, Domingo."

"You are a true angel. I love you. I will be home immediately."

He hung up, declined an invitation to play frontón at the military camp, and hurried across the hotel's glass-roofed patio to the garage.

The one-way streets were in his favor, and he was home in ten minutes. He found his mother in the library, placidly crocheting.

"That fool Florinda is not as good a cook as Petra," she said as he kissed her hand. "I don't know whether our dinner will be fit to eat. Take off your coat, Domingo. This room is warm enough."

He flung his coat over the arm of a chair, stretched out on the sofa. "My head aches," he told her petulantly, and she nodded.

"It should, my heart. Now tell me everything from the beginning."

How much does she know, he wondered, staring at the embossed ceiling.

His mother said placidly, "Cardito is so much like your father. Lovable but stupid. Cardito and Brunhilda, they are Vázquez to their fingertips. Now you and Sofía are Faustos. I can see my father in both of you, the long bodies, the narrow heads, the rich hearts and the good brains. Of course, there is one difficulty. We Faustos sometimes let our hearts rule our brains."

He turned on his side so that he could see her. He wondered if his eyes were telling him the truth about her, if her hair really gleamed with silver, if her skin were actually as soft, as fresh with youth as he imagined it to be.

"I thought you had guessed the truth," he told her, "the other afternoon. You are very wise, my mother."

Her mouth twitched in a slight smile. "I do not believe in leaping to conclusions," she said dryly. "Besides, if you had wanted an affair with the girl, you would have removed her from the house. Allowing her to stay here, and in her condition, was the act of a young stupid."

An idea frightened him a little. He said quickly, "You have not told this truth to my uncle Agapito?"

"Not yet. I wanted to know your own plans."

He thought of what he wanted to say, sorted the ideas, chose the words carefully. "If my uncle Agapito knows Cardito is old enough to be a father, he will consider him old enough to manage. It may not be in my uncle's mind to have a lawyer in the family, anymore than a musician."

The inference was received by his mother, considered, rejected. "The law is an old and honorable profession. In colonial days the law and the church were the only professions open to young men of good family."

"My uncle Agapito is not a historian. He may put law on the same level with medicine, necessary but not adequate as a money maker."

Doña Otilia pursed her lips, raised her brows until her forehead wrinkled. "Have you heard that Irineo Miranda and Wilfrido Vidal are going to propose for you on Wednesday night?"

"Don Jonás told me."

"You could stop that proposal by telling your uncle that you are in love with Serafina, and intend to take full responsibility for the child."

He stared unseeingly past her head at the long brocade drapes that hid the windows behind dark cream folds. "Dressed in yellow," sang his mind. "Dressed in yellow, dressed in yellow."

"Would you like me to do that?"

"What I like is of no consequence." She bit off a snarled length of thread, expertly retied the smooth sections together. "This thread gets worse every year."

He lit a cigarette, frowned at the match before he blew it out. "The child is Serafina's. She is consumed with the thought of it. She intends to name it for Santa Catarina. I have no right to say what she shall do with it."

His mother bent toward him, her eyes shining pools. "I was frightened that you would agree with me. I am very pleased with you, Domingo."

His amazement shook his voice. "You want me to tell them the child is Cardito's?" At her nod, he sprang up, began pacing the floor. "No, I will not have my uncle messing in Cardito's affairs. While the boy's sick in the hospital, my uncle will snatch up Serafina, the girl will disappear, without a yea or nay from Cardito. How do we know how much he cares for her?"

"A servant girl?"

"We are not walking in the past. Already Mateo, a servant, is working in our firm. And my uncle's fine wife Tecla is not very far removed from an *jacal*."

"Domingo!"

"Look at her short body, the broad hands and feet, the coarse texture of the hair. Serafina has better blood in her than Tecla."

"Domingo, are you in love with Serafina?"

Startled, he swung toward her. For a moment the memory of Márgara was so strong that he could almost feel her under his hand. He forced a laugh. "I do not rob cradles, Mother."

"Verónica is only twenty."

"Verónica was older at birth that Serafina is now. And I am not in love with Verónica."

"Unless matters are very carefully handled, you will marry Verónica within the year."

"I know," he said bitingly. "With ten bridesmaids dressed in yellow. She has even bought the pattern for their dresses. This does not amuse you, my Mother? You do not even smile." His hands tugged at his hair, pulled it out of its usual carefully brushed state.

"I haven't seen you do that since you were a little boy," she commented, putting her crocheting in her lap and leaning back to watch him. With an abrupt movement, she tossed him the mass of snarled thread. "Straighten this out. It will give you something to do with your hands. It's amazing how much easier thoughts come when you have something to do with your hands."

"I wish my life were as easy to unsnarl," he said as he plucked futilely at the knots.

"Your father loves you very much, Domingo. He thinks that the Miranda marriage would be most suitable."

"You do not think so. You told me . . ."

"I know. But I am a woman, lacking in true judgment. Perhaps your father is right. Verónica belongs to our world."

"Our world is finished. The old ideas no longer fit . . ."

"Perhaps," his mother said thoughtfully. "Not for Cardito and Sofía. They are the new generation, cradled in new ideas. For me, there were only restrictions and no freedom. For them, there is only freedom and no restrictions. But you, my oldest, came too late for the one and too soon for the other. You cannot stand in a vacuum between the new and the old."

"I like the new world, the free world."

"Naturally. But will your father permit that liking, Domingo?"

He looked up at her, his face strained and old. She said gently, "Your father's desires have always carried much weight with you, Domingo. You are a dutiful son, your mind, your every thought molded by tradition, by custom. To break a mold is easy. To replace the mold, that is the difficult thing."

"I suppose so," he murmured, his mind busy with the implications of her words.

They heard the doorbell ring. Doña Otilia stood up.

"There is your uncle now. I'll tell him you're waiting in here to see him. Do not anger him too much. He makes a powerful enemy."

Domingo, restlessly objecting to being left like a beast awaiting the slaughter, followed her to the parlor where they found Brunhilda and Jorge Palafox, but no don Agapito. The great man had left word that he wanted Domingo to come to him that night after ten.

He hopes the waiting will make me more nervous, Domingo thought, so that I will be easier to handle.

It needed a definite effort to listen to Jorge Palafox' enthusiastic speeches about Monterrey. Brunhilda could not understand why he liked it so much.

Jorge said, "Everyone knows everyone else. I like to walk down the street and see familiar faces. México City is so big there is no opportunity to casually greet one's friends."

"These casual meetings are not always convenient," Domingo said dryly, remembering his efforts to speak in peace to Márgara.

Jorge laughed, shrugged his shoulders. "I have the soul of a small town. And yet I like a city. I like the bustle, the smell of business. To get both the smallness and the greatness in one place. The idea delights me."

Brunhilda, who had no intention of spending the rest of her life in Monterrey, said quickly, "After a year of it you would be very bored. The same faces day after day can become quite monotonous." She pouted at her sister, who entered in time to steal the spotlight from her. "Why are you shivering, Sofía? I can't understand how your coldness can get more cold."

Sofía laughed, shrugged out of her coat which Jorge took for her, and held her hands to the gas flame. She told her family that Cardito was better, but restless with staying in bed. He was having many visitors, most of them his fellow students. She added casually, "Mateo came to the hospital to bring Cardito some fruit. I thought it nice of him."

Jorge said, "He's a very clever young man." Again there was that overtone that Domingo could not quite fathom. "He has almost persuaded me to build a factory here."

"You, a factory?" Brunhilda's laughter trilled. "You're a banker, not a manufacturer."

"Bankers have much to do with manufacture. No, I've had an idea for a long time of building a big photo-finishing plant, something like the giant ones they have in the States, that would serve the Republic. The difficulty, of course, is the water."

Water, Domingo thought. Mateo was saying something about water the other day.

"But yesterday afternoon," Jorge continued, turning to Sofía,

"Mateo showed me some chemical reports on Monterrey water. It would be ideal for such a plant."

Domingo smiled in his mind. He tried to keep the amusement from his voice as he asked, "Has he shown you a suitable site?"

"We've seen two or three. He prefers one on the Saltillo Road, and I'm inclined to agree with him."

"That's near the *colonia* that's named for you, isn't it. Sofía?" Brunhilda asked.

Sofía shrugged, moved across the room and took a bridge table from the large armoir. "Sunday is not a day to discuss business. Does anyone want to play bridge?"

Domingo, glad of the chance to freshen his mind with the cold science of cards, agreed. Jorge obviously wanted to do whatever pleased Sofía, and Brunhilda would not leave Jorge, so they played until doña Otilia called them to dinner.

She apologized to Jorge for don Rafael's absence. He had not been well, and it was so cold, the doctor thought it better to keep him in bed. "He went to the hospital early this morning to visit Cardito, and he came home exhausted. The boy's illness worries him."

Turning to lighter subjects, she kept the conversational hoop rolling with practised ease. Her school days had been spent at a convent in Tours, and she and Jorge shared many memories of France. Brunhilda pouted because she could not find entry into this twosome, and Sofía retired into her aloof world. Domingo poked at his food, cursing Serafina's father between every bite.

He excused himself at the end of the meal, and carried his coffee upstairs to his parents' room. The gas was turned on full, and the heat made Domingo gasp for breath. Then the stuffy feeling slid away, and he sat down near the bed, where don Rafael was wrapped in blankets.

For the first time he noticed a resemblance between his father and his uncle Lucio in the delicate wax skin, wrinkled with age, and the finely spun hair. With his head resting on the high pillows, don Rafael's flesh fell away from the bones, and the high curve of the cheek, the set of the eyesockets, were twins to Lucio's.

"Domingo," his father said in the dry voice of age, "I am just a little tired, I think. Just a little tired."

How frail he is, Domingo thought. He said carefully, "Lozano was in error, Father. Serafina's child is not my child."

"I know. I told him he was a rogue and a liar."

"She is going to have a child," Domingo admitted. He adjusted his words, examined them, liked them. "She informed her family that the father is a bellboy in one of the hotels. Her father beat her, and she was in great pain. She was a servant in this house. Where else would she come but to this house for aid?"

"You told this to don Jonás?"

"What was the use? He didn't know Serafina—the helplessness of the child."

Don Rafael's thin hands plucked at the blanket nap, rolled little balls of wool. "Jonás Miranda," he said with fastidious reproof, "has had enough to do with servant girls. He should know how to handle the situation. What does he suggest?"

"To give the man a little money and a great fright."

"You think that would be clever?"

"If we can frighten him into leaving the city—yes, I think that would be clever."

"I leave the matter in your hands." Don Rafael turned his cheek toward the pillow. Thinking the old man had slid into sleep, Domingo tiptoed toward the door. His father's voice stopped him.

"Do you think Jorge Palafox will make a good husband for my daughter?"

Domingo, thinking of Jorge's plans to add another factory to Monterrey's sum of six hundred, said, "A very good Monterrey husband."

"Perhaps we can make it a double wedding, yours and . . ." The sentence died into silence. This time don Rafael was really asleep.

Domingo shut the door carefully behind him, his lips pressed tightly together. The late afternoon sun broke through a thin seam in the clouds, and for a moment everything the light touched: the gallery walls, the top of the patio trees, the balcony railing, the sky itself, was gilded. The color engulfed Domingo. "Dressed in yellow, dressed in yellow," the imp sang in his ears as he hurried down the stairs. "Yellow, yellow, yellow."

His mother stopped him at the foot of the stairs. She had wrapped a shawl around her against the evening chill, and her body was a blurred outline in the approaching darkness of evening.

"Did you tell your father, Domingo? About Verónica, I mean."

"No," he answered slowly, wondering why his brain should be so tired while his body tingled with excitement. "I wanted to tell him, but he looked so—so helpless somehow."

She said nothing, watching him, her face expressionless.

"How could I tell him?" he cried. "My father is an old man. He wants that marriage . . ."

Still she said nothing. The twilight was deepening fast, and it was difficult to see her face. What was she thinking behind the mask of that face? What did anyone think behind the mask?

He went past her into the areaway. From the parlor floated the laughing voices of his sisters and Palafox. They seemed to be playing a game of some kind with Mexican cards. He could hear Sofía chanting, "The three of gold, the horse of swords, the queen of cups."

For a moment he beat his fist against the thick plaster wall. He knew now that the feeling of excitement was merely a slow rage climbing through his veins.

He hesitated a long while at the telephone. It had been in his mind to call Tito. Friends since childhood, whenever one was involved in difficulties, the other was always ready to lend a helping hand. But for the clearing up of the Serafina affair, Tito of the waltzing body would be as helpless as himself. The world above did not know how to contact the world below. There was only one person who could help him now.

It was good to hear Mateo's quiet voice sounding as though it knew the difference between two and four. After a brief conversation, Domingo left word with Florinda that he was taking the car, and did not know when he would be home again.

His rage had thinned, become a jellied substance that floated on the surface of his mind. He was determined that the Serafina problem be solved before he went to his uncle's. It would not do to fling himself, weaponless, against don Agapito's golden wall.

Mateo was waiting at the gate of a small house set back in its own yard near the Alameda. He got in the car without a word and Domingo drove to the carpenter's shop. Serafina's cousin, Jaime, tried to hide when he saw Domingo, but his father dug him out, and with many tears running down his cheeks the boy admitted all that had happened.

"I didn't want to make any trouble," he sobbed, "but he beat me so hard. You can see the bruises." He thrust out one thin arm.

Domingo's doctor's mind reacted with added rage at the sight of the purple marks.

Mateo grunted without sympathy. "A beating is a beating, to be endured and forgotten," he said coldly. "What does this fiend look like? For we must find him tonight."

Serafina's uncle had a photograph of the man, taken at his wedding. It was a large oval picture, and showed Pancho Lozano in a rented full dress suit standing beside his new wife. His face was oblong, with thick curly hair parted on the side, a heavy mustache and a pouting underlip. His narrow eyes looked dull. He was drinking even then, Domingo reflected.

Mateo said, "At the moment he is doubtless in a *cantina.*"

"Doubtless," Serafina's uncle agreed, nervously pulling at his belt. He gave his son a cuff on the ear that sounded loud but obviously did not hurt. "You coward, go with these gentlemen to hunt the drunkard. And don't come back until you find him."

They drove to the Avenida Madero, where Mateo, armed with a list of possible *cantinas,* got out. "I'll try this side of the street and you, that one."

Domingo did not want to separate, as Mateo's efficiency was good to lean upon, but the ex-chauffeur shook his head. "I have an idea of what he looks like. Besides, I know the men who run these bars. I think I'd do better without you."

He walked quickly across the street, and Domingo found a place beside the parkway that divided the avenue into two sections. Mateo's bluntness offended him for a moment. He realized, however, that the man was right. The people below had never trusted the people above, and would join together to protect one of their own kind. But he could not sit and wait in the car. He ordered Jaime to lead the way, and they began to search through various saloons.

Some were large, with special rooms for eating, where family groups gathered to consume plates of *machacado,* of platters of barbecued ribs, called "Needles." Others were so tiny there was hardly room for the bar. These holes-in-the-wall were patronized exclusively by men. In all of them there was laughter, the haze of cigarette smoke, the fragrance of frying meat tinctured with the sour smell peculiar to beer, the yellow glare of unshaded lights, and the shrill cacaphony of music pouring out of radios.

273

After the tenth bar, Domingo called a halt. "Are you sure," he demanded, "that your uncle can be found in these places?"

Jaime's eyes drooped, the lashes heavy against his cheeks. "Almost sure unless he gets very drunk."

"Let us say he is very drunk. Where would he go?"

The lashes fluttered but did not rise, and the young face settled into lines that were too wise for the soft skin, the childish roundness of cheek and jaw. "I don't know, s'ñor Domingo. Who can follow the mind of a drunk man?"

"I think you do know."

Jaime withdrew a step, then, with a movement too quick for Domingo to follow, he snapped sideways and darted through the swinging doors into the street. Domingo hurried after him, but the Sunday evening crowd was thick, and the boy had found refuge in it.

Muttering profanely, Domingo dodged through the traffic, and made his way to the car, where he found Mateo, hat tilted over his eyes, sitting behind the wheel.

"I lost the boy," Domingo said furiously, climbing into the front seat. "He's more afraid of his uncle than he is of his father."

Mateo shrugged. "His father beats him with love, but his uncle to hurt."

A truck, out of control, shot past them. At the intersection, the driver's door opened, and he was slung halfway out. The trailer swooped to one side, sideswiped a car that had stopped for a red light, then swung the other way and hit the wall of a furniture store. For a moment action ceased. Three men were jammed in the truck's cab, a woman perched on one of the men's knees. The window framed her terror filled face, then she was jerked backwards as the driver swerved into a sidestreet. Police whistles blew, people shouted, a mass of Sunday night revelers converged upon the victim car.

Mateo gave a low exclamation, tossed his cigarette out of the window, and put the car in gear.

Domingo, who had been staring in horror at the accident, snapped his head around. "Where are you going?"

"To follow that truck."

"Man, that is a job for the police. We're hunting Pancho Lozano."

"That truck will lead us to him." Mateo, honking and yelling at the same time, cleared space through the crowds.

A police car, siren at full blast, darted into the narrow street ahead of them, and they were able to pick up speed in its wake.

Domingo had to yell to be heard above the noise. "Are you crazy? What has that truck to do with Pancho Lozano?"

Mateo settled deeper in his seat, his hands clutching the wheel. His deep voice cut through the sound without effort. "The woman in the cab, I recognized her. She's from Baca's."

"What the devil is Baca's?"

"You mean you don't . . . no," Mateo said slowly, "you would never have heard of Baca's."

He said nothing more until they turned back onto Avenida Madero. By this time they had lost the squad car and the truck both, but Mateo did not seem overly concerned. "It's all right," he said. "I know where Baca's is."

"I don't want to be mixed up in any police raid," Domingo told him sharply.

Mateo shrugged. "You won't be. The police weren't close enough to recognize the woman, and the truck won't lead them to Baca's, I can tell you. Not if the driver wants to stay alive."

The excitement of the chase finished, Mateo expertly lit a cigarette with one hand. Domingo had never seen him smoke while driving, and this small action seemed to say, "I am no longer a chauffeur, but a man of position."

"When you are ready to speak about Baca's," Domingo said meekly.

Mateo laughed. "It's a saloon where *mezcal* is the principal liquor sold. But they sell other things to any man who has the price."

"You think we'll find Pancho Lozano there?"

"I think so. Two or three of the bartenders hinted at it, but I was too stupid to understand the hints until I recognized the woman. I think Lozano's love for drinking is greater than his love for the honest life of a carpenter."

He said nothing more until they entered Villa Guadalupe. Once, when the bullring was out here, the town had made much money from Sunday crowds, but now that the two coliseums had been constructed in Monterrey proper, the plaza was empty, and the gaudy food stands were deserted.

Night had fully taken possession of the land, and the houses were dark shadows. Mateo turned into an unpaved sidestreet, that wound in and out around cactus fenced corrals from which came the sour odor of pigs and chickens, and the musty sweetness of cows. Then the town proper was behind them, and they were following a ribbon of hard packed dirt through wide fields toward the mountains.

"I hope you know where you're going," Domingo muttered.

Mateo said without rancor, "Boys who grow up on the streets learn queer paths"

Domingo leaned his head against the door, stared out at the wide fields, where no man had planted corn or ever would. These fields belonged to the dry sand, to the prickly thorn bush, the gray sage, the white blossomed *anacahuita,* and the low growing cactus. Here and there, age weary *yucas* lifted their bent arms to the sky. These plants needed strength to live in such fields, strength to battle the absorbing sand, the drought, the blazing sun. It was a struggle for existence, Domingo realized, of which he knew nothing, and Mateo everything.

Then the moon rose above the mountains. Its light was so brilliant, the headlights of the car were almost unnecessary. Strange, Domingo reflected, with Márgara that moonlight had been warm with enchantment. Tonight, with Mateo, it was cold as money.

He turned toward the ex-chauffeur. "Aren't we nearly there?"

"Another kilometer, I think."

"How does Lozano get out here—and the other customers?"

Mateo's shoulders rose, to be outlined with moonlight. "Baca's makes arrangements for its patrons. There, on the fold of the hill, see that light? That's Baca's."

"After we get there, how will we get away?"

Mateo laughed softly. "It can be managed."

The light had blossomed now into a yellow window set in a low adobe house. Mateo swerved the car off the road, turned it so that it was pointed toward town, and put on his brakes. He opened the glove compartment, took out the gun that was always kept there, glanced at Domingo, and said dryly, "I'd better keep this. You'll find some brass knuckles in there. Put them on, and then keep your hand in your pocket until you need to use them."

As they approached the door he said in a low voice, "When the fight starts, run for the car. Don't pay any attention to me."

For a moment Domingo hesitated. His mind told him that venturing into this business was a stupid plan. There were other ways to contact Lozano, safer ways. Yet, at the same time, another element in him that he had never known existed, was charging his blood with bubbles of excitement. For weeks he had been encased in a prison of inaction. This promised fight was as exciting as the lure of the Xtabay.

He patted Mateo's shoulder. "We leave that house together, friend."

Mateo did not answer, but his shoulder twitched under Domingo's hand. He opened the door, and they went into the room.

At first the light blinded Domingo, and then he saw a low room, whose walls had once been whitewashed, but were now filthy with dirt. A few unpainted tables were scattered about the cement floor, and at them were sitting a few men and women. A green painted bar ran along one side of the room, and a man in a torn pink shirt leaned over it. Two gasoline lanterns hung from the ceiling, another was on the bar near the man's elbow.

There was neither curiosity nor apprehension in the stares that followed them to an empty table. Mateo sat down, tipped his hat back, then gestured for Domingo to do the same. He lowered himself cautiously to the chair, realizing that eyes were appraising the cost of his clothes, and his tenseness, as well as Mateo's calm.

"We want beer," Mateo called to the bartender.

After a long moment, the man said, "We have nothing but *mezcal*."

"Cold beer," Mateo said, "with thick foam."

The man reached under the bar, and Domingo saw Mateo tighten, then relax as the man brought them two bottles of warm beer without glasses. Mateo took one of the bottles, clamped the top between his teeth, gave it a twist. He spat the top out on the floor, and pushed the open bottle toward Domingo. He then did the same with his own bottle. He glanced up at the man.

"We'll pay you when we've finished drinking."

"And when will that be?"

"When Pancho Lozano stops hiding in a closet, and comes out to meet us like a man."

Domingo could feel a ripple pass over the room, as though these people had stopped breathing for a moment, and were now breathing again.

He glanced cautiously around, and was struck by the fact that although the men, in their pink and green and lavender shirts, were all individuals, the women were merely duplicates, one of the other. All of them had on close-fitting, sleeveless satin dresses, their arms brown and flabby against the sheen of the cloth. Their lips were heavily painted, and their faces coated with a white powder that made their thick brows and beaded lashes look pasted on. Their hair hung free, in heavy lusterless ringlets, small spit curls outlining temples and cheeks. The white light from the gasoline lanterns threw heavy shadows across their mouths and throats. From the men came the dank odor of sweat, from the women the reak of cheap perfume.

One of the women rose. Undulating on spike heels to a juke box, she pushed a slug into the slot, then punched down a record number. She stayed there until a scratchy raucous version of "Beer Barrel Polka" filled the air. Finally she turned and came toward their table. Mateo said, without moving his lips, "If she chooses you, dance with her."

Her black eyes were wide and staring, the pupils shrunken to pinpoints by dope. She bent forward, stared at Mateo, turned her head toward Domingo. She lifted off his hat, examined the inside of it, dropped it on the table. One of the men laughed, but when Domingo glanced toward him, the sound was snipped off as by scissors. She tugged at his shoulder. He stood up.

The brass knuckles were still on his right hand, and Mateo had said to keep that hand in his pocket, so he kept it there. He put his left arm around her waist, and she felt soft as meat without bone. Her two palms came up to his shoulder, and they began to dance.

The dope did not seem to affect her dancing. It was like pushing air across the room. He could feel her in his arm, but there was no sensation of weight, of having to maneuver another person. Her head lolled back until he saw her face from chin to forehead, rather than from forehead to chin. She moved closer to him, and the heat from her body penetrated his clothes. Now and then she laughed, her face instantly smoothing into black lines again.

The thick powder, the half closed lids, the complete lack of expression should have looked like a mask, but it was not a mask. Márgara's face was a mask. This woman's face was drawn by an amateur, the space from nose to chin too long, from hairline to eyebrows, too short.

No one else danced. When the record stopped, she turned away from him, collapsed at an empty table, folded her arms and rested her cheek on them. Domingo hesitated a moment, then told the bartender to take the woman a glass of *mezcal*. He rejoined Mateo, who was drinking the warm beer.

The bartender stopped at their table, stared at Domingo, then jerked his head toward the girl. "She's Lozano's woman. And he's jealous. He'll be here in a minute."

Mateo found a cigarette, lighted it and passed it to Domingo, then lighted one for himself. Although Domingo could not see Mateo speak, he heard, "When Lozano comes in, he'll start trouble. Go straight to the car and wait there for me."

Mateo leaned back, hooked his arm on the back of his chair and stared insolently at Lozano's woman.

For a moment Domingo disliked Mateo's calm air of command, until reason told him that this was Mateo's world, not his, that he was allowed here only on sufferance. It struck him as odd that Mateo had even brought him, was actually turning against a man from below in the service of a man from above. If there had ever been any question of Mateo's loyalty, it was dissipated now in this room. The dislike faded into gratitude, and he, too, turned to look at the woman.

She had drunk the *mezcal* and was facing them. To Domingo it was as though the other people in the room were puppets, that no one was alive in it save himself, Mateo, and the woman.

Her dope filled eyes narrowed. She's tired of playing, Domingo thought. What is she going to do now? His right fist clenched tighter around the brass knuckles.

She pulled the back of her hand across her mouth, then gave a piercing scream. The room shivered with the sound. The second time she screamed, a door hidden to one side of the bar snapped open, and a small muscular man with an oblong face came through it.

The woman buckled her fingers on her hips, began to laugh. It made Domingo a little sick to watch her open mouth, crimson with rouge on the lips, the yellow pink of her tongue, to hear the shrill sounds, to know that there was no brain commanding the action.

Lozano walked toward them, his hands dangling free, his weight on the balls of his feet. He walks like a bullfighter, like Mateo's brother, Domingo thought briefly. Then he saw the man's eyes. They were swollen and bloodshot, and there was hate in them.

Lozano reached a table, gave it a push with his hand. Two of the men sitting at it were tumbled to the floor by its weight. They scrambled to one side, knives flashing. Lozano paid them no attention. All of the men were standing now, their knives reflecting the white glare of the gasoline lanterns.

Mateo did not move. Domingo felt his mouth go dry with fear. He forced himself to remain silent.

Lozano paused between them, rested his fists on the table top, looked at Domingo, then at Mateo, then at Domingo again.

"Why did you dance with my woman?"

Mateo had given no cue for these speeches. He took a deep breath, and then, without warning, the thick jelly of his anger exploded. He could feel his eyes widen, his nostrils flare. All the arrogance of his ancestry was in him as he answered, "Because it amused me."

"So?" Lozano looked at the hovering circle of men. "He says it amused him."

Some of the men laughed, but there was no gayety in the sound.

"What do you want here?"

"You," said Domingo. He wanted action. Without thought, his foot caught Lozano's leg, jerked him sideways so that the table crashed to the floor and Lozano with it.

Mateo put a bullet through the lamp on the bar, and the released gasoline ignited, turned the bar into a blazing torch. Domingo wrenched sideways from the gleam of a knife, released his right hand from his pocket. He thrust it into something soft and yielding, and heard a surprised grunt.

Women were screaming, but he was too busy to listen to them. Guns in this small room were useless. The bullets could just as easily hit friend as foe. Mateo must have known that, Domingo thought groggily, because there were no more shots. He warded off another knife thrust with his arm. A river of fire crossed his cheek. The pain added to the wildness in him. He had never before felt the lust to kill, but he felt it at this moment. His right arm swung of its own volition, and he stood with feet spread apart, his weight well-balanced, his lips pulled back from his teeth in a wide grin. His enemies were no longer men but giant cats, outlined by the flames of the burning bar.

A cat darted toward him from the right, another from the left, knife talons raised high. He twisted sideways, and his hands caught two heads, smashed them together. Then all the cats were tumbling toward him. He flung back his head and loudly yelled, the deep lung yell of delight.

(A Vázquez had yelled thus at the infidel Moors of Granada. Another had yelled against Zachary Taylor's *yanquis* from the top of the Bishop's Hill. Still another had yelled against the French in the battle of the Fifth of May. All of Domingo's heritage was in that triumphant sound.)

Something tugged at his back. He tried to break free, heard Mateo's voice through the blood roaring in his ears, "Let's get out of here!"

Domingo wanted this fight as a man craves liquor, but the practical voice killed the excitement. With the passing of battle madness, he realized that Mateo had chosen their table with a view to quick exit, and the door was very close. Back to back, they fought their way toward it. It was not until they were outside that Domingo discovered Mateo had Lozano's body draped across one shoulder.

The enemy was shooting at them. They had to dart into the field to escape flying bullets, and Mateo fell to one knee. Domingo, ahead of him, whirled and ran back, tugged at Lozano's body. "I'll take him. Can you walk?"

"I think so," Mateo gasped. At the first step he collapsed again. "Go on. Go on! If they catch you, you'll be buzzard's meat."

Domingo hesitated only a second. Lozano was limp weight. He could not manage both at once, and Lozano was the prize they had gone to Baca's to get. He stumbled across the field, dumped Lozano in the back of the car, pulled the man's head around and pressed his fingers on certain nerve centers in the thick neck. Lozano, already half conscious, slumped down again into helplessness.

As Domingo raced across the field toward Mateo, he thought gravely that a knowledge of medicine was invaluable in a fight.

The ex-chauffeur was stretched out at full length, protected by a clump of *anacahuita* bushes. He was guarding his shots, making each bullet pay for its passage. Luckily, the fire from the bar had spread to the house, and the men were more concerned with saving their women than in rescuing Lozano. A few of them, however, were still shooting.

Domingo, crouched low, swerved from one side to the other, finally dropped on his knees beside Mateo. "I'm going to pick you up. It will hurt."

"That's better than being dead," Mateo muttered.

Swinging him to the fireman's carry, Domingo snatched the gun from Mateo's hand, fired rapidly as he turned, and then ran at full speed to the car. The vagrant idea occurred to him that Diego Rivera's colorful dramatic sense would delight in this scene: the weighted figure running across the *yuca* studded field to the car, and in the background the tangerine, violet and green of the flames, outlining the jerking silhouettes who were trying to drag terrified women out before the roof collapsed.

He dumped Mateo on top of Lozano, climbed under the wheel, and pushed the gas pedal to the floor. Not until they were a kilometer's distance from Baca's, did he draw to a stop.

Mateo was unconscious, but Domingo, working quickly, soon brought him back to an awareness of his surroundings. Luckily the bullet, which had passed through the side, had not touched the ribs. Domingo did a round bandaging job with part of Mateo's shirt and sat back on his heels.

"Now that the heroics are over," he said wearily, "what do we do with Lozano?"

"Nothing." Mateo grinned through pain clenched teeth. "We put a little note on him, and dump him here in the road. They'll find him by morning."

"What kind of note?"

" 'With the compliments of Domingo Vázquez de Anda,' would be nice, I think."

This psychology, which belonged to the people below, was difficult for Domingo to fathom, but he dimly understood what Mateo meant. Having been defeated by Domingo in the eyes of his friends, Lozano would no longer attempt to blackmail him. "I had best stay away from dark streets for a while," Domingo said. "He might try to put a knife in me to avenge his honor."

"He might," Mateo agreed. And then, shyly, "I knew you would not leave me, s'ñor Domingo."

Domingo made no answer, but pulled Lozano's lax body into the road, and fastened the note to his chest. Then, making sure that Mateo was as comfortable as possible under the circumstances, he said, "I'd better get you to the hospital."

"For a small wound like this? There is a doctor in my *barrio* who will take care of it very well. If you would drive me to my mother's, please?"

He's a servant again, Domingo thought. He's grateful to me for saving his life, and now he's a servant again.

Mateo's mother was a dignified woman who asked no questions, but sent her youngest son off for the doctor.

This busy little man was also gifted with silence. After taking care of Mateo, finishing with an injection to make him sleep, he turned his attention to Domingo, expertly cleansed and bandaged the knife wound on his cheek, and then rushed off to attend his other patients.

Mateo was still awake when Domingo stepped to the bedroom door to see how he fared.

"The doctor said you would be on your feet in a week," he said awkwardly.

"Less than that," Mateo answered cheerfully.

Domingo nodded, not knowing what to say. Mateo said, "I was going to show the house with the green bathroom tomorrow morning. Perhaps you can attend to it, s'ñor Domingo."

"It's your sale," Domingo said. "I'll tell the man he must wait until you recover." He put his hand on the door, turned so that he could not see the face on the bed. "Also, men in business together—titles are foolish, don't you think?"

He left quickly. He did not want to be late for his interview with don Agapito.

XXI

Don Agapito's house, in the exclusive Bishop's Hill district, had central heating, glass brick, and a canopied roof deck. The Mexican architect who designed it was a fervent admirer of Frank Lloyd Wright. A decorator had been brought down from New York to furnish it. There was a pleasant array of colors, proper pictures on the walls, and no books on the shelves. These were filled, instead, by Tecla's admirable collection of luster ware.

Domingo, while he waited in the long living room, beautiful in bleached wood, felt as he had so often in the past that people lived in this house, but they kept their homes someplace else.

A silent footed manservant, dressed in white, came and told him that his uncle was waiting for him in the study.

Domingo obediently followed him up the curving stair to the small room where don Agapito was sometimes allowed to find what he called his "few minutes of relaxation."

It was fitted like an important man's office, with built-in filing cases, and a huge desk that, so far as Domingo was concerned, served no other purpose than to frame don Agapito in his portrait of "Banker at Home."

Don Agapito was sitting behind the desk now, the inevitable cigarette in his hand, his charming smile illuminating his face.

His man-of-the-world attitude, Domingo thought cynically. He doesn't want me to feel too self-conscious about Serafina. He shook his uncle's hand, and relaxed in the feather softness of a large chair. How much his uncle loved the various shades of yellow, as witness the pale wood of the furniture, the beige drapes and upholstery. Even the cigarette lighter had a thin patina of gold.

If his eyes saw the taped bandage on Domingo's cheek, he courteously refrained from comment. Instead, he inquired after don Rafael's health, and managed obliquely to point out how much the Miranda engagement meant to the old man's tenuous hold on life. "I call him an old man when he is five years my junior. But then, age is a matter of the mind."

284

He's getting sententious, Domingo thought. That means he's dangerous.

He said quietly, "My father's happiness means a great deal to me. He has had too much of selfishness lately."

The thrust told. It pleased him to see don Agapito's eyes jerk at the corners, the quick wetting of the lips. "Brunhilda should have used more tact. But the past is finished. At least it will be finished with . . ." he hesitated, reluctant to give point to the conversation, ". . . with the Serafina affair. I am disappointed in you, Domingo. Yes, a little disappointed."

Domingo fought his temper, was pleased to watch it come under control as he repeated the story he had told his father, and later of his adventure with Mateo.

While he talked, he could see don Agapito's eyes gleam at mention of the fight. He interrupted only once to ask, "The wounds were serious?"

"Not mine. A scratch on the cheek. Mateo fared much worse, but the doctor says there is no cause to worry."

"Possibly. These street-cultured men have an amazing vitality. Continue, please."

Domingo finished the adventure and said, "This Lozano has the instincts of a bully. To be taken and then rejected—it will make an amusing story for his friends. So amusing, Mateo thinks the man's pride will drive him from Monterrey."

Don Agapito lifted a paper knife from the desk, admired its brass sheen under the yellow light of the brass lamp. "The plan was yours?"

"To frighten him, yes. I don't like blackmailers. The plan of action was really Mateo's."

"I like this Mateo," his uncle said, and Domingo could see that the great man was pleased by the way he ran his finger up and down the blade of the paper knife. "I understand you have taken him into the firm."

"It was that or lose him to another real-estate office. He has a talent for salesmanship."

"Yes. I heard of the Palma incident. Very clever." Don Agapito replaced the paper knife at its precise angle to the brown desk blotter. He tapped out a cigarette, lit it, leaned back in his broad-armed chair. "A very ambitious man. He would make a good husband, don't you think?"

This twisting away toward Mateo puzzled Domingo. Determined to remain agreeable, he said pleasantly, "I imagine he's too wrapped up in his ambition to be much concerned. . . ." His voice faded into silence as he saw the expression in his uncle's eyes. For a moment his carefully held temper almost evaded him, but he dominated it in time. "You think he would marry Serafina for money?" The horror in his voice made his uncle smile.

"Not money, no, but an advance in position. I think he would marry Serafina for that, yes, if he is ambitious enough, and I think he is."

"No," Domingo said. And again, "No!" The chair was too soft under him. He stood up, paced across the pale cream rug that made a cool spot on the glistening brown tiles. "Serafina is a good girl, a sweet girl, but she is not the wife for Mateo. He'll marry a girl from above. He's got the mark of the new rich on him already."

"Perhaps," don Agapito agreed doubtfully. "No matter. There are many ambitious young men. Don Wilfrido wanted money the other day for a protégé of his, a bullfighter. And bullfighters have no need to apologize for servant wives."

Domingo bit hard on his lower lip. The image of Serafina, the eyes too large for the heart shaped face, swam into his mental vision. He said coldly, "Perhaps Serafina does not like bullfighters."

"Women of that class, concerned with children—what do their husbands matter to them, really?"

"It's very easy to say, 'Women of that class.' But Serafina is not of 'that class,' of any class. She is a human being with a mind and heart of her own. You will not find her easy to dominate, I can tell you."

Don Agapito blew a plume of smoke into the air. His attitude held a tinge of disappointment, as though he had felt a small pride in his nephew, but now the pride was being stripped away. He said, "Sentimentality, Domingo, is a curse of your mother's family. I regret that you have inherited so much of it."

That was the end of the conversation, really, Domingo thought, reviewing it later. They had gone on talking, but don Agapito had neither been convincing, nor, in turn, convinced. To him it was a simple matter: marry an ambitious young man to Serafina, and the Serafina affair would be finished. But it was

286

not that simple to Domingo. Serafina's fragility, her pride in her child, endowed her with a Madonna aspect that filled him with protective awe.

There was one thing in her favor. No one except the boy cousin knew where Serafina was. Domingo made a point of locating Jaime and threatening him with a punishment more terrible than any beating Pancho Lozano could give him if he told.

The boy's eyes were a man's eyes when he said proudly, "I told my uncle about you, but I didn't tell him where Serafina was. He wanted to know, but I didn't tell him that."

"I trust you," Domingo assured him, and added a gift of money to the compliment.

Then he went to find Márgara and tell her the reason behind his engagement to Verónica. He carefully evaded injecting Verónica as a threatening note, because at the least hint of danger, Márgara would vanish with her father into unknown darkness. It was not pleasant to recognize that she feared the exposure of her secret more than she trusted her love for him. Her love was a matter of three week's growth. She had lived with her fear for thirty years.

So Domingo put the whole weight of his confession on his father's frailty, his bitter disappointment over Brunhilda, the pleasure he took in his son's engagement.

"Engagement," Domingo told Márgara desperately, "is not marriage. I'll find someway to escape that net. My father is really ill. His spirit is ill. My engagement is a medicine to him."

She caught his hand up to her lips, stroked his fingers. "Do you think I cannot understand? And my whole life fastened to my father?"

She moved away from him, toward the far side of the car. They were sitting looking out over the city, on top of the Bishop's Hill. The Palace screened don Agapito's home from their view, screened all of the wealthy colony. From where they were sitting they could see nothing but small, inexpensive houses, the houses of the semi-poor, with the tall arch of the pale sky above them, and in the distance, the folded slopes of Saddle Mountain.

Márgara whispered, "The church teaches, 'Honor thy parents, even when it breaks the heart.' That is what the church teaches."

Domingo stared unseeingly in front of him. "I remember when

I wanted to be a doctor, and my uncle Agapito convinced my father I should be in the real-estate business. He told me, 'It is not a son's place to question the commands of his father.' I grew up with that teaching, Márgara. It is the only teaching I know."

"It's the only teaching I know," she said under her breath.

She said then that the book between them must close. "To have half is not better than having nothing. The half is a sharper sword in the heart."

"But not so soon," he cried.

She turned to him, touched his shoulders, clutched at him. "No," she answered violently, "not so soon. We will go to Saltillo again—once more. Promise me."

"Yes," he said, kissing her. "Yes. Yes!"

The effect of his talk with Márgara stayed with him through the rest of the week, helped him to pass the difficult proposal evening with dignity and assurance.

For him it was merely a matter of waiting. He did not see don Jonás (although he had telephoned the elder Miranda to tell him that the Pancho Lozano disturbance was finished), and rigid etiquette prevented his speaking to Verónica.

If he could be said to have a reward, it was in the improvement of his father's health. Don Rafael even came down to the parlor to sip a little brandy with the triumphantly returned, and slyly joking, Irineo Miranda and don Wilfrido Vidal.

"The pleasantest proposal I ever had occasion to make," don Wilfrido assured Domingo. "We had a most stimulating conversation about José Elguero's posthumous volume, *Yesterday, Today and Tomorrow*. You remember, Rafael, the journalist who wrote for the *Excelsior* in México City. You surely must remember that magnificent sentence of his, 'Heroes are always costly, especially when they are politicians.'"

"But didn't you discuss Domingo and Verónica at all?" Brunhilda's eyes widened with disappointment.

Irineo laughed and struck his knee with his hand. "Why should we? Don Jonás knew why we were there. We knew why we were there. We knew he was going to accept our proposal. Should we waste good time talking about that, when we had so much more exciting matters—matters of history, of philosophy, to take up our time?"

Brunhilda swung her head around toward Domingo. "Are they teasing me?" There was a flare of anger in her.

Domingo winked and handed her 'a glass of wine. "Calm yourself, my sister. It is me they are teasing. Did you decide on my wedding date?"

It was easier to talk about the engagement now. It was almost as though he were discussing someone he vaguely knew, a chance acquaintance whose destiny was of small importance.

"But certainly." Don Wilfrido nudged Irineo with his elbow. "Shall we tell him or let him perspire a little?"

The old jokes, Domingo thought wearily, and they meant nothing to him. He simply did not care. When he refused the bait, their faces filmed with disappointment. The wedding would be in December, they told him. On December 15th. For ten months he would be a free man, and then, farewell to freedom.

Don Wilfrido grew suddenly serious, put his hand on Domingo's knee. "But don't believe them, any of them, when they tell you of the marriage trap. Without marriage, a man is only half a man. Without children, he is no man at all. When they put your first son in your arms, you will know what I mean. There is never a love that quite touches the love for your first son."

Domingo's eyes rose to his mother's. She was sitting quietly beside don Rafael. But she caught her son's glance, raised her brows, thrust her chin out a little toward the marble topped table. They were in the formal parlor, where the Louis XVI furniture was not comfortable to anyone. Since this was a state occasion, the discomfort had to be endured.

Domingo could not imagine why the table, bare except for a double bowled Victorian lamp and a book, should be important at this moment. And then he saw that the book belonged to Cardito, was one of his law books. My eldest son has already been born, he thought, and was glad of Jorge Palafox's entrance, glad of the respite from an emotion that he did not want to feel.

Sofía and don Lucio came with Jorge. They had been at the hospital, trying to entertain Cardito, whose enforced idleness was making him cross.

Don Lucio embraced Domingo, patted his shoulders, said, "To think of you married. I can't endure it."

Everyone laughed at the feeble joke. Don Lucio told them he had some really pleasant news. "Not a calamity such as these crows bring." He waved his hand toward Irineo and don Wilfrido, and his voice had a cutting edge to it.

Domingo pursed his lips in surprise. It had never occurred to him before that don Lucio could have likes and dislikes in the manner of ordinary people. The shy little man deeply loved don Primitivo; he deeply hated don Agapito, but beyond those dominating emotions, don Lucio· led a shadow life, passing through the family as a gull's shadow passes over water.

His mother cried, "But is that not wonderful news, Domingo?"

"I am sorry, mother. I was thinking . . ."

"You can't expect a newly engaged man to follow a conversation with intelligence," don Wilfrido guffawed, rocking back and forth on his chair.

His mother raised her shoulders, but her eyes did not echo the laughter. "To think of having Cardito home on Sunday. All of my children together again. Really together."

The four Vázquez de Andas, Domingo thought. Cardito home again, safe again.

"Until December," Sofía murmured. She had sat down close to her mother, and she seemed oddly ill at ease. She knows I don't love Verónica, Domingo thought, but I wish she wouldn't pity me so obviously.

Then he knew what was making the room feel stuffy and close. It was not the jokes of the men, but the pity of his mother and Sofía that he resented.

He got up, busied himself with pouring more glasses of wine and brandy. At the moment his desire for Márgara was a pain throbbing in his chest.

Dimly, as through water, he heard Jorge Palafox say, "This gathering is a pleasant memory to carry away with me."

"You are leaving?" Brunhilda cried, her voice too shrill.

"But yes. Tomorrow, I think."

There was a babble of voices that drowned Palafox's, but Brunhilda's tones cut through the noise, stamped it out of existence.

"You said you were going to stay at least two months . . . that you were going to buy land for a factory."

"I have bought it," he answered.

Business came into the room, sat down beside Jorge, gestured for silence with the primness of a schoolteacher.

"I closed the deal with Mateo this morning."

Brunhilda's eyes were suspicious. "Mateo's sick."

Jorge nodded, turned to face Sofía. Domingo had the impression that Jorge was trying to say something to Sofía in a code known only to the two of them.

"I know. I went to his house. Do you mind, Domingo? Mateo knew what I wanted."

"I am glad. This sale meant a great deal to Mateo."

"I know." Jorge's tones were colored by the reserved note that always came into his voice when he spoke of the ex-chauffeur. "He's a remarkable person. And his mother is a charming creature. She reminds me of my French grandmother for some reason, I don't know why. That same bird-like dignity. Birds are very dignified, or is the word 'self-assurance?' "

He was still facing Sofía. Her fingers fluttered at her throat. She was more unsure of herself than Domingo had ever seen her. Then she rose in the fluid movement that was part of her training, and hurried from the room with a mumbled, "Forgive me."

"Such manners," don Rafael gasped. "Domingo, fetch Sofía back at once. And tell her I expect a proper apology . . ."

"Please," Jorge interrupted. "Forgive me, don Rafael, but . . ." He paused, embarrassment on his face. "I told Sofía this afternoon that . . ." Again the pause. It was difficult for him to speak in the room filled with curious people. He said steadily, "I was hoping that you would give your consent to our engagement, don Rafael."

"To Sofía?" The name was a breath from Brunhilda.

"Unfortunately she does not . . . the idea is not agreeable to her." He stepped across the room, raised doña Otilia's fingers to his lips. "It has been an honor, señora."

Then he was shaking hands with don Rafael, with Irineo Miranda and don Wilfrido. He bent over Brunhilda's lax fingers and turned to Domingo. "You have been kind to a stranger. And so has Mateo. A very remarkable man, Mateo."

"Very," Domingo agreed gravely. What a nice thing etiquette is, he thought, setting up all the rules for one to follow under any circumstances. Keep the emotional scenes to a level balance.

Nothing must tilt the balance too much one way or the other. "Of course, if you're building the factory you will be back with us soon."

"I will try to return in December for your wedding."

"And for mine," Brunhilda said without inflexion. She did not glance around at her family. Her eyes were steady on Jorge's face. "I was waiting to tell it until after Domingo had his little hour. But I'd like you to know before you leave. I'm marrying Tito Gómez in December, on the fifteenth, the same day as my brother. It will be amusing, don't you think? A double wedding?"

Don Rafael started to speak. Doña Otilia twitched his sleeve, silenced him with the gesture. Jorge Palafox spoke the proper words, then there were more bows, more courtly phrases, and don Lucio took Jorge's arm, guided him toward the door. He said over his shoulder, "I will be back late. Don Primitivo, Jorge and I are going to celebrate the new factory."

After the door shut behind them, don Rafael exploded to Brunhilda, "And what is this nonsense about Tito? I thought . . ."

Her chin was high, belligerent. "Don't pretend you don't like him, Father, because you do. I'd much rather be married to Tito than Jorge Palafox. He's so much more comfortable, so much less exciting. Sofía has good judgment. We are not cut out for excitement, we Vázquez." As she whirled, her skirts billowed around her. The closing door caught the hem, and they heard the goods rip.

Domingo wondered if she would ever wear the dress again. It was the same turquoise moiré she had worn the night she returned from New York three weeks ago.

"So many marriages," don Wilfrido was saying. "But that is the way. You lose one bird, and soon the whole nest is empty. Congratulations, Domingo, on Mateo's sale of a factory site. It should make a pretty profit."

Business smiled, preened herself. "I am more important than engagements," her phantom lips told Domingo before she faded from view.

Again the farewells, the courteous phrases. The two men seemed unaware of the broken ambitions that had been in the room with them, the shards floating about their heads; or perhaps they were covering ugliness with the patina of good manners. That had been the philosophy of the creole since Cortés first set foot on Mexican soil. "Good manners cover everything, including the devil's tail."

In the spell of the same philosophy Domingo escorted them to the front door, his face reflecting nothing but courtesy.

Before stepping into the street don Wilfrido tapped his arm. "Agapito called me this morning. He said that you and he have a plan for my bullfighter. I am most interested. Perhaps you can come to see me tomorrow or the next day?"

The shock made no impression on Domingo's new armor. He said, "I regret—with Mateo ill just now—next week, perhaps?"

"Of course. Patience is a good whetstone for curiosity."

Domingo shut the door. Brunhilda must have been waiting for the sound of its closing, because he could hear her begin to scream. Unable to endure the thought of his sister's hysterics, he caught up his coat and fled down the street, toward Márgara, toward his safe enchanted world.

Márgara was not at the studio. Domingo could hear the telephone ringing and ringing, but no one answered. For a moment, after he hung up, he was frightened. Where was she? What had happened to her? Then he remembered that she had told him Bárcenas loved the movies, that they often went in the evenings. He wished childishly that they were all in San Antonio where six English movie houses and four Spanish might give him some chance of locating her. But Monterrey's twenty major houses, and at least thirty neighborhood theatres removed any hope at all.

Thrusting his hands deep in his pockets, he wandered up Morelos Street, staring in the windows of camera stores, bookshops, Chinese stores, and *Arabe* stores. His eyes saw meters of Chinese silks, Swiss organdies, Irish woolens, toys and costume jewelry brought in from the States; books magnificently bound in leather; graceful religious images from Spain; fine silver from Taxco, perfumes from Turkey; embroidered slippers from Cairo.

His ears heard the chattering voices of people. Coveys of shopgirls in their best finery flirting with radio mechanics, with students, with *conscriptos* in uniform. Sober business men strolling with their plump wives and herds of children. And there were tourists, sometimes romantic couples, sometimes in groups of four or five.

Through it Domingo passed, his eyes open, his ears clear, but he saw nothing, heard nothing. He was intent on the image of Márgara, the sound of Márgara's voice.

At the Central Market, moving through force of habit, he turned right and followed the pink wall to Padre Mier. He dodged through the one way traffic, oblivious of shouted insults and grinding brakes, and went into don Primitivo's saloon.

As he had guessed, don Primitivo, don Lucio, and Jorge Palafox were sitting at a back table, all of them mellow with beer. Don Lucio was trying to give Jorge a mandolin lesson, to the clearly phrased disgust of the other customers.

"Eh," don Primitivo boomed, seeing Domingo, "here is a rooster with no need of solace for a broken heart." He shouted to his brothers to bring more beer. "An engagement demands celebration."

Jorge smiled, tried to look happy over Domingo's happiness. "Now we will talk. I have had enough of this instrument."

"An insult," don Lucio said, hugging the mandolin.

"I lack the talent," Jorge said placatingly. "A man needs talent to conquer the chords."

"Not talent," don Primitivo corrected, "earth-fever. The trouble with you is that you have no country."

"I'm a Mexican."

"Are you? You're a Frenchman, an Englishman. You don't think with a Mexican brain."

"Indeed?" Jorge raised well-bred eyebrows. "My people came to Mexico some centuries before yours. There is an avenue named for one of my ancestors in México City. Which of us has the greater right to the name of Mexican, you or me?"

He's drunk, Domingo thought. He would never make such a boast if he were sober. The three of them are drunk, and so am I, but not on the same kind of liquor.

"Your ancestors have nothing to do with it," don Primitivo snorted. "Listen, there is a Spaniard who owns a grocery stall in the market. All his words are up in the front of his mouth, sweet as a sugared song. His wife comes from his own province."

"What does that prove?" Jorge took the mandolin from don Lucio, twanged two of the strings.

"Ay, but you've not heard the end of it. They have a son,

294

eighteen. He's just been shipped down to a military camp in the south as a *conscripto*."

"Magnificent," Jorge said. "A young Spaniard in the Mexican army."

"A young Mexican," don Primitivo corrected him. "The way he holds his head, the way he walks, the way he puts phrases together in a sentence, even the accent. His parents took him back to Spain two years ago. Everyone he met asked how long since he'd left the Republic. They could see the eagle stamped on his forehead."

"It's the climate that does it," don Lucio commented gravely. "I took a correspondence course once on the science of weather."

"I remember," Domingo said, accepting a large stein of beer from don Primitivo's youngest brother. "You failed that course."

"I did not fail it." Don Lucio's head moved back and forth with injured pride. "I was simply not interested in all of it. But I remember it said that climate fashions the individual. That's why an African does not look like an Englishman."

"The air," don Primitivo agreed with a courteous bow to his friend that was as courteously returned, "the water, the food, these things fashion the bones, change the skin, mold the shape of the brain."

Jorge Palafox lit a cigarette. Domingo thought, he's changing back into the magazine illustration. For a little while he has been human, but now he has left us for his own strange world of great fortunes, where a man is not Mexican, or French, or *gringo,* or any nationality at all. Don Primitivo is right. Jorge Palafox is not Mexican, poor creature. He is only a drawing in a smart magazine. Sofía must have sensed this unreality in him. She is not stupid, my sister.

"I've lived in México for ten years," Jorge protested. "My bones are still the same, my skin, my brains. I consider your argument valueless."

Don Lucio glanced at Domingo. "Are we arguing? We are simply stating a truth. It was in the course."

Don Primitivo settled more comfortably in his chair. "You were twenty-five when you came to México. The earth of France and England molded you, not México. You are not Mexican, you poor boy, and this evening proves it."

"What would I be doing if I were really Mexican?"

"Do you think a real Mexican would take a girl's prim 'No' for an answer? He would hire musicians to play under her window every evening. Wherever she turned she would find him looking at her—here is Domingo. He has won Verónica Miranda. Follow his example."

"Yes," Domingo said. "By all means, follow my example." He took another long drink of the beer. He was tired of this talk of Verónica. Márgara was his girl. It was Márgara he wanted to see, to touch, to hold.

Jorge Palafox was saying wearily, "Sometimes a girl means 'No' when she says it, especially when there is another man."

"Another man? For Sofía? Ha!" said don Lucio.

Don Primitivo spread out his hands. "We know Sofía better than you, my young rooster. She is a well guarded castle that needs . . ."

"Let us discuss history," Jorge Palafox said quietly. The tone of the Palafox was in his voice, that he had inherited from viceroys and governors and other men of command.

"By all means," Domingo said, "let us discuss history." Another man for Sofía, murmured the back of his brain. What nonsense. She was really being loyal to Brunhilda with the cold code of honor as silver cold as herself, poor girl. The front of his brain ignored Sofía, clung to the warm mystery of Márgara. He turned eagerly to don Primitivo. "What do you know of Dr. Velarde?"

This switch to the Revolution startled the two older men. It was difficult for their set minds to move so quickly from one subject to another. Don Primitivo blinked his eyes, ran his thumb up and down his chin.

"Huerta's evil man?"

"The same."

"Why Velarde?" don Lucio wanted to know. "Why, out of all history, Velarde?"

Domingo shrugged, not wishing to appear too eager. "Is he not an enigma in México history?"

"He's dead," don Primitivo commented. "I read it in a magazine. There was quite an article about him. He died in Brooklyn."

Domingo could hear the ghost voice of Márgara saying, "My father took me to a night club in New York . . ." If Velarde had died in Brooklyn, then Bárcenas must have been in New York because of Velarde. Domingo said aloud, "Irineo Miranda and Isaac Fuentes were speaking of Velarde the other day. I was interested because I remembered nothing about the man beyond his name. Don Isaac seemed to despise his very memory."

Don Primitivo took out a large handkerchief, loudly blew his nose. "I was in the north with Villa at that time. I don't remember much about him."

"I remember him," said don Lucio. His eyes turned inward, his face dried skin over bone. "I knew a girl in México City. She was dying of cancer. Such agony. It was after the Ten Days, and all the pain killing drugs were being sent to the army. I'd heard about Velarde. I went to him. I begged him to help her. He said he had no drugs. I said, 'Better for her to die, then.' Yes, I said it. I asked him for something to give her. He was a short man, no taller than myself, with black eyes in his face, very black, without pupils. He said, 'I'm a doctor. My duty is to save life, not destroy it.' 'She is in great pain,' I said, and he said, 'A normal expression of cancer.' Later he cut out the tongue of Ruperto Martínez." The expressionless voice paused, and the men stirred slightly, not looking at each other, their eyes embarrassed.

Don Primitivo asked gently, "She died?"

"Yes, she died. I was glad I was in Veracruz when Velarde left the Republic. I've never liked being in crowds, but I was glad to be in that one."

Jorge said politely, "The crowd in Veracruz was interesting?"

Don Primitivo said, "It was in all the newspapers, even in our Revolutionary sheets. I cut the story out of *Los Sucesos* because —well, you will understand why I cut it out." He yelled to his brother to bring a scrapbook, the 1914 scrapbook.

Domingo blessed don Primitivo's lust for human interest. Perhaps this clipping would give a hint of Bárcenas, if he were clever enough to read between the lines.

The scrapbook came, and Jorge looked at it with curious eyes. Don Lucio and Domingo had seen it many times, its cover of fine monk's cloth embroidered with pansies, thistles and violets possessing a sentimental value. Doña Otilia had done this work for an old man she had never seen because he was a friend of her brother-in-law's. The pages, large sheets of brown wrapping paper, were fastened together by ribbon striped in the colors of the Republic: red, white, and green. On the first page, in brilliant shades of brown and yellow, was a sun-splashed portrait of don Primitivo's own beloved hero, the man of gold, Pancho Villa.

Don Primitivo bent over the large book, his lower lip thrust out, his glasses low on his nose. He carefully licked his thumb before turning each page, muttering low phrases to himself caught from the wealth of material in front of him. Domingo knew that the scrapbook would be worth many times its weight to such men as Irineo Miranda and the Engineer Néstor Cortés. To don Primitivo it represented the gleanings of a long life devoted to the study of human beings. If he were asked to put a price on it, he would undoubtedly screw his face up in astonishment and ask, "How much is the worth of a man?" For him, the scrapbook was, in a sense, the measure of his own worth, his own contribution to the art of living.

Domingo passed his tongue over his lips. In that scrapbook might be the story of Bárcenas, not as it was known to Márgara, but as it was known to the Republic in the foggy days of 1914.

"Ay," wheezed don Primitivo. "Here it is. You see, I remembered the newspaper. *Los Sucesos.* And here is the date, June 10, 1914."

"Velarde was in Paris by June tenth," don Lucio objected. "General Angeles saw him in Paris before then. As I remember the day of the crowd, it must have been May the fifth or sixth. Of course I'm not certain. I was not interested in the calendar in those days."

"No," thought Domingo pityingly, remembering the days after he lost Doris. All you want is for the days to pass, for time to enclose you and deaden the memory.

"The paper," said don Primitivo flatly, "says June tenth. At any rate here is the story." The base of the book indented a crease on the curve of his stomach. "This account is written by a young journalist, as a memory of the event." He took a drink of beer to freshen his throat. His voice deepened to the proper monotone level as he began to read:

I recognized Velarde on the train as it pulled out of the station, bound for Veracruz. I knew that he and Huerta had quarreled, that he was leaving the country. The conductor said the man gave his name as Lozano. What a lack of imagination for a pseudonym. There are a million Lozanos in the Republic. But if it was Velarde, as I suspected, and he was going into exile, his wife and children would be with him.

"Children?" Domingo interrupted.

Don Lucio explained impatiently, "Velarde had a wife and two children. Boys or girls, I can't remember. Continue, friend."

"Hum!" said don Primitivo, glaring at the interruption.

Domingo penitently hung his head, and the great man continued:

Yes, they were on the train. It was not easy to mistake the señora. She was so very beautiful, a creole from San Luís Potosí. No one who knew her could understand why she chose to marry Velarde, an Indian from Nayarit. Perhaps she glimpsed the genius in the young medical student. She could not have seen the blackness festering in his soul.

His shadow, the Ratkiller, was not with him. . . .

"Huerta would not release that little man," don Lucio said.

"The Ratkiller?" Jorge asked curiously.

"An ex-bullfight veterinarian," don Primitivo explained. "Later he turned police informer. Gossip said he betrayed three hundred men to their death. I will now continue reading."

At the first station I sent a telegram to my friend, de la Torre. . . .

"Antonio Rivera de la Torre," don Lucio said precisely. "I knew him very well. He was editor of the Veracruz paper *El Dictamen* in those days. The American authorities put him in prison until Velarde sailed. I took him cigarettes and little cakes every day. He liked little cakes."

"Very interesting," don Primitivo said with tart courtesy. His finger ran down the lines of faded newsprint.

When the train arrived in Veracruz . . . but let me tell you. There is a bridge under which the train passes. This was lined with people. As soon as the train appeared, these people began to sing. The music shook the heavens, it twisted the soul with its cruelty. They sang the one song that broke the heart of an Emperor:

Farewell, Mamá Carlota,
Farewell, my tender love.

299

Don Primitivo laid the scrapbook on the table and glanced around triumphantly. "Did I not tell you it was the song of great satire? And my own father handed General Riva Palacios the envelope on which to write the words."

Jorge Palafox picked up the scrapbook, stared down at the clipping. He continued to read aloud in a faintly shocked voice:

> When the train reached the station, the avenue to the Hotel Nueva Diligencia was lined with people. The *yanqui* General Funston, afraid of the crowd's temper, sent a troop of cavalrymen to protect Velarde. The people begged Funston to turn Velarde over to them. "He is Mexican and we are Mexican," they said. "This is no quarrel of yours."
>
> "While I am in command here," Funston answered, "it is my quarrel. This man shall sail on the French boat *Festa*. And he shall be guarded until he sails."
>
> So he sent a troop of cavalrymen, and their horses blocked off the crowd. But they could not block off the sight of Velarde. Many of us knelt down, looked under the bellies of the animals. We could see him walking through the center of the street, carrying his own bags, because no *cargador* would touch them. Who would aid the murderer of Ruperto Martínez? Many in the crowd had mounted pictures of Martínez on posters, held them up for him to see.
>
> Did he see them? Who knows? Was he thankful that his wife and children had been spared this indignity, that a taxi driver had already driven them to the hotel? The quarrel was not with them. It was with the Indian from Nayarit, the doctor who had betrayed his profession.
>
> This was his hour of payment. He was afraid. It was not in his face but in his eyes. They rolled constantly from side to side. And the weapon used against him was sharper than any sword, the weapon that was a song. It rolled back from the buildings, it covered him with its melody. The words were engraving themselves upon his brain:
>
> Farewell, Mamá Carlota,
> Farewell, my tender love.

Jorge Palafox replaced the scrapbook on the table, repressed a faint shudder. "You are right," he said. "I lack the brain of a Mexican. Who but a Mexican could have turned a song into such fearful torture?"

Domingo hardly heard him. He was aware only of a great disappointment. Velarde, who fled to Paris, met Angeles of the

300

high ideals, and fled again to Brooklyn, to die there. Velarde, whom Bárcenas hated with such overpowering hatred that the mere thought of his hatred made Márgara shake with terror. Velarde, it was all Velarde. But what of Bárcenas? Where in all this fog of history had Bárcenas any position?

After Jorge Palafox left for México City, Domingo's life settled into a dull routine, shot through, like metal thread, by his infrequent meetings with Márgara.

His acceptance of Verónica was in the plain of his training. For generations, the men and women of his family had married according to the dictates of family. He merely slipped into the groove which was already worn smooth for him. And December was very far from February. Too much could happen in the intervening months for him to worry much about it. This, too, was a part of his training, incorporated in the texture of air and earth.

> Valentina, Valentina,
> Today I drink sherry.
> Tomorrow, if they kill me,
> I will be dead.

sang the words of the Revolutionary hymn. Birth, and life, and death could happen between February and December. Ten months might be ten years or ten centuries, for to the dead there is no time, and to the living time is of no importance when one is in love with the Xtabay.

Love made him tolerant of Tito's tears. On Thursday morning Tito came and wept in the office from sheer joy. "I have waited so long," he said. "So long. And now Brunhilda has consented. To think she gave up the magnificence of the Palafox for me." It was a beautiful thought. The more he contemplated it, the more he wept.

At home Domingo passed stern orders. Tito must never learn the truth. "What truth?" Brunhilda demanded, her full lips curved in a pout, her eyes venomous as they contemplated Sofía.

Don Agapito took the news with amazing self-control. In spite of his fine plans for Brunhilda, it did not really matter to him which niece married Jorge so long as the Palafox fortune came into the family. But Sofía's betrayal of Vázquez de Anda interests stunned him. He could not comprehend her reasoning. When she wearily explained that she did not love Jorge, he flung up his hands in amazement. Love, he declared, was not a proper subject for women's minds. They were romantic, the lot of them, and needed the guidance of a practical mentality. He did not argue with her, however. As he told Domingo, he had never been able to argue with women. "They jump to conclusions. How can a man follow through on a thread of argument when his opponent jumps to conclusions?"

So don Agapito left Sofía to the outer cold, and turned his attention to Tito Gómez. He listened to Tito's advertising schemes, and watched with interest the success of the Bárcenas plan.

Monterrey's society followed Tito's carefully laid trail, and Bárcenas had so many customers other photographers began to complain in loud voices. They need not have worried. Bárcenas refused to make appointments. Many a day no one answered the loud knocks on the studio doors. Unfortunately, this seclusion merely whetted Monterrey's appetite. She was ready to buy. What was the matter with Bárcenas that he took no interest in selling? Then a photographer on the Avenida Madero cashed in on Bárcenas' reputation, advertised photographs in "The Bárcenas Manner," raised his prices above the level of his competitors, and Bárcenas was left in peace at last.

In spite of Bárcenas' indifference, don Agapito could understand the cleverness of Tito's scheme, and highly approved of Mateo's and Tito's plans for the new middle-income property.

The sale of Santa Sofía to Jorge Palafox was much discussed in Monterrey. It was true that Monterrey already possessed six hundred factories. Nevertheless, another factory meant more wages to tinkle in the shopkeeper's tills, and Mateo swept into the gossip-light as one of the new young men worthy of watching. Domingo was constantly congratulated upon his cleverness at recognizing and polishing the rough jewel of Mateo's talents.

Through this whirlpool Domingo moved with indifference. Save for his daily visits to Cardito, his thoughts centered on Márgara, were absorbed by her image.

A second visit to Saltillo over the weekend had been made impossible by Cardito's return from the hospital. Doña Otilia was disappointed because all of her family could not be together for Sunday dinner, but Tecla's sister's child was being baptized in Saltillo and Sofía had been chosen as one of the godparents.

"She did not want to go," doña Otilia said, "but I insisted. To be chosen as a godparent is a great honor."

Domingo, sensitive to his mother's tones, looked at her curiously. Her voice lacked a conviction that was puzzling. Then Cardito came downstairs and Domingo promptly forgot this minor mystery.

Remembering that Mateo had betrayed his own class to help the boy, Domingo suggested that he be invited to the dinner. Doña Otilia looked at him with veiled eyes, but made no comment. Cardito thought it an amusing idea. It was Brunhilda who refused to sit down with an ex-chauffeur.

Don Rafael said curtly, "The man is no longer a servant. And he made us a good profit on the Santa Sofía sale. I think it an excellent idea, Domingo. Invite him."

"I will not . . ." Brunhilda began rebelliously.

Tito, to everyone's surprise, told her to hold her tongue. "I'm going to need Mateo in my business. After we're married, you will thank your patron saint for Mateo many times, I can tell you." The firm command in his voice, his automatic acceptance of his position as the ruler of Brunhilda's destiny amused Domingo, but his nerves quivered at the thought of Brunhilda's incipient hysterics.

There was a stillness in the room that made Cardito twitch his shoulders with nervousness, then she tossed her head and relaxed. Her, "As you say, Tito," startled Domingo more than any tempest. For a brief moment he saw her, not as he imagined her to be but as she really was, trapped, like himself, in the box of her world. The gloss of her *yanqui* independence slid away from her even as the engagement ring slid on her finger. She was settling like a dove into the nest of Mexican domesticity, and, Domingo reflected, in ten years she would gasp in horror at the freedom of young moderns.

But when Domingo spoke to Mateo, the ex-chauffeur raised his hands in sorrow. The satisfied Palma had promised to introduce him to other Monterrey-minded friends in Saltillo. Plans had already been arranged for this weekend. Also, it would come as a small vacation. The doctor had advised rest to give the wounded side time to heal.

Domingo said, "Sofía will be at her cousin's. Perhaps you can drive her back in the afternoon."

"It will be an honor," Mateo assured him.

That was why, at the three o'clock Sunday dinner, neither Mateo nor Sofía sat at table with them. Cardito dominated the room. His jokes, his student's humor, made them all laugh. Tito contributed some new Monterrey anecdotes to the gayety, and for the first time since Brunhilda's arrival, don Rafael's cheeks had a touch of color in them.

After dinner, don Lucio played them a few selections on his mandolin. Brunhilda even agreed to accompany him on the piano for such selections as "Over the Waves" and "Farewell for End of the Dance."

Don Rafael's hand moved in rhythm to the music and it amused Domingo to watch Cardito listening with the cynical politeness of the young for the old. It was only a surface amusement, however, because the illness had somehow changed Cardito, made him more reticent. The feeling of camaraderie between the two brothers was gone. It's my fault, Domingo decided. Every time I look at him, I think of Serafina, I can't help it, and that builds a wall neither of us can climb. The boy is puzzled by it, but I must not tell him. I must not.

He heard Brunhilda saying, "How gay we are. If Mateo were here, we should all have to be very polite, not gay at all."

Doña Otilia chuckled softly. "My daughter," she said, "you remind me of a venerable female in Veracruz whose mother had been a lady-in-waiting to Carlota. This doña Fulana had a room in a House of Guests owned by three impoverished old maids, who insisted that their clientele have the best social references in the Republic." Her laughter took on an impish tone. "But times grew difficult. It was sometimes necessary for the old ladies to accept one of the new rich, in particular one man, very nice, you comprehend, but of the type of—well, Mateo. Can you imagine our doña Fulana, poor as a country saint, insisting on sitting with her back turned to the bewildered man, even at meals? He could not imagine what he had done to offend her."

"She was right," Brunhilda said, striking a loud chord.

Don Lucio said mildly, "The romantic world of the creole is finished, Brunhilda."

Don Rafael pyramided his hands, rested his face against them. He spoke with the deliberation of a man who knows his pronouncements mean the difference between light and dark in the minds of his family. "I was lately reading an essay by Vasconcelos." He paused to give weight to the name of the famous Mexican philosopher. "He contends that we have produced a new race in the Republic, the *mestizo*, half Spanish, half Indian, combining the brilliance of the one and the strength of the other. It is the *mestizo* who will inherit México. It is his by right. México produced him and must return to him."

Brunhilda said coldly, "Nuevo León is a creole state, father. We have no place for the *mestizo* here."

"It will not stay creole long, my daughter. As long as we possessed our broad grazing lands there was no reason for the *mestizo* to leave the wealth of the south. But when Colonel Robertson built our railroad, when industry absorbed us, the *mestizo* came, lured by our money. Now that he is here, he will stay."

Brunhilda said violently, "He cannot conquer us. We are the great families still."

Tito laughed. "Ay, little cat, open your eyes. Ten years ago Nuevo León was a creole state, but not anymore. The *mestizo* is everywhere."

Cardito's dry young voice said abruptly, "The *mestizo* is the middle class. Without him there can be no democracy."

"Words," said Brunhilda. "Fine words that mean nothing."

"Listen," said Cardito, his eyes filling with fire, the orator's tone coming into his voice. "In the rest of South America the creole still holds the whip hand. Look at Perú. Lima is a creole city with processions to honor the arrival of the Spanish ambassadors, the Afternoon of Mantón to open the season's bullfight, and a snap of the fingers for the Indian starving in the mountains. Perú today is the México of eighteen forty. We are the only Latin-American Republic which has evolved a middle class, and that middle class is the *mestizo*."

Domingo smiled at his brother. At twenty Cardito was already thinking like a man. Other boys of his age, especially those with stern fathers, were still children. Pride in the boy filled him with a new warmth. The Serafina affair must not be allowed to stop this growth.

Domingo saw very little of Márgara during that long week. He saw Verónica twice, but both times she was so rigidly chaperoned by her family that he had no opportunity to talk to her.

Finally, at the Thursday night promenade, he walked her around Plaza Zaragoza, alone with her as was his right, while her mother and Tecla smiled at them from a bench to see that they stayed on the plaza, did not wander off through the dark streets behind the Cathedral.

Verónica said quietly, "If I had it again—that moment at my feast day party—I would repeat what I did. I love you, Domingo. I fight for what I love."

He said, trying to keep his voice light. "You make a dangerous enemy, Verónica."

"I don't understand you, Domingo. You say you love the Bárcenas."

"You know I love her."

"Then why don't you fight for her?"

This was dangerous ground. He shifted rapidly, trying to find a surer footing. "Perhaps there are reasons of which you know nothing . . ."

"Reasons!" Her voice was a whiplash. "Your father's been ill. You don't want to hurt him. So you give up the woman you love, and become engaged to me."

"That is a good reason, isn't it?"

"An old-fashioned reason, Domingo."

"Old-fashioned? Is that what you call obedience to your family's wishes?"

She shrugged indifferent shoulders, smiled and bowed to her mother and Tecla as they passed the gossiping women. "We have a new freedom, Domingo. Do you think Cardito would do what you're doing? Not Cardito. He'd say 'Strengthen your heart, my father, but I'm not going to marry Verónica. Fulana de Tal is the girl I love.' That's what Cardito would say."

Domingo jerked his arm in muscular reaction to the jerking in his mind. There was no doubt of it—all details of the Serafina affair must be kept from his brother. "Yes," he said slowly, "you're right. But as you say, I'm old-fashioned."

Verónica shook her head thoughtfully. "I don't think you are, really. I think you're in love with me."

"Ay, Verónica, must we start that argument again?"

"If you really loved the Bárcenas girl you'd fight for her, in spite of anyone, even your father. The way I've fought for you."

Domingo sighed, shook his head. "Sometimes you love a

person enough to give them up. You don't understand that, do you, my little romantic?"

She glanced at him with an odd expression trapped behind her lashes. The slowly pacing crowd had brought them back to Tecla and the señora Miranda. Verónica stepped out of the circle, asked solicitously if her mother was tired. Tecla frankly concealed a yawn with her square tipped fingers. "I am. Take your old aunt home, Domingo."

As he drove them through the narrow streets he thought he recognized the figure of Pancho Lozano, under a street light. A second glance assured him he was mistaken, but the resemblance was strong enough to start his mind revolving about the problem of Serafina.

Perhaps it would be best, he thought, to move her away from Tía's, but where would he take her? She loved the little town, she was happy with Tía. More important still, she was safe with Tía, because he doubted if even Pancho Lozano would dare cross Tía's wrath.

Late that night he drove to the carpenter's house on Areola Street. Serafina's uncle assured him that Pancho Lozano had left Monterrey. At least he had not been seen in any of his favorite saloons since Mateo and Domingo had given him such a fine lesson in manners. Remembering it, Serafina's uncle laughed loudly and insisted on giving Domingo a glass of sherry.

The small cousin, curled up in one corner of the room, said nothing, but he followed Domingo out to the car. "My father," he whispered, "is mistaken. My uncle came to the house yesterday. He wants to know where Serafina is staying."

"Did you tell him?"

"He beat me . . ."

Domingo caught Jaime's thin arm, shook it. "Did you tell him? If he gives Serafina another beating, it will kill her. You know that."

The boy tried to jerk free. In the light from the dashboard his face took on that aging sly look. "I had to stop the beating." Something in Domingo's expression made his voice split, climb higher up the scale. "I told him you'd taken her to Laredo."

Domingo's grasp on the thin arm loosened, but Jaime made no attempt to run away. "In the opposite direction. Do you think he believed you?"

"I followed him to the bus station, saw him leave."

"He'll be back," Domingo said slowly.

The boy was confident now, a man grown to himself and the world. "Not that one—not for a long time. I sent word through my friends, shine boys, street vendors, to spread the word in Laredo that she was there. Not the street nor the house, nothing fancy. Just that she's been seen."

Domingo laughed with relief. "The great fraternity of the street, eh? I should have been born a beggar. I'd be a wiser man today." He took his wallet from his pocket, took out a fifty peso bill. "You might spread some of this among your friends."

The boy's fingers closed talon-like around the money. He kissed the paper and was a child again. "I've done favors for them. Let them whistle." He climbed out of the car, slammed the door shut. The moonlight touched his black curls, dug hollows in the round cheeks, turned him into a small faun. "Eh, s'ñor Domingo, if you had been born a beggar, who would there be to give me money?"

"A true philosopher," Domingo retorted, and drove home with a sense of relief. At least one of his problems had been solved for a while.

XXII

That was Thursday. On Saturday he called his house and said that he had to go to Saltillo on business. His father sounded faintly worried. "You might bring Sofía home with you tomorrow."

"She's gone to Saltillo again? What important event this time?" He did not like the idea of Sofía being in Saltillo. It was the capital of the state of Coahuila, true, but it was small in size, and it would be very easy to run into her at the wrong moment.

"No event, Domingo. I think she's running away from Monterrey gossip. Everyone points her out as the girl who turned down Jorge Palafox. And if she stays at home—well, she and Brunhilda are fighting all the time."

308

"My hours may not be convenient to her."

Don Rafael said irritably. "Your mother told her to go. Sofía had already left when I returned from Agapito's." His voice demanded sympathy that his wishes should count for so little in the house where he was master. "No matter. Bring her if you can."

Domingo hung up and drove to Zaragoza Street to fetch Márgara. He intended to tell her about Sofía, but Márgara looked so young, so happy, so untouched by anything but her love for him that he could not force himself to brush her pleasure with even a shadow of the world that was outside their own enchanted circle. He was confident that Sofía would refuse to leave Saltillo at nine on Sunday morning. Some of her friends were doubtless returning in the afternoon. Let her ride with them. This weekend belonged to him and Márgara. Sofía had no place in it.

Once more the trip to Saltillo was a delight. Today was the seventh of March. It was the coming of spring. As though aware that the cold month of February had gone into its long sleep, the valley flung aside the bleakness of winter and brought out its new clothes. Yellow buds were opening on the cactus. Golden poppies lounged across gray rocks. The *huisache* trees had strung small yellow balls along their limbs, and the perfume was so sweet it made the head ache. The flowering thorn added its perfume from feathery fronds powdered in topaz.

"Everything is yellow," Márgara said contentedly. "Spring is buying her freedom from winter with lavish gold."

"Ten bridesmaids dressed in yellow," Domingo's memory reminded him. He did not care. December was lost in the haze of the future. This was March, this was spring, and Márgara was beside him.

The mountains were not connoisseurs of music, and did not care when Domingo and Márgara began to sing the old songs that grew out of the earth.

> Shadow of our Lord, St. Peter,
> The river lures me,
> And thus your love would my poor love allure.

They sang of the mosquito with a lance so sharp it pierced the heart. Because they were happy in love they sang the sad songs of lovers less fortunate:

I told you nothing.
There was naught to say.
You went to another.
To another belongs your heart.

Finally they reached Saltillo, pretended to settle themselves into the serious dignity of a couple who had exchanged rapid vows in front of the civil judge to satisfy the law, and solemn vows at the altar to satisfy the church.

But Márgara was firm about one thing. She would not return to the hotel of their previous adventure. "You would have to sign your name as Felipe Angeles again. No, Domingo, no. Call it superstition if you like. But he was executed. I will not have his shadow standing over us."

So they went to another, smaller hotel, where Domingo chose the moon as a pseudonym, and signed his name Luna. Unfortunately the dining room was closed. They had to return to the first hotel after all to get something to eat.

As Domingo started to push open the glass doors, he stopped in amazement, caught Márgara's arm and drew her into the shadows.

"What's wrong?" she whispered, pressing against him to quiet the trembling that always invaded her body when she was afraid.

"Quiet," he muttered. His brows drew together in an angry line as he stared through the glass. At this late hour the lobby was nearly empty. The clerk was reading an English mystery story. Across the tiled floor from the desk was a jewelry counter, designed to catch the tourist's eye. Cold rage invaded Domingo as he watched Sofía lean against the counter, one arm held up to display a silver bracelet.

His eyes seemed to be fitted with telescopic sights. He could see the purple amethyst carved into a flower shape and sunk in the silver, the graceful curve of her arm to the shoulder, and on the shoulder, resting there possessively, a man's hand, Mateo's hand.

The plump woman clerk was smiling at both of them, pointing out the bracelet's artistry. Her lips moved, then Sofía answered, tilting her head slightly toward Mateo. He pulled his mouth to one side as though doubtful, finally nodded and took out his wallet. Money passed across the counter, and while he waited for his change, Mateo took Sofía's hand, examined the clasp more intently. With a quick glance at the clerk, who had turned her back on them, he lifted Sofía's wrist to his lips. Domingo could see her laugh, could see the expression of adoration on her face.

Márgara pressed against him, whispered, "Isn't that your sister? The one who came to the studio with Verónica Miranda?"

"For God's sake, quiet!" Domingo cried. "Let me think clear for a moment, Márgara."

"Domingo, what are you going to do?"

"Something. I don't know. I've got to do something."

When he looked through the glass again, he saw that Sofía and Mateo were strolling, arm in arm, toward the small bar at the right. As they disappeared inside, he said, "Would you be afraid to stand here alone for a few moments?"

She begged him not to make a scene. He shook his head impatiently. "I'm only going to speak to the clerk."

It was the same clerk who had been on duty two weeks ago. He was well trained. Out of the hundreds of names that crossed his desk every week, he sorted out the right one, attached it to Domingo. "Ay, the señor Angeles. There is something I can do for you?"

"I saw a couple buying some jewelry. I believe I know the man, but I'm not sure. He is staying here?"

"The señor Chapa? Yes."

"And his wife?"

"As you say. And his wife. You do know them?"

In the mirror behind the desk, Domingo could see his face. It was stern and set, the lips tight beneath the thin line of mustache. He took out some money, folded it, thrust it under the edge of the register card-holder. "They are old friends. It would be amusing to surprise them." A secondary Domingo stood to one side, admired his primary's calmness.

The clerk's eyes shifted slightly, glinted with a wisdom as ancient as Serafina's street-taught cousin's. "An agreeable surprise I am sure. The hotel . . ." he hesitated. "A quiet surprise, perhaps?"

"Very quiet. The room number?"

"One twenty. On the left side of the patio."

Domingo nodded, said, "I will return later," and went out

to Márgara. He put her in the car, turned toward the railroad station. "The train from México City has been running late. It may still be in the station. I'm sorry, Márgara. When you get into Monterrey look for a porter named Ramírez. Tell him I said to take care of you."

She said in a low voice, "No need of that. I've been taking care of myself for a long time, Domingo."

The train was still in the station. He bought her a seat to Monterrey, lifted her hands to his lips. "Forgive me, my beautiful. I'll telephone you in the morning."

She nodded, made no answer, nor any gesture to detain him. As he strode away from the Pullman he glanced back over his shoulder. He could see her head resting against the window. Her hand rose, waved to him, and he waved back.

It didn't occur to him to wonder what Márgara might be thinking of all this. His entire attention was focused on Sofía. The cold, remote Sofía. For Brunhilda to be mixed up in an affair of this type—that he could understand. But Sofía!

Little by little small discrepancies from the past slid into place to form the entire mosaic. It had been there for him to read from the beginning: Sofía's lost handkerchief, Mateo's comment on a woman disrupting a man's ambition, the woman in white in the patio, Sofía's patience when she was teaching Mateo how to order a meal, her fierce defense of anything that was Mateo's, including the drunk brother-in-law. Yes, it was all there.

Jorge Palafox had guessed the truth. He had even said so in an oblique fashion. "There's another man," he had said, and someone laughed, called Sofía an impregnable fortress. Sofía, the fastidious. Sofía, carrying on an affair with a servant.

It's the new freedom, Domingo thought in violent revulsion. It's come too fast. Our girls have no standards left to guide them, and no judgment to aid them. And me, like a blind fool, so intent on Cardito, I forgot Sofía was only twenty-two. Doña Petra tried to warn me, but who would have guessed it of Sofía? Saints in Heaven, Sofía!

He parked the car and walked through the lobby without noticing the anxious-eyed clerk. The patio was the same as it had been two weeks ago, but then he had turned to the right. Now he followed the left arcade, paused in front of number 120. He raised his hand to knock, hesitated. Sofía had always hated locked doors. He touched the knob, turned it softly, gently eased open the door.

The room was a duplicate in reverse of the room where he and Márgara had stayed. Somehow it cheapened the ecstasy that had been his and Márgara's.

Sofía was sitting on the bed, one leg tucked under her, arms thrust behind her, propping up her body. Mateo, in his shirt sleeves, was at the dresser, carefully measuring brandy into two tumblers.

It was Sofía who saw Domingo first. Her eyes widened. She said, "Mateo!" in a choked voice.

He turned toward her curiously, saw her staring at the door, completed the circle and faced Domingo. His street training did not let him jerk with surprise. Instead, he replaced the bottle carefully on the dresser-top.

Domingo stepped into the room, away from the door. "Wait outside, Sofía," he said quietly.

She stood up, and for a moment it was not Sofía he saw, but doña Otilia, a young, slender doña Otilia. Then the illusion passed as Sofía moved toward Mateo, thrust her arm through his. "Don't be a fool, Domingo."

"I gave you an order, Sofía. Obey it."

Mateo said, "I give Sofía orders. No one else."

Domingo ignored the ex-chauffeur, kept his eyes fixed on Sofía's face. He could see her chin come slightly forward in her lifelong signal of stubbornness. "Mateo's old-fashioned," she told him. "He thinks a wife belongs to her husband."

"In the office of the civil judge," Mateo said. He pointed at a valise propped open on the luggage rack. "The documents are in there if you wish to examine them."

Domingo made no move toward the valise. Instead he went to the straight chair and sat down. Mateo lifted one of the brandy glasses, pushed it into his fingers.

Sofía said, "I'll get some water," and started toward the bathroom. Mateo caught her arm, guided her to the bed where they both sat down.

"No need of water," he told her. "At the moment he needs it straight."

She smiled, laced her fingers in his. "As you say, Mateo."

It was the same tone Brunhilda had used to Tito last Sunday, the tone of all Mexican women to the men who have conquered them, the tone Márgara never used.

Domingo propped his elbows on his knees, buried his face in his hands. "How could you do this thing, Sofía?"

"How could I not?" she asked, and the story was in her voice. From the moment she had seen Mateo in the station restaurant, she had known he was her man. When the steel strikes the flint there is fire.

"I took advantage of him," she said, leaning against Mateo's shoulder. "I was a shameless one, I can tell you."

Domingo said between dry lips. "That night in the patio, the woman in white was you."

"When he turned around and saw me he was furious." She laughed, remembering Mateo's anger. "He told me I was a shameless wench."

"Not wench," Mateo said. "I never said wench."

"You thought wench," she told him, rubbing her cheek against his shoulder. "But I wouldn't go. I put my arms around his neck and told him to make me go."

Mateo looked thoughtfully at Domingo. "I know what you're thinking. It's true I'm a practical man. It means a great deal to me to marry a Vázquez de Anda."

"Such ambition," Sofía said, her plaintive sigh ruffled with mirth.

"I owe you a debt," Mateo said. "You saved my life a week ago."

"Now who's being practical?" Sofía demanded. "You'd never have gone to Baca's in the first place if it hadn't been for Domingo."

Domingo asked slowly, "So you know about that?"

"Mateo tried to lie about it, but he lies very badly. Naturally I was curious. Wouldn't you be curious if your bridegroom had a bullet wound in his side?"

Domingo rose, crossed to the dresser, set the tumbler carefully on the glass top. "What shall I tell our father?"

Sofía came to him, put her hand on his shoulder. "Don't worry, Domingo. Uncle Agapito is very pleased with Mateo's salesmanship. He'll convince our father that Mateo is the perfect husband for me. I'll have a grand wedding in the Cathedral, and all Monterrey will agree it's a fine marriage. Don't worry, Domingo."

"Uncle Agapito?" Domingo repeated blankly. "You'd use Uncle Agapito . . ."

"Why not? Brunhilda did. Besides, Mateo's not afraid of Uncle Agapito. In fact he's convinced me that Uncle Agapito is not such an evil man."

Domingo looked around at Mateo. The muscular young man was relaxed on the bed, his face as much of a mask as Márgara's had ever been. This, however, was the mask the *mestizos* had inherited from the Indian, the mask that had strengthened them, given them power to fight the tempestuous blood of their creole ancestors, the mask of patience.

"If Mateo has convinced you that our uncle Agapito is an admirable character," Domingo said dryly, walking to the door, "then Mateo is truly a maker of miracles."

Mateo rose, said, "I'll be back in a little while."

"But, Mateo, where are you . . ."

"I'll be back." The clipped phrase sliced the question in half, told Sofía she was not to ask questions. She was a wife, now, the wife of a middle-class man, and for such there could be no questions. He shrugged into his coat, opened the door for Domingo, and the two men went out together.

"There is a bar down the street," Mateo said, "where the beer is fairly good, although not as good as don Primitivo's."

Domingo, his hands deep in his pockets, said nothing, but walked through the lobby with his new brother-in-law. The clerk watched their passage with relieved eyes. A respectable tourist hotel cannot afford a scandal, and Domingo's manner, the size of his tip, had not been reassuring. Yet here the two men were, walking out of the hotel together, as quietly as though they were really the friends Domingo had pretended.

Can I be friends with him? Domingo wondered, as they went into the small *cantina*, and found a table in a deserted corner.

Mateo said seriously, "Do you still think I am a seeker of opportunities?"

"Aren't you?"

"In a sense, yes." He looked at his palm, concentrated his attention on the clear lines. "A gypsy told me once that I would always get what I wanted. Do you believe the future is written in the hand?"

"I have never had my palm read," Domingo answered courteously. A section of his brain said, he has the mask of patience, I have the code of good manners. What is the difference, really, in the end?

Mateo let some beer trickle down his throat. "Jorge Palafox offered me a very good job in México City handling his bank's real-estate business. It paid a bigger salary than any I could get here in Monterrey."

"You are fortunate. When do you and Sofía leave?"

For the first time Mateo's obsidian eyes took on expression. "You don't understand. It was the job or Sofía. It could not be both. He loved Sofía. He was willing to gamble to get her." Mateo paused, lit a cigarette. The rancid odor of burning wax overlaid the sour fragrance of the beer as he dropped the match in the ashtray, poured a little beer over it to keep the coal from smoldering on the wax matches left there by other customers. "He said I could make a big success in the Capital, even enter politics, with a special license on my fine car. He described the car with much eloquence. Imported, you understand, with many gadgets. Very expensive. He also suggested a tailor, so that my suits could match the car, or the car my suits."

Domingo had a sudden vision of Jorge Palafox, not quite real in his magazine illustration attitude, trying to buy Mateo with an imported car. Mateo, who had grown up on the streets, Mateo who said there was a hundred centavos in every peso, the quiet, unimaginative, strangely talented Mateo. His chuckle grew into a laugh. "He should have made such an offer to your brother, the embryo bullfighter."

"That one? Zas! He'd sell his soul for enough money to buy an entrance to the ring."

"Your soul, I take it, demanded a higher price?"

"I prefer the word Sofía." Mateo's eyes were steady, and there was a glint in them that frightened Domingo a little. He'd seen this glint before in don Agapito's eyes, and in the eyes of other men who had built Monterrey into an industrial power. He's completely ruthless, Domingo thought, as ruthless as the city that bred him. Sofía sensed this in Mateo from the first, and surrendered to it, just as, in the end, Monterrey will surrender. Poor, delicate, overbred Jorge Palafox could never compete against this strength. Jorge, like Uncle Lucio, tried to buy life from a correspondence course. But Sofía didn't want a second-hand life, any more than Monterrey wants it. For them the raw product that can be forged into shape.

He remembered that flashing vision when he thought he saw his mother standing in Sofía's place. The resemblance between mother and daughter was very marked. In the Vázquez de Anda house it was doña Otilia who took command in the moments of crisis. It would be the same with Sofía. Mateo might think he gave the commands, but it would be Sofía's hand on the driving reins. Jorge Palafox could never have endured the sapping power of Sofía's determination. Him, she would have destroyed. Mateo, she could mold into any shape she wanted, and the shape she wanted was power.

Sofía-Monterrey, Monterrey-Sofía, the one the symbol of the other. Not Sofía Vázquez de Anda, but Sofía the entity, the new generation who, like Saddle Mountain, rejected the conservative line of the ranges, and stood alone, in solitary grandeur, dominating the valley, with her hands on her hips, her head pressed against the sky, her arrogance flaunting in the wind, mocking the enmity of the rest of the Republic, wearing their crude jokes proudly, and in the wearing, defeating the jokes at their source.

He remembered his uncle Lucio's words about the city, "Only the strong can dominate it." Perhaps Mateo had the necessary strength. At least he came closer than anyone else, and Sofía had chosen him.

Domingo impulsively stretched his hand across the table, his slender, delicately boned hand. Mateo enveloped it in his broad muscular grip. To Domingo's Spanish mind it was an emotional moment. The hand of the creole lay in the hand of the *mestizo*, and between the palms lay the happiness of Sofía.

Domingo returned to Monterrey because he could not endure the thought of spending the night alone in a room redolent of Márgara.

During the long drive it occurred to him for the first time what Márgara must have been thinking as she waved to him from the train window. He, himself, had placed her in the position where his rage over Sofía resolved itself into humiliation for

317

Márgara. Anger filled him, directed this time at his own thought-lessness.

Verónica had said that obedience to one's parents was old-fashioned. Brunhilda had not considered her father's wrath, nor had Sofía. What they wanted they reached out and took, without a thought of the consequences.

Domingo's eyes narrowed as he peered through the wind-shield at the smooth road unwinding over the mountain pass. Doña Otilia had told him he was too closely bound to the old generation ever to be happy with the new. He decided that she was wrong. It was really a matter of choice, and the choosing was now. He would follow the new. Márgara was his girl. Let don Agapito dig into her past, discover anything he liked. Márgara was the important one, not the sacred purity of the Vázquez de Andas. It was mere surface purity. Hidden in the footnotes of their history was theft and cowardice and blood, as there was in every history. Tomorrow he would call the family together, tell them about Sofía, and tell them about Márgara. He firmly pushed the thought of his father's frailty out of his mind. The new generation did not take into account the illness of old men.

When he opened the large gates to the back patio, he was surprised to find the entire house and all three patios blazing with lights. Sofía must have telephoned the news of her marriage, he decided, as he garaged the car.

Then he heard Florinda's shrill voice calling, "Doña Otilia, the s'ñor Domingo has arrived. It is you, s'ñor Domingo?"

"Yes," he shouted, and hurried through the patios to the gallery stairs. His mother was waiting at the top, a lavender wool shawl spread over her shoulders, hiding her white nightgown. Don Lucio circled her like a small puppy, eager to give aid but not certain how to do it.

"We have been telephoning all over Saltillo for you," don Lucio said fretfully.

Doña Otilia held her voice under rigid control. "Lucio, go and telephone Agapito that Domingo has arrived. Petra, is that you sulking in the shadows?"

"I am not sulking," the cook snapped. "I want you to get out of this cold."

318

"Turn off the lights, and send Florinda to bed."

"I'm going to make you some chocolate."

"As you please." Doña Otilia beckoned Domingo to follow her into her room. He noticed with sudden terror that don Rafael was not in his bed. "Sit down, Domingo. I have bad news for you."

"Where is father?" He realized the words were stupid even as he asked them. If his father had been dead, doña Otilia's shawl would have been black, not lavender.

"With Agapito. I tried to keep him at home, but you know how he is when he gets stubborn."

Domingo reached for his mother's hand. "Don't worry, Mother. I saw Sofía in Saltillo, had a long talk with her . . ."

"Stop chattering, Domingo. Listen to me, please."

He had never heard this tone in doña Otilia's voice. This, added to the snapping of her fingers for a cigarette, meant that she was truly nervous. She never smoked unless she was faced with a crisis she did not quite know how to handle.

"This afternoon, about six, after you left for Saltillo, your uncle Agapito came for a brief visit. He had a long talk with Cardito, upstairs in the boy's room."

"Cardito," Domingo echoed.

"Don't interrupt. When Agapito came downstairs, he was very pleased. Then he told us the news. He has decided to make Cardito his heir in the bank."

"Cardito a banker? But he wants to be a lawyer!" The words shot out before Domingo could stop them.

"I used the same words to Agapito. He pointed out that you would inherit the real-estate office. Since he had no children of his own, Cardito was the logical choice. He had thought of Tito, but he admires Tito's talent as an advertiser. Your father agreed with Agapito's reasoning."

Domingo could keep still no longer. He jumped up, began to pace the floor. "This is absurd. I won't have it. Cardito has a fine talent as a lawyer. I will not permit his being shifted into something he will hate as I hate that real-estate office. Uncle Agapito shall not destroy Cardito. I won't let him touch the boy."

His mother, who kept her eyes closed during this tirade, said now, "I don't think that choice is yours, Domingo."

"And who has a better right? If I accepted his bastard as

319

mine, do you think that . . ." He stopped, turned away from her. "I'm sorry, Mother." The piled emotions of the evening snapped together, pressed down upon him. His skull felt too small for the throbbing brain. He flung himself in an armchair, moodily stared at the tip of his shoes.

"There is one person with a better right," his mother answered coldly. As he glanced sideways at her, she nodded. "Cardito himself."

"Cardito?"

"He has run away, Domingo."

All the muscles of Domingo's face relaxed. There was a roaring in his ears, and the room blurred. His doctor's hidden sense warned him that he was dangerously close to fainting. He bent forward, dropped his head low between his knees, felt the blood tingle as it rushed to his brain, cleared it, made thinking possible again.

"Are you sure?"

"He left a note. It was addressed to you, but when I discovered he was gone and found the note, I opened it and read it." She unfastened the cuff of her full sleeve, took out the note and handed it to him.

He rubbed his eyes with his fingers, shook his head. "I can't . . ."

She ignored his weakness. He could hear the paper rattle between her fingers as she unfolded it, and then she read in a precise voice:

My dear brother, I am not an animal to be pushed from pasture to pasture. I borrowed a hundred pesos from the box in your room. In time I will repay it. If you will remember, I ran away once before and found myself a job. I am doing it again. But I am older now. I will not be such a fool as to stay within reach of Uncle Agapito's long arm. That is why I am borrowing the money.

She stopped reading, added with an air of surprise, "He underlined the word 'borrowing.' "

Domingo took the note from her, re-read it again for himself. He noticed that it was signed with Cardito's full name: Ricardo Vázquez de Anda y Fausto. He had to smile at the childish pride of the signature. "He's such a little boy," he murmured.

Doña Otilia snorted. "Pure Vázquez de Anda. Just like your father."

Don Lucio came into the room, hesitated near the door. She said, "Either come in or go out, Lucio. Don't hover."

He said meekly, "Agapito wants Domingo to go to his house immediately."

She thanked the little man, waved him out of the room. Then she went to Domingo, pressed his head against her softness. "When I worry, I speak too sharply. Domingo, find Cardito for me. Your father and Agapito mean well, but they lack the Fausto brains. Especially Agapito. He wants to roll over everything with a steam tractor. And Cardito is just like him. When two tractors meet, they explode. And all that is needed is a simple twist of the key. A clever twist, Domingo, done by a man with brains, not brute force." She wiped the tears from her eyes. "Make them stop whatever they are doing and use common sense, Domingo."

"Of course, Mother." He kissed her hand, went downstairs to the hall telephone, put in a long distance call to Saltillo. Mateo's voice at the other end sounded thick with sleep. But the sleepiness vanished as though wiped away by Domingo's news. Once Mateo asked him to wait. Domingo could hear a rapid conversation somewhere in the background. While he waited, doña Petra, carrying a tray of chocolate, paused beside him.

"Who are you calling at this hour?"

"Mateo."

"That one? Since when is Mateo to be told family secrets?" Her servant's pride was hurt. I am the privileged one, she implied, not this young upstart.

Domingo thought, everyone will know it by tomorrow. He said, "He's part of the family now. He married Sofía last Saturday."

Before she could comment, Mateo was speaking again, saying that he and Sofía would leave for home immediately. "Don't make a move until I get there. If the papers get hold of it, no telling what scandal they'll print, including the Serafina affair."

"Come to my uncle Agapito's," Domingo said, ignoring the tone of command. He understood Mateo's attitude, Mateo, the practical, the efficient. Since the evening of the fight, as though to compensate for having been carried to the car by Domingo, Mateo had released the bonds of his forceful personality. It is compensation, Domingo reflected, for having to owe his life to me.

In this case, he felt Mateo was right. It would not only be Serafina who was affected, but Márgara, also. If reporters ever get hold of her! He shivered, crossed the patio to go to the car. A sobbing in the darkness halted him. Doña Petra was crouched on the bottom step of the stairway, her shawl pulled low over her face, her body shaking with her tears.

"Eh, doña Petra." Domingo knelt beside her, put his arm around her. "Do not weep, little old one. We'll get Cardito home safe again."

"Cardito," moaned doña Petra. "He's a man. He can take care of himself. It's Sofía."

"Ay, doña Petra. I know. But the world moves, and the future is already yesterday."

"I told you to watch out for her. When you hired Mateo I said to myself, 'He's all man, that one.' I kept Florinda out of his reach. But you wouldn't guard Sofía."

Domingo had to bite down on his lower lip to keep the laughter out of his voice. Poor Sofía, indeed, he thought. It should be poor Mateo. "Never mind," he said comfortingly. "By the time we are through with Mateo, he'll wish he were back in the simple peace of a chauffeur's life. We're a wild lot, we Vázquez."

She nodded, let him help her to her feet. Then she tugged at him until he bent his ear close to her mouth. "Don't tell doña Otilia I said this. If you do, I'll swear I never spoke the words. But it's not the Vázquez blood that's wild. Doña Otilia's own father . . ." she hastily blessed herself, kissed the back of her thumb. "All I ask of you, niño Domingo, is to let me see Brunhilda's face when she hears about Mateo. It will be such a lovely moment."

At his nod, she stumbled up the steps while he went to the garage.

Domingo parked his car in front of his uncle's house, put it in gear to keep it from sliding backwards down the hill, then relaxed and lit a cigarette.

Good drivers, aided by the downward slope of the road, could return from Saltillo in forty-five minutes, and Mateo was an excellent driver. Mateo was the stone falling toward the placid pool. Mateo was the knife in the hunter's hand.

It did not occur to Domingo to feel pity for the stone, sorrow for the knife. His mind was fixed on the water of his uncle's serenity, on the crouching lion of his uncle's arrogance.

He bent forward and the light from the dashboard illumined his face, sunk hollows at the temples, narrowed his cheeks with shadow, darkened his chin to the illusion of a beard. The face was no longer Domingo's face but the face of Spain, a Spain three centuries dead, the Spain that had followed Cortés to set the mark of its branding iron on quivering Indian flesh, the cruel white metal of Spain stripped of its dusky beauty, its gold in the firelight, its castaneted romance. The Spain that had conquered three quarters of the world was in Domingo's face as he bent forward to look at his watch.

Thirty minutes more to wait. He ran down the car window, tossed out his cigarette so that it made a flashing arc toward the checker-board of lights that was the hospital. A line of dark houses hemmed the further side of the Saltillo Road, and beyond them were the broad plains and the wall of mountains, a wall of blackness against lighter blackness. The moon had set long ago, but the stars tufted the sky with glittering hardness. He looked up and wondered if somewhere Cardito was also looking at the stars. Most probably Cardito was curled up sound asleep, his round child's face untouched by worry.

Domingo's doctor's mind gnawed at the problem of Cardito. The boy was still too weak to expose his body to bad food and over-exertion. A guilty conscience touched Domingo, whispered that this was all his fault. Márgara had drugged him with love, had dulled his judgment. He should not have left Cardito so much alone. The mischief was done. Regrets could not change the past.

His second cigarette finished, Domingo climbed the steps to the front door. When he reached the study he found his uncle framed by the big desk, and don Rafael sunk apathetically in the large soft chair.

Don Agapito snapped, "Lucio telephoned thirty minutes ago that you were in town. What has kept you so long?"

Domingo raised his brows, pulled a chair forward and sat

in it, thrusting his long legs out in front of him. "I was waiting for Mateo. He should be here in ten or fifteen minutes."

Don Rafael said gently, "Mateo may be a member of our firm, my son. He is not yet a member of our family."

Domingo said, "He is now," and told them the story of Mateo and Sofía.

Neither man moved nor interrupted. Don Rafael's face whitened a little, became a bit more tired, but the blow of Cardito had padded him so that the blow of Sofía bounced away from him like a stone dropping on sponge rubber.

Don Agapito lit a cigarette, frowned, said, "This is utter nonsense. Luckily the marriage is only a civil wedding. We will have it annulled. Mateo will go to México City. That will end it."

Domingo kept his eyes fixed placidly on the ceiling. "Jorge Palafox tried to bribe him with a job in México City. Unfortunately Mateo is in love with Sofía."

Don Agapito snorted, moved his lips in his charming smile. "If the price is big enough, he'll go. I know ambitious men."

"Not this one," Domingo said.

Far off in the depths of the house he heard the front doorbell ring. There was the sound of voices, of steps on the stairs, then Domingo lifted himself to his feet as Sofía came in, followed by Mateo.

"Father," Sofía cried, and went to don Rafael, kissed his cheek, sat on the arm of his chair. "This news about Cardito. It is dreadful. What are you going to do, Domingo?"

Domingo sat down again, looked around at Mateo, who seemed to be calculating the dimensions and possible cost of the room.

Domingo said dryly, "It lacks sound-proofing."

"A disadvantage," Mateo agreed, sitting down by Domingo. He accepted a cigarette from him.

Don Agapito hissed with irritation, then murmured, "We will not discuss Cardito for a few minutes. Sofía. . . ."

"Don't lose your temper, Uncle," she warned, looking at him with a face as set as his own.

Again the charming smile. "My dear niece, when do I ever lose my temper?" The smile spread, veiled the ice-sheathed eyes. The beautiful voice chose the correctly mellow tone. "You are to be congratulated, Mateo. My nephew told us of your marriage."

Domingo pulled his Spanish rapier from the hidden case in his mind, swept it in a broad arc. "Our uncle infers that you have made your fortune, Mateo. The marriage is to be annulled, and you, sufficiently well paid, will go to México City."

He watched the brass paper-knife snap between his uncle's hands, and smiled placidly. The tense silence that followed was broken by Mateo who bent across Domingo, said courteously, "Forgive me," and ground his cigarette out in the copper ashtray sunk into the wood of the chair arm. He said, "A very clever idea, that."

Domingo looked down at the ashtray, jiggled it a little in its setting. "Very clever," he agreed.

Don Agapito's voice stripped itself of warmth. "Domingo put it bluntly. That comes of his *yanqui* training. I, too, shall be blunt. What is your price, Mateo?"

Mateo glanced around the room, shrugged, let his gaze linger on Sofía who was still poised on the arm of her father's chair. She flipped her bag open, took out a lipstick and mirror and repaired her mouth make-up.

Mateo said politely, "She weighs fifty-two kilos . . ."

"Fifty-one, stripped," Sofía said.

"Sofía!" don Rafael gasped.

She smiled, patted his cheek. "You are a sweet father." Then she looked around at her uncle, a mischievous smile tugging at her lips. "A *gringo* was buying some strawberries in the market the other day, and strawberries are seventy-five centavos in set price. But you know how *gringos* love to bargain. So the vendor added ten *centavos*, took off ten *centavos*, and everybody was happy."

Don Agapito pushed his chair away from his desk. "This is preposterous."

"Yes," Mateo said gently, "I think it is." There was amusement in his voice, and something else, a calm certainty of his own power that pleased Domingo.

Don Rafael put up his hand, touched his daughter's arm. "You must be married here, in the Cathedral."

"Of course, my father." She bent and kissed his thinning

hair. "I did not really elope. Mother knew about the wedding. Tecla's brother-in-law was one of the witnesses."

"Tecla," don Agapito whispered, staring at the door as though he expected a penitent Tecla to be cringing there.

Sofía laughed, and it was the free laughter of pure mirth. "Tecla doesn't tell you all she knows, my dear uncle."

Don Rafael said wonderingly, "Your mother is a very remarkable creature, my daughter." He shook his head, muttered peevishly, "I wish she were here now. I wanted to bring her, but Agapito thought women were not necessary to this meeting."

As Domingo listened to the pettish voice he tried to imagine this same scene as taking place in the 1920's instead of the 1940's. Of one thing he was certain. There would have been no words glistening like water drops on a tin tray. In the Twenties the gun was still close to the hand, family honor more important than happiness. Don Rafael would have left Mateo's blood on the sidewalk to ferment a new legend as tragically stupid as the Miranda's.

Domingo glanced at the placid *mestizo* face beside him. Greater legends had grown from even more stolid flesh. But this was the 1940's, the age of the practical man, of social progress. No room here for legends. No room, no room, sighed his mind, for the Xtabay.

Domingo snapped his thoughts away from the dangerous paths that led always to Márgara, and said quietly, "Has everyone forgotten Cardito?"

The great page flipped over. With its turning, a change enveloped the room. They were allies again, against the common fear of Cardito.

Don Agapito shifted his body to a more comfortable position. The raised eyebrow, the tilt of the head told them that for the moment he was willing to ignore the case of Mateo and Sofía while his executive genius contemplated the more pressing problem of a vanished nephew. "Otilia read me the note. Young boys think themselves very clever. He told Domingo he was going some distance from Monterrey, so that we would not search for him in Monterrey. He is doubtless at one of his friend's houses at this moment. You know his friends, Domingo. Think of the one most apt to hide him, then go there and get him."

"No," Domingo said.

326

They all looked at him then, even Mateo, with puzzled wonder.

"What's wrong with you?" Sofía demanded.

Domingo shrugged. He had waited a long time for this moment. Ten years, he thought, is a very long time. He stretched himself, and enjoyed the feel of his muscles sliding one against the other.

"Why should I bring him home? So that our uncle can tear up his ambition and fit him into a mold he was never meant to fit? So that he can spend the rest of his life as a man without substance? So that he can turn into a creature who sips life from correspondence courses? We have one such buzzing bee in our family. I see no reason to create another."

"Domingo," don Agapito snapped. "These are foolish words in your mouth."

"Are they?" Domingo rose, walked to the desk, bent across it so that he could look into his uncle's eyes. He saw the iris, small layers of golden brown flecked with gold. In the shining black pupils he could see his own head reflected, elongated, magnified. "You did it to Uncle Lucio and my father. You did it to me. But you're not going to do it to Cardito." Then, as the cat releases the mouse for a little while, he turned to the others. "I'll find Cardito. I promised our mother I would. But I'm not going to bring him back here to crush him under the weight of the bank. No one is going to bring him back."

Don Rafael said thinly, "You can't blame Agapito for what he has done to you or to the rest of us. Life does not say, 'Here are the riches of the world. Enjoy them.' She makes you sweat and weep for what you want. I know."

"And what of Mateo?" Domingo asked softly. "Mateo did not fold his hands and whine, 'What use to fight? The very blood in me will hold me back.'"

"So that is why you brought Mateo here tonight," don Agapito said thoughtfully. There was a new respect in his glance as Domingo swung back at him.

"Mateo has the strength to fight. He got it because there was no one pressing him down into the earth. Cardito shall have that strength, too."

"If he comes back," don Agapito said gently, "he'll be a banker."

"Then he'll not come back."

"I think he will. Remember, if you can find him, so can I. It will take longer, but I will find him. And then he will come back."

Domingo shook his head. "I'm afraid you don't know our Cardito very well."

Don Agapito looked past him to Mateo. "You think I am losing my power, my knowledge of men, because I accept Mateo's marriage to Sofía?"

"How kind of you," Sofía murmured.

Don Agapito said, "Sarcasm is not becoming in a woman." He set his hand on the chairarm, and the curve of his body turned him into a painting, rich with yellow and browns. "I accept it because Mateo has an unusual talent. I know that talent does not always appear in carefully tended gardens. It flowers in strange places, but wherever it blooms, the talent is greater than the plot of earth from which it springs. If I had known from the beginning that Sofía and Mateo were—attracted to each other, I would have fostered their marriage as carefully as any gardener hovering over a rare bulb. The Vázquez de Andas need Mateo's talent. Our earth requires rich nourishment." He tilted his head slightly toward Sofía. "At first I was angry because I don't like elopements, sly plans in the darkness. I am not a man of slyness. My fighting is done in the sunlight, not in the shadows. But now that I have had time to consider it, I realize that you could not have chosen a better husband in all of Monterrey."

Domingo felt a touch of nausea. How clever you are, he thought sickly, as he watched Sofía and Mateo smile at each other, then, together, smile at don Agapito who made them a present of his own charming smile. Ay, Mateo, Sofía, he thought desperately, you whipped him to the wall, and now he's found a way to climb to the top, to trap you again, to keep you under his domination. But he did not say this aloud. No use to say it. The spell had been woven, the magic was greater than truth.

Don Agapito picked up the broken paper-knife, tossed it in the wastebasket, found another knife in the drawer, and ran his finger down its shining length to the sharp point.

"Inbred families have little strength, Domingo, and we are too inbred. You blame Lucio's correspondence courses, your father's sickly life in the real-estate office, your own broken dreams on me. And now you blame me because Cardito, in a childish rage, runs away from home for a little while. I am not to blame for all this. The fine instrument can become so refined it will no longer give forth music. I am the last strong Vázquez left. We will leave Mateo to judge. He is a practical man. Lucio wanted to be a university professor. Do you know what the University of México City pays its teachers? Eighty pesos a month. Could you live on eighty pesos a month, Mateo?"

"I could starve on it," Mateo said carefully.

"Lucio would have had to find some sort of business outside of his professorship. As it is he makes a fair living in a drugstore which I bought and gave him. He has his correspondence courses, his nightly glass of beer with don Primitivo. Is he not more successful, really happier now than doing what he thought he wanted?"

Domingo said nothing, watching him, waiting for the rest of the specious argument. Don Agapito lifted his shoulders, glanced at his brother. "Rafael wanted to be a musician. But musicians are strange creatures. They eat like everyone else. So I bought a real-estate office and gave it to him. I never ordered him to give up music. He gave it up himself."

"A man can go just so far without training," don Rafael muttered.

"You could have made enough money in the office to get the training."

"I was married," don Rafael said.

"Precisely. A man owes a certain obligation to his children. Rafael thought it would be nice to have a musician in the family. He chose Brunhilda because she was the only one of you four with any aptitude. But she's a lazy little creature, and completely without a brain, as you all know. When he wanted to send her to New York she came to me in tears. The thought of studying music was unendurable to her. Me, I have no children. The four of you are as close as I will ever come to being a father. Brunhilda is soft and pretty. I gave her two years in New York. Two years of enchantment."

You gave them to her? Domingo thought with sickness for this hypocrisy. What of the money sacrifices my father and I made to keep her there? You bought her clothes and a fur coat, but what

329

else . . . ? Saints in Heaven, do the rest of us mean nothing in your scheming?

"You might have given one of those years to me," Sofía was saying, the old resentment tinging her voice.

Don Agapito cocked an eyebrow at her. "You never asked me for one. Besides, I doubt if you would have enjoyed it as much as Brunhilda did. You would never have poured out that enjoyment into long letters to please a lonely old man." He opened a desk drawer, took out a thick pack of letters fastened together with a rubber band, tossed them on the desk. "Perhaps it was selfish in me. I admit it. I am selfish." He let them bask in the warmth of his selfishness. "It gave me pleasure to give pleasure to a little girl."

Domingo said doggedly, ignoring the hypocritical note. "Putting Cardito in a bank will not give him pleasure."

"Listen, Domingo, I have watched Cardito carefully. In that filing case are typed copies of every speech he made to the student's syndicate. There is a full report on the counselor Farías and his quarrels with Cardito. Banking is not altogether a matter of figures. It demands a certain knowledge of figures, true, but most of all it demands the ability to say 'no,' when everything inside you wants to say 'yes.' Cardito may have the ambition to be a lawyer." Don Agapito touched his heart and then his temple. "But he has the brain of a banker. Many times in his student career, it would have been very easy to say yes. But he said no. That banker's brain of his will bring him back to me. In the end I will win. It would be much simpler for all of us if he recognized that fact now."

"Did you point that out to him when you were talking to him this afternoon?"

"Yesterday," the practical Mateo murmured. "It is now Sunday."

Domingo held a tight rein on his temper, courteously inclined his head to Mateo. "Yesterday afternoon?"

"Naturally. But Cardito is young." This time it was don Agapito who looked straight at Domingo, bending forward so that he could see his face reflected in the unshifting pupils. "He believes that his own desires are more important than anyone else's."

"For him they are," Domingo answered softly. "You fight for yours, why shouldn't he fight for his?"

"Because he lacks the strength, Domingo. I told you the strain had run thin."

"By your measurements, perhaps. Not by mine. You say a banker must know a great deal about human beings. Perhaps you do. But you don't know enough. In even the most decadent of us, there is one core you can't touch."

"Even in you, Domingo?"

"Yes, even in me. For ten years I've let you blindfold me, propel me any way you wanted me to go. But I'm through with it now."

"You will feel differently," don Agapito said with indifference, "after you marry Verónica Miranda. Marriage, as your father can tell you, is a matter of responsibilities, whether you want to accept them or not."

Domingo did not look around at his father. He drew a deep breath, said steadily, "I am not going to marry Verónica Miranda."

There was a long sigh behind him. At first he thought it was from his father, and then he realized that it was Sofía. She came to him, ran her arm through his.

"I'm so glad," she said. "Ay, Domingo, I thought you were never going to speak those words."

"The engagement has been formalized," don Agapito said, lighting another cigarette. "You will marry her. It is natural for young men to shy at . . ."

"I said I wasn't going to marry her, and I'm not. I'm going to marry another woman."

Don Agapito's hand hovered over the desk before he set the lighter carefully on it. "Don't be a fool, Domingo. Serafina is a very pretty girl, but unlike Mateo, she lacks the proper talent."

Don Rafael said sharply, "Serafina? How can you marry Serafina, Domingo? That would be incest."

Domingo blinked his eyes, opened his mouth to speak, but don Agapito shot words past his shoulder. "You mean that Domingo is not the father of Serafina's child?"

Don Rafael rose, his shoulders oddly straight after their years of bending. "Did I tell you that? Did Domingo?"

"Domingo spun some tale about a bellboy, which I accepted. . . ."

Don Rafael looked at his eldest son. The sternness of his fatherhood was in him as he said, "You may not marry Serafina. I forbid it."

331

Sofía tugged at him, said, "Father, sit down. You're too weak . . ."

"Leave me alone, Sofía. Did you hear me, Domingo?"

Domingo raised his hands. "I never had any intention of marrying Serafina. But who told you the truth about her?"

"Cardito, naturally. After the Lozano episode I went to Cardito and made him tell me the truth."

"That day in your bedroom when I was talking to you, you already knew. . . ."

"Naturally. I wanted to be frank with you. But you obviously had made certain plans in which you wanted no interference, not even from me." There was pride and sorrow both in don Rafael's voice, pride in Domingo's action, sorrow at being shut out of his son's confidence.

Domingo felt his head beginning to pound. He sat down, then realized his father was still standing, and stood up again. "I'm sorry, father . . ."

Don Rafael came to him, patted his shoulder. "I am not such an old stupid as you think, eh? Now about this woman you want to marry. Do I know her?"

"No, you don't know her."

"She must be someone undesirable," don Agapito commented, "or he would not have permitted the Miranda engagement."

Domingo's eyes blazed, so that his uncle instinctively bent away from him. "Stay out of my affairs! Is that too much to ask? I don't want you meddling with my life anymore. I'm through with you. Leave me alone!"

He snatched up his hat. Without a glance at any of them, he ran from the room, and out of the house.

The sky was cold with dawn. Domingo could feel a trembling that passed through his limbs like rippling water. His doctor's mind told him the reason for this ague. For two weeks he had lived for the thought of tonight, Márgara soft in his arms, his body tuned to the need of her. Now she had been snatched from him in a tempest of events that merely intensified the need.

He crawled into the car, set it in motion, put his foot savagely down on the gas pedal. The car quivered, leaped like a wild thing to the dangerous curves. Tires screeched in protest as he twisted the wheel.

Somewhere in the night Márgara lay alone, her arms empty

of him who loved her. Somewhere in the night Cardito lay, his body fragile with illness. And between the two Domingo spun, a top to the master cords stretching, both equal in tension, neither releasing.

He found his bed at last, and flung himself across it, fully dressed. Sleep closed him in a box of darkness that held him through the morning and the afternoon.

XXIII

Doña Otilia told Domingo that Sofía was at Mateo's house, and Brunhilda was upstairs in her room, exhausted with hysterics over the marriage news.

He said thoughtfully, "Indian earth in Spanish wine. Are you glad, my mother?"

Her crochet hook flashed in the lamplight. She said yes, that she was glad. Sofía had confided in her from the beginning, and even then she had been glad. "Mateo has a virility that Sofía needs. He is all man, that one. And wise, Domingo. Very wise."

"Is it wisdom?" Domingo wanted to know, and his mother shrugged.

"Call it cleverness. He has an idea about Cardito. I want you to go and see him now, Domingo. To please me."

The woman who opened the door of Mateo's house was as Jorge Palafox had said, solemn with the dignity of birds. There was no embarrassment in her as she stood aside for Domingo, only a grave amazement that some day a child of Chapa would carry the name of Vázquez also.

He blinked his eyes against the harsh glare of the overhead light. An upright piano, the front hidden by fringed red silk, stood against one green painted wall. The settee, the rocker, the arm-chair, were Austrian cane, and the small square table had a doily of organdy embroidered with fantastic pansies.

Sofía rose from the rocker. He bent to kiss her fingers, and when he straightened he saw that Mateo had come into the room.

"I hear you slept today," Mateo said, his obsidian eyes brushed with laughter. He said to his mother, "If we could have coffee. . . ."

She nodded, went into the kitchen, taking Sofía with her.

"Sofía wanted to come here," Mateo explained, "until we could move into our own house. Don Rafael has offered to give us one for a wedding present."

He chattered amiably of houses, and the expense of a mansion against the inconvenience of a cottage until the women returned with a loaded tray. Mateo's mother poured a tablespoon of black liquid from a cruet, then added steaming milk. The aroma of coffee perfumed the air. As she handed him the cup, Mateo said proudly, "My mother makes her own extract. Jorge Palafox named it true nectar. Eh, my mother?"

"I have been a cook for thirty years." She turned toward Domingo, her folded arms resting on the curve of her stomach. "I should know how to make good coffee."

Sofía put her arm about the older woman's waist. "If Domingo is to take the ten-thirty plane there is no time for chatter." She pressed the woman against her gently, and the elderly face relaxed from pride, became sweet with love.

"So you have dissected Cardito's mind, you wise ones?" Domingo flicked his eyes across each face.

"He's not in Monterrey," Sofía said. "He wants to be a lawyer, so he would go to a place where he could get schooling."

Mateo said, "I thought of Saltillo. It has an excellent university, but Sofía said no."

Domingo considered Saltillo, rejected it. "He could not get both a job and schooling there. Also, he knows too many people. He used to go over with student groups."

"We finally decided that it must be the Capital," Sofía said.

A faint smile touched Domingo's lips. He carefully replaced his cup on the table. "Could there be any doubt? Naturally he wants to lose himself in a big city. For him it is romantic."

"Very," Mateo said. "The life of a student starving in a *pensión* would attract Cardito." He put his fingers to his lips, whistled shrilly. A young boy thrust his head through the kitchen door, stared at Domingo with wide-eyed wonder. "My youngest brother," Mateo introduced casually. "You, brilliant one, argue with central. Tell her I want to talk to Jorge Palafox in México City. When she gets him, call me."

334

Domingo said sharply, "I don't want Jorge Palafox mixed up in this."

For a moment Mateo said nothing. Then he lifted the coffee tray and put it in Sofía's hands. "Take these into the kitchen, my beautiful."

She put the tray down, tossed her head like a restive colt. "Cardito is my brother. I have a right to hear, even if it concerns Jorge Palafox."

Mateo drew a long breath, said, "Young wives need strong hands."

He went to her, locked his hands around her waist, lifted her out of the room and shut the door.

Domingo laughed and his glance crossed the face of Mateo's mother. He could see the secret smile behind her face, the smile of a matriarch secure in her power—a power so great it had no need to assert itself, a power she knew Sofía would learn in time.

She said, a chuckle fringing her voice, "Is there no jealousy in you for Jorge Palafox, my Mateo?"

He shrugged. "As long as she does not talk to him nor of him, what difference?" He took an envelope from his pocket, became the man of business. "Here's your plane ticket." He hesitated, said, "Domingo," feeling the word with his tongue, tasting it, liking it. His eyes were shy on Domingo's, and Domingo smiled at him. The eye-meeting was deeper than a clasping of hands, than the embrace of arms on shoulders. They held each other with their eyes, and were no longer master and man, but brother and brother.

"Domingo," Mateo repeated, and the word rose and became a chanting. With the shame of a practical man for emotion, he said quickly, "There is a ten o'clock plane for México City. I will arrange for Jorge Palafox to meet you at the airport at midnight. . . ."

His brother called through the closed door, "Jorge Palafox is on the telephone, and Sofía is talking to him."

The matriarch's laughter burned as Mateo shot across the room, tossing over his shoulder, "You owe me ninety pesos for that ticket," just before he slammed the door.

Later, Domingo told Sofía, "It's eight now. At nine you and Mateo can pick me up on the north corner of Plaza Zaragoza. I have private business, important business . . ."

"Sh," his sister said wisely, with an oblique glance at Mateo. "I know what private business is."

She said nothing more but remained standing by Mateo's mother while Mateo went to the corner with him. That image of Sofía beside the bird-dignity of the older woman stayed with Domingo through the bus trip downtown. Both had accepted each other and their mutual love for Mateo so completely that no adjustment was necessary. The woman was Sofía grown old. Sofía was the woman grown young. Mother and wife woven together, until the warp could not be distinguished from the woof.

Then the bus let him out at the proper corner, and all thoughts of Sofía, of his family, even of Cardito slid from him. "Márgara," sang the tapping of his shoe leather against the worn building steps. "Márgara," the wind sighed through the gallery. His knuckles tapping on the studio door spelled her name.

After she opened the door he drew her outside, held her close, breathed deeply of her hair. When she said his name, he shook her slightly, begged her not to speak. She was quiet in his arms. He kissed her forehead, the lobes of her ears, drew his mouth across her cheek until he found her lips. He could feel them move under his, warm and sweet. They opened slightly, and he pressed her closer to him.

"Márgara," he whispered, "how I have needed you, my Márgara."

She inclined away from him, murmured, "My father is inside." With her hand pulling him, they went to the gallery steps, sat down close together. He unloosened the pins in her hair, played with its coiled length while he told her all that had happened. She gasped when he repeated his defiance of his uncle Agapito.

"You actually told him you were going to marry me?"

"Certainly, my beautiful. I am tired of this stupidity. And my father took the news very well," he added with brief surprise.

He could feel her head move against his shoulder. "But my father, Domingo. I don't know. You must give me time . . ."

"There is no time." He looked at the luminous dial of his wristwatch, frowned at the racing minute hand. "My uncle Agapito will try to find you . . ."

"Ay, Domingo."

"Quiet, I have a plan. My old nurse has a house in Santa Catarina. Even my uncle Agapito is afraid of her tongue. She's already taking care of a girl named Serafina." He rapidly explained the Serafina affair, ending with, "Her father is hunting for her. The poor creature needs protection from him. I doubt if he'd try any mischief if she were guarded by Tía Nicanora and you and your father."

"Domingo, you don't understand . . ."

"Hush, my beautiful. I have to go now to catch the plane. Here is a note for you to take Tía Nicanora." He laid the envelope in her hand, pressed her fingers over it. "In this way, you will be safe from my uncle Agapito, and Serafina safe from her father. It is the best plan."

She said rebelliously, "I don't know."

He laughed, kissed her with rapid little kisses. "Don't argue, my own. Don't you know that good Mexican wives never argue?"

He waited to hear the docile note in her voice, but it was lacking as she repeated, "I don't know."

He had no more time to waste, so he kissed her again and ran rapidly down the stairs. Always the Xtabay, he thought contentedly.

> And she will escape you like a bird flying . . . where does he go, the man who follows the Xtabay? Who knows?

Does it matter where he goes, Domingo wondered, as long as the green and gold enchantment surrounds him?

México City at night has a magic of its own. In the poorer district behind the University, the buildings wear a patina of history, for most of them were built in the early sixteen hundreds. They had housed the laughter of people before the giant cathedral had known their prayers.

Domingo's car raced through the narrow streets, dodging through traffic with the complete disregard of mortality that has always marked the city's taxi drivers.

Nervous with the tension that followed two weeks of anxiety while Jorge's competent detectives traced Cardito through law school records, Domingo clung to the cab's seat and tossed a steady stream of profanity at the chauffeur.

The man shrugged happily while he peered through his windshield. The glass was so covered with decalcomanias of bullfighters, the Blessed Virgin of Guadalupe, and a nearly nude hula dancer that it was difficult to see the street.

Finally, there was a swoop to the right, a sickening sound of rubber skidding on asphalt, and the car came to a halt in front of a two-story colonial building, hooked at each end to other buildings, so that the entire block was a wall of carved stone. A chipped coat of arms was over the proper door, with two long iron-barred windows to either side of it.

The driver outlined this achitecture with his hands. "A mother and two daughters," he said. "I collect windows and doors, señor. It makes my job more interesting. And I label all of them. There's a grand-aunt with five nieces in the next block. If you'd like to see them I'll take you there. It's a rare sight, one big window with five little ones trailing away from it."

"Undoubtedly," Domingo said dryly. "You are sure this is the house?"

"You gave me the number. There it is in front of your nose."

"Wait for me."

The driver muttered something, and Domingo asked sharply, "What did you say?"

"You have the accent of a Monterrey man."

"Does that mean something?"

"Did you hear about the Monterrey man who gave away all his money to charity?"

Domingo looked at the driver in surprise. "You must be mistaken, friend."

The driver shouted with laughter. "Of course I'm mistaken. What Monterrey man would be such a fool?"

Domingo's mouth twitched in quick anger. The high singsong voice, so different from the deeper northern tones, offended him more than the words.

"Very clever," he snapped, ringing the bell.

A girl answered, her hair dangling down her back in two plaits. She kept the door half open, peering around the edge at him. "The lady owner says if you are a student, not to let you in. She is tired of students."

"I don't want to rent a room," Domingo explained hastily. "I'm looking for my—for Ricardo Vásquez de Anda."

"Such elegance," she sniffed. "The only Ricardo we have here is Ricardo Fausto."

338

Naturally the young fool would take his mother's name, Domingo thought. The girl was already closing the door. He said quickly, "A friend. He can give me the address I need."

She asked suspiciously, "You're sure you don't want a room?"

"I'm not a student," he reassured her, and let her see the gleam of silver in his fingers.

Her eyes brightened. She instantly swung the door wide open. "True proof. No student ever has any money. That's the way you can tell they are students."

She led him down a short passage that opened into a patio. A broad corridor branching off served as a sort of dining room. Here a group of five boys clustered around a table. One of them was dealing a game of *monte* with a deck of greasy cards, being careful not to molest small stacks of copper coins piled in front of him. Another, blond as a Flemish potrait, with a sulky baby face, was strumming a guitar, most of the other boys softly whistling the melody. A lantern dangled above their heads, suspended by a string from a heavy crossbeam stained to blackness by the dirt of time.

The card dealer yelled at the girl to bring them wine. She indicated Domingo. "A visitor for Cardito."

He could hear the boys muttering amongst themselves as he followed her up wide marble stairs, chipped at the edges, to the gallery. His sensitive historical sense told him that other figures were also mounting these stairs: men with short velvet capes over slashed doublets, women in the wide paniers of seventeenth century Spain, young men and women who had knelt to the Emperor Iturbide, to the tyrant Santa Anna, to the Austrian Maximilian, to the Indian Porfirio Díaz. After the Ten Days the elegance disappeared. No one cared anymore if the fine marble stairs were kept in immaculate condition, if the pomegranate trees in the patio withered. Certainly this servant girl did not care, did not even feel the presence of the ghosts as she said over her shoulder, "Those vultures hope Cardito will have sense enough to borrow money from you."

"You don't like students?"

Her shoulders rose and fell. "One gets used to them. The body can get used to anything but hunger. Of course, a few are different. Cardito is different." Her voice deepened, softened.

Dear saints, not again, Domingo thought disgustedly. He

looked at the shapeless blue serge dress that did not wholly conceal the youthful curves of her body, at the face that still lacked the nostril calipers of maturity.

This girl was very different from Serafina, whose delicate child-ishness was coiled now about another child. Cardito's attitude toward Serafina puzzled Domingo. He knew that Cardito must have a good reason for it, and yet. . . . He shook his head in perplexity. Did he really know his younger brother whom he so much loved?

The girl knocked on a paint-blistered door that had narrow slats instead of panels. "Cardito's a good rooster, but careful of his money. Those vultures downstairs will get poor pickings no matter how much he gets off you. Me, I like a careful man. Who wants to spend the rest of one's life gnawing *tortillas* to pay for one evening of fun?"

Cardito's voice yelled, "Don't bother me. I'm busy."

Her eyes were proud. "He knows his own mind," she whispered. Then she shouted, "A gentleman's here to see you." She turned, gestured toward the door with her thumb. "If you bang long enough he'll open for you if only to get rid of you." Her fingers lifted toward him and Domingo dropped silver into the greedy palm.

Not until the level of the first steps shielded her did Domingo say quietly, "Let me in, Cardito."

There was silence from the room. Then Domingo heard the creak of bedsprings, the swish of slippers crossing bare tiles. Cardito opened the door, looked dispassionately at his brother. "You have a trick of finding me." He stepped to one side, and Domingo entered the room.

It was a narrow cell with a high window that let in some air and less light. The bed was a brass frame, white paint peeling away from the metal, with a finger-thin mattress, unbleached muslin sheets, a towel covering the pillow in lieu of a case. A blanket was flung in a rumpled heap across the foot. There was one chair, and a rickety table, a wad of paper trying to keep it solid on the dusty floor. A single brick on the table served as a base for a candle, although an empty electric socket dangled from the ceiling.

Domingo picked up the candle, set it down again. Cardito said defensively, "The señora agreed to take fifty centavos a week off my rent if I burned no electricity. Law books are expensive."

A tightness came into Domingo's throat. He said roughly, "How do you live?"

"I've got a job as waiter in a student's restaurant near here. No tips, but I don't belong to the waiter's syndicate, and they get the jobs with tips. What matter? The hours are convenient." Cardito sat on the edge of the bed, gestured Domingo to take the chair. "I'm sorry you came. No matter what you say, I'm not going back."

Domingo said, "I don't want to take you back. But this— you're going to have to get out of this place."

"I'm contented," Cardito said. He could not control his curiosity. "I thought you were sent to lecture me in Uncle Agapito's best style."

"He'll not make a banker out of you, Cardito. I promise you."

"Naturally not. I wouldn't allow it."

"So certain, Cardito? Then why did you run away?"

"It was easier than arguing. And Father would just have gone to bed. You know how Father is. When he doesn't get his own way, he goes to bed." The young voice was cruelly indifferent. He stretched out his hand. "I'd like a cigarette if you have one. I can't afford them." There was a pride in this last sentence, as though being so poor had a value that no man with money could understand. He took a deep breath of the smoke, let it trickle from mouth and nose. "I've never been much impressed by our father's illnesses. Look how he behaved over the Serafina affair. Very childish, I thought."

Domingo stared at his brother, hearing the words but not understanding them. "How long had you known Serafina was with child?"

"From the first, I suppose. I told her she had better get out of the house. But Serafina said she was afraid of her father. Did he beat her up very much?"

Domingo forced himself to speak quietly. "Enough. Quite enough."

Cardito made a small face of disgust. He had not shaved lately, and the beard was a down on his cheeks. "She's been beaten before. She'll get over it." Laughter bubbled past his lips. "Father said Lozano accused you of being her man. This shocked father more than anything else. According to father no man of sensibility— and he thinks highly of your sensibilities—would keep the girl so close to our mother. 'What was I to do with her?' I asked him. He had no answer for that, I can tell you."

Pain clamped a screw against Domingo's heart. The slow twisting was an agony. "Have you no feeling at all for Serafina?"

Cardito looked astonished. The candlelight spread shadows across his eye sockets, gave him the anonymity of the blind. "She's a servant girl, amusing to kiss a little, to love a little. What else does one feel for servant girls?"

Domingo remembered how he and Sofía had feared the advent of Jorge Palafox. The degenerate son of a great family, they had feared. But they had not thought of Cardito, so deeply loved, so carefully protected. The pain in his chest turned another notch of agony.

"What did you expect would become of Serafina?" He crossed to the bed, stared down in wonder at his brother. "Didn't you have any sense of responsibility?"

"Why should I? There was always Uncle Agapito to pay her off."

He jerked back too late to escape the force of Domingo's blow across his cheek. He sprawled on the bed, his eyes sulky above the smoldering anger.

Domingo breathed deeply to quiet himself, nursing his right hand in his left. He spoke in low dead phrases, telling Cardito what he thought of him. The boy's lips curled away from his teeth, but he made no other movement.

When Domingo's voice was finally silent, Cardito said frigidly, "My life is my own. I pay for this room with money I earn. For the first time in my life I can do as I please without begging permission to breathe from you or my father."

"Permission? Do you think we . . ."

"From the time that I was a baby you've stood over me. Cardito must do this, Cardito must do that, Cardito can't have candy, it's bad for him. He has to go to bed early. Cardito must get so many hours of exercise . . ."

"Saints in Heaven, Cardito, I was trying to keep you well."

"You should have practiced your medicine on a more grateful patient then."

"Have I ever denied you anything, Cardito? Did you ever wish for anything that I didn't try to get it for you?"

"A bone to make a puppy grateful."

The contempt slashed like lightning across the night of Domingo's mind, cut to the clearness beneath, made him realize many things.

This sullen creature curled on the bed was not Cardito. Here was a child afraid in the presence of an ogre, and the ogre was himself. It was all plain now. The events turned in Domingo's mind, settled into a pattern. Don Rafael had told the boy of Lozano, of Domingo's attitude, and the boy waited for the accusing words. But the words had not come. In trying to protect Cardito, Domingo had released a greater fear. In his mind the elder brother was no longer friend but crouching enemy. So the boy ran away, and now, faced with responsibility, he crumbled into cowardice.

"When I hit you," Domingo said between stiff lips, "why did you not hit back at me?"

Cardito raised his hands to his mouth, his eyes cringing. He said nothing, but his eyes spoke for him.

"No," Domingo said thoughtfully, "how could you?" A laugh forced itself through his throat, into his mouth. "In the deep tropics men dare not eat fresh meat, even lately killed meat. They put strips of it in the papaya fruit and let the pectin pre-digest it. When the meat comes out it is gray and tasteless, just as you are now, without the savor of a man. I put you in the papaya, and there is nothing left."

"Is there not?" Cardito came to his feet, his hands tense in fists. "You want the truth and I'll give it to you. I didn't run away from Uncle Agapito's bank. All I had to do was fold my arms and sit still, and what power in Uncle Agapito then? I ran away from you."

Domingo's pain had reached that level of numbness more terrible than pain.

The voice went on. "All the time I was in the hospital I thought of the weeks you'd be fussing around me, forbidding me to breathe for fear I'd get a relapse. And I was right. That week I spent at home was more than I could endure."

Under the astringent powers of the cold young voice Domingo's portrait of Cardito washed away until the primitive picture was revealed. The poise of the head, the line of the nose, the curve of the mouth was pure Vázquez de Anda, pure don Agapito.

Domingo pulled the brim of his hat down until his eyes were hidden in the shadow. "You have a message to send our mother?"

343

"She's a wise old one," Cardito said, and even for her the coldness did not warm.

"You stand in your field," doña Otilia's voice whispered in Domingo's mind, *"everyone in his private field, and no bridge to link them together."*

Domingo laid the package of cigarettes on the bed, then went out, closing the door gently behind him.

The servant girl was sitting on the steps. As she heard him coming, she moistened one finger, pulled up her skirt, pretended to doctor a run in her stocking. The young leg was pitifully thin. A tendency to rickets in early childhood, Domingo thought automatically.

Her lashes fluttered provocatively. "Did he get any money from you?"

Domingo took a card, wrote something on it, then pulled a hundred peso bill from his wallet. "I won this on the lottery. Would you like to have it?"

Her eyes were avid. As she stood up, her shoulder rubbed his arm. "What do you want for it?" The deepened sex tone in the baby voice sickened him.

"Do you know the Palafox bank?"

"Who doesn't?"

"If Cardito gets sick, take this card to the bank. Insist on seeing Jorge Palafox. When you do see him, he'll give you another hundred pesos."

"I'll see him," she promised, thrusting the bill down the front of her dress.

"Do the same if Cardito moves away from here. Give don Jorge the new address."

"I swear it by the bones of my mother."

"Keep this money a secret between us with no words to Cardito, or don Jorge will move his hand. What good little servant girls if don Jorge moves his hand?"

Her eyes rolled sideways in fear, and Domingo, sure of her silence, stepped past her and went down the stairs. The same boys were still playing cards, while the blond one strummed his guitar. Domingo could feel their attention following him to the sidewalk.

He was surprised to find the taxi waiting. He got in and gave Jorge's address. The driver repeated it indifferently, then his voice jumped an octave with awe. "That's the home of the Palafox."

344

"Does it matter?"

"You Monterrey men! Is there no money your fingers have not touched?"

He was still muttering to himself as he put the car in gear, drove away. Domingo, slumped in a corner, did not glance through the window at the receding house.

It was good to be in the crisp freshness of Monterrey again. While telling his family all he thought they should know of Cardito, he wondered vaguely why they did not question him in close detail. He did not realize that the pain of his meeting with Cardito had left white streaks in his hair, dark shadows around his eyes.

Because of the common anxiety over Cardito, don Agapito and Domingo had set up a truce, their every word to each other attended by exquisite courtesy. At first the elder Vázquez tried to get more precise information from Domingo, but Tecla and doña Otilia effectively blocked him off, glossed over his words with rippling words of their own, until finally he sat back in a fit of private sulking.

The tactless Brunhilda also tried to cut through Domingo's reticence, but Tito, after a signal from doña Otilia, told her to keep silent, and she was silent.

Mateo and Sofía were not present. The two sisters met only through necessity, and Brunhilda was so overly sweet to Mateo that even doña Otilia's placid nerves could not endure the strain. Domingo had promised them to come to their house later in the evening.

He was glad to park his car and open the gates of the small *chalet* on Calle Washington that don Rafael, following the etiquette of Monterrey fathers, had presented to the young couple. It amused Domingo to notice that it was the house with the green bathroom, redecorated now with a stained glass window.

He teased Mateo about it, who shrugged and led the way into the tiny dining room. "I told you that men bought houses for strange reasons. Can you imagine a greater luxury than stained glass in the bathroom?"

Sofía hugged her brother, petted him, gave him iced beer, told him the details of her quiet Cathedral wedding at early Mass. Her brown dress belonged to her premarriage days, but there was a

345

change in her. He finally realized it was the shawl over her shoulders. She sat the the table, her arms crossed, her hidden hands pulling the shawl tight across her breasts. In hundreds of houses in this middle-class section other women in shawls were sitting in dining rooms, content to preserve the parlors for funerals and weddings and other affairs of state.

Mateo had taken off his coat, and was urging Domingo to do the same. But Domingo shook his head. In a sense he, too, belonged to the magazine illustration world of Jorge Palafox, he thought bitterly. It would take a long time for him to break through into the life of the middle-class.

It was odd, he reflected, that he felt much closer to this pair than he did to his family in the Padre Mier house. To his sister and her husband he told the truth, his cold voice sparing neither Cardito nor himself. After he finished, Sofía concerned herself with darning Mateo's socks. Mateo tilted his chair until the back was resting precariously against the ornately carved sideboard, one of Serafina's uncle's better products.

"My brother, Manuel, that would-be bullfighter, is the same. These boys are all alike. They involve themselves in a situation that's too big for them, so they run away from it, and then they have to argue themselves out of the knowledge that they are cowards."

Sofía carefully wove her needle through the raveled black cotton. "What Mateo means . . ."

Mateo interrupted her. "I'll tell him what I mean. The beatings I've given Manuel, and he not lifting a finger to defend himself. Then, after the crisis is finished, he comes crawling back, all tears and repentence until the next time. Cardito will show up one of these fine days."

"Mateo's right, Domingo," Sofía said. "You know he is."

"It's a terrible thing," Mateo said, "but you can protect too much. I learned my lesson on Manuel. My youngest brother must take what comes, and learn to smile under it. Cardito would have been better off if he'd gotten more whippings and less cotton wool."

Domingo asked slowly, "You really think he'll come back then?"

"Didn't Mateo say he would?" Sofía asked in a voice that

would not permit any argument with Mateo's slightest comment.

The men laughed at her indulgently.

Domingo said, "Perhaps you are right, Mateo, but . . . can one want a thing too much?"

The two looked at him, and he said, "I wanted to be a doctor, but I gave it up in obedience to my father's commands. He said then that eventually I would understand. I think he meant that my talent wasn't big enough, just as his talent for music had not been big enough. True talent is ruthless."

"Mateo knows," Sofía murmured. Brother and sister looked at Mateo who shook his head.

"As you say, true talent will refuse to be caged. But with Cardito, I don't think it's true talent. I think it is nothing but selfishness. I am sorry, but that is what I think."

Domingo nodded, "If you could have seen him cringing on the bed. It was the cringing—the terrible cringing!" He shuddered, then laughed a little. "Do you believe me completely a fool?"

Sofía put her hand over his. "Don't worry too much, Domingo. Remember the only faith is in . . ." the three said in chorus, "Peace in the cemetery, and wealth from the lottery."

Impatient to see Márgara, Domingo went to Santa Catarina the next afternoon. She had gone to the village on an errand, Tía Nicanora told him, but Bárcenas, who had taken a fancy to Serafina, was with the girl in the sun drenched patio at the back.

"I must see Márgara first," Domingo said, and started toward the door, when Tía stopped him.

She whispered confidentially that she was worried, that the photographer and Dr. Mancini were battling over Serafina's health.

"Mancini demanded to see the old man's permit to practice medicine. Of course he hasn't any. Then Mancini threatened him with the law, told him to keep his veterinarian's skill for animals."

"Veterinarian," Domingo whispered. "Ay, God, the Ratkiller."

"What did you say?"

"Nothing. Mancini is right. Remember that, Tía. Mancini is right. What in God's name is keeping Márgara?"

"The plaza, I suppose. She likes to sit there and watch the tourist cars go by."

He walked slowly toward the plaza, but with each step his feet dragged more and more until he was hardly moving. He sat on the outthrust ledge of a house and stared unseeingly at the gray dirt of the street. For Velarde there had always been the excuse of his genius, but for the Ratkiller there was nothing but contempt and disgust. Huerta must have paid his favorite executioner well to enable him to bribe his way out of certain death from Obregón's firing squad, with enough over to carry him to Europe, to New York, to all the hidden holes his rat's mind craved.

No wonder Bárcenas hated Velarde, who had trained him to kill, and then deserted him, leaving him to carry out Huerta's constant orders to kill, and kill, and kill again.

Perhaps he finished his saga of death with the murder of Velarde himself. Or perhaps Velarde had died before his arrival, thus cheating Bárcenas of his last most favored crime. Then he returned to the country he had betrayed, hunting a peace he could never find. Everywhere he went, men of his own generation would finally mention the Revolution, Madero, the martyr, and Huerta who martyred him. Huerta, naturally, introduced the subject of his satellites: the genius, Velarde, and the slime-loving Ratkiller.

There could be no escape for Bárcenas, ever, from the stories of his crimes. That night when he came into don Primitivo's saloon, it was not Jorge's resemblance to don Santiago Palafox that frightened him. It was the song, "Farewell, Mamá Carlota," the song that had tortured Velarde in his last Mexican hours. To the Ratkiller it must have seemed as though Velarde were walking down the street again between rows of people contemptuously singing, "Farewell, my tender love."

The Ratkiller. How many men had he murdered, really? Did he himself know? Had he kept a special account book, checking off each name as he came to it? Had Márgara seen that book? Did she know the tally? Márgara, the green and gold. Márgara, the Xtabay. What did the legends whisper of the devil woman, who enchanted men with her beauty, then drew aside the firm sweet flesh to show the skeleton beneath?

With a horrified gasp Domingo whirled and ran to his car, jumped in it, cut through sidestreets to the main highway, set the pedal close to the floor, until the vast Saltillo Valley was a blur on either side.

The houses of Saltillo jolted him to consciousness. He had not meant to drive so far, but now that he was here, he felt hungry. He turned through the narrow streets until he reached the exit to Torreón where a small *merienda* shop offered *tamales* of the frontier (with meat or raisins), and the best *atole* north of San Luís Potosí. He was surprised at his own hunger, until he remembered that he had not been eating very well lately—not since Cardito had disappeared, really. The chocolate *atole* was so good that he had a second cup. A false peace held him and he knew it was because his mind would not accept this new agony. He had been hurt so much lately that he wondered if there was anything left to ache.

He went out to the car again. It had rained a little while he had been in the *merendero,* and the air was fresh and sharp. Saltillo residents were driving up for an early supper. The sound of their laughing, carefree voices made him realize how isolated he was from any laughter. When he climbed into the car, he knew he was too tired to attempt the return trip to Monterrey, so he drove to the hotel.

It was scraping sensitive flesh from bone to choose the same hotel where he had experienced such happiness with Márgara, but the Spanish aestheticism that had decreed the Inquisition drove him to it. Better to trample over familiar paths than to run away like Cardito.

He strode toward the desk to meet the eyes of the same clerk.

"Why," the man fluttered nervously, doubtless wondering what surprise Domingo was going to introduce tonight. "A good evening to you, señor Angeles."

Domingo grunted, started to write the famous name, then held his pen suspended over the register. Two voices spoke in his mind, almost together. "He brought me little cakes in Paris," Márgara said.

The other voice belonged to don Lucio as he argued a date with don Primitivo. "General Angeles had already left Paris on June tenth." *And the Ratkiller remained in Mexico until after Huerta's fall in July, 1914.* There had been a picture of him in the México City jail in the Casasola collection.

Domingo flung down the pen, asked for a telephone with such sharpness that the clerk had to swallow twice before pointing it out to him. The booth seemed small and stuffy until a curious Néstor Cortés assured him that General Angeles had left Paris in June to join Villa's forces, and remained in México until his execution.. But why this interest in Villa's gray lieutenant?

349

Domingo mumbled some reply, hung up, managed to make his way to the bar where he ordered a double brandy, then forced himself slowly to sip it. As he stared into space, he recognized the one great truth about himself. He had always, since he was a boy, reasoned a problem through to its conclusion, only to discover, too late, that most of his difficulties had been set up by himself. It took the unimaginative Mateos of the world to really see the truth for what it was.

No longer tired, Domingo turned the car around and headed it toward Santa Catarina. The image of Márgara shimmered in front of him, the skeleton sheathed again in warm sweet flesh. It was only then he realized that it was flesh, not magic woven from the green and gold jungle mystery. The Xtabáy was gone, and in her place stood Márgara, daughter of Bárcenas, a woman like Sofía, like Verónica, a woman in love, no legendary creature of enchantment.

The mystery of her remained but it was simple human mystery. Don Lucio had it with his memory of a woman's pain, doña Otilia had it behind the veil that shadowed her eyes. Serafina had it too, as she curved her body around the child unborn. Each soul in its private field had this same mystery, and Domingo realized again that he had built too much from too little. He had taken the mask of a face, had charged it with the electricity of his own imagination until he produced no human woman but a burnished painting out of all proportion to the original.

His world of illusion shattered as he drove into Santa Catarina. He saw her, then, standing on the plaza.

Years later he wondered how he would have reacted if he had seen Márgara outlined against the brightly painted saloon, against the drugtsore, against the church. But she had chosen the corner of the Juárez house, and as he saw her silhouetted against it, the bust of Juárez smiling serenely down at her, the imagination that had made Domingo see the stocky Indian patriot clear, now curved around Márgara, engulfed her. The broken shards drew together, formed a new whole. The jagged cracks became smooth under the gloss of the old enchantment.

It was not the daughter of Bárcenas who turned to greet him, but the Xtabay. He held her close against him, breathing the perfume of her, content to be enmeshed again in the curling tendrils of the secret jungle.

350

XXIV

She still would not reveal her father's secret. It belonged to Bárcenas, not to her. For the first time in years, she said, her father was really happy, hovering over the quiet Serafina. "For us there can be no marriage yet, Domingo. I don't want to pierce his happiness with any outside thing, even my own happiness."

Domingo, watching the man and the servant girl together, could only agree. At first he had felt a lance of jealousy as he saw Serafina turn to Bárcenas instead of to himself, but he came to realize that these two were so remote from the world of reality that they could find no companionship save with each other.

The man guarded Serafina's fragility like an angry cock. Dr. Mancini protested at Bárcenas' highhanded method of regulating Serafina's diet and exercise. "He's no doctor," Mancini raged. "I refuse to permit this murder."

Domingo soothed the Italian storm, begged Márgara to caution her father, pled with Serafina to be sensible. The two women smiled secretly at each other and assured him they were in all things sensible. He felt cut off from them, as though Márgara, Serafina and Bárcenas walked along a path he could not follow.

Irritated by this feeling, he stayed away from Santa Catarina, not in a fit of sulks, he assured himself, but with the plantive hope that during his absence they would realize their need for him and draw him again into their confidence.

He was not surprised to find the real-estate office humming with activity. Mateo and Tito were deep in plans for the new *colonia*, and Domingo found most of the desk work delegated to him. It surprised him that he actually enjoyed this aspect of the business. For the first time in years, he woke in the mornings glad to go to the office.

Don Rafael refused all contact with the business, spending his hours in the parlor creating little tunes, whose only value was his own enjoyment of them. And in the background, don Agapito hovered, watching Domingo with puzzled eyes. They met on occasions, but the courtesy, strong as mountain rock, was between them.

The news of Cardito that filtered to them through Jorge

Palafox was bad. The boy had started drinking, abandoning his law studies little by little. Domingo took this news in silence. The knowledge came to him that where he had failed with Cardito, he must not fail with Cardito's child. He felt as responsible for that child as though it were his seed and not Cardito's that had fertilized Serafina's womb. This was an attitude that don Agapito found exceedingly foolish.

He summoned Domingo to his office to explain that arrangements had been completed for Serafina's future. Mateo's brother, the bullfighter, needed money to gain technique on the great bull ranches of San Luís Potosí, and later to support him while he forced entry to impresarios' offices. Don Agapito explained this in a patient, courteous voice.

"The girl's uncle contends that you have her hidden away someplace. Stop being stupid. Bring her back, and let this marriage take place before the child is born. Manolo is content with the money and will solve the entire difficulty."

Domingo rose, feeling very tall in the low-ceilinged office.

"Is this why you sent for me?"

Don Agapito bit down on his thumb, finally struck his fist against the desk. "I know that stubborn expression. What's wrong now?"

"Nothing, except that Serafina is not going to marry Manolo. She's not going to marry anyone."

"Domingo, you astound me." Don Agapito pushed back his chair. The sun streamed through the slats of the venetian blind, laid a checkerboard of light and shadow on the curve of his cheek, on his shoulder and arm. "No plan I ever make seems to please you. Why do you hate me so much?"

Domingo turned his hat between his hands. "I think it's because you've never given anyone else the right of free choice."

"Ay, so now I'm a tyrant. A dictator. I suppose my portrait should be decked with flowers, as in the old days we used to festoon the portraits of don Porfirio."

With a faint smile, Domingo put on his hat, went to the door. "If the idea amuses you."

"Don't leave, Domingo. We're not finished. I am willing to make concessions. If the boy Manolo is not suitable we can find someone else."

Domingo drew a deep breath, turned around. "The boy

Manolo, any boy, has nothing to do with it. It is Serafina that is important."

"Indeed? Then why don't you want her protected?"

"By a bullfighter?"

"Manolo will be good to her in his fashion—in the fashion she understands. I've been thinking about you a good deal, Domingo. Sit down, my boy. I want to tell you a conclusion that I have reached."

Domingo shrugged, relaxed in the red leather chair. A telephone bell tinkled softly. Don Agapito spoke into the instrument briefly, then replaced it and sighed, "Always interruptions. No matter. Business can wait for five minutes."

"Business can wait? In Monterrey? A miracle."

Don Agapito pursed his lips, shook his head sorrowfully. "To you, business is a necessary evil because you are a medieval man. You should have been born in the time when the Moors still ruled Spain, and Castilla was a struggling kingdom. For you the spirit is more important than the flesh. Save the soul is your way and let the body go hungry."

"Serafina is not starving."

His uncle came around the desk, sat on the corner of it, one thin leg swinging back and forth like a pendulum. "But even the medievalist knows the value of a bargain. If you will be sensible in this Serafina affair, I will bring Cardito back from México City and no more will be said about his coming into the bank. Let him be a lawyer if he wants it."

Domingo took out a cigarette, lit it, drew a deep breath. The smoke trickled out with the truth about Cardito, and as he talked, he watched his uncle's face close, watched the flesh whiten over the bones and the lips press into colorless lines.

Domingo's mouth curved slightly into a smile as cruel as Spain. "I turned Cardito into a shell of nothing, because I wanted to protect him from you. In a way, you and I are together guilty. But this child will not suffer for our guilt. It will not be pushed into the path of a greedy bullfighter so that we can escape the consequences of our own crime. If we did that, we'd be no better than Cardito, cowering from responsibility in a third class student's boardinghouse."

Don Agapito's hand clenched on the desk. Looking at the bowed figure, pity touched Domingo. Something clicked in his mind, and he realized suddenly that he had triumphed, that he was the strong one now, and his uncle a weak old man, struggling still for power, but helpless with the power stripped from him.

He stretched out his arm, touched the flaccid shoulder. It was the first time he had ever touched his uncle of his own free will. "You called me a medieval man. It is you who are the true medievalist. You want your safe little shell, with no change within it. For you change is an evil thing."

The words came halting, torn from the throat. "I've changed Monterrey. I've made her strong."

"In the past, yes. But the past is dead. You are standing still now, and the city is flowing forward without you."

Domingo went to the door, opened it, so that the bank's interior, men moving quietly from cage to cage, was visible for a brief instant before he pushed the door shut. "Dark as a cave, and almost silent. Is that like the Credito Industrial, with the light streaming through glassbricks, with as many women as men circulating through the vast rooms? Your type belongs to the dead cities, to Guanjuato, and Queretaro, existing on the bones of their past. Monterrey is a living city, that consumes itself as it grows, so that it always rises, newborn and vital from the fire. And every child born here is a part of the city's future. Remember that, when you try to put the hand of your influence on Cardito's child."

He walked out of the office, his feet light on the ground, his hands sunk in his pockets, the air fragrant in his lungs. The long battle between himself and his uncle, he knew, was finished at last, and it felt strange to be the victor. There was sweetness in victory, he thought, a dangerous sweetness. Taste it too much, and it could become as enervating as cocaine. No wonder his uncle had loved this feeling of power, had been reluctant to let it go. In a way don Agapito was like don Porfirio Díaz, two men who had known power so long they did not realize the world about them was changing, was taking power into its own hands and needed their guidance no longer.

With these thoughts, Domingo went home, where he continued to assert that he no longer intended to marry Verónica in spite of the formal engagement. The Mirandas and Vázquez could keep up the pretense if they liked. As for himself, the church would be empty of his presence on December 15.

Don Jonás raged, the señora Miranda cried, don Rafael

354

sulked, but through it all Domingo remained detached and calm tempered.

For some reason he could not fathom, Verónica did not keep her threat to spread gossip about himself and Márgara. He decided that her own pride would not permit her to say she had lost him to another woman.

One morning she called him at the office, and asked him to take her to lunch at the Arcos. "Late, Domingo, about three. No one will see us, and I want to talk to you."

He said he could see no reason for conversation, but after her promise not to make a scene, finally agreed to it.

She was very quiet in the car, and in the restaurant maintained an appearance of sparkling conversation for the waiter's benefit. The only other customers were sitting at a far table against the wall, the same pair of young lovers who had been there the day he had come here with Sofía and Mateo, when Mateo was only a chauffeur and Sofía was planning how to trap him into marriage.

That seemed years ago instead of a mere six weeks. Domingo stirred his coffee moodily. "Well, Verónica, what do you want to say to me?"

"I only wanted to ask you why you lied."

"Lied?" He frowned with puzzlement. "When did I lie to you?"

"How cleverly you picked up my suspicions about the Bárcenas woman. You learned the lesson from my pretty tale of loving Tito I suppose."

"Verónica, what are you talking about?"

"What all of Monterrey is talking about. This servant girl of yours."

"Serafina?" Domingo chuckled, shook his head. "So Monterrey has found that out. Well, too many people knew the secret, I suppose."

"Domingo." Verónica stretched her hand toward him, then quickly drew it back. "When Sofía married Mateo, it was different. Mateo was already a success. Men admired him as a new talent. Mateo was never cut from servant's cloth, and everybody knew it. But this Serafina—a true servant. No matter how much you love her, in the end she'll ruin you."

"I had no idea you were class-conscious, Verónica." He

watched her narrowly, wondering what knife blade she had hidden in her sleeve.

"I'm not, Domingo. I ask you to think of Serafina for a moment. I've met the girl, talked to her. She's a sweet, pretty little thing. But she has no more brains than Brunhilda. When her prettiness fades, what's left?"

"This interest in my welfare touches me deeply, Verónica."

The light cynicism in his tone made her flinch. The eyes that came up to meet his were as steady as his own. "I love you, Domingo. I've said it from the first and I'll keep on saying it until you believe me."

Domingo, staring deep into those eyes, did believe her for the first time. Embarrassment made him turn aside. "Forgive me, Verónica. I've not been kind to you. We're a selfish lot, we Vázquez."

"I was selfish, too, Domingo. I should never have tried to trap you, but I was desperate. You simply wouldn't look at me, and when I spoke to you, you'd brush me away as though I were a little girl."

"You were a little girl."

"Yes, I was. A stupid, headstrong, romantic little girl."

Domingo chuckled. "Your father warned me about your romanticism. He said if you ever heard about Serafina, you would stick a knife in me."

"Like most fathers he sees me with his own eyes."

Here it is again, Domingo thought, the new attitude. The loving tolerance of the old, in place of the blind obedience.

She was saying, "Because I love you, Domingo, I'm sensitive to every tone in your voice. And when you speak about Serafina, there's nothing there. It's empty."

"I'm not in love with Serafina. I never was. And her child is not mine. Will you believe that?"

"If you say so." The obedient voice. The voice of Sofía for Mateo, of Brunhilda for Tito. The voice that Márgara would not recognize. Is it the fierce unbroken spirit I love in her, he wondered?

"Domingo, I was right in the first place? It is the Bárcenas? Please, I must know."

He recognized her need. "Yes, Verónica."

356

She relaxed then. Her face lengthened, lost its youthful freshness, turned from a girl's into a woman's.

"You can take me home now," she said dully.

There was no speech between them as he drove her home, but as he helped her out of the car, he held her hand for a minute. "You once made a threat against me, Verónica. Do you still mean to do it?"

She looked past him at the bricked-up famous window. "No, Domingo. I have no weapons left."

She went into the house, and something in the way she shut the door, an extra theatricality in the gesture, made Domingo shake his head in wonder over the strangeness of women. Somehow Verónica had closed the link between herself and her legendary aunt, so that the legend was alive again in Verónica, and the story of a new self-sacrifice for love was in the making.

A few nights later Domingo was playing chess with his father, his mother sitting near them, the inevitable crocheting in her lap, when doña Petra came to the door. "There's a boy who wants to see you, niño Domingo. I tried to chase him off until tomorrow, but he . . ." she gave a sudden shriek and saved herself from falling by grasping at a chair as a small streak of humanity flashed around her, a screaming Florinda at his heels.

The boy caught Domingo around the waist, lashed out with his heel at Florinda, who promptly burst into tears.

Domingo banished the two excited women from the room, and settled the boy in a chair.

"Serafina's cousin," he explained hastily to his shocked parents while he poured a few drops of sherry between Jaime's frightened lips.

"Eh, and what's wrong with you?"

"My uncle came back from Laredo. He tried to beat me again, but I got away from him. Then he followed me out to Santa Catarina. I only went to warn Serafina. I didn't mean to lead him there. He's given her a terrible beating. I stole a ride on a tourist's car and got here as soon as I could."

Domingo kept his voice quiet in order not to further terrify the boy. He could hear his mother's quick breathing, the drumming of his father's fingers on the chess board.

"Where is your uncle now?"

"I don't know. But you said if he ever beat Serafina again, he would kill her."

"Nonsense," doña Otilia said calmly. "Serafina is a fine strong girl. A beating can't possibly hurt her." She rang for Florinda, gave orders that Jaime was to be put to bed in the servants' quarters. "At night everything is always terrible," she told him gently. "Tomorrow morning you will laugh at your fears."

After he was led away, she said, "Fetch my shawl, Domingo. You're going to take me to that girl."

"No," Domingo said.

"No," echoed don Rafael.

They might have saved their breath. Doña Otilia was a soft plumpness on the front seat as Domingo turned the car toward Santa Catarina.

When they arrived, they found the house an ocean of excitement. Tía Nicanora, a gun in her lap, was sitting facing her bedroom door. A chair, tilted under the knob, effectively kept it from opening in spite of the banging and pushing against it from the inside. When Tía saw doña Otilia her mouth opened in surprise. She tried to smooth her hair, while she glanced helplessly from her former mistress to the door she had evidently been told to guard.

Márgara, wrapped in a long white apron, a towel hiding her hair, came out of the kitchen carrying a heavy basin of water. Seeing Domingo, she hesitated, used her shoulder to brush some escaping strands of hair from her eyes.

"Put more water on to boil, Domingo," she said. If she noticed doña Otilia, she gave no sign as she hurried into Serafina's room, slamming the door with her foot.

"You'd better do as she says, Dominguito," Tía Nicanora said in a quavering voice, her eyes still fixed on doña Otilia.

"Move!" his mother snapped, and he hurried into the kitchen.

All of the buckets were empty, so he had to fetch more water from the patio well. At last three pails were set on the long brazier, and he was free to return to the parlor.

Only Tía Nicanora was sitting there. Of his mother there was no sign. The banging on the door had finally stopped, as though the prisoner had given up in despair.

Tía extended the gun to Domingo. "You'd better keep this. I'm such a bad shot I might kill the man."

He said, worried, "Did Bárcenas get that violent, that you and Márgara had to lock him up?"

"Bárcenas?" Tía sniffed. "It's not Bárcenas in there. It's Dr. Mancini."

Domingo felt his muscles stiffen, his hands grow icy. "Mancini!" His voice shot up out of control. He finally battled it down to place. "Have you women lost your wits? Who is in there with Serafina?"

Even as he asked the question, he read the answer in her eyes. He said, "Ay, God, why did you create women!"

He leaped to the door, started to pull the chair aside. Tía hung her weight on his arm, dragged him back.

"You touch that chair and as big as you are, I'll spank you. Doña Otilia!" she shrieked. "Come out here, doña Otilia!"

Doña Otilia opened Serafina's door, said, "We have no time for nonsense," and shut it again.

Tía, breathing heavily, pointed to a chair. "You sit there and behave yourself."

"Listen to me, Tía, Mancini is a doctor."

"He's a stupid fool. And his grandfather was a coward."

"I don't care about his grandfather. Serafina is a very sick girl . . ."

"And she's in proper hands," Tía said flatly, snatching the gun from him before his stunned senses could stop her. "If you compose yourself, I'll tell you what happened."

"Mancini," Domingo repeated blankly. "I am in a dream, a nightmare . . ."

"Nothing's happened to you. It's already happened to us. Bárcenas and Márgara walked down to the plaza to fetch some bottles of beer. They were hardly gone when that drunk madman broke into the house, with Serafina's cousin attached to his shirt, trying to hold him back. Can a thin weed hold back a tornado? I went at him with a chair, but he knocked me against the table. My head struck the point." She rubbed her head now with tender fingers. "When I came to, the madman was gone and so was the child, and Serafina was lying on the floor in a pool of blood." Her voice rose excitedly. She lifted her apron to her eyes to stem her tears. "I ran out screaming for help. A neighbor hurried for Dr. Mancini. Luckily, before he arrived, Bárcenas and Márgara came. That Márgara, she's a wonderful soul." Tía's sobs conquered her voice. Her chair squeaked as she rocked back and forth.

Mancini started pounding on the door again, shouting threats at them. Tía went to the door, yelled at him to be silent, then returned to her chair and her story. "Bárcenas was like a man transformed. Once when your mother was ill, a great doctor came down from the States. He had that same smoothness, that same—I don't know how to explain it, but you'd trust a man like that with anything you had. He only said one sentence. He said, 'There's a chance for the child.' Then Mancini arrived. Such a shrieking and howling as you never heard. Márgara trapped him in that room, how I don't know, and left me here to guard the door with the gun. It's not a very good gun. It never goes off when you want it to. And it always goes off when you don't want it to."

She waved it back and forth, and the muzzle swung toward and away from Domingo. After some anxious maneuvering he managed to get it safe into his own hands. Then he rose as his mother came toward him. She said quietly, "It's a little boy," and burst into tears.

Márgara, weary, white-faced, followed her. She sank down on a chair, said through pallid lips, "He won't leave her. He just stands there holding the baby, but he won't leave her."

When Domingo started toward the room, his mother stepped in front of him. "No, leave him alone. He's had a great triumph. Leave him with it."

"No other doctor could have done it," Márgara said. "That's always been his genius, doing what no other doctor could do." Her voice broke and she began to cry.

Domingo stood very still. Far away, music was playing and he wondered vaguely where it came from until he realized it was his own blood singing in his ears. All of this was untrue, of course. Serafina was not dead. How could the lovely voice be still, the graceful body move no more?

It had never occurred to him during these long weeks, that Serafina, growing more remote from life day by day, might finally reach the final barrier and pass it, leaving behind her the stone where the shadow of her hand had rested.

A voice nagged at him like a tormenting fly, a voice that kept saying, "Domingo, Domingo." He tried to push the voice aside, but a hand caught his hand, twisted until the pain shocked him back into the room.

"Domingo," his mother said firmly, "time for sorrow later. Just now we have the problem of Dr. Mancini."

Yes, of course, Mancini was locked in Tía's bedroom—Mancini, whose grandfather had been a coward. Domingo looked around for Tía Nicanora. He wanted to tell her how funny he thought it was that anyone should still be concerned over the cowardice of Mancini's grandfather. But he saw Márgara instead. A white-faced, silent Márgara. Her eyes were large and liquid with fear. The sight of the fear was the final spearhead against the shell of his grief. Awareness flooded him, and he said, "We've got to get Bárcenas out of here before we release Mancini. Get your father, Márgara." She nodded, hurried to the bedroom. He said, "Tía, after we leave, release Mancini. Try to soothe him, tell him it was all a mistake. . . ."

"He knows it was no mistake," Tía snorted. "The words I said about his grandfather were no mistake, I can tell you."

Doña Otilia said quickly, checking Domingo's anger with her hand on his arm. "Don't worry, my son. I will be here. I don't think the doctor will disagree with . . ."

A scream from Márgara interrupted her. The girl rushed into the room, her eyes wide with fright. "My father. He's gone. And he's taken the baby with him."

XXV

His mother told Domingo afterwards that he stood there so silent for so long they thought at first he had not heard Márgara.

To himself there was no space at all between the words of Márgara, and the curve of air around his face as he pressed the car toward Laredo. Márgara was crouched beside him, bent forward, peering through the windshield.

He knew she must have told him to go to Laredo. She would know better than anyone the road her father would follow.

She said on a hysterical note, "I didn't want to tell them back there, but he took your gun, Domingo."

Domingo's hands relaxed in panic. The car skidded sideways across the road. It took all his strength to battle it back under his control. "How did he get it?"

"I saw him come in and bend over you. I thought he was saying something to you."

"I don't remember." Domingo lifted his hand to his forehead.

She said impatiently, "You were dazed with grief. . . ."

How could she hold such a tone in her voice with Serafina dead? Serafina, who had talked with the saints. Santo Domingo, protect her soul. . . .

"I saw him take the gun, but I thought he was afraid you would shoot Serafina's father."

. . . Intercede for her in purgatory. She was as clean of sin as any flower. . . .

"It never occurred to me he would want the gun for himself."

. . . Protect her, Santo Domingo, and all that is hers. Keep her child safe until I can reach it. Serafina's child, a boy, another Cardito. No, Catarino. She wanted him named for Santa Catarina. Catarino, Tinito.

The name spun itself into a covering web, and the child was no longer a darkness in the womb, but an entity, living, dominating, individual to itself, ceasing to be a part of Serafina and Cardito, now humanly Tinito, his flesh soft and warm, his blood bright with life, his eyes humid with the secrets of his own inner texture. Tinito, fragile in the present, great with future strength.

It irritated Domingo when Márgara began to moan a little. He said, "Are you sure your father went to Laredo? That he, himself, isn't hunting Serafina's father?"

She thought carefully before she answered. "If he hadn't taken the baby, I would have thought that, yes. But I think now that the operation, the fear of Mancini, has made him go back in his mind to the early days so that all he wants is escape. The child is part of the pattern. He may have taken it because he loved Serafina, but in the other escape there were children too. I'm sure he has gone to Laredo. Please, Domingo, hurry!"

The car swung into Hidalgo Street leading them through Monterrey, where they lost considerable time. Once free of the military camp, Domingo was able to pick up speed again.

"I don't see how he could get there ahead of us, Márgara."

"Dozens of tourist cars leave every hour for Laredo." She added simply, "And he has a gun."

Domingo thought, and he has the child. I must not think of that. If I do, I shall go blind with fear and never catch them. He said desperately, "Talk, Márgara. For God's sake, talk to me."

Márgara, recognizing a need for speech, haltingly began. It was all there, the flight from México City, the pressing crowds in the streets of Veracruz. "The posters about Ruperto Martínez. I can remember them still. But there was no truth in the story. Huerta needed a scapegoat for the Martínez murder, and having quarreled with my father found it convenient to pin it on him. Do you believe that? My father was a doctor. He could kill for science, but not for cruelty."

She's already talking about him in the past tense, Domingo thought pityingly.

She said, "He was a very great surgeon. A true genius. The French recognized that genius. But finally the Martínez rumors followed him even there. The new humiliation killed my mother. As for me, I think General Angeles broke my heart when I was seven years old."

"Angeles? What did he do, Márgara?"

"He ate at a restaurant near our house. He was Mexican, and I was a Mexican child. He would play with me, bring me little presents. Then one day he found out who I was. I'll never forget the way he turned away from me. He was a cold, proud, beautiful man. I cried until I ran a fever. My father searched Paris for him, to implore him to come and speak to me. But he had returned to México, to fight with Villa. I never saw him again."

"You loved Angeles," Domingo said. "I think you love him still."

She said, "He has always owned the best of my heart."

She went on with the story. A widower now, with two chil-

363

dren, her father went to London, but still the Martínez rumors followed him, so they fled to New York.

"To Brooklyn," Domingo said.

"No," Márgara said, "New York. Brooklyn came later, much later. In New York someone recognized us and we had to move on. We went west to Chicago, to Detroit, to Los Angeles, but there was always the recognition. Do you know how terrible it can be to have to run away from the contempt of your own people?

"My father's money was slowly disappearing. He didn't dare practice medicine, the only thing he knew. My brother and I spoke good English. As we grew up we found jobs, but they never lasted long. The Martínez rumors were always at our heels. At Los Angeles we were forced to turn east again, to Denver, Oklahoma City, Dallas, and finally Brooklyn.

"My brother was killed in a traffic accident in Brooklyn. His name was also my father's. The papers mistook him for my father. I can still remember the headlines in New York's *La Prensa:* 'The Murderer of Ruperto Mártínez Dies in Traffic Accident.' My father wept over that headline. The one man he never killed was slowly killing him."

The one man, Domingo thought, but what of all the others who died because he believed more in science than humanity?

Márgara was saying dully, "Then my father realized that so far as the world was concerned, he ·was dead. He could risk a return to México."

"Why, Márgara? Why did he want to come here?"

She shook her head. "I don't know. I'm not Mexican enough to understand. The blood is in me, but not the feel of the country. He had it. He wanted to come here to make his peace with his own earth. He took the last of his money, used it to buy forged papers. But fear was with him still. We wandered from Chihuahua to Yucatán, and always a pair of staring eyes would send us into darkness. Finally we reached Monterrey, opened the studio. Photography, you know, has something to do with chemistry. You need a license in México to be a chemist, but not to be a photographer. And we made a little money. Enough to live on."

After a pause Domingo said, "I was a blind fool not to guess the truth long ago. But his body has changed so much. There is no resemblance to the photographs, none at all."

He said nothing more until they safely passed the steep descent of the Mamulique. "You told me he hated Velarde . . ."

"The very sound of the name. It was as though he had turned into another man, not only in body but in mind. To my father, Velarde, the idea of Velarde, was equal with the idea of Satan."

"My poor Márgara."

She said fiercely, "Don't pity me, Domingo. I don't want pity."

He raised her hand to his lips, and then she was wildly crying. He wanted to stop and comfort her, but the magnet of Tinito was stronger than his pity for Márgara.

The car had slowed a little with the impulse. She said harshly, "Drive on, quickly. Don't you understand? He has a gun."

They reached New Laredo at last. Márgara directed him down a sidestreet to a house with a witch's lizard painted over the door. "This old woman specializes in smuggling people across the border." Márgara explained as she banged for entrance.

A giant of a man swung the door open, glared suspiciously at them, then at the car. Márgara said something too low for Domingo to hear, but it must have been a signal of some sort because the man grunted, stepped aside for them.

The room was low-ceilinged, and smelt of filth and unwashed bodies. The only light, coming from coals glowing in a brazier, was no light, really, but a shadow, pink as a shrimp's back. An old woman crouched in its gleam, thin gray hair straggling over her face.

Domingo caught Márgara's arm, pulled her close to him, but she jerked free, went and stood over the woman. Although the ancient creature had a network of wrinkles for a face, her black eyes were young, young as the curve of the world, young as Hecate. When she smiled her gums shown clear. Márgara, bending over her, had the clean lines of a sword, but the old woman crouching on the floor, had no lines at all. She was a blob of shadow in the shrimp-pink light.

At first she made no answer to Márgara's questions, but she finally admitted that a man and child had been there. After that her lips closed over her gums, her chin and nose nearly meeting. Domingo thrust some folded bills into her curved hand. She

raised the bills, smelt them, tasted them. She told them to follow the giant.

He led them through back streets to the high cliffs that
lined the Mexican side of the Río Grande. The moon had set
long ago, and the sky was torn with glittering star points. Domingo
took deep breaths of the dusty air. It was crisp after the turgid
smokiness of the witch's house. He wished desperately that he
had some sort of weapon, but it was too late to fetch the gun
from the car. Bárcenas was ahead of them with the child. He
had to be stopped on this side of the border. Domingo did not
want to be faced with a charge of illegal entry to the United
States. Once in prison he could do nothing for Tino, and don
Agapito was not one to forget a defeat.

They crept through a narrow split in the cliff, down which
they had to scramble, clinging as best they could to loose rocks
and weeds. Then they were on the rocky shore of the river itself, which luckily, at this time of year, was a narrow trickle of
water.

"They should be just ahead of us," the giant grunted. He
did not trouble to lower his voice. The cliff saloons above them
were bombarding the night with music, radios turned on full
blast.

The music pounded, the wind, caught in the cañon of the
river, whipped around them, time flowed sluggish as the water,
and always ahead of them Bárcenas and the child. They could
see only the shadows of their own bodies.

That great drum beating, Domingo thought dully, was his
heart. His hand was grasping something, and it came to him with
aloof wonder that it was Márgara's arm caught between his fingers. He was half carrying her as they stumbled forward, and yet
he had the sensation that she was also carrying him. He knew
that she had forgotten him in her desperate attempt to reach
her father, just as he had forgotten her in his anxiety for the
child. But his hand on her arm fastened them together, held them
back when they both wanted to run, linked them each to the
other in a bondage neither wanted.

His throat closed, and the ripple of the water enticed him.
He longed to fall on his knees, drink deep of the water, but he
stumbled onward, Márgara ahead of him. Her hair slipped from
its pins, spilled over her shoulders, brushed his fingers. Somewhere,

in the remote past, he had lived through this scene, and now he was living through it again, his throat parched with thirst, the woman running in front of him, the water luring him.

Shadow of our Lord, St. Peter. . . .

The words of the old song tossed about in his mind, its minor cadences mingling with the laughter and song from the cliff saloons.

The river lures me, the river lures me.

Is there no ending, St. Peter, to this nightmare? Santo Domingo, protect the child. Santa Catarina, hold safe your namesake. Blessed Mary, Mother of God, be merciful. . . .

A thin scream pierced through the blaring music, followed by a strange cracking noise that echoed against the cliffs. Márgara gasped, plunged forward, her feet twisting on the rocks. Domingo, caught off balance, stumbled, fell to one knee, dragging her down with him. She turned against him, beat at him with her fists. The giant, who had leaped ahead of them, came toward them, said hoarsely, "We must return."

"What happened?" Was it himself who asked that question? Was it Márgara? Was it both of them?

"The fool just killed himself."

A great cup of silence descended on his head. There was a nothingness about him. Even the river was still.

Sounds of distant laughter, screeching music shattered the cup. Márgara smothered a scream, crumbled to the ground, her body rocking back and forth in pain. Domingo did not even see her fall. His mind was focused on the child. He ran through the darkness, his feet unaware of the slippery stones.

An arm reached out, caught him, swung him aside. Someone behind them yelled, and Domingo realized that it was the giant giving him safe conduct to the other guide.

He tried to speak, found his mouth too dry, had to swallow before he could whisper, "The child?"

A rumbling voice answered him, was drowned by the laughter and music of the cliff saloons. A hand guided his hand, and he felt the curve of a blanket with something soft and warm within it. The blanket came into his arms. He could feel it moving, and when he dipped his head toward it, he heard the whimper of a baby.

The rumbling voice said, "We've got to go back."

Domingo obediently turned, followed the pressure of the grasp on his arm. The climb up the cliff was a fantastic series of twists and turns, of balancing forward and back, of each helping the other, the child swinging safe between them. On the top at last, Domingo paused with a horrified gasp at his own forgetfulness. The child was consuming him, shutting out the thought of anyone, even Márgara.

"There's a woman down there. I've got to go back and fetch her."

"The giant has her," the rumbling voice assured him, prodding him toward the witch's house.

Márgara was there, slumped on a bench, her eyes humid with tears.

"Domingo, they won't move him. They're leaving him on the stones . . . the cold stones. . . ."

The crouching hag snorted, but it was the rumbling voice of Bárcenas' guide that answered Márgara. "Don't be a fool, woman. By this time the immigration authorities are swarming like ants around that body. Do you want to put us all in jail because of an empty shell?"

Even here, thought Domingo, the practical mind.

Standing in the room's center, the baby tight in his arms, he looked around at the rumble, was surprised that it emanated from a hunchbacked creature little taller than a dwarf. A giant, a dwarf, and a straggly-haired witch. These were the people Márgara knew. These were the product of her terror-wrapped life.

She demanded to be told what had happened, and the hunchback answered her.

"Everything was all right, me in the lead, he following with the child." The hunchback rubbed against Domingo with a dog's gesture. "I didn't know it was a kidnaping," he whined. "You can't blame me when I didn't know."

Márgara spoke, and her tone held a sharp insistence. She knows how to deal with these people, Domingo thought, and his arms closed tighter around the child, pulling it to him, protecting it from the filth of this room that lay on mind as well as body.

"No kidnaping, fool. Tell your story."

"I'm telling it. Everything was all right, and then a crowd of drunks began shouting. You know how they do. There was a lot of laughter with the shouting. This fellow started to cry. He begged me over and over not to let them sing. As though I could silence a crowd of drunks ten meters above my head."

"They started to sing," Domingo said. His eyes met Márgara's and they both knew why Bárcenas had fired the gun. " 'Peace,' said the old maxim, 'peace in the cemetery.' "

"Don't drunks always sing?" the hunchback wanted to know. "It was a good song, too. I like it." He hummed a little of it:

> I carry my forty-five
> With which to kill traitors.

"That's when he went crazy. He squealed like a goat in the slaughter pen, and the next thing he'd shot himself through the brain. I got the child away from him as he fell. I don't like these crazy ones," he said, and spit to one side before tipping a bottle of mescal to his lips.

He had lost his dog-like attitude now that he felt no danger, and there was insolence in the angle of his head.

If we had not come when we did, Domingo thought, the child would have disappeared, and I'd never have found him. He might have been hanged twenty years in the future, and I'd never have known he was Cardito's son. Serafina's son.

Domingo wanted to speak to Márgara, but the image of Bárcenas, broken and vulnerable on the stones of the riverbed, sealed his lips. Through all of Bárcenas' years, the stones had played their part: the stones of Nayarit mountains where he had been born; the rain-washed stones of México City where his heart had turned to stone in his serving of science; the gray stones of exile, and finally the white stones of the riverbed. Everywhere stones, and he broken on them, his genius seeping out with his blood to stain the stones that cradled him.

Domingo looked around at Márgara. She was not crying. She was beyond tears. She let him guide her to the car, but when he suggested a hotel, she shook her head.

369

"It's already dawn."

"I've got to take this baby to the hospital, Márgara. It needs care."

She shrugged indifferently, and he turned through dimly familiar streets until he found the hospital. As he transferred the child to the nurse's arms, he looked at it, really looked at it, for the first time, and it came to him with a little shock that no one ever truly visualizes a new-born child. This spider creature, thin in legs and arms, was not the butter-ball of his imagination with dimples for knuckles, and creases at wrists and ankles.

Then the nurse expertly covered the small head, still crimson from the womb, and as she walked away, the true vision dimmed and the imagined picture was once more paramount. The image took on Serafina's delicate beauty, and added to itself the memories of Cardito's fat babyhood as Domingo returned to the car, where Márgara sat quietly smoking.

"We'll have to wait about an hour."

"It doesn't matter."

How flat her voice. The years with Bárcenas had given her a center. With the passing of that center, she was as limp as tumbled cloth.

"The bridge will open soon," she said. "Then I'll cross to the other side."

He opened the car door, slid in beside her. Here was Márgara, here was his love. His mind told him this, but his heart made no response. Yet the code of his upbringing opened his lips, spoke the words. "I thought you would stay with me."

"Monterrey is too full of him. I could never live there."

She turned slightly toward him, her face not yet a mask, but already leaving the warmth of life. "It's your city. You could never live any place else."

If I were a doctor, his mind whispered, I could stand beside Tino, see that he was given proper care. He savagely wished that in his medical readings he had paid more attention to the care of new infants, especially following the mother's death. But of this knowledge he was woefully ignorant.

His lips said, "There are many cities in the Republic."

His mind said, He is doubtless with a wet-nurse. Is that what they do with newborn infants? And even as his mind spoke, the image of Tino, cradled in a woman's arm, lips blindly seeking upward, took possession of Domingo, so that it gave him a little shock to hear himself saying, "Many cities. The colonial jewel of Guanajuato, the bustling commerce of Guadalajara. We could find a home."

"Not in the Republic." She smiled faintly, her eyes remote, turned inward. "It is not my country. The customs here are strange to me. I don't understand them." She gestured with her chin toward the International Bridge. "That's my world across the river."

. . . Tinito's face was small as the palm of a hand. It was crumpled and red, with soft bones that rested warm and safe against the smooth curve of the full breast. The tiny lips were sucking milk, greedy as any small animal. . . .

"In the States is happiness." Her voice tugged at him, pulled him toward her. "Could you be happy with Dr. Velarde's daughter?"

His hand touched her hair, but there was no tingle of excitement.

He who cuts a lock of hair from the Xtabay, shall be her master . . .

but the desire for mastery was gone. "Dr. Velarde saved Serafina's son."

"Ay, yes, the baby." That flat tone, as free of emotion as a piece of silver. "My father wanted to keep that baby." The feeling was coming now, flowing over the silver, enriching it, burnishing it with gold. "Could we take him with us?"

. . . The mouth had consumed one breast, was starting now on the other, hungry gums pressing close on the pink nipple, pulling the brown breast away from the brown body. . . .

"I thought perhaps your family would have plans for him," Márgara said.

The image of don Agapito, gilded with triumph, rose up before Domingo. The man was smiling, the charm sliding through the smile, whispering, "I shall win in the end. Leave the child, Domingo, and I shall see that he disappears, so that no head may turn on the street to watch him, no mouth may whisper, 'There walks a son of the Vázquez de Anda.' In the end I shall always win."

"No!" Domingo said, the word cutting sharp against his lips.

"My uncle Agapito would put him in an orphanage. I can't have that, Márgara. Serafina didn't want him in an orphanage."

. . . Is it true that you are dead, Serafina? Will I never hear your voice again, never hear you laugh . . . ?

"Domingo, we can take the child with us. My father would have liked that. Perhaps he'll grow up to be a doctor, like my father. You wanted to be a doctor. He may have inherited it with the Vázquez blood. It would be so wonderful if he could . . ."

"No!" Again the sharp cutting of the word. Strange how so rounded a word could be so sharp. "He'll be what he wants to be, not the product of a plan!"

"Domingo, there's no need to get excited. . . ."

. . . The brown breast was emptying its richness into the hungry mouth, the breast brown as toasted earth. . . .

"What are you thinking, Domingo?"

"I can't go to the States, Márgara."

"Why not?"

"That child is a Mexican. He has the right to be a Mexican. He can't grow up in the States, or Europe, or any place else but here in the Republic."

She was formal now, and stiff. "You'd give up—us—for this baby? Does the love between us mean nothing?"

Love? It was a word, too. What did it mean, really? Affection, trust, enchantment? The green and gold depths of the jungle? Love. Did it mean the silent room, a woman sorrowing in it, the door forever barred? Did it mean the breaking of customs, the merging of the world below with the world above? Did it mean a young girl in the sunlight, chickens pecking corn from her extended hand? Love, love, how broad a word was love. Love was a child, soft in a blanket, eyes turned inward still toward its creation. Tino, Tinito, for you the great love, the love above all loves. There is no love so great as the love of a man for his son. Tinito, my son.

"I hate this country, Domingo. It's never meant anything but sorrow and terror to me. Are you trying to chain me here because of a baby—a servant girl's baby?"

Márgara, is this you speaking? What has happened to you? Where is your beauty and your magic? Where have you gone, Márgara, that you have left me here with a stranger?

"You told me once in Saltillo that you would never leave me

in the dark again." She was bending toward him, her mouth soft against his mouth. His lips felt her breath, felt the moving of her lips as she spoke. "We could be happy, Domingo, the two of us."

. . . The brown breast was empty now, and the small head turned, a bubble breaking on the lips, the eyes already heavy with sleep, the brain clear of anything but the mystery of life. . . .

Domingo tried to find words, but there were no words. He wanted to say to her, "I failed with Cardito, who was more my son than my brother. Because I stole all sense of responsibility from Cardito, this child was born. I owe this child a debt, and I must pay it. It is a debt greater than any promise made to you, than a man can make to any woman. It is a debt to the future, from me who have failed in the present.

"I loved you once, Márgara, my green and gold, my Xtabay, but there is always a Ulysses of common sense to drag the enchanted back from the jungle magic. You and I, we've known our time of happiness. This child must know his, too.

"And this is his country. You can't understand that, Márgara. You never had a country. You're like Jorge Palafox, only a name written on the pages of history. Poor creature, poor Márgara, you pity your father, but he had something you will never possess. Something I cannot steal from the child he saved from death. Perhaps this child is the final total of his payment to the México he betrayed. I don't know. But I do know that Mexican air must be in Tino's lungs, its water in his blood, its earth in his bones. That is the right of his heritage, and I cannot steal it from him."

These were the words he wanted to say. They formed a nebula within his brain, but they would not break free. He could only shake his head, murmur, "Forgive me, Márgara."

He saw the mask come back, cover her face, transform her once again into the woman he had first glimpsed in the shadows of the photography studio. All that had been was gone as though it had never been.

He drove her to the bridge, and she walked away from him, her body a green arrow that lost itself in the early morning crowd.

And you will follow the Xtabay, and you will never find her, you poor creature.

He realized vaguely that there was something wrong about the bridge, and then he saw that the huge National Lottery sign, which had stood there for years, was gone, toppled by a recent storm. The old maxim returned to him, "Mexicans have faith in two things: peace in the cemetery, and wealth from the lottery." In three things, Domingo thought. The future of our children.

The baby was a warm bundle on the seat beside him when he reached Monterrey.

In spite of the mourning for Lent, the warmer days were bringing out the crowds, and all the fields were beautiful with bloom. The cold of winter was finished, the sun had come to warm her city, and Saddle Mountain arrogantly reared cantle and pommel to the clear blue sky.